TAKING
FLIGHT

TOMES OF ASCENSION

Printed in Australia

Original cover artwork by Shoshanah Graves

Cover design by Lizza Creative

Internal design by A to B Editing

Second edition 2024

Paperback ISBN 978-1-7637423-1-4

eBook ISBN 978-1-7637423-2-1

Hardback ISBN 978-1-7637423-0-7

The author acknowledges the traditional owners of the land and pays respects to Elders past, present and emerging.

A catalogue record for this work is available from the National Library of Australia

TAKING FLIGHT

TOMES OF ASCENSION

A.G. CHARLTON

My endless thanks to my best friend Malik and everyone else who helped me and believed in me along the way. This book would never have happened without you. We finally made it.

To every author who inspired my love for fantasy, and made me dream of telling my own stories.

To Shoshanah Graves, for your fantastic work on bringing Syline to life in the cover. Thank you.

To my dog Felix. You slept beside me every day when I first wrote this story. You're gone now, but never forgotten.

Prologue

THIS WAS NOT WHAT LAURALEE had expected.

When her mother told her she was being sent to the walled city of Russenholde to apprentice beneath Lady Jane, she had expected high society, mingling with the nobility of the hardy folk, manipulating and controlling the whims and mood of court. After all, the only other time she had met Jane, the woman had seemed the perfect socialite, dressed in the highest fashion and speaking with the cocksure confidence of someone used to getting exactly what she wanted.

Instead, Lauralee found herself trudging through the ancient, mouldering aqueducts beneath the city. Rats squeaked just out of sight, and foul-smelling grey water sloshed about her wax-coated boots. The wax was supposed to stop the stench seeping in permanently and with only two pairs, she hoped it worked. They were on an incline, heading steadily down, and it was all she could do to keep just her boots, and not the rest of her, in the filth as she slipped and slid her way down.

Infuriatingly, her new mistress had the magic to float bare inches over the putrid water's surface. Apparently, that magic couldn't be extended to Lauralee. Her mother and she could not use magic. Something about their blood, but for just that reason she always carried scrolls to dispel other's spells before they could cause her harm. She was very tempted to use one of those precious scrolls now to drop Jane into the sludge.

If any were to see them, they'd be hard pressed to find a pair more out of place. Jane still projected that same impression she had first given Lauralee, with her beautiful auburn hair, flickering to an orange-red at its curling tips. It hung in long tresses over the elegant, tight fitting black gown she wore to show off her shapely figure, which, miraculously, picked up none of the filth that infested this place. A wand hung lazily in her right hand, dancing between her fingers as she twirled it idly. Meanwhile, Lauralee looked every part the vagabond adventurer, with her close-cropped white hair, pale, almost boyish features, garbed in her travellers' leather cloak, which she did her best to hold from the muck.

Neither belonged down here, as far as Lauralee was concerned. Jane had not even told her their reason for coming to this place, with none of her guards, without her husband, without any of the protections and guardians she would normally surround herself with. Lauralee supposed she should be honoured. Mostly, she just wanted a bath.

"We're nearly there," came Jane's melodious tones, and Lauralee nearly stumbled into her mistress's back.

After staring at it in the dark for so long she hadn't noticed it growing closer. She pulled herself to a halt hurriedly and the filth around her ankles sloshed loudly, echoing in the tunnels. Jane spun with silent grace in the air, turning to face her and said, "Don't look so dour, darling, you're about to bear witness to a very important moment for us all. Besides, didn't your mother tell you your face will stick that way if you wear a frown too long?" A smirk played across her lips as her manicured hand reached over to pinch Lauralee's cheek. Lauralee flinched in response. Her sisters and aunts might've been habitually physically affectionate, but Lauralee still felt uncomfortable at the touch of anyone but her mother.

"You still haven't told me what we're doing here," Lauralee said, trying not to sound like she was sulking.

"That is because it is a ward's duty to observe and learn by silently doing so. If you had any part to play here, you would know, my dear. For now, all you need to do is watch, so you can tell your mother all about this in due time. Now, come along, we shouldn't keep them waiting."

With that, she spun back around and drifted forward, a globe of light materialising at the tip of her wand as she went. Lauralee, curious as to who "they" were, followed. They came to an unnatural intersection; the wall of the aqueduct had been broken in on one side, providing access to a natural cavern, from which a strange smell rose; like burnt bread or roasting fat. Lauralee was surprised she was able to pick out the smell over the greywater, but something about it tingled in the back of her throat, catching in her mind.

Jane drifted into the cavern and touched down upon the dry rock. Lauralee followed eagerly, having dry ground beneath her feet was a small reward for the journey so far. Before they continued, Jane turned to her and without a word of explanation, incanted a short spell. Lauralee flinched as the wand pointed at her, then stood relieved as the greywater, along with its scent, slid off her cloak and boots.

"So jumpy," Jane tittered. "You do need to learn to relax dear, though I suppose you do take after your mother," she mused as she turned and walked down through the tunnel without another word. Lauralee hurried to keep up.

﹦

IT WAS ANOTHER FIVE MINUTES of walking before the cave opened up. They stepped into a natural atrium which thrummed with the eerie blue glow of bioluminescent fungus. Standing at the bottom of a craggy depression in the centre of the room, half in shadow, were two figures.

The smaller of the two turned to face them as they approached. It wore dank, mouldering robes, coloured grey, tinted blue by the fungus light, which clung to its form in the same way cobwebs cling to rafters. Though shorter than its partner, it was tall, head and shoulders over Lauralee and stood with an awkward, stooping posture extending one arm towards them in greeting as they approached. That arm seemed to short-circuit something in Lauralee's mind. Looking at the figure, she knew something was off, unnatural, but couldn't figure out what.

A moment later, it clicked. The arm reaching toward them was not the only one on its left side, the other hanging slack in its sleeve, starting some halfway down the creature's chest. Its hood sat strangely, as if it were draped over horns. Most of its face was lost in shadow, but what she could see was smiling, wide and predatory, lips melted to teeth where flesh had run like wax spread wide in a shark's all too cheerful grin.

She looked past it to its fellow, her eyes roving, looking for anything else to focus on, but its companion was no better. Hulking, huge, it stood an easy eight, maybe nine feet tall. It would have been even taller, had it not stood in a painful stoop, back bent almost double beneath the weight of… what? At first, she took it to be covered in armour, plate mail, akin to a knightly bodyguard. But that wasn't armour. It was thick and grew in random protrusions, with waving fronds of vegetation growing from it. It was like someone had ripped a chunk from a coral reef, animal life and all and wrapped it around what, at a stretch, could be called a man.

No, she wasn't quite sure she could bring herself to call this thing a man. Its massive arms scraped the floor with chitinous pincers, and its head – god, its head. The flesh of the scalp was ripped back to meld into its verdurous carapace, keeping its head pulled hard upright, while its eyes, having escaped their sockets, waved on stalks made from skin and muscle twined together like cord. They turned to stare straight at her. They were so red, and yet all too human. There was so much pain in those eyes.

Lauralee had seen many terrible things since becoming her mother's daughter, done terrible things too, but she doubted any moment would sit as stark in her memory as this one. She felt something her mother had promised her she'd never have to feel again, felt something she was not meant to be able to feel. That cold shudder running down her spine. Looking into those eyes, all she wanted to do was run.

"The Scholar does not like to be kept waiting," said the smaller of the two. Its voice was like a man screaming for help as he drowned. Each word bubbled up from somewhere deep within him, through a morass of fluid. She was sure it drooled as it spoke. Something hissed on the floor.

However terrifying they were, Jane seemed none affected, gracing the creature with an indulging smile as if she was humouring a petulant child's bravado.

"Well, then it is a good thing you are not the Scholar, isn't it? Besides darling, have you not heard of being fashionably late? It would've been uncouth if I'd shown up right on schedule."

The creature stared at her silently for so very long. Was it trying to make sense of what Jane had said? Or was it just deciding whether or not it should kill them? Lauralee didn't dare lower a hand to her knives, but she did edge subtly behind Jane. The creature's head ticked to one side hard, like an owl eyeing prey.

"You will be on time if you have further dealings with the Scholar, or payment will not be given," it announced. It was so bizarre, its words were that of a clerk, a merchant, but its voice, its body, were the sheer stuff of nightmares. What payment?

"I will keep that in mind if, for some reason, I wish to return down here," Jane said, reaching into the satchel hung at her side to retrieve a massive, silk-wrapped tome. Suddenly the atmosphere in the cavern shifted, a mantle of dread settled over Lauralee as she saw a change come over the creatures before her. They stood more alert now, puppet strings pulled taut as if there was something else gazing through them. The robed ones' two left arms reached for the book, and Jane pulled her hand back.

"My payment?"

Another voice spoke from its lips. It was deep, rumbling, and spoke with a natural poetic cadence that rolled in and out. It put Lauralee in mind of the tide.

"You will find, Lady Jane. That I'm very generous. With those who serve me. I have your payment. I have included extra. A spell-book, a gift. In it, details. Tools. Information you'll need soon."

"Icaria, I presume?" Jane purred, not skipping a beat. That must've been the Scholar's name, Lauralee supposed.

"Indeed, that is I. A pleasure, meeting truly. You are as I guessed."

"Quite, well, it's not truly face-to-face, now, is it? But then I suppose it will do," Jane said in a mellifluous purr.

Rather than reply, the creature twitched a hand and its hulking aide turned, loping to the side, where it picked up what looked to be a coffin by a chain hung from a forged metal ring in the lid. It dragged it to them, as the robed creature produced a large tome of its own from within its robes and held it out with its right hand. Its two left hands sat waiting. A short silence ensued, before it was broken by Jane.

"And my creatures? The forces you have promised to me?" Jane asked, still holding the tome.

"They await your call. They are hidden for now. They are close indeed. Close to your manor, your home."

Jane grinned and, only then, finally, did she extend the book. The robed creature, the servitor of this scholar, this Icaria, took it and proffered the other to her. Jane accepted, slid the book smoothly into her satchel, and looked to the coffin.

"It is asleep, yes? Will it wake if I remove it from the coffin."

"No." The burbling, gasping voice had returned. "Powerful enchantments will keep it asleep for some time. But it will need to be returned to the coffin in time to keep it at rest."

"Good, then I think that should be all, yes? I look forward to calling upon your creatures later to inspect them. The book has the details?"

"Yes." With that, the creature turned and began walking away, its companion following. Once they were gone, Jane's smile grew wider and she stepped close to inspect the coffin, undoing the locks to crack it open, before peering inside. Her smile grew truly predatory then.

"What were they? What is that?" Lauralee asked her mistress, arms gesturing helplessly between the creatures and the coffin they'd left behind, beginning to approach it in desperate search of answers. A glance from Jane warned her away.

"Them? They're not important. Not anymore. They've served their purpose until I have a future need for them. Servants of some ancient mad wizard who thinks themself a god, not knowing what they've given up. I heard tell of them through some hearsay rumours and was able to get their attention enough for an exchange of letters, surprisingly nice handwriting. Did cost quite a few servitors of my own, though."

She reached a hand into the coffin, her smile turning almost tender for a moment, then she leaned away, closing the coffin, and twirling the red feather she had retrieved between her fingers, smelling it with relish.

"So, what did they give up?"

"She's a demigod, Lauralee, and now, she's mine. Even if that fool wizard thinks the tome can grant him divinity, having the real deal is so much greater. Come."

She summoned up an arcane well of force beneath the coffin, keeping it suspended unsteadily off the ground as she began to pull it along by the chain. She dropped the feather absently as she continued on past Lauralee, who stood wishing she had taken the chance to peer into the coffin, but imagined the contents wouldn't stay hidden from her much longer. She had so many questions she wanted to ask, but that wild, dangerous look in Jane's warned her they could wait for now.

—

AS THEY DEPARTED, NEITHER WOMAN took note of the feather left on the floor. Its tips began to smoulder and burn until it was wholly alight. Within those flames, within the light of the burning divine feather, a silhouette began to form. In moments, the feather was nothing but ash, and nestled atop it was a small red songbird. Looking around, it let out a chirping song before taking flight, making its own way from the caverns.

Chapter 1

SYLINE SAT UPRIGHT IN BED with a gasp. She found herself shivering, despite the clammy sweat that covered her from head to toe.

"Alexis!" she called. A moment passed. "Alexis!" she said louder, her heartbeat pounding in her ears.

Footsteps padded quickly down the hall outside her room, and the door opened to reveal her maid. Her short white hair was polar opposite to Syline's own black, waist-length hair. Her soft, sky-blue skin and arms covered in tattoos only made her all the more exotic. Alexis hailed from the tundra elves of the east, though her family had migrated when she was young. She was dressed still in her own pyjamas, having been woken in her quarters nearby by Syline's call.

Alexis hurried over to her, worry in her large eyes.

"Are you alright? Did you have that dream again?" she asked, stepping over and placing a hand to Syline's forehead. "You're freezing and you look pale as a ghost."

"I… I had a nightmare, yes, umn, yes, the halls again…" she mumbled but, despite the embarrassment, she was glad when her maid stepped in and embraced her. She was glad for the warmth. Alexis was the only person she had told about the recurring dream, those awful empty halls. She didn't want her family thinking she was any stranger than they already did.

"So, you call me like I'm your teddy-bear. You scaredy cat," Alexis teased, giving her a squeeze as she did. Syline managed a little smile as she pulled away from the embrace.

"Would you mind drawing me a bath? I feel frozen to the core."

"Sure, sure, I'll sneak one in myself afterwards before your sisters get up," her maid said and headed for the door. After a moment dawdling in bed, Syline followed, not feeling like being left to her lonesome in her room.

AFTER HER BATH, HER DAY proved quite relaxing. She and her maid shared breakfast in her room, well before the chefs had arrived to make breakfast for the rest of her family. She passed the day in quiet self-study watching snow begin to fall from darkening clouds outside her window, preparing herself for her lesson tonight with her tutor, the old wizard Anatoly. Only in the early afternoon was she called outside for her other lessons. Her daily duelling practice with her mother, the Falcon of Russenholde, Kassandra Petranski.

SYLINE WAS THE SECOND-ELDEST DAUGHTER of the nation's greatest general, Peter Petranski. Once an adventurer, her father was now the leader of the nation's border guard, defending it from the creatures that came from the north when the oceans and rivers froze. Creatures Syline, like most, had never seen. Things like trolls and wyverns were nothing but stories her brothers told to scare her. The nearest Syline had ever seen to a monster was the hellblooded in town; those humans who had devilish heritage somewhere in their bloodline, and they were still at heart, people. Her father took his sons with him for months at a time, training them in war and battle against the greatest of foes.

His four daughters and the matters of estate and noble politics, he left to his wife, Kassandra. Famed for being the greatest duellist in the land, she had once been his partner in adventures across the world. Her keen, amber eyes gained her the nickname "The Falcon of Russenholde". She stood austere and perfect, her black hair braided down to her waist and framing her hard, high-cheeked features as she watched the two girls before her.

Steel clashed against steel as Syline and her younger sister, Magdova, duelled. The pair were nearly identical and separated by only a year, yet, despite being the elder, Syline almost always lost these practice matches. The duels were scored on touches, not injury, and the frailer, thinner Syline had always struggled to compete with her sister, not just in skill, but in grace and cunning with the blade. Magdova moved like a dancer, her steps elegant and assured, whilst Syline moved methodically, transitioning from stance to stance, each one practised just as their mother had shown her. She was a good student if nothing else.

Syline saw an opening. She stepped in with a jab for her sister's shoulder. Magdova slid beneath the jab and threw her shoulder into Syline's chest. Off balance, Syline stumbled back. Her guard was open and Magdova knew it. Syline took a harsh slap from her sister's blade to her sternum. With a whimper, Syline landed on her rump in the snow. It had been brushed out of the ring by the servants, but overhead, the clouds grew darker, and Syline knew they'd be in for a storm this evening. She hoped to be warm inside for her lessons by then.

"Point for Magdova," their mother called, as Syline's sister gave her an apologetic smile, helping her to her feet.

Syline returned the smile with one of her own as she came up, before looking off to her mother. On either side of her sat her other sisters. Katarina, or Kat, as everyone actually called her, the eldest at twenty-two, five years older than Syline and already a professional duellist in her own right, sat to her left watching with interest. She had short hair and had taken after their mother, from her sharp, sculpted features to their mother's talent with the blade. Syline suspected, if it were her and all her other siblings versus Kat and her twin brother, the pair would best them easily. On her mother's right was Kassandra Jr. the youngest of all of them and their mother's last hope for a "normal" noble daughter. Syline and Magdova had each found their own paths in magic and art, Kat had dedicated herself to the blade, and their brothers were all soldiers after their father's heart. If their mother wanted to have any chance of allying their family with another through marriage, it'd be through Kassandra. She sat hugging her knees to her chest and shivering into her cloak. She was too young to be joining in on the duels just yet.

"Yes, Syline?" her mother asked, noting Syline staring their way.

"Nothing, Mother," Syline replied, stifling any comment she was going to make about Magdova's rough play. She didn't want to seem like a poor sport.

"Alright, then. It's best of three. Take one off your sister," she said, giving her an empathetic smile.

Syline gave her mother a nod and a smile, before turning back to Magdova, raising her blade vertically and tapping it to her breast in a warrior's salute. Magdova grinned and returned it.

"You're welcome to try," her cocky younger sister said as they each whipped their blades down to the side, signalling the beginning of their duel.

She and her sister each searched one another for weaknesses and openings as they circled one another. "The dance", as Magdova liked to call it. Syline kept her footwork stable. Meanwhile, Magdova was moving easily across the snow, but not with true purpose in her steps. She had confidence she was fast enough to respond to anything Syline threw out and was letting her defence falter for it. Magdova was cocky and Syline was sure she could take advantage of that. Syline stepped side-on and swung for her sister's shoulder. Her sister greedily threw her blade out wide to defend. Syline turned her arm out of the swing and let loose a swift jab at her sister's torso. Magdova gasped. She threw herself back and straight out of the ring to try and evade.

"Syline's point," their mother said. "Magdova! Don't underestimate your opponent! You're getting sloppy with confidence. Imagine if you faced Kat or me with that footwork!"

"Sorry, Mother!" Magdova squeaked out beneath the admonishment. She raised her blade up to her breast in another salute. Taking a long steadying breath, she narrowed her eyes and levelled her steely gaze at Syline. Her sister was taking this duel seriously now.

Good, even if she lost, Syline thought, she wouldn't make it easy for her and she'd do it without her sister's roughhousing. The pair exchanged a smile as she raised her blade up to her breast in return, then they each swept them out to the sides. The deciding match began.

For the last time that day, the pair began their dance, but this time, the mood was different. Now, both were taking it seriously. Now, both knew, the moment their attention wavered, they could truly lose. For Magdova, it was about maintaining her streak, while Syline was determined to break it. This time, Magdova wasn't seeking to punish her sister; she was out to overwhelm her. She thrust forward, and Syline parried it out to their side. Magdova turned it into a swipe at Syline's chest. She slapped that down and tried to counter, but her sister's blade was there already, stabbing at Syline again and again. Magdova was abandoning defence, but in the process, she was forcing Syline to abandon offence with how fast her attacks came.

Magdova knew her greatest advantages over her older sister were physical. Syline could slap the blows aside, but her sister's aggression gave her no room to counterattack. Syline found herself slowly backing towards the edge of the ring. She had to find an opening. She had to break the assault, or her sister would just drive her out.

As Magdova went for another jab, Syline thought she'd found it. She threw herself past her sister back into the centre of the ring, throwing a passing cut at her sister's shoulder. Magdova dodged it almost casually, but now Syline had her chance; she could bring up her own offence now. Her sister turned, slashing at Syline's shoulder. Syline brought her blade up to counter it and just like that, she had lost. Her sister had used the same trick she had on her, but to much more violent effect. Syline had tried to get her blade in the way as her sister twisted to jab at her chest but got caught on the knuckles by the blunted blade. The shock had her drop her blade, but her sister, intent on proving her victory, pressed on, jabbing Syline once, twice, thrice in the stomach. She pushed her elder lookalike back until Syline stumbled out of the ring, yelling for her sister to stop, that she had won.

"Magdova!" their mother said. "The match is over! This is sport, not combat."

Magdova froze in place with her arm cocked back for one final jab. Magdova looked that way, then lowered her blade. Syline stared at her, holding her hand. Only her gloves had stopped the blade cutting her. Even blunted, the point would likely still leave a bruise.

"Sorry, Syline," her younger sister said, letting out a little sigh and shaking her head. She sheathed her own sabre and stepped over. "I got a bit carried away there." She gave her an apologetic smile.

Syline looked at her sister for a moment, ready to retort, to tell her off, to call her a bully, a buffoon, cruel, even. But she didn't. Her sister was competitive to a level Syline wasn't. That's how it was and sometimes you do get a little hurt in these duels. Even Syline had left her sister with bruises from over eager swings a few times in the past. That was what she told herself to push down her anger. To hide how frustrated she was at her sister. How annoyed she was about how desperate her sister was to maintain that streak. How angry she was about how her sister got so brutal when she looked like she might win even once. She didn't tell her off. She just shook her head, stepped in and hugged her sister.

"It's alright Mags. It happens," she said, flexing her hurting knuckles behind her sister's back. "Good to know you're that scared of losing to me," she teased, although a bit flatly. "I'll need to make those fears come true next time."

Their mother smiled and, after a moment of watching the pair, called to them.

"You two are finished for the day. Syline, get Alexis to find you a balm for your knuckles. The both of you can take it easy 'til dinner."

Parting, the pair each nodded to their mother and disappeared inside.

AFTER HELPING BALM HER KNUCKLES, Alexis went off shopping with the other maids, and Magdova left for her lessons with her tutor. Syline was left alone to stew. Her sister might've apologised, but her knuckles still ached and she was still frustrated over the whole incident. Syline was passing the time by doing a bit of reading, a bawdy novel her mother would surely confiscate called *The Dragonslayer's Lance*. She was comfortably settled in the window love seat in her room when her mother creaked the door open and stepped inside. Syline quickly slid her book under a pillow as her mother shut the door behind her.

"How're your knuckles, little sparrow?" she asked as Syline turned to face her properly.

Syline held out her hand, clenching and unclenching.

"It's not as bad as it looked," she said. It still ached, but she didn't want to seem like a poor loser.

"I'm glad," her mother said with a smile as she sat down beside Syline and put an arm around her shoulders. "You did well that second round."

"But I still lost," Syline said bitterly, a little frown peeking through. She hadn't won at all this month. Today was the closest she had come in a while.

"I know you did, but you did so with grace. That's more than I can say for how your sister won today."

Syline managed a bit of a smile at that but shrugged. She was trying to push them down, but tears quickly began budding at the corner of her eyes.

"I just… it's been so long since I've managed to win even one match. It just feels unfair. I try and I try, but she always wins."

"Come here," her mother said, standing up and walking to the mirror above Syline's dresser. Syline followed, and her mother wrapped both arms around her, pulling her to stand in front of her. Her mother was almost a head taller than her.

"It might not come as naturally for you as it does Kat and Magdova, but I still see so much potential in you, my little sparrow."

Syline shook her head a little.

"I could never compare to you or Kat," she mumbled.

Her mother's grip on her tightened.

"To be fair," her mother started, "I'm not sure I could compare to Katarina now. She's got the kind of talent that comes once in a generation. But, in some ways, I despair for her."

"Why?" Syline asked, confused.

"Because Kat has eyes only for duelling. She's so much like her twin, Ulrik, in that. He'll be a fine general, but you should see him on the dance floor. She might be the finest duellist I could ever hope for, but martial skill isn't all I want you girls to take from it. Duelling is what I know best, so it's how I teach, but from it, I want you girls to learn manners, cunning, how to read others and how to think for yourselves." She smiled softly and fixed one of Syline's curls behind her ear, before continuing, "You might not have as much raw talent as Magdova, but you also pay a lot more attention to what I tell you. Perhaps with a little extra training. How would you feel about a few extra lessons, just the two of us, maybe three times a week?"

Syline smiled up at her mother, emboldened by her words for her. She wiped her eyes clear of the tears.

"I'd like that, Mother."

"Fantastic, in fact, I'm so certain you'll beat her soon, that I'm going to give you half your prize for it now."

Syline cocked her head slightly to the side and watched through the mirror as her mother pulled a small black box out of her coat pocket. She opened it to reveal twin platinum hair pins, each one bearing the family crest: twin sabres crossed over a torch. The torch in this case bearing a tiny blue jewel to symbolise the flame. Syline felt her breath taken away and just stared as her mother took out one and used it to pin one side of Syline's long curls back.

"Do you like them?"

"I love them!" Syline squealed and inspected herself in the mirror.

Her mother embraced her tight and leaned down to kiss into her hair.

"Then be quick to win the second, little sparrow," she said, giving a playful grin, before releasing her and starting to walk for the door. "Take it easy for now, though. I'll see you at dinner."

Syline watched her mother go with a barely restrained grin, before turning to inspect the hair pin in the mirror once more. She'd have to be sure to win the next as soon as possible.

DINNER THAT EVENING WAS SERVED just as the sun began to set. Tonight, it was medium rare venison seasoned with rosemary and salt, along with mashed potatoes, drenched in perhaps a little too much gravy. There was grilled toast on the side that had butter practically oozing off it. The sight and smell of the meal were almost as good as the taste, the heady scents of butter, salt and still cooking fats filled Syline's nose.

If Syline was thankful for one thing about all the exercise her mother forced them to do, it was that it certainly worked off the heavy meals the family enjoyed, otherwise she'd barely fit into her training leathers. Ever since their mother had ruled no magic, art or books at the table, Magdova and Syline had become quick eaters and needed to be dragged from their hobbies by their youngest sister, Kassandra Jr. All three arrived together and sat down as one, quickly falling into conversation.

Magdova was incredibly jealous when she caught sight of Syline's new hair pin, but soon enough forgot about it as she spoke to the enraptured audience of her sisters, about her next painting. She spoke about how she and her teacher had been having disputes over the changing artistic styles in popularity, and to prove her case, she was doing a piece on one of the ancient bridges that linked this island with the next. Neither Syline nor Kassandra understood a lot of what she said, but their sister's passion for it had them captivated.

Those bridges had always been of interest to Syline, who loved ancient mysteries and mythology. Large land masses were exceedingly rare, so the ancient bridges, linking the world's numerous islands that made kingdoms and borders beyond those of a coast even a possibility. They had been around longer than any recorded history and their stone and woodwork did not decay with time. The Church of the Wanderer insisted that the Wanderer built them when he journeyed across the world at its conception. With few better explanations, even other religions accepted that as fact. Whenever the family went on trips outside the city, Syline always made sure to carry her own little iron talisman of the Wanderer, a gift from her father. It took the form of a disc, representing the world, with the arc of a bridge across its centre. She thumbed the talisman in her pocket, thinking of her lessons that night as Magdova finally trailed off, losing steam around when the maids were clearing away their empty plates.

After dinner came a dessert of caramelised figs served on vanilla ice cream, with maple syrup drizzled over the whole ordeal. Kat and their mother seemed ever so slightly put off by the dessert. Instead, the pair of them just had coffee as they talked about the duels of the day. Their mother would occasionally stop to drag Kassandra Jr from servants or Magdova, to force her to talk about politics and court for at least a little while. Eventually though, dinner came to an end, and while her sisters were happy to hang around and talk to one another until the end of time, Syline was eager to be away.

Once she was excused from the table, she practically sprinted to her room, gathered up her satchel, coin purse – in case she got hungry or wanted a coffee on her way home – her study journal, and spell-book, wrapped a scarf around her neck and put on her beloved witch's hat: tall, with a crooked tip and a sash around the brim. She thought the hat, more than even the wand, made her look the part of a mage. She kept her plush toy sparrow in her pocket. She was seventeen now and, while her sisters occasionally teased her about him, she'd had Malir since she was little, and she wasn't about to throw a gift from her parents away. Besides, she didn't have a familiar yet, so, until she did, Malir would have to suffice as her arcane companion. She had always preferred to walk, even in poor weather, such as tonight. The snow had only grown heavier as the hours dragged on and looked fit to sit at the flurry it was now until the morning. Syline was making her way for the door and tightening her scarf when her mother called her back.

"Syline, you're forgetting your sword."

Syline had a certain pride about being a young wizardess. Magdova's passion might be for art, and Kat's the blade, but Syline defined herself by the wand. Her mother thought differently and Syline turned to find her right behind her, the blade in hand.

It was a beautiful blade. Clean, unblemished steel with a golden crossguard detailed with a silver engraving of their house sigil. Well weighted for Syline's hand too; she couldn't have handled a larger or heavier sabre. Kassandra handed it to her as she gave her a one-armed hug.

"No Petranski woman is complete without her blade," she told her, as she had dozens of times before. "Stay safe alright?"

"I will, Mother."

"And have fun, little sparrow. I love you."

Syline smiled up at her mother and gave her a brief squeeze.

"I love you too, Mother."

With those final parting words, Syline stepped out into the cold and pulled her scarf up over her mouth. She exited the manor's gates and started up the main road towards the King's palace and the attached great library where she would meet her tutor. Overhead, the weather broached upon a blizzard; it had never let up all day and it looked like a storm was brewing on the horizon, ready to break at any moment.

Chapter 2

IN A WORLD DIVIDED INTO fragmented islands and long archipelagos, the city of Russenholde had the privilege of being one far larger than most. Capital to the kingdom of the same name, though not the oldest or the most powerful militarily, Russenholde garnered plenty of respect. Many travellers wished to settle there, thanks in large part to its plentiful resources: iron, good farmland and a fish population that never seemed to fade. Its strong walls kept many safe from the dark wilds, and the streets within were cramped, winding and labyrinthine in all but the richest quarters, to cope with this. On top of having such a sprawling city, the island had room for a great many farms. It even extended northward into wild untamed forests and foothills tended to only by the nomadic tundra elves who laid claim to them.

In the winter however, the island's farms became little more than frozen plains and the farmers took to the greenhouses, controlled by the court wizards, making the streets more cramped than ever in the colder months. Workmen and labourers bumped shoulders with displaced farmhands and livestock.

Through those age-old winding streets, Syline made her way for her nightly lessons, negotiating between those same displaced farm workers. The streets were still busy this early in the evening, light seeping from windows, lanterns hanging from tent stalls that would be open an hour or so longer, and cold vendors nodding to Syline as she passed, all working together to give the city an air of life amidst the gathering dark and chill. She occasionally had to sidle between stalls to make way for a carriage or politely push her way through a group of townsfolk or merchants heading one way or another. Syline moved faster than most city goers. After all, her lessons with her magic teacher – an ex-court mage himself – were the part of the day she looked forward to the most.

Not even the biting snow whipping against her robes could smother the embers of excitement building up in her chest for the rest of the evening. She did, however, take the time to wrap her scarf about her face to stop it freezing her lungs, for the snowfall had only grown harder since she'd departed. The wind whistled and wailed around the elven "onion-tipped" towers, which reached for the sky in the richer areas. The brightly coloured architectural style had become more and more popular of late, pushing in amongst the high sloped roofs of the city.

Seeing an amassing crowd of workmen leaving for home, Syline cut down a side alley to avoid getting caught up in the flow of foot traffic. These side-streets made up much of Russenholde and one could find all manner of impromptu stores, taverns and seedier establishments hidden within them – if one knew where to look. During the day, the sheer amount of foot traffic made these side-alleys safe for just about anyone to venture through, but as the sun was setting, Syline's heart started to race. She felt eyes on her from windows up above. She could hear howls of laughter and far more canine growls from a hidden tavern. Dog fighting, she guessed. She was convincing herself away from looking in the window when she heard him.

"Hey missy, come 'ere a second," a voice drawled from behind her.

Syline whipped around and found a man, stumbling towards her from yet another hard-to-find tavern, tipsy, but brawny. To the frightened Syline, it seemed like he was practically twice her size, his biceps as thick as her hips. He looked like a lumberjack, or maybe a blacksmith or ice fisher. Fear rushed through her.

"I'm afraid I'm quite busy. I'm sorry, sir," she managed, backing away from him. Quite proud of herself for keeping a stammer out of her voice.

"Aw now, don't be like that, pretty girl like you." He took a few steps closer to her and Syline saw his hand come to rest on a long knife on his belt.

She acted first. She had to. She could see other thugs like him emerging from the same tavern, watching with amusement. She feared this could turn ugly at any moment if she didn't get away. Syline drew out her long duelling sabre and held it in a forward guard intended for fending off someone taller than her, like Kat. She hoped it would work well enough on a brute like this.

"My name is Syline Petranski, daughter of Peter Petranski, the King's foremost general! I-if you don't want his wrath raining down upon you, leave me alone, sir!"

The man took a halting step back, eyes widening in alarm and hands coming up in submission. Whether it was the volume of her voice drawing attention, the content of her words, or perhaps the blade in her hand, he seemed put off his course. The man gave a great shrug of his shoulders.

"Ah'm sorry, ma'am, didna realise you was a noble." He took a few more steps back then turned away and scampered into the other brutes, who began to jostle their fellow. Laughing at him, taunting him for backing down so easily.

"You shouldn't threaten a girl no matter who she is, you big brute," Syline muttered at his back, keeping her eyes on him as he cursed out his friends, eyeing her over his shoulder until she hit the next main street over, where she finally sheathed her blade and quick-stepped away from that alley and the men within.

With them out of sight, she began moving quickly along the main thoroughfare, still heavy with the traffic of tradesmen and women, quick enough that she'd have been told it was unseemly by other noblewomen, and cowardly by her far more warrior-like mother. She made for the perceived safe-haven of a cafe she frequented at this end of the main road that led to the library some five minutes away. It was always open late for court wizards departing the archives and King's palace late in the evening, and with such a clientele, she didn't think anyone would be foolish enough to follow her in there.

—

STEPPING INTO THE CAFÉ, SHE found it a refreshingly warm reprieve from the chill evening air. The smell of coffee grounds permeated the place and the tinkle of the bell above the door was a balm to her nerves, familiarity easing the tension coiling her heart. Gustaf, the owner, a dwarf from far to the west, was a bald man with cherry red cheeks and teeth stained by a long habit of chewing a mix of tobacco and coffee grounds. He turned to beam at her as she shook snow from her shoulders.

"Lady Petraska!" His voice boomed, his accent foreign.

"Petranski, Gustaf."

"Petranski, Petranski, right. I'll remember this time!" he said, giving her a cheeky grin. He did that every time she entered the place. It was somewhere between endearing and annoying, but she could never quite settle on which. "What will be?"

"The honeyed smile, please. I'll take it to go. I'm headed for the library."

"Just leave mug at front desk! I collect tomorrow," he said, bobbing his head with a nod, as he turned to begin making her drink. She placed the payment for it on the counter, to a call of "Thank!" from the man, but he did not turn around to count the coin, leaving her with a moment of silence.

Besides him, the place was almost empty. There was one other woman sat by the window, reading. Syline approached the front of the shop to check through the window to see if the man was following her, looking this way and that up the street, without daring to duck her head outside. The snow fell thick now; it was hard to see far past the light of the shop, but she saw no sign of him. A shudder ran through her. She knew she was being silly; no one would be foolish enough to chase after a daughter of the king's general, indeed, the king's god-daughter, but still, the thought of running into him in the burgeoning dark raced through her mind.

"Are you alright?"

The voice almost jolted her out of her skin. It was the woman. Looking at her properly, Syline could see she was probably around her age, her short cropped white hair had made Syline mistakenly think she'd have been far older. She wore a maid's skirts, but had a thick, traveller's leather jacket thrown over them.

"Hmn? Oh, yes, I'm, I'm fine. Thank you." Syline's cheeks felt flushed. She didn't want to admit to this woman she was nervous to leave over something so silly. Desperate for something to change the topic, she took note of the book the woman was reading.

"Oh, is that the *Wyvernclaw Tales*?"

The woman paused, blinking at her, before looking down at the book she read. She paused to mark her page with a red bookmark, styled to look like a mote of flame, closing it as she replied.

"Yes, it is, volume two." She looked back up, giving her a smile. "Have you read it?"

"I'm reading the third volume now. Where are you up to?"

"I'm about halfway. Cain has just found out where his powers come from. Were you getting a coffee? You're welcome to sit with me if you'd like."

"I can't," Syline stammered. "I'll be late for my lessons at the library. I'm just taking my drink to go. But," she trailed off.

"But? You seem nervous about something."

Syline sighed. She'd been caught. Her eyes trailed to the door as her hands came to hug her biceps.

"I… there, there was a man, a thug. He harassed me in an alley near here and I embarrassed him. I'm just a little rattled and a little scared he may have followed me."

"My mistress is expecting me back at the library soon." The young woman stood up, draining the last of her own drink. It was the same syrup and cream heavy concoction Syline had ordered. A dreadfully sweet mix Gustaf had brought from his homeland, which hearsay said, was even colder than Russenholde.

"Why don't I walk with you? I doubt he'd be fool enough to bother two armed young women," she offered with a small smirk, nodding to a sword Syline had failed to notice on her hip.

A sigh of relief slid out of Syline, though she tried to stifle it.

"I'd like that," she began, before giving a small curtsy. "I'm Syline Petranski," she said as she stood back up straight, "and you are?"

"Lauralee Lupa. I am Lady Jane Petrov's personal assistant. She's doing some study at the library presently."

"Lady Petrov? Oh, I've always wanted to meet her, maybe you could…"

"Lady Petraska! Your drink ready!" Gustaf interrupted.

A little grin crinkled Syline's features.

"Coming, Gustaf!" she called back, before finishing, "Maybe you could introduce me to her some time?"

Lauralee cocked her head at that but gave a small nod.

"Perhaps," she said, waving for Syline to collect her drink.

When Syline returned, the other young women offered her arm to her, like a knight would to a lady. Syline had walked with her father's soldiers like that in the past, even the prince once, but having another girl protecting her felt a tad embarrassing. Despite that, she took Lauralee's bicep with one hand, huddling close by her side, sipping her drink with the other as they ventured out into the cold. She couldn't say if it was gratitude, or the overwhelming sweetness of the drink that kept a smile plastered across her lips the whole way there.

—

THE GRAND LIBRARY WAS A special place in the city, at least as far as Syline was concerned. Attached to the castle itself, the four-storey building sat inside the king's personal holdings and was devoted to study and the archiving of history. The place was filled to the brim with the smell of old parchment and melted wax from an endless number of burned-out candles. The college where most court mages gained their full tutelage might be two nations away in the Magocracy of Sigillite, but Syline felt near certain that this library held more knowledge than that place ever could. She wasn't there already because one needed a certain level of mastery and because of a number of arguments across which her mother had made very clear Syline wasn't ready to leave home yet, and that she'd tear her poor mother apart with stress if she moved away from home, let alone the nation. Either way, Syline was happy enough to continue her tutelage in private, for now.

The first floor was a public library for those who wished to advance themselves, tended to by a number of librarians, including a lovely blind dwarf girl Syline liked to talk to. But it was the second floor that Syline headed to tonight. Divided into ten sections for each of the noble families of the city, private records, artefacts and family histories were gated behind lock, key, and the assurances they were in a place protected by the king himself.

Some families had large cabinets full of prized weapons and magical tools, others had filing cabinets full of documents. One even had dozens of spell-books from each of their past wizards in the family. The Petranski family, however, wasn't known for being a family of readers; financial records, a few books on hunting and war dictated by Syline's father, and a ledger on active hunters, were all that adorned their bookcase. The rest of the private area was taken up by a reading table with two chairs and a blackboard. It was here Syline's private lessons were conducted and nowhere in the world did she feel more secure than in this little section of the library.

Syline had just bid farewell to Lauralee, promising to catch up some time to talk more, and letting the other girl have what she'd failed to finish of her drink, as thanks for her guardianship, when her tutor called out to her, having heard her enter.

"Syline, dear, do hurry up; I'm all set up and ready," came his deep, but soft tones.

Her tutor, Anatoly, had once been a very prodigious court mage, but now he had retired to the role of archivist. Like most men of her land, he was naturally broad and powerfully built, but age had stooped him. His hair had receded long ago, though his long, well-trimmed beard stood strong. Still, when Syline was around, the man's eyes shone with energy and glee.

Anatoly had retired from the role of court mage after his wife and daughter had died in childbirth. It was a few years after this that Syline had met him and begged him to take her under his wing. He'd taken her by surprise by agreeing without hesitation, and Syline certainly didn't mind the way he doted on her and treated her like his own; it helped make up for her own often absent father. Syline was used to spending a few hours listening to his stories, learning new spells and advancing herself alongside her ageing teacher, alone. They'd never had guests in their lessons before, apart from the few times her mother or father wanted to sit in. That's why she was taken aback – shocked even – when she turned the corner into her family's little sanctum.

Sat beside Anatoly, giving her a faintly nervous smile, was a young man. Probably only a few years older than her, his skin was tanned, and his arms were lean but very well-muscled. Curly black hair spilled down his shoulders, framing a boyishly handsome face. Tattoos around his eyes, that gleamed like fresh oil, marked him as a sorcerer, for only they needed such things to help bind their powers. He wore sleeveless red robes, pippets and badges upon it, marking him as one of her father's men. The fetishes, amulets, and tools of an accomplished battle mage hung off the robe and his wrists. A faint scar sat on the corner of his lip. Magdova would have described it as "rakish" or "dashing" and Syline had a hard time disagreeing. He gave her a rather limp salute, as if unsure that was appropriate for the situation. With a giggle, Syline curtsied back.

"Syline, let me introduce our guest for tonight," began Anatoly, gesturing to the young man. "This is Ioann Voronyakogtya, a sorcerer in your father's forces. His unit is on leave here and I thought it would be a great chance for you to learn about sorcerers. It's not like we have any permanently here in the city."

"It's a pleasure to meet you, Miss Petranski," Ioann said. His speech was a little halting, like he was talking to a superior officer and reminding himself to be polite. Syline was a little put out; she didn't often talk to men even close to her age and if he was going to treat her like that, she rather doubted she'd be making a friend.

"And, since he's here, I thought I'd do what your mother apparently never has, and teach you how to talk to boys," Anatoly said with a grin, splitting his old features.

"What?!" cried both Syline and Ioann, each looking at him in alarm, blushes gathering on their cheeks.

Syline's old tutor cackled, slapping his knee as he wiped tears from the bags under his eyes.

"I'm sorry, I'm sorry, I couldn't resist! The pair of you are both so shy."

Syline felt a moment of camaraderie with Ioann when he glared right along with her at her tutor, who simply looked all too pleased with himself.

"Oh, don't be such poor sports," he said, still grinning. "Sit, Syline, sit. We might as well start the lesson. Today, we'll be studying a basic fire spell. Obviously, elemental spells are key to many battlemages' arsenals, and Ioann has made the subject of our lesson something of a signature of his."

Syline couldn't help but gain a giddy grin at that. Usually, Anatoly was quick to dismiss any combative magic as beneath researchers and intellectuals, such as themselves. He'd taught her some basic magic for self-defence, but only at her insistent begging and liberal application of fluttered eyelashes and whining. Whatever he might think, Syline still considered it the most exciting kind of magic.

"Habere ferrum pugione art feuer," Anatoly incanted and summoned from his wand a long line of sapphire-blue flame with orange just touching its edges. It was around the length of a short sword and emitted a constant roaring sound as it devoured the air around it.

"We'll be revisiting it when you eventually learn about enchanted items and medical magic. It sees common use in both. Obviously, it has great combat applications though and that's what we'll be focusing on today."

Syline practically had stars in her eyes as the lesson continued. Her teacher ran her through the incantation. Incantations were based around shaping the magic as it was produced, and similar phrases were used in many spells. Syline was familiar with the opening phrase of the spell, but she'd never worked with the shaping phrase, nor the one that conjured the flame. She'd never worked with elemental magic before and it turned into quite a tongue twister. It took her quite a few tries on the elemental phrasing before Anatoly was happy with her. That wasn't even working in any spell or efficiency suffixes to alter the output of the spell. Having Ioann sitting off to the side, quietly looking embarrassed, didn't help. His discomfort and shyness were only making Syline feel all the more awkward, and she kept stumbling over herself whenever she caught his amber eyes.

Anatoly found it hilarious.

"Alright, that should do it. We'll wait 'til we're outside 'til you cast it in full. Don't want to risk anything catching alight. When we're out there, Ioann can show you *his* rendition of the spell, as well." With a quiet groan as his old knees panged with pain, the old mage led the way to the stairs but was quickly outpaced by his younger companions.

Of the three, Ioann seemed the most eager as they made their way out of the library, practically leaping down the stairs. Syline was momentarily distracted, waving to Lauralee who caught her eye, carrying a stack of books back to Jane's holdings. The maid looked from Syline to the sorcerer Ioann and grinned, mouthing, "Nice," to her. Syline blushed and hurried after Ioann.

—

THE THREE STOOD TOGETHER BY the small carriage station attached to the library. The snow fell heavily now, each snowflake thick, and gathering on the ground swiftly in great swathes, but a spell from Ioann had it so none of it ever touched them.

"Alright, Syline, try casting the spell now, please. Now that we're not at risk of burning anything down," her mentor told her with a playful little chuckle.

Syline ignored his jibe, instead focusing on the pronunciation. The arcane language was something to be mastered in and of itself, many of the words rolling, complex sounds that pushed the ability to form them. She held her spell-book open, reading from it and letting the words come forth, one after the other.

The spell completed; she felt the magic rush through her. It felt warm as it pooled in her fingers, bursting forth as a short dagger of fire from the tip of her pointer, around the length of her hand. It was bright blue, just like Anatoly's. A bright, giddy grin split Syline's lips.

"Well done, Syline! But you'll need to limit your output, or you'll wear yourself out in no time!" Anatoly turned to Ioann. "Now, our guest here is a bit of an expert in his own rendition of the spell. Ioann, can you show us?"

"Sure. You might want to, er… you should stand back a bit."

Anatoly placed a hand on Syline's shoulder and guided her back a few steps.

Ioann said no incantation, held no magical focus and carried no spellbook. He held up his arm and let out a roar as the tattoos on his face and ones hidden beneath his coat glowed cherry-red. His arm from the elbow down was encased in pure, sky-blue flame with purple and white shades around its edges. Extending well past his fist, his flame "dagger" was almost six feet long, far better described as a great sword. Probably just to show off, the man swung it along the ground, leaving a great rent of melted snow in its wake. The snow that even got close to him vaporised into steam from the heat of being near it, leaving a slowly widening patch of rising steam and clear cobblestones around him.

Syline looked down at her little flame dagger and quietly dismissed it before exclaiming, "That's amazing, Ioann!" The man grinned bashfully and dismissed the flames.

"As I said, Ioann here is a hunter for your father; he has something of an acclaim for that spell. After all, not many mages are known for rushing headlong at their enemies. How long can you keep that up, Ioann?"

"Usually for around ten minutes or so, sir. Then, I'd need around half an hour's rest."

"See, Syline? A sorcerer is a unique kind of person. Their magical energy returns to them much faster than anyone else's and in far, far greater quantities. We wizards need the ink to tap into magic at all, for the ink acts as our conduit into our own souls, from which we draw our power. Sorcerous magic is different, however, their souls have words of power, words of the arcane, written into them; in fact, it's sorcerers who discovered much of our founding lexicon for the language of the arcane, by discovering the words tied into their souls. It comes so naturally to them that, without training, many are unable to control their magic and produce spells purely by accident. Incantations are useless to them. Their power can even be given to another to grant a wizard their nearly infinite reserves for a short time. Though, doing so will take the magic from the sorcerer for good, perhaps even kill them." He said it all with his usual studious manner, but Syline saw Ioann's discomfort written across his face. "Ah, not that we'd ever do such a thing in Russenholde. The practice is forbidden, but not all lands are so moral."

Ioann gave a small nod, a frown written across his face.

"I've heard of the mage seekers to the far south."

"Indeed," Anatoly said, now frowning himself, "but let's not get too lost on such grim topics. Tonight was meant to be fun for the pair of you. To get back on topic, there's also the key aspect sorcerers have, that makes them natural battle mages, but also serves as their greatest weakness."

Anatoly stepped away from the pair of them and looked first at Syline.

"Syline, dear, try casting the spell again, but make it as powerful as you possibly can, okay?"

Syline nodded, feeling a bit flustered. She knew she couldn't possibly compare to the kind of power Ioann had just shown, but that didn't mean she wasn't going to try. She repeated the incantation, adding provisors to increase the output and will more strength into the dagger. When it reemerged, it was about a half a length longer than before, almost entirely white with a centre of blue right at the tip of her finger. She couldn't help but grin with pride and hold her hand up to show it off. Anatoly clapped, as did Ioann, but Syline very quickly felt herself running short with familiar nausea that told a mage they were reaching their limit. She dismissed the spell before it exhausted all her magic.

"Fantastic work, Syline. See, for a novice, that is very impressive. You could likely soften metal to uselessness with that, even if you can only keep it up for a few moments. You practise enough to have a good magical reserve for someone your age. Now, Ioann, I want you to make your own blade as small and tightly controlled as possible."

She thought she heard Ioann curse under his breath, and already, the sorcerer looked embarrassed. He didn't roar this time, but instead stared at his arm in intense focus, his brow furrowed. The flames emerged from just past his wrist, encasing his fist in them. Unlike Syline's and the blade he had displayed before, it seemed very unstable. It was around the length of his arm now and flickered and spurted at random, sending sparks and bursts of fire pushing from it off to the sides rather than being one focused length. The shape of the flame fluxed and the heat seemed to be fluctuating just as often. With a strained release of breath, the flames surged up into their previous size, and, with a sigh, Ioann dismissed them and shook his head with an embarrassed chuckle.

"Powerful, bombastic spells come naturally to sorcerers. The difficulty for them comes in reducing the amount of power, rather than increasing it. Already, Ioann is quite renowned for his control of the spell by sorcerer standards. Most sorcerers wouldn't even manage the blade, their magic would escape in great bouts of fire, explosions and blasts."

"But that's partially thanks to these tattoos, ma'am—"

"Syline's fine," Syline said with a little smile his way. She saw one come to Ioann's face as well, before he cleared his throat and nodded.

"Er, right, Syline, the ink doesn't quite work the same way for me like it would a wizard. The tattoos, they sort of… they rein me in, stop it pouring out nonstop and put a cap on how much I can give."

"So, while a wizard's speciality comes in surgical, precise spells of various utilities, a sorcerer can cause great destruction or amazing effects. For them, the sign of a master is being able to rein it in."

Syline was wrapped up in it, but she couldn't get the image out of her head of that huge blade of flame Ioann had summoned, and how amazing he had looked holding it. Sorcerers might not be as controlled or scholarly as wizards, in fact, she could easily see Magdova as a sorcerer with the wild bursts of energy they seemed to spur off, but they were still amazing in their own right. She listened to the pair's explanations and further lessons in enraptured bliss, occasionally giving a question or providing her own thoughts on a topic. Sadly, Ioann didn't stay the whole lesson, leaving early to evade the coming blizzard with a promise that he'd try and meet Syline for coffee sometime before he left for the hunt once again.

Anatoly teased her mercilessly for the giddy grin and blush she gained the moment Ioann wasn't looking. Syline had no defence but to pout at her tutor.

Chapter 3

AFTER IOANN LEFT, THE LESSON turned more to discussing the theory, history, variations and applications of the spell that had come throughout the years. Syline wouldn't pretend for a moment that this wasn't one of her favourite parts. As much as she loved magic, she loved stories of the past just as much and hearing the tales of famous wizards renowned for the spell set a thrill in her heart. When the lesson finally came to an end, snow still pelted hard against the window.

Anatoly looked to the window with a tired sigh as he stood up.

"Would you like me to walk you home? Gods know a girl your age shouldn't walk the streets at night alone as you do. Besides, your mother terrifies me, and if anything were to happen to you, it'd be my head on the chopping block."

"Actually–" Syline started.

"Yes, Syline?"

"Do you mind if I stay a bit late? I kind of want to do some reading here before I go home."

"Reading you couldn't do at home?"

"Please? You know I love it here."

The archivist gave a grand sigh. Like her mother, he found it hard to be harsh on Syline, and unlike her mother, he didn't have a stern streak laced into him. He fished out the keys from his pocket, and, immediately, Syline's eyes lit up with glee.

He held them up.

"You'll lock up when I leave and I'll let your mother know. This storm's getting worse. If you don't come home soon, it'll be too bad for you to come home, so you'll be better spending the night." Anatoly placed the keys down on the table and leaned over to peck her on the cheek. "Have a good evening, little sparrow. Stay safe."

After Anatoly left, Syline spent a fair bit of time dawdling in the Petranski's holding in the library, running back over her notes and practising the flame dagger spell to light candles that had run low around the room. Once she had the variations of the incantation in mind, it was none too difficult to lower the power of the spell to a simple, weak flame, just enough to light the candles and give her some practice. While she was practising, Lauralee popped her head in to wish her a goodnight and let her know that she and her mistress were leaving now. Syline reaffirmed her promise that they would catch up some time. It was rare she met someone who shared her taste in adventure novels.

She was rooting through her bag for *The Dragonslayer's Lance* when it occurred to her that she should lock up the library. This late, it was shut to the public, and only court wizards and nobles, who had the keys, were allowed entry. Tonight, that included her, something which she was rather smug about. As it stood, she was alone here, bar the scant few guards patrolling outside. The library was her kingdom this night, no court wizards were there and, as much as it made her feel smug, that smugness came with a rush of excitement and fear both.

Making her way down the steps, her eyes glanced to the windows by the door, and she was surprised to see the silhouette of a man cast in black against the snow by the lanterns hung on either side of the door. At first, she assumed it was just one of the guards passing by on their patrol. But he was heading straight for the door, and she recognised the silhouette, the big, brawny shoulders, huge arms, and loping gait.

It was the man from the alley.

Panic gripped her heart and Syline sprinted for the door as fast as her legs and her entangling robes would allow. The door began to open, the man's hand appearing on its edge and Syline simply threw herself against it. She heard a muffled cry of pain through the slammed door as she frantically pushed the key into the lock. There was a splatter of blood around where his hand had been. Turning the key, she slumped against the door, panting as she watched the handle rattle, once, twice, then the man seemed to finally give up. She breathed a sigh of relief and began to back away from the door, just in time to see as the man's face appeared in the window. She thanked the Wanderer that the first-floor windows of the library were barred on the inside, but still the man's glare made her quiver in fear.

The man turned his head like he had heard something. He looked back at her and slammed his hand against the window, leaving a bloody trio of fingerprints. A guard must've heard his cry and the man had no intention of getting caught as he ran off into the night. Even with him gone, Syline felt her breath coming short to her as she ran to lock any other entrance to the library. The shadows cast by lanterns around the building were long. More than once Syline could have sworn she saw one move or one that was just a little too close to a human shape. She prayed it was just her fear and paranoia in the wake of the man. She didn't run into any more trouble as she locked the two backdoors into the library, the one out into the carriage stands, and the one back into the palace itself, which really, she didn't need to lock, but it made her feel better.

Finally, beginning to convince herself she was safe, she made her way back to the Petranski holdings and locked the bar door behind her. A long sigh shook the fear out, relief and safety washing over her now that she knew for near certain no one would be able to reach her. There was no way she'd be going home tonight. She'd just have to stick it out in here. She could make it up to her mother in the morning. She dragged a chair over by the window and grabbed a pillow she had left here the last time she stayed overnight, along with the spare pair of robes stashed under a cabinet. Finally, fetching her book from her satchel, she nestled herself down in the chair, pillow at her back and both robes cocooning her against the freezing cold outside.

"I'm okay," she promised herself. Reaching into her scarf she produced her little plush sparrow, Malir, and hugged it to her breast as she said once more, "I'm okay."

Opening her book, she eventually started to sink into the tawdry tale and forget her worries, hidden away in her little nook of the world as she was. She couldn't help but imagine the dragon slayer as Ioann, and the princess he saved, as herself. Eventually though, she found herself placing the pillow onto the arm rest and laying her head down. Hugging tight to her proto-familiar, Syline soon enough dozed off in the seat, content and warm in her own little domain.

―

THE SOUND OF GLASS SHATTERING and the screeching of the harsh wind pulled Syline out of her slumber. It must've only been a few hours or so, for it was pitch black outside, and only a couple of candles still burned around her hideaway, flickering limply at the end of their wicks. Sitting up, Syline unwound herself from in amongst her robes and climbed to her feet. A thief? Someone coming to steal from the library? The thrill of excitement and fear ran through her. She tried to rationalise that no one would be fool enough to try and rob the king's own library, but memories of the man from earlier pushed those illusions away. Some would be fool enough.

The man. What if he had come back for her yet again? She approached the barred door of the Petranski holdings and looked out into the library, conjuring a tiny mote of light at her shoulder with a muttered incantation and a flick of her wand, fetched from the table. It drifted through the bars and she used the moving mote of light to try and discern just what had happened. There, from another of the locked noble holdings, snow drifted between the bars of the door. Only the most determined thief would try and steal from the second storey in a night like this. Surely, the wind would blow them from here to three kingdoms over if it caught them wrong. That meant it most likely wasn't a thief, but Syline knew just how much damage wild weather like this could do to books. Already she could imagine the pages destroyed beneath the melting snow's touch.

Fancying herself a bit of a little hero, Syline unlocked the door and walked that way, holding Malir to her breast as she did. The dark library made her uneasy, especially with the whistle and howl of the wind outside. She recognised the holdings as that of the Petrov family – known more for their merchant connections than anything else. They brought a lot of money to the capital at least, and – much more interestingly – it was said that their matriarch, Jane, who Syline had come this close to meeting tonight, was a wizard from a foreign land.

She'd always hoped for the chance to sit down and talk to her, but she seemed quite an unapproachable woman. Maybe Lauralee could give her an "in" with her.

Syline looked through the bars of the door and moved her magical light through them ahead of her, using it to probe the area. Just in case there really was a thief. But the room seemed empty but for innumerable chests and ledgers, and, in the centre of the room, a desk upon which sat an open book. The writing upon it gleamed like oil, even dry. A sure sign of the ink. A spell-book. To have a spell-book ruined by weather, especially for a learned mage like Jane, she could think of nothing worse. Who knows how many years' worth of curated spells were hidden in that tome! She knew a mending spell. Surely, they'd thank her if she fixed that window before it caused any problems.

It looked as if the wind had shattered the window with bluster alone, or perhaps, a chunk of ice had been kicked up into it. Either way, snow was falling heavily in through the window. The wind was coming this way and blew inside eagerly, making Syline shiver and pull her robes closer around her. That spell-book made up Syline's mind for her. She couldn't imagine how shattered she'd be if she found her spell-book sodden and worthless, the ink run off the pages by silt and snow. No, she wouldn't let that happen to Jane's book. Especially after the family, well, family servant Lauralee, had been so kind to her. Putting Malir back in her pocket and pulling out the keys, she tested each one on the door. None worked.

"Broken bridges," she muttered, cursing the private nature of nobles. She should have known; she'd given the key to her family's sanctum to Anatoly herself, after all. She'd have to break the doors lock to get in, but she'd be able to mend that with the spell she'd use to mend the window as well, but first she'd need to be able to touch the shards of glass to even cast the spell. It was a motto of her father's, one that her mother tried very hard to make sure none of the girls took as their own. "Better to ask for forgiveness than permission."

Better yet, if she repaired the door, no one would ever need to know what she'd done. Her heroics could stay her little secret and keep her out of trouble. If she did get found out though, maybe then, she'd finally get to speak with Lady Jane.

Her mind made up, she found herself staring at the lock. Wondering just how she was going to manage this. With a grin and a nod to herself, she set off to fetch her spell-book as her little light moved to float just above her head. Grabbing her spell-book off the table, on a whim she threw her satchel over her shoulder, as well. Walking back to the door, she flipped through her book until she found the spell she was looking for, one that conjured balls of arcane force. A simple, but powerful offensive spell that was one of the few Anatoly had taught her. She bookmarked it under her thumb as she flipped forward to her notes from that evening on the fire dagger.

From her outstretched finger came the length of flame. She had it burning bright, its centre tinged blue. She'd only need it for a few moments hopefully, so the drain on her reserves wouldn't be much an issue. She held the flame against the lock. Holding it right where it connected to the door, Syline watched the metal slowly grow to a brighter and brighter red. When she was confident it would be enough, she released the spell and the breath she didn't realise she'd been holding. Stepping back, she flipped to the page she'd bookmarked and took a moment to consider. She'd want the magic left over to perform the two mending spells and she didn't want nausea that came with bringing herself to her limit in magic. So, for her next spell, she'd use the bare minimum, a kick should finish the rest.

She spoke the familiar incantation and from her fingertip two glowing blue distortions in the air flew forth and into the heated metal, warping and buckling it. She hoped that would do the trick. Putting her spell-book away in her satchel, she put her back to the balcony railing, giving herself a run up as she launched a kick against the warped lock. It buckled, sitting awkwardly in the door frame, but didn't break fully just yet. One more kick broke it. Syline stumbled forth into the room. She felt a strange, tingling sensation across her skin. Looking back, she saw a blue skein of magic peeling away from the door frame. An alarm spell. Syline knew it herself, she should have guessed Jane, a far greater wizard than she, would have had one in her vault. That was fine! The lock would be repaired, the window would be fixed and she'd be back asleep in her own holdings before anyone was the wiser. It'd be fine. She hoped. Besides! Even if they did find out it was her, she wasn't doing anything bad. She was helping Jane. They'd probably thank her for her initiative.

Collecting herself and adjusting her robes, Syline moved for the window and fetched out her spell-book once again. The mending spell was one of the most useful spells a clumsy young wizard learned. Able to repair anything to how it once was, though the larger the item and the more cataclysmic the breakage, the more it would take out of you.

The spell tumbled from her lips and a golden, crackling glow overtook the window and each and every one of its shards. They floated past her outstretched hands as, one by one, the pieces fitted themselves back into the window and became one with the remains of the pane as if it had never broken. Syline stepped back and admired her handiwork, but her eyes couldn't help but stray to the spell-book open on the table. Snow marred its surface. She stepped over and used the hem of her robe to do her best to dry the page, and as she did, without even thinking about it, she began to read.

It was an advanced spell, one that combined elemental with teleportation magic, something she hadn't even begun to study. It was well past what Anatoly would let her touch, but reading the page, she felt she could grasp the basics of it. From the looks of things, the spell would cause a huge burst of lightning from the user's feet, at the beginning and end of their teleportation, and the spell could be modulated to extend the range of distance travelled and increase or decrease the power of the lightning, even shut that portion of the spell off entirely.

Idly, she started flicking through the pages of the book, keeping her thumb on that page so she could get back to it when she left. Getting to scan a spell-book as great as this would be her secret little reward for her good deed. As she read on, she became more and more amazed; this book seemed to have every single spell. Ones of her level and ones far, far above it. Spells that broached into an archmage's level of mastery. Interspersed were pages in a language she didn't understand, strange, curling symbols more like art than language. She dismissed those as a fancy of the mage, for all around them were spells she could only dream of casting. But the further she read on, the more she felt her stomach sink. Some of these spells she did recognise, not because they were famous, not because they'd made the careers of an innovative mage, nor because they'd saved lives or been the focus of some fable.

No, she recognised these spells because they were illegal. Spells to drain the life energy of others, to create undead, to summon illusory assassins that would kill without a single clue leading back to you. Just owning a spell-book with these spells could get you sentenced to death. What were the Petrovs doing with a spell-book like this? Were these spells legal in a foreign land, or were they up to something sinister with them? She turned the book back to the page she'd found it on, thinking it best she mend the door and head back to her holdings when a prickling on the back of her neck led her to look up.

A silhouette was in the doorway, the little light hovering at her shoulder extended only so far as to show the hem of a woman's scarlet evening dress, leaving the rest of her in shadow. She was quite a bit taller than Syline and she felt herself locking up like a deer before a hunter's lantern. She'd been caught.

"Now, just why are you in there young one?" asked the woman, striding closer into the light. Her skin was porcelain pale, her auburn hair having just the slightest hint of red at its tips, which perfectly matched her deep red lipstick, and beautiful scarlet evening dress, entirely inappropriate for the weather tonight. Her voice was soft, curious, but her eyes burned with a terrible intensity, and with barely… barely contained fury.

"W-well, I was spending the night here and I heard the window break under the storm, and I thought it might be a thief because there was a man following me before and I was scared what he'd do, but then it was just the wind, but I saw all the snow getting on your books and I thought about how hurt I'd be if my spell-book was destroyed by the weather and yours was so much bigger than mine, so I just thought I was doing something nice." Syline trailed off, rambling and wilting, fearful under the judgemental eyes of the foreign wizard.

"You thought it would be alright to break into my family's holdings, as long as you were doing it for a good reason? Fitting for your family, your 'lineage of heroes'. You're Syline, yes?" The woman let out a small, melodic chuckle as she took a step closer. "Did you really think it was a good idea, even though this room is under the king's protection, Syline? Even though knowing now you've been in here, I could have you punished, imprisoned, executed even? Kick up enough fuss, and the king would need to make an example of you, regardless of who your parents are. But it's alright as long as you were doing something good. Ah, the road to damnation is full of good intentions and the naïvety of youth."

A little bit of bluster worked its way up through Syline's fear. Naïvety? Jane should be grateful! She'd saved all these documents! If she was going to threaten her for helping her, Syline was rapidly changing her mind on how much she wanted to talk to the foreign mage.

"You'd go with me if he saw this spell-book! This book's full of illegal spells! Spells that carry the death sentence." Jane's expression darkened and Syline's counter-threat slowly fell from a petulant squeak to a frightened mumble. "Just for recording them."

Jane glared at Syline, her arms hanging by her sides. A moment passed in silence. Her lips twitched slightly, then turned fully into a snarl.

"Oh, Syline." Jane's hiss cut the silence like a hot knife. "You really shouldn't have looked through it. I was going to let you go with a cuff on the ear, but now…"

She left her threat to the girl's imagination as she stalked forward. Unthinking, Syline picked up the book as she stumbled backwards. She was in danger. The woman was just a wizard without a focus, yet, somehow, Syline knew, if Jane caught her, she'd receive much, much worse than a cuff on the ear. Seeing her grab the book, Jane's composure broke even further, irritation turning to fury as she hurried towards Syline.

"Give me the book!" she yelled.

The terrifying woman broke into a sprint towards her, teeth bared, revealing sharp fangs, her arm back ready to strike her, fingers tensed into a claw. Syline froze up and didn't even move until the woman's fingers scored across her shoulder, nails slicing clean through her robes and flesh. She screamed and the woman replied by grabbing Syline by the robes and hurling her into a nearby bookshelf. Syline flew as if a man twice Jane's size had thrown with all his strength, hitting the bookshelf hard and slumping to the floor. Even as the books rained down around her, Syline held tight to the spell-book. She was going to die here. Jane wasn't going to arrest her or ask for recompense. She was really going to kill her. Her finger still marked the page of the teleportation spell she had first seen. Frantically, she opened the book to it and began to read by the light still hovering at her shoulder, as Jane stormed towards her to follow up and finish her off.

Perhaps it was fear that let Syline cast as she did; the knowledge that her life may very well be on the line, but, in that instant, she cast the spell so fast the woman barely touched her by the time it was complete. Syline cast it flawlessly, each phrase pronounced to perfection, and the world went white.

—

Suddenly, the room was full of lightning. As Jane felt her foot hit the young mage's shoulder, the girl exploded into electricity, pain filled Jane's form and she fell to the ground screaming. Black and white spots danced across her vision, and she felt her body shake uncontrollably. Blood was leaking out the side of her mouth – she had bitten her lip in her seizures. When the shakes and tremors finally came to an end, she opened her hand. In it lay a platinum hair clip, marked by two sabres, crossed in front of a torch burning with a gemstone flame.

"Syline Petranski." She let out a ragged breath. "You stupid girl."

It was cold. It was so damned cold. Wherever the spell had taken her, she couldn't see a damned thing. She was completely surrounded by snow. It was so hard to move. So hard to think. She struggled to pull her wand from her pocket and begin an incantation that would protect her from the cold. Black spots danced across her vision as she tried to pull on reserves she didn't have. The wand fell from numb fingers. She couldn't even move her head to see where it'd fallen.

She was going to die. That realisation came in with the cold, numb, distant. Something she could do nothing about.

Her eyes were heavy. At least if she was going to die, she'd likely do so in her sleep, that was a comfort. Something landed on her chest, light enough to be barely noticed through her robes, but it still made her force her eyes that little bit wider.

A songbird, of all things, something that had no right being out in this cold, at this time of night. Gold eyes met her ice blue ones as it turned its head this way and that, taking her measure. It began to sing, a beautiful, cheerful tune. The sound was like the battlehorn of summer, for through Syline, warmth rushed in a charge. A cosy, comforting warmth that reached from the tips of her fingers to the end of her nose. It was like being wrapped in a blanket and tucked in to bed. Despite the absurdity of it all, Syline let out a little yawn. By the time the bird's song had finished, she was fast asleep, still filmed in the otherworldly warmth. The bird hopped to and fro on her chest, looking about. Setting its sights, it took flight and disappeared into the darkness.

Chapter 4

WHEN JANE RETURNED TO HER manor, arriving in a burst of flame in the hidden chambers she and Lauralee convened in, she did so in a mess. Her hair was singed and still smouldering in places, her dress was ripped and torn, her own blood was splattered across her lips and chin and someone else's dripped from her claws.

Lauralee was aware Jane was known for her temper but seeing her like this reminded her just how different it was for one of their kind to be in a temper, than it was for a normal human to be. Lauralee stood at the corner of the dark room, having been organising Jane's notes from the evening. She hesitated to speak, lest whatever fury Jane had burning within was unleashed on her. But in the end, as Jane's breath came to her in furious, shuddering gasps through clenched teeth, curiosity overcame Lauralee.

"What happened, my lady?" she asked, and Jane's head whipped to her like a predator sensing prey.

Okay, that was a mistake. Jane flexed her hands, as if ready to pounce, but seemed to force herself to calm. She stood up straight, running a hand through her hair and adjusting her dress as a long, ragged sigh left her.

"An idiot child with more guts than brains. That Petranski girl you were flirting with, broke into our vault when someone smashed the window, thinking she'd fix it for us. It would have been sweet if she hadn't started reading my tome. She's disappeared with it. I'm amazed she managed the teleportation spell I'd been studying when she left, but it did quite a number on me. Took the book with her."

The switch to this show of calm was quite startling to Lauralee; she guessed much of it was a cover. A trained, practised control of her temper. Syline had broken into the vault. The timid girl, clinging to her because some thug harassed her. It amazed her what sides of people came out, just like Jane's fury. Lauralee hadn't expected this side of the sweet noble girl she'd met in passing.

"She took the book? Then what will happen with your project? I met her. I could find her again, I'm sure. I have her scent. I can silence her before she reports it to anyone important."

Jane looked as if she considered it, raising an eyebrow in amused surprise.

"You'd kill her?"

"Of course, my lady. If that's what the Mother's Hand needs."

Jane smiled; Lauralee's words seemed to calm her in a strange way. She walked towards the table Lauralee had been working at, pausing to place a hand on Lauralee's shoulder.

"You'll go far, Lauralee. Don't let emotion cloud vision, that seems to be a lesson you're already taking to heart. Your mother breeds them well, it seems. No, no, there's no need for you to bloody your hands with her. She might have gotten lucky casting that spell, but a beginner like her? She'll be lucky if she's not already dead. She'll be blessed by the gods themselves if she can walk tomorrow. Most of the watch is in my thrall. I'll have them begin scouring the city for her. We may even be able to wipe her memory and bring her into my thralldom if they don't get overzealous. If they do, well, we'll manage; a noble daughter disappearing invites questions, so there's a good chance I'll be receiving a visit from her mother tomorrow. Besides, the spells were a gift. The main concern were the writings on the goddess and the beasts and I'd already removed those into their own binder. No, she's an irritant, but she can't distract us from other more important matters. She'll be dealt with by tomorrow's end, I'm sure. You, meanwhile, my dear…"

Jane seemed so calm in how she spoke now, but it was then Lauralee noticed Jane's fingers were trembling on her shoulder. Nervous quivers that had her clenching her grip on the young woman, sharpened, painted nails within a hair's breadth of piercing in. It all still simmered there; she was still cooling down.

"You have another mission. Do you remember that cult we spoke of?"
Lauralee nodded.

"They're due to attempt a summoning tomorrow. As their patrons in this, it's due that we have someone there to greet their new lords and instruct them on our plans for Dawnsteel and receive a scroll from them they should have prepared for us already. Your mother said you can still use scrolls, yes?"

Lauralee nodded.

"Good girl, good girl. Take these then." She handed her two scrolls. "Teleportation, one to take you there, one to come back. Study the map in the back, the ritual site is marked. Don't get involved with them if you don't have to, you're an observer until the summonings are done, then you need only instruct the demons and leave."

Lauralee nodded one last time, then dared to ask, "What are you going to do now, my lady?" She did not comment that she'd never seen a demon and was quietly petrified at the thought.

"Our research is far from done my dear, from what we've managed tonight." She picked up the books Lauralee had been organising. "I do believe I'm ready to have my first taste of this god."

She licked her fingers clean of Syline's blood as she spoke, delighting in every drop.

━

PUSHING ON THE SOUTHERN BORDER of Russenholde was the city of Dawnsteel. The primary god of the region may have been The Wanderer, the god of open roads and long journeys, but Dawnsteel was a city for Soel, the Glorious Dawn, the god of daylight, fire, and justice. Where Russenholde fostered hunters of monsters and worse, Dawnsteel held its own special kind of warrior: The Morning's Fury, hunters of men and their dark machinations. The servants of the Glorious Dawn hunted cultists of demons, fey and other vile things and were unrelenting in their quest to purge the land of darkness.

Amberly Penzare was one such hunter. She was a tall, beautiful half-elf, white hair framing well-sculpted features and her skin carrying the faintest blue tint when caught in the right light.

Children had been disappearing from Dawnsteel; from the avenues, from the parks and from even their beds. Evil's audacity knew no limit.

Other members of the Morning's Fury investigated other places around the city en masse and encouraged the citizens to come together in prayer, but her instincts had led her here, down in the old catacombs to the east of the city.

While the others clambered in the light for safety, Amberly knew the only solution was to descend to the dark and face it head-on. She'd found nothing though and cursed herself a fool. Every moment wasted was another child lost and she'd been pacing these dark, empty tombs for hours, guided by the scant light that penetrated through holes in the ceiling above. She'd found nothing but rats and the dead, and for all the questions she had, the dead told no tales. There was one more layer beneath her, one in total darkness. She'd need her torch to descend any deeper, and to do so would throw any attempt at stealth out the window. Still, nothing for it, it was this or retreat and admit she had been wrong.

She brought the flint bangle on her wrist to a striker, kneeling with her torch before her. Once, twice. Come now, the third strike should do it, she thought.

"Hold, dawn soldier," came a voice in the darkness.

Fire and ashes, Amberly cursed herself for letting herself be snuck up on, hand going for the longsword on her hip.

"I said hold!" the voice hissed once again. "Shitting hells, if I were here for a fight girl, I wouldn't stop to introduce myself." A silhouette emerged from the dark of the stairwell headed down. It was tall, masculine. It looked as if he was wearing some kind of horned helmet, but she couldn't make it out clearly in the darkness.

"And just who would you be, stranger? Out for a morning jog amongst the dead?" Amberly said, keeping her tone light and jovial as the man stepped from the dark, a hole in the ceiling made a spotlight of what little sunlight could break through. A familiar figure, if one that made her slightly uneasy, even now. Red skin, tattered wings at his back, eyes of pure black, seeming to drink in any light that fell upon him and ram horns sprouting from the sides of his head. A devil. He was dressed in a mix of leather and chain, his clothing fine and beautifully made, his black hair stylishly waxed back.

"No, personally, I prefer a route with fewer rats and a lot less mould," the man quipped back, a playful grin on his lips.

"Good morning, Laes. What brings you to this lovely neighbourhood?" she asked, taking a step closer to meet him in the spotlight.

The devil had been a friend to her for months ever since he had rescued her on a whim. She'd wound up way in over her head against a cult of fiend worshippers. He'd been there on the command of someone higher up in Hell who wasn't happy with fiends "moving in on their territory'. Since then, the pair had always seemed to run into one another and, while not the most conventional duo, they'd started to share information to help the other and their respective allies in the fight against demonkind. Seeing him here sent a rush of both stress and relief through her. If Laes was here, her hunch was right. The children were here.

"I'm here for the same reason as you, Amberly; the child-stealers crossed a line they shouldn't have, and now, I've no choice but to step in. But, they already have demons down below. Too many for me to handle alone."

"Demons?" Amberly clenched her hand around her hilt and her face twisted in rage. The Morning's Fury hunted many things, but none brought fury from her like demons. Just the word...

"Yes, demons. Now, don't light that blasted torch unless you want the whole of the Abyss to know we're coming."

She swallowed her fury and forced herself to focus. With just the two of them, she knew running in yelling bloody murder would just get them both killed. She knew that. She told herself that again and again, but it wasn't easy. Every impulse in her body told her to run past the man, to dive headlong into that which took all she loved away from her, but, after a few moments, she managed to quell the rage.

"Okay, Laes, I'll follow your lead." She gestured into the dark as her blade hand stiffened about the hilt. "Lead the way."

—

SYLINE WAS ALONE.

The young noble daughter wandered the halls of her family home, bare feet padding against the marble tiles. Portraits of her parents and landscapes of their nation, Russenholde, hung dark upon the rosewood walls. Dust hung heavy in the air, and cobwebs thick in every corner. She called out for her sisters, her mother, her servants, anyone. The only answers she received were her own echoes bouncing back at her from the darkened corridors. So it had been for the last three weeks, any time she shut her eyes, she found herself here, in this necropolis, this terrible, haunting rendition of her home.

She couldn't shake the sense that something had changed this time. Each breath was becoming more and more difficult, her throat felt closed off and each step made her body ache all the more. She was so cold, so damnably cold. She was making for the parlour and its grand fireplace, when she heard a great wail. That was her mother's voice.

Heartbeat pounding in her chest like the drums of war, Syline threw herself up the stairs, sprinting down the hall to her mother's room. Her mother lay upon the bed, clutching at her stomach with one hand. Black blood spilled out between her fingers. With her other hand, she reached out to Syline.

"Mother!" Syline screamed, rushing to her side. Not knowing what to do she grabbed her mother's hand in hers. The air shifted, dust flitting in a new direction. Syline held a corpse's hand. Its face twisted in a rictus of horror, empty eye sockets staring at something the way Syline had come. Trembling, Syline turned.

Something stood by the far wall. Its flesh was grey and pallid, veins flush against the skin, eyes sunken in their sockets with dried blood rimming around them like old tears, and hair hanging slack like some terrible hag from a horror tale told around campfires. In its grasp, it held a grey hand, severed from its owner. Syline screamed, feeling her thoughts empty from her mind, her entire body frozen as she realised what she was looking at. She was looking at a mirror. That realisation hit right as her hideous double caught flame within the mirror. It flailed as it burned and, panicking, Syline did too, before realising, whatever terrible inferno had affected her reflection, it had indeed affected it alone.

In moments, on the other side of the glass, her double was naught but embers and ash. Syline cast a look at the corpse on the bed beside her, seeking comfort where there was none to be found, before, legs quivering, she began to move towards the mirror. Her foot creaked on the floorboards. A crack splintered up the mirror, glowing with heat. Another, then another, spiderwebs of fractures laced their way across it. Syline turned to run but was too late. The mirror exploded into fire and ash, covering her, burning her as shards of glass filled the room, lacerating across her back.

She would have screamed, but she could barely draw breath as the figure swirled into being in the doorway, given flesh by the ash and dress by the flame. A woman clad in hellfire with bone-pale skin stood before her. Her body shifted and reformed constantly. Lips split to reveal fangs as she took a step forward, flames spreading beneath her gait.

"Give it to me," the woman snarled. "Give it back!" She reached out for Syline with grasping claws emerging from the conflagration.

Syline just froze. She would have died had she not been yanked aside by a being larger still. Cloaked in the night, his features naught but eyes gleaming like stars, his grip kind, reassuring, cool, in contrast to the blistering heat of the woman. Around his neck, the symbol of a bridge crossing the globe.

"Run," the god told her, "or ruin shall fall."

The being stepped to interpose himself between her and the ash and flame. Behind him, Syline saw the window. She ran to it and leapt through the glass into a blizzard. Compared even to the shards tumbling around her, the blizzard hit her like a thousand knives, lungs burning with the cold as snow ripped across her, blinding her and leaving her body in freezing agony. She crashed amidst the falling glass into the tundra below, sinking deep into the snow. Compared to the terrible heat of being near the woman, she found herself freezing. She struggled to lift herself from the snow, but more and more of it fell down atop her until all was cold. So damned cold.

—

SYLINE WOKE UP SCREAMING. SHE lay on her back under at least a few feet of snow. A warmth that had filled her all night, was slowly beginning to fade. She couldn't remember casting it, but she must've managed a spell to protect her from the cold. She knew if she had not cast it, she would only be a frozen corpse found by scavengers, but, as it was, winter's chill was just beginning to creep through her sodden clothes.

She found she could at least move her arms, the space around her large enough to wiggle and shimmy them until she had them in front of her chest. Taking a shaky little breath, she started clawing her way up through the snow. When she got out, she'd have a thousand new problems to face but, for now, the most important was getting back out into the sunlight. Overall, it took her only about three minutes of shimmying, clawing and pushing to clear the snow above her enough to sit up. Her torso pushing clear of the cold and she looked around, eyes squinted as she squirmed and kicked to clear her legs enough to pull them out after her torso.

She was outside the city, right at the edge of the treeline. Sat in a mound of snow that had piled up beside a large oak, its leaves weighed down by last night's blizzard. She could see the walls to the north of her, perhaps a fifteen-minute walk away. Syline started to take stock: she had broken into the Petrov's private sanctum, read its spell-book full of illegal spells, been attacked by the Petrov matriarch herself and managed to cast some terribly powerful teleportation spell that had thrown her clean out of the city.

The weight of these events hadn't really hit her while she'd been digging herself out, but recalling them now, left her needing to lean against the tree for support.

Lady Jane had said the sentence for stealing the book would be death, but the book was full of illegal spells. If she could let the king or a court mage see it and show them where she'd gotten it, everything would be okay. Everything would be okay once she reached the king. A thought flashed to her mind. She looked down and spotted the book lying closed in the hole she'd just vacated. Quailing at the thought of it being destroyed, she hurriedly grabbed at it and brushed it free of snow. She did a cursory check of the pages, making sure none had been too damaged by the snow before putting it in her satchel. It was a tight fit getting it in there alongside her journal, her own spell-book and *The Dragonslayer's Lance*. After a few moments of trying to get it in, she sighed and tossed the tawdry tale into the snow. At the moment, she couldn't care less about finishing it.

With the book safely away in her satchel, she let a little bit of pride enter her heart. Anatoly would have never thought she'd be able to cast a spell like that! Sure, she had passed out afterwards, but she'd done a lot of casting leading up to it, and she'd still managed to do the incantation perfectly! While someone was trying to kill her no less! Some part of her knew she was just trying to distract herself from how scary this all really was, but still, she allowed herself a moment's smugness at her masterful casting.

Doing one last brush down of herself, Syline set her eyes on the southern gate and set off wading through the snow. She didn't go unseen as she approached the walls. A young girl in dark blue robes tended to stand out against the stunning white of fresh snow. When she was about a minute out from the gate, she spotted a man in shining chainmail descending from the wall, coming to meet her.

Thank the Wanderer, she thought. If she could get a guard to escort her to the king's court, then she could bypass any troubles she might face along the way. Any worries of the Petrovs trying to stop her would just slip away if she had a guard with her. It's not like they could go against the king's orders as openly as that. She waved to him, beginning to jog through the snow in his direction. The guard waved back and stepped out of the shadow of the wall towards her. Something seemed off though. The way he trudged towards her. The way his hand rested squarely on his sword's hilt. The way his eyes sat on her, predatory, like a wolf watching prey.

She pulled up short. A terrible sense of dread filled her; the Petrovs had many, many connections. It was rumoured that the merchant family smuggled goods into the city without paying a tariff. Who knew how many of the guards they had in their pocket. She couldn't go back home. The risk of getting caught would be too great. She was no sneak-thief; she had no confidence she could steal her way through the city in the night. She had to get out of here. The guard was–

The guard had started running. He must've sensed her hesitation and wasn't going to let his prey get away. He had drawn his sword and held it ready as he sprinted through the snow towards her. He wasn't trying to capture her; he was trying to kill her!

Twice in two days was too often to have people running at you with death in their eyes. As much as it terrified her, Syline was almost just as angry. This was ridiculous! She'd done nothing wrong! They were the evil ones, not her! Almost without thinking about it, she drew her sword, if only to show she'd not go down so easy. Fear still plagued her heart, however, and at that moment, no spells came to her lips; she could remember no incantations that might get her out of this jam.

The guard was ten paces away, closing fast and he brought his sword up for a downward swing. It was up high, gleaming in the morning light. It was an easy counter for her, and one that her body acted upon before her mind was truly aware of it. Slapping his blade aside, she made a jab at his forearm, only cutting a nick in his clothing, trying to scare him back. He took a half-step back to avoid further blows as she leapt away from him, trying to put distance between her and the man.

"Why're you doing this?!" she yelled, anger outplaying fear, affront defeating fright. She searched her brain and found an incantation, one fresh in her memory from the day before. Murmuring the words, she fetched her wand from her pocket, and the finger of flame extended from it.

As far as off-hand weapons went, a fire dagger seemed like a pretty good one.

The guard eyed her in a new light, a bit more respect. He moved into a defensive stance and began to circle her, rather than running in to put her down like a defenceless lamb. She did the same, beginning "the dance".

"Lord Gehrman Petrov wants you quiet. He didn't say dead or alive, but better safe than sorry, hey? 'Sides, I always wanted to bag a noble's head."

"Don't you know who I am?! You can't just kill me, I'm the daughter of Sir Petranski! The king will have your head, you villain!" Again, Syline refused to let fear take her, anger welling up at her position in the world changing so very suddenly, and in a manner so entirely out of her control. This wasn't a contest, this was real; no structure, no rules and no reward in sight but to not die.

"I think you'll find" – the man rushed her, catching Syline's side with his elbow, pushing the breath from her lungs – "that I can."

She swept her blade for him as she stumbled off to the right. He took a small cut to the bicep but accepted it with only a grunt. His hand darted for her wrist and grabbed her blade-arm in a crushing grip. Syline screamed as she felt her bones creaking. The world slowed. Her eyes graced the walls, the gates, no one was watching. Her mother couldn't call off this duel. He wouldn't apologise for playing too rough over dinner later. She was going to die if she didn't win. He was really going to kill her. He brought his blade back, aiming to stab it through her gut.

Syline brought the flame dagger right for his eyes. The flames lapped over his face, blistering the flesh and searing the eyes. The man squealed like a stuck pig, releasing her, to fend her off as he stumbled towards her, swinging wildly with fist and blade. He caught her collar with his hand, and she saw a grin spread wide. He had no intention of letting this fight end. Grabbing her, the man hefted her up by her robes, the girl struggling as he went to repeat his prior attack. Even half blind, with her in his grasp, he couldn't miss. He brought his blade up for the killing blow.

Syline's fire dagger guttered out. The magic was beginning to drain on her and she couldn't risk weakness at this moment, nor did she want to ruin the man by repeating that trick. The thought of ruining an opponent, someone her mother had always taught to treat with respect and camaraderie, rattled her to her core. With the hand now free of the flames, she held her fingers flat and jabbed them into the one weak point he presented holding her up like this: his throat. The man spluttered as she rammed her fingers just above his Adam's apple. She felt his grip shake, but his will was stronger than the blow. Eyes still shut, he spat in her face, then resumed his previous grin and slowly pressed the sword's tip against her stomach. She felt it pushing in against the wool of her robes, the thick fabric the only thing protecting her now.

"Keep struggling girl, and I'll make it slow."

He wasn't someone she should show respect. He wasn't a friendly rival to test in play combat. This was real! She was going to die unless he did. She had no other choice; it was do or die. Him or her. That was what she told herself. She had no time for choices or second thoughts. As the man's blade slowly pressed through her robes, pricking her stomach, Syline screamed her frustration and pulled her arm back. She stabbed forward. She felt the blade pierce his flesh and heard his strangled gasp as it pushed through his ribs. Momentum carried it deeper and bright scarlet blood spilled out over her blade. He collapsed, as she fell to the earth and snow. She had to experience the feel of her blade moving through flesh all over again as he slowly slid off it.

In his last moments, he stared up at her with scared, blinded eyes. He seemed confused, as if he didn't know what was happening. His eyes begged for answers, his lips mouthing words he had not the breath to speak. He didn't look like the same man in those moments, it was as if he had awoken from a dream. Syline felt her gorge rising, felt tears streaming down her cheeks. She turned and took off running for the woods before someone in the city saw them out there, her blade held in a loose grip down at her side.

—

SYLINE RAN FOR WHAT FELT like hours. She ran until each step left her legs burning, left them feeling as if she had hot coals in her muscles and daggers in her knees. She didn't think as she ran. She only focused on getting away from there. From him. Her mind blank but for the thought of fleeing the scene of her most terrible crime. She only stopped running when she'd arrived at the edge of the island. She stood at the edge of the scant woods, trees at her back and the great frozen river that separated the islands ahead of her. She could see the southern bridge, far along the coast that would take her along the main road towards Dawnsteel. Once she stopped, it was like everything caught up to her all at once. She collapsed to her knees as all the fear and pain overcame her. Exhaustion and the thought that she had killed a man pushed her stomach up to her throat. She vomited, violently. She vomited until she brought up nothing but water, and by the time she was done, her eyes watered, her nose ran, and her breath came to her in big, whooping gasps. She stumbled away from all that she had just excavated from her stomach and collapsed down against a tree. There, she caught her breath and struggled to get her reeling mind under control.

She'd killed a man. If she'd had any chance of getting out of this now, it was well gone. Even if she could call it self-defence, she couldn't fight the fact that she had just taken someone's life. She couldn't... she couldn't go home. She couldn't see her mother, or her sisters again. She'd never have another lesson with Anatoly unless she could find some way to fix this. It all simply became too much for her. She curled in on herself, hugging her knees and crying into her robes. She just couldn't take it; she didn't know how to survive on her own like this. She'd only left the city on outings with her whole family in the past. What was she going to do? Where was she going to go? How was she going to fix this?

Crying was all she could do for a long while, but by the time she had run out of tears to shed, she found her heart felt a bit lighter. Her feelings vented to the world. As if she had to get that behind her to have any chance to keep moving.

She slowly got to her feet, brushing herself down once again. From her pocket, she pulled out her plush sparrow, Malir. Overlarge and overstuffed, she needed his comfort right now and hugged him to her breast as she looked around. Her eyes settled on the bridge and she watched a trio of men go across it on horseback. It was a walk to cross that bridge, but they'd make it a lot faster on horseback. There were closer islands, but they weren't linked by the Wanderer's bridges, so, naturally, they didn't fall into the "main road" that was traced by their path.

She could just make out the shape of spears in the men's hands. They were looking for something. Someone. Chances are, they were looking for her; it would've been long enough by now. Chances are they'd found the soldier's body and knew she was out of the city. She could fancy they'd been sent to find her by her family, that they'd take her home safely, but after how the guard had met her, she didn't dare risk that. She had to get moving before they went this way, but she couldn't follow the main road. That's where they'd expect her to go. That meant she had little choice but to cross the frozen rivers and move along the bridgeless islands until she found a town these manhunters wouldn't grace. She could plan further from there.

Now, she had some kind of a plan. Some kind of light at the end of the tunnel, however faint a one it might be. She had the spell-book and she had her sword, and she had Malir. She gave the little toy a kiss on the head before tucking it back into her robes. She wiped her sword clean on the snow and then wiped it again with the hem of her robes before sliding it back into its sheath. With that done, she took one last look over her shoulder, thinking to herself that this was what she had always wanted. She'd always wanted her life to be more interesting after all. To have an adventure of her own. That was certainly what this was, but it had come in a way she would have never expected. One far scarier than whatever she had been prepared for.

Maybe that's how it always goes for real adventurers, she mused to herself, as she stepped off the coast onto the frozen water, beginning her long walk to the bridgeless island on the horizon.

Chapter 5

MAGDOVA STOOD WITH HER EAR to the door, Kassandra at her elbow. It'd been a long time since she'd heard her mother this angry, and the fact she was losing her composure like that, was enough to scare her. Anatoly had arrived, shepherded by their footmen, pale-faced and sweating and the tirade hadn't slowed since the door had closed. Finally, it opened and Anatoly emerged; the large man looked like a shell of himself, fret and guilt weighing on his shoulders. Hope flared in his eyes for a split second as he turned to look at them, but it died just as quickly.

"Hello, Magdova. I'm sorry, did we worry you?"

"Is Syline going to be alright?"

His lips thinned to a line, quivering before he gave the pair a small nod and a pat on the shoulder.

"We'll find her, don't worry."

"Magdova?" Her mother's voice came from inside the study.

Anatoly's grip tightened on her shoulder for a moment before he set off, disappearing down the hall. Magdova turned to watch him go. Before looking into the study, Kassandra slunk behind her, fearing they were in trouble. Their mother was sitting at the grand oak desk, head in her hand, covering her right eye. Kat was seated on a sofa by the hearth, looking their way.

"Were you two listening in?" her mother asked, but there was no accusation in it.

"Is Syline going to be alright?" Magdova asked plaintively.

"We'll find her. How long have you been listening in?"

"Just when you started yelling."

A sorrowful smile slid up her mother's lips as she waved them to the armchairs on the opposite side of the desk. Magdova sat as bid, but Kassandra squirrelled her way to her mother's side, trying to give comfort with a hug about her stomach. Their mother placed a hand on her head, stroking her hair tenderly.

"You wouldn't have heard the footmen then. It seems there was a break-in at the archive last night; something was stolen from the Petrov's vault and, judging by the bloodstains, Syline decided to play the hero and tried to stop the burglars."

Magdova gasped. *Syline, what were you thinking?* she thought. *You can't even beat me with a sword.*

"So, they kidnapped her?"

"Hopefully." Her mother sighed, knuckling her eye. "Once the burglars know who she is, chances are they'll issue a ransom. If they harmed her, they would know they, and their whole family, would hang. We can get her back when they show themselves. Until then, I'm mobilising every border guard in the city to hunt for her. Kat's going as well," she said, looking at her eldest daughter.

"And they better hope the border guard finds them first," Kat said, burning with anger.

"According to Anatoly, Jane Petrov was there last night with a maid Syline struck up a conversation with," their mother continued. "I'm going to talk to her now and see if we can figure out who might've stolen whatever they took. That might give us a clue. Either way, I've also sent a runner to fetch your father and brothers and bring some of their forces home from past the northern border. Once they find him, I'm sure he'll be home with all due haste, and the border guard have some of the best trackers in the land."

"So, she'll be alright?" Magdova felt like a broken record, but she didn't know what else to ask. "Can I help loo–"

"No," her mother answered instantly, lowering her hand to meet her eyes with her own. They were rimmed red, puffy and raw with recent tears. "Neither of you are to leave the house without guards and my permission, do you understand?"

"Yes, mother," Magdova said, flinching as if she'd been struck. Her mother's gaze softened and she reached out to put a hand on Magdova's head.

"I can't lose you as well."

Kassandra had begun to cry, fear overcoming her; their mother wrapped her arms around her youngest and picked her up, holding her close as she stroked her back.

"She'll be alright, I promise."

Squeezing her youngest daughter, she carried her over to set her down by Magdova.

"Can you keep your sister company until I get back? It's your job to keep an eye on Magdova and make sure she doesn't run off."

"I understand." Kassandra nodded, mollified.

"Good girl," their mother said, leading both from the room, Kat not far behind.

"I'm off to see the Petrovs now. I'm sure this will all be settled before you know it."

Magdova thought, the way her mother said that sounded like a prayer.

JANE WAS WAITING FOR HER when the footman opened the door and stood in the grand foyer of the Petrov manor. The woman was a beauty; Kassandra always wondered how Gerhman, the fat old miser, scored someone like her.

"Dame Petranski." The other woman slid in close, taking one of her hands on both her own as she kissed Kassandra on the cheek. "I heard. I'm so sorry. I promise, our footmen are at your disposal. I'd have sent them already after these thieves, but I had a feeling you'd be visiting and I'm sure you'll know how to use their efforts better."

Well, that was easy; Kassandra was grateful. The foreign woman kept to herself outside of the big social events, and though Gerhman was an old friend, he'd become a lot more insular these last few years as well. She'd feared getting their help would've been like getting blood from a stone.

"Thank you. Can I ask what they stole? I think that could be a big help in narrowing down our suspects. There aren't many brave, or stupid, enough to break into a nobleman's vault.

"A spell-book, one given to me by my teacher in my homeland. I'd been studying it just that night, too. It seemed like Syline was trying to stop them, correct? I'm so sorry she's gotten herself hurt or worse for my sake."

"That's the Petranski in her." Kassandra said with a conflicted, sad sense of pride. "She'll be alright and I promise we'll get your book back."

"I appreciate that, but please, Syline should be in your mind first; I just want her to make it home safe. I'll have my men reporting to your doorstep tomorrow morning."

Kassandra nodded, looking past her into the foyer.

"Would it be alright if I came in? I heard that Syline spoke with your maid that night; I'd like to ask her a few questions if I can."

Jane shook her head softly.

"I'm afraid she's not in today. She had to hurry home to look after her mother. She should be back in a few days; I'll let her know to visit you the moment I see her."

"Alright, thank you, Jane. Thank you." Kassandra sighed, the world feeling so very heavy. "I suppose I should get back out there. My men and I will be raiding some known criminal hot spots today to see if we can't turn up any leads."

"You're a much braver woman than I am, but I promise, however I can help, I'll be there."

"Thank you, Jane, you're a good woman. I'm sure we'll speak again soon."

After a little more idle small talk, Kassandra left, forcing herself to confront the reality of the situation once again. Syline was gone and she had no idea where to go. What kind of criminal steals a spell-book? Dead ones when she was done with them.

<hr />

"WELL, LET'S BE OFF THEN," Laes said as he drew his own sword. It was about the length of an arming sword but was made entirely of matte black metal. Its edge was covered in serrated sections, chips and cracks, each one faintly glowing with a red light. Amberly had the feeling that, despite those cracks, that blade would probably be tougher to break than any blade she'd ever held or faced. It looked like it was worth a king's bounty from the magic within it alone.

"Follow my lead and don't you dare light that torch. I can see just fine in the dark, so I'll get us in position before the fight begins." Laes grinned at her before turning on his heel and walking with all the confidence in the world down the stairs, disappearing into the dark.

Taking one last deep breath, Amberly hurried after him. Catching up to the devil, she placed a hand on his shoulder and whispered to him,

"How do you expect me to follow your lead if I can't bloody see you?" She could sense the blasted devil was grinning, even when she couldn't see him. He playfully patted her on the hand and kept on walking.

"Then stick close, paladin. We've got quite a walk yet."

Amberly shook her head gently, a wry grin on her features. Inwardly, she enjoyed Laes' playful nature, but, of course, she wasn't going to admit that. Nor would she voice her suspicions that he only had her keep her torch unlit so she'd have to hold onto him, the flirt.

"So," she began, quieting her voice. "I've always meant to ask, what kind of devil are you?" she asked as they began down the winding stairs to the next floor. He was taking it slow, so she did not tumble, and it didn't go unnoticed.

"I know there are a few that make contracts and you fit the description of a Lachelnder Dieb, but the codexes said they smell like roses and honey. You smell good, but not like that," he said.

"Vanilla and lavender; it's perfume."

"Ah, good choice, my lady." She heard a snicker from him before he continued.

"And I'm a half-devil, actually. My mother was a lovely woman, a bit too drawn by my father's devilish good looks." Even he seemed annoyed by that pun, audibly groaning when he heard her snicker. "If that's funny to you, I regret our partnership."

"Oh, come on, it's funny because you're the one saying it. Wait, so are you a hellblooded? I've met hellblooded folk. You look a bit like one, but you've got a totally different feeling to you."

The man seemed to concede the point, and she felt him pat her hand with a pleased little hum.

"I'd been told the Morning's Fury study to sense the aura of others. You'll be pleased to know that your own is *sickeningly* good, though, is that...? Never mind," the half-devil cooed to her.

He couldn't see her frown. His smug tones were not half as endearing as he likely thought them.

"You're right, I'm not a hellblooded; it's a common misconception, actually. Hellblooded are the descendants of half-devils like myself, or the children of warlocks who've promised their children to the hells. They belong in this world. At the end of the day, they're just normal people with a few odd quirks, whatever the goodly priests might try to put upon them." The devil had the same infuriating tone of a teacher condescendingly praising a student for being at least *half* right.

"If you don't belong in this world, then why, Laes, do we run into each other most every time I go out alone?"

"Would you believe true love draws us to each other? Our fates and souls aligned?"

"No, I wouldn't," she said, laughing under her breath.

"Fine, fine, I made this kingdom my haunting ground a while back. There are more warlocks than you'd think, though, have no fear. I don't support worshipping me anywhere but the bedroom. They're not the cult sort. As for right now, these child-stealers broached upon a line they shouldn't. They took children from a warlock bound by contract to me. The children aren't bound for me, but the contract requires that I protect my warlock's family. They drove a hard bargain," he said with a soft chuckle, as if remembering the warlock fondly.

"You sound like you like them. What, a pretty widow? Going to pay her a visit for some worship when we're done here?" Amberly teased.

"No, no, I was hoping I'd get to take you to dinner," the devil replied without skipping a beat.

Despite herself, that got Amberly blushing bright as a cherry and she was more furious at herself for letting it get to her than the devil for trying it. After all, what else should she expect from him? She'd just have to fight fire with fire. She just hoped devils still felt the heat.

"Oh, is that so?" she cooed to him, stroking down his cheek with the back of her hand. She felt him jump at the touch and almost laughed. "Well, I'm sorry to say, but as handsome as you are, Laes, I don't think you're the kind of guy I could see walking down the aisle with. You'd probably catch fire. I'll think about it, though. Depends how much you impress me today. I don't date weaklings."

The devil chuckled. "Are you sure you're a Morning's Fury? You're a bit too fun for that bunch."

Together, they descended into the dark. She could hear the sibilant voices of the cultists in the distance and, beside them, the cries of children and the awful, grating growls of demons. Their howls and screams sent a shudder through her, a cold wind from years past: a red tide of demons, screaming horses, broken carriages, broken bodies, her mother asking her again and again to just look at her. Look at her!

"Look at me, Amberly! Amberly!"

She felt Laes shake her shoulder. She could just make out his silhouette as a darker patch in the lightless hall.

"You're okay, Amberly, I'm right here. Those demons can't reach you anymore and we're more than enough to take the ones ahead."

"I'm... I'm fine. Thanks, Laes..."

The half-devil didn't move for a few moments, then she felt him let go of her.

"Alright, just stick close, okay? I don't want to have to come back and find you in the dark."

Another exultant roar filled the halls. Amberly felt rage rising in her breast, and this time, she didn't fight to quell it. She'd wet her blade with demon blood this day.

—

SYLINE WAS ALONE.

The walk to the island she planned to make her home for the night, was a long, cold and lonely one. Along the way, the sun dipped into the horizon and, by the time she reached her destination, it was just barely giving off the last few rays before nightfall. Trudging up the shore of the empty island, Syline could at least take solace in the fact that no one lived here. Often – especially by worshippers of the Wanderer such as herself – islands with no bridges leading to them were considered bad omens, places the god of travels did not intend for mortals to visit. Many went unsettled for just that reason. Though, with a kingdom as mighty and as reliant on its lumber trade as this, quite a few of the bridgeless islands here had been settled all the same.

This one, however, was too small and too lacking in viable resources to be considered worthy of the notice of the great beast that was the kingdom's economy. Perhaps they just hadn't expanded out here yet? It was large enough to support a lumber mill at least. She suspected it was one of the many islands dark rumours were spread of, where the dead were said to walk and devils broke into the world. Druids might like it here, she thought. The trees were old and tall, and the little rustles in the underbrush told her there was indeed life hidden in the island. Rabbits, foxes, and perhaps a few bigger creatures, it was a private kingdom all their own until she'd paid a visit. She suspected they'd each found their way here from other islands during previous winters and had gotten trapped when the seas and rivers melted once more, leaving the population of the island to grow, alone.

Syline's legs burned. Her side and wrist ached as she completed the final leg of her journey. She'd checked them halfway through her trip across the frozen waters and found both mottling purple and red from the guard's assault.

She trudged through the island's brush to reach a pond. At least around it, the trees were thick enough to give some nice cover from the wind and snow. Syline left her satchel leaning against one of the trees as she set to gathering sticks and bark. Her stomach growled, but she had no idea where she'd find herself food, so she focused on the problems she knew she could solve. The first of those was the cold. A wizard never lacked a fire starter; she just needed some firewood.

After she'd gathered enough that her arms began to go weak beneath the weight of it, Syline returned to her satchel and set to building her fire. Her father had shown her how to do this once and though the memories were vague, they were still there. Soon enough, she was satisfied and murmured a sigil, a type of minor spell named after the mage nation Sigillite, so simple that one could learn them off by heart without the need to constantly refresh themselves on it. It was one of sparking, one of the most important ones a wizard can know, just for how often they'd find a use for it.

The sparks caught on her kindling and soon enough her little fire was burning nicely. She kept a small pile of spare kindling and wood beside her, should she need to help it burn brighter as the night wore on. For now, Syline was quite pleased with herself. Three trees were very close to each other where she sat, so the wind would have a hard time catching her fire to any significant degree and the heat from it wouldn't disperse too far. Now that she was at least warm, Syline packed some snow in her mouth, letting it dissolve. At least she wouldn't go thirsty this time of year. She packed some snow under her robes against her bruised side and wrist to help with the swelling on the bruises. At least, as cold as she was, she didn't feel their aches as much as she might have.

While her mouth froze from the cold of the snow and the rest of her body gradually warmed up, Syline sat down to take out her stolen spell-book. For all the trouble it was giving her, she hadn't actually gotten much of a look at it yet. Crossing her legs, Syline placed the huge tome in her lap and started reading. For now, she didn't bother with the spells she thought would be beyond her level to cast. No point thinking too hard on that which she couldn't even touch. The spell-book really did seem to be that of a true master, the sheer number of even simple spells they had in here was staggering. She had heard Jane was an adept mage, but this was the tome of a legend. Spells she expected to be able to cast but of a variety she'd never even heard of; spells to seal doors completely, spells that spewed cones of flame, spells that would change her appearance to any person she could think of.

Despite her growing excitement, Syline made a point to avoid anything that looked like necromancy. She wanted no part of that. She had heard tales of the destruction a necromancer could bring and how the stronger spells of the school left a taint upon your soul.

For now, Syline decided to give herself something constructive to do; she started picking out the spells she believed could be cast and would be useful to her, ones that she could see herself using regularly. Getting out her inkwell and quill, Syline began to scribe those spells down in her own spell-book. This tome was a masterful source of knowledge. In fact, it practically felt like a free pass to her. A ticket to greatness. If she held onto this book, she would always have the next layer of spells to graduate herself to. Greater and greater spells until she was casting ones on par with an archmage.

However, the tome was also gigantic, and she found the handwriting rather difficult to decipher. Although beautiful, to be sure, it was also overtly flowing, to the point where telling which letter was which became at times a chore. She'd never be able to find a spell quickly in the tome, and she was convinced her perfect casting of that lightning teleport spell was a fluke. Having relevant spells in her own spell-book would make her life a lot easier.

Syline was beginning to almost enjoy this task when she spotted movement out of the corner of her eye. She looked that way and spotted a rather large rabbit, hopping between the trees. Syline's stomach growled.

The rabbit looked up. Syline forced herself to stay perfectly still until the rabbit went back to rustling about in the snow, looking for its dinner.

Once it did, she slowly and carefully turned the pages of her own spell-book to her spell of arcane missiles. Once a target was chosen in the incantation, the spell would guide itself to them, making it difficult for the missiles to miss. She hated to kill such a cute little rabbit, but she was so damned hungry. She simply had to eat. She began the incantation. The rabbit looked up and darted into the underbrush. It was too late; she was already through the targeting verse. Two of the little balls of bluish light peeled off from her wand and into the underbrush. The only sound was a little meaty thud.

Hoping the rabbit didn't suffer, Syline placed her spell-book back in her satchel and got up to fetch the rabbit. Pushing her way through the underbrush, she found it lying limp just a metre or so from where she'd seen it push into the brush to escape her. It looked as if the missiles had broken its neck. At least it died quickly. She picked up the rabbit's body, holding it by its ears, as she'd seen chefs in her home do when they were making roast rabbit for her family. She carried it back to the fire, laid it down in front of her, and realised a new problem.

She had no idea how to prepare a rabbit.

She bit her lip, staring into the glassy, unseeing eyes of the rabbit. Her mind went soaring back to the guard. How she'd killed him, how his eyes had been so afraid, so very terrified right before they had gone dark. She could only pray that its death had been quicker, less painful than his. She couldn't have killed it for no reason. She wasn't going to kill an innocent little thing like this and then not do something with it. She'd have to figure this out. Without a knife – or any real implements – at hand, she went for the one tool she did have: her huge tome of spells. Surely, there'd be something in there that would help with this. She started going through it, page by page, searching for any spell that she thought might help. Illusion, no. Fire spells might help cooking it, but she couldn't eat it with the fur on. She didn't know how summoning spells could help here; she couldn't summon a chef.

That would have been too easy.

She scanned the pages one by one, just flipping through them until she found an insidious little spell, one she could only imagine the nefarious uses necromancers put to. The spell was for sculpting and shaping the form of a corpse. She doubted any necromancer had thought to use it like she planned to right now. Syline studied the spell over and over. This was necessary. It might be necromancy but it's not like she was using it for anything evil. She was just using it to prepare her dinner. Hell, looking it over, there were a few other spells labelled necromancy that didn't fit with what she'd expected. There was one that was just for sleeping comfortably in a suit of armour. Maybe…

She shook her head but steeled her heart. Right now, she was entirely on her own and could only rely on herself. She'd have to get used to doing what was necessary to survive. Syline let the unfamiliar incantation leave her lips, and felt the magic pervade her form. She looked down at the rabbit.

The spell allowed one to completely reshape a corpse but did not grant any life to it. First, she made the skin split and cleanly fall off the body. She then let the head fall off. It was too disconcerting seeing that, the flesh and bone parting cleanly under an invisible knife. She grabbed it by the ear and flung the head away into the woods. Some animal would probably enjoy the meal. Finally, she got to the parts she'd be able to eat. She vacated the guts from the rabbit and threw those away as well, gagging as she did, leaving only the meat: breast, back and the upper half of the legs. She'd at least eaten enough rabbit to know what parts usually went into the meal.

With the rest of the rabbit discarded into the woods, Syline placed each piece of meat into a little mound of snow nearby to keep them fresh. She fetched one of her cleaner and straighter sticks from her collection of firewood and pierced each piece of meat with it, making herself a little rabbit kebab. Separated from the rest of the animal, it was much easier to just consider them food rather than some poor little creature she'd just killed.

As she began to rotate the meat over her roaring fire, the impact of what Syline had done finally started to affect her. She'd never killed anything in her life, and today she'd killed both a man and a rabbit. She hadn't even really thought about killing the rabbit other than satisfying her own hunger. What was she turning into? She didn't stop rotating the meat – the smell of her coming dinner was simply too good to ignore – but as she did, Syline felt tears begin to gather in her eyes. Sure, she could rationalise both of them, but still, she had killed the rabbit so easily. Would killing other animals, or even people, be so easy in the future? Would killing hellblooded, dwarves, elves, or even humans be as easy to her as killing this rabbit? Just an act to satisfy her needs? Sure, plenty of men and women in the world killed things every day, but Syline had never had to before. It was hitting her just how coddled a life she had had until now.

Her father raised her brothers to be huntsmen from childhood, but she and her sisters had an easy life. Yes, she'd trained constantly as a duellist, but she was never expected to have to fend for herself, let alone kill. They were supposed to run the city side of things, whilst her father and brothers were forever holding back the dark of the wilds. She only got to see her father once or twice a year. He'd never seemed to know what to do with her. Kat kept up with her brothers easily, but Syline? She was soft, she was born for city life, she didn't belong out here. No one else would think twice about that rabbit, but all she could see when she looked at her dinner before her was the rabbit's empty, dead eyes. The guard's empty dead eyes. His lips, trying to say words that he had not the air to speak. His life probably flashed before his eyes. Gods, what if he had a family? What if the rabbit had babies that would starve without it? Is this how the world was? Kill or be killed every day, regardless of who you left behind…?

Syline's tears and thoughts of self-hatred were interrupted by something landing on her leg. Looking down, she found a small raven sitting on her and staring up curiously. In shock, Syline screamed, rearing back from the bird. The raven reacted similarly, flapping up into the air with angry caws. It landed a few feet from Syline and went back to staring at her.

Her shock abating, Syline stared back. She wondered just why a raven would come – of course, she had a fire, food and soft robes. She probably looked like a fantastic nest to it right about now. She looked at her kebab of rabbit meat. Surely, she could afford to give up a little bit at least. She wanted her meat to cook a bit longer, but she didn't think the raven would mind its part being a bit undercooked. She brought the stick out of the flames and peeled off the top piece, the little bit of meat the back had provided. She wasn't sure what was left would really fill her up that much, but right now, a little companionship would really do her about as much good as that meat would.

She placed the meat down right by her leg, returning the kebab to the flame. The raven eagerly bounced over and snapped it up. Then, showing absolutely zero fear of her, it leapt right back into Syline's lap. It nestled down between her legs and into her soft robes.

Syline's eyes budded with fresh tears as she felt a giggle overcome her.

What a ridiculous bird. The raven looked up at her and made its best facsimile of her giggle with a warble deep in its throat. Warily, she reached out and began petting the raven down its back. Her family owned ravens as messenger birds. She knew they were intelligent and affectionate birds once they got to know you. Kat had one as a pet and she'd been begging her mother to let her make one her familiar.

The raven continued its gentle warbling, finishing its meat and resting its head under its wing, perfectly at ease. Maybe, she'd just found her familiar. She'd always heard animals had a certain sense for mages, and sometimes it was the familiar who chose the mage, not the other way around.

"Is that what this is?" she asked the raven. It lifted its head, staring at her. "Do you want to be my familiar, little one?" She didn't know what kind of reply she expected, but it seemed this raven had already taken a liking to her and had definitely made its decision. It hopped up onto her shoulder, and affectionately butted its head into her cheek, making that same warbling noise deep in its throat.

"I'll… I'll take that as a 'yes'." With the raven on her shoulder, Syline got out the master spell-book. Forming a pact with a familiar was a spell in and of itself, and she was sure she had spotted it in there. Scanning through, she let out a little victorious "aha" as she fell upon the page.

"Ready, little one?"

She didn't wait for a reply this time, the bird gave her one anyway though. Climbing down from her shoulder, it took roost in her scarf, small enough to comfortably sit there just above her breast, only its head poking out as it looked up and let out a caw. She ran through the incantation. The spell could be resisted by the animal if it wished. They could sense what it would do and, if they didn't wish for the bond, they could refuse. The raven most certainly didn't, and small runes appeared from its head to the tip of its tail, running down its form. The runes formed her name in the tongue of magic, naming the raven as her familiar. They faded just as quickly. The moment the bond was formed, she could sense it. She didn't know what to expect, but she could feel the raven's presence with her in a new light, as if, in its own small way, the raven was present in her very mind.

She could sense how it was feeling as if they were her own emotions. She could feel warm, easy contentment from it, along with the fading traces of loneliness. The raven was able to communicate with her in a primitive way through their bond, and it sent to her mental images of two other ravens, far larger than it, being torn apart by a large, white mass of fur she picked out as probably being a lynx or some other wild cat. She sensed it had been wandering for a long time, looking for somewhere it belonged, but ravens on other islands had rejected it. Ravens had their own languages in a way, and each murder's dialect was slightly different. It didn't fit with any of them and was again and again left isolated until it eventually found her.

Once more, Syline bit back tears. She pressed her head down and kissed the top of the raven's head.

"Don't worry, you'll be safe with me from now on, dear." She pulled out her rabbit kebab from the flames, pulling off a piece of the breast and giving it to the raven.

Her heart felt a great deal lighter now. She might have killed the rabbit, but in her own way, she felt like she had rescued this little raven. The rabbit was delicious and each bite eased her heart a little more. She told herself she couldn't feel bad for killing a rabbit; it was just part of the food chain. If she hadn't killed it, something else would. If she was going to provide for herself and her new little familiar, she'd have to get used to doing what needed to be done.

As her raven fell asleep in her scarf, Syline finished off her meal, feeling much better. Tomorrow, she could go to one of the lumber towns, try and find herself a bodyguard to help her find somewhere to hold up more permanently, until she figured out a plan to go home. Right now though, Syline closed up her satchel and pulled Malir out of her pocket. She placed it in her scarf next to the raven for her new familiar to cuddle up to and nestled into the tree behind her after adding a little fuel to the flame. Syline soon fell asleep, doing her best to ignore the ache of her tired muscles and bruised body. She was feeling like she might really be able to do this.

She might really be able to succeed in this adventure.

Chapter 6

DESCENDING INTO THE DARKNESS OF a demon-filled catacomb with only a half-devil to guide her was, perhaps, not the greatest decision Amberly had ever made. But, so far, it wasn't going all too poorly for her. Laes would occasionally reach back to guide or use one of his wings to nudge her in the right direction when they had to round a corner or suddenly double back.

Amberly was deprived of her sight down here, but the scent alone told her the demons were near. That same pungent stench, like rotten eggs and faeces mixed in some awful concoction over a fat-fuelled flame. That scent was one she would never forget, not since the day those who bore it slaughtered all she ever knew. She remembered it so vividly, overpowering even the stench of blood as she had lain there, hidden beneath a blanket and her mother's corpse. The demons had killed both her parents then, and only her mother's body had kept her safe and hidden. Stifling tears, she was bathed, enveloped in the stench of demons, with nothing but their laughter and her mother's paling features for company until the Furies came.

"Turns the stomach, doesn't it?" Laes whispered to her. He paused for a moment, then shook her gently.

Amberly turned to look at him as if waking from a dream. "What?"

"The stench, demons. Turns my stomach, at least. A lot of devils are…

sort of allergic to demons, being near them makes us ill. It's the best weapon the wild dogs have against us. Anyway, get your sword ready. If the stench is this bad, they must be close."

For the longest time, the only light had been the deep ruddy-red that emanated from Laes' blade. She kept hers ready by her side as the pair slunk around another corner. They could see torchlight now, growing against the walls. Laes gave one last look back at her before pushing forward. On impulse, she gave the half-devil's shoulder a light squeeze – a show of solidarity – before releasing him. She could see now. Slinking forward beside Laes, she made her way down this last hallway. They emerged into the half-light of a large crypt lit by three torches burning in the mummified hands of the owners; corpses propped up in garish poses with wire and nail.

In the centre of the room, three children stood, all with bizarrely serene smiles on their faces, eyes vacant, their backs to one another, forming a loose triangle. Abasing themselves on their knees before them were figures in simple brown, satin robes, seemingly praying to the children. Beside them, propped up in the empty coffins of the crypt, were the corpses of other children, their bodies devoid of skin. The ground all around was splattered with blood and scattered with vicious-looking hooked, bladed tools. At the back of the room, Amberly spotted eyes glinting in the dark, another figure, hidden in shadow, watching, but not participating. All Amberly could make out of them was a feminine figure and a shock of white hair.

Amberly felt the hate rising in her; it was all that stopped her vomiting then and there. She had never been somewhere that smelled as utterly horrid as this place. Piss, ash, shit and that awful, invasive smell of demonkind. She began praying repeatedly to Soel to give her the strength to crush these cultists, to stand strong and not give in to her body's own weakness, to slaughter them before they could harm any more of these poor children. She started to raise her blade when Laes caught her bicep. He nodded off to the left. In the shadows of a side room, they could just make out other children peeking out fearfully, arms wrapped in chains.

"You get their attention and try and get them away from the children," Laes began. "I'll start –"

"Can you help us, miss? Please?" a small voice at Amberly's side interrupted. They looked down. It was a fourth child with the same serene smile on his face as the three by the cultists.

"Of course, dear." Amberly's instincts had taken over. She reached for the boy and placed an arm around him. "I need you to hide for now though, ok–" Her voice cut off, strangled when the child grabbed her wrist. She felt the bones crack under the crushing grip. Far, far too strong for any child.

She screamed.

"Shit!" Laes cursed beside her and his hellforged blade lashed out at the boy's wrist, taking off the arm at the elbow. The child hissed like an angry cat, leaping backwards. Seams showed around its eyes and lips, like its skin had been stitched onto it. "They're skin stealers, Amberly! Protect the side room!"

Spots played across Amberly's vision at the pain as she stumbled back from the thing in a child's skin. Its serene smile turned vicious as the skin peeled off its form. What stood up from within the child was far larger than it had any right to be, considering its diminutive host, standing easily six feet tall. The awful thing seemed made of little but sinew and bone, its eyes nothing but lights within a terrible, predatory skull, somewhere between a big cat and a bull. The smell hit Amberly full on now. Even Laes grimaced in her peripheral vision. Only her fury kept her stomach in check. They well and truly had the cult's attention now. The cultists were yelling and rushing for their weapons as Amberly and Laes retreated to guard the door to their remaining hostages.

"A good eye, devil," hissed the first of the demons, now missing an arm but flexing its other long, clawed appendage as its fellows broke free of their child hosts, advancing towards the duo.

"Please, your kind might think themselves clever, but you can't hide how ugly you are, no matter whose skin you wear."

The beastly demon cackled as it leapt at Laes. The devil dipped low, his blade carving a long line through its gullet as Amberly's stabbed viciously into its shoulder. Her blade burned with the holy flames of her god as she roared a battle cry.

"Fear, darkness! For the dawn has come!"

The first of the demons screeched, crippled on the floor, before Amberly decapitated it with a vicious swing.

"Not bad, knee scuffer," Laes complimented her with an easy smirk, turning properly towards the advancing foes. The cultists seemed eager to hide behind their demon lords. They'd be easy pickings once the real threat was dealt with.

"Not bad yourself, hellspawn," Amberly teased in reply.

She blinked back the black spots in her vision, hastily praying to her god for healing as two more demons rushed in. The wonderful warmth, her god's touch, filled her and the pain in her wrist faded just in time for her to meet their charge, and just in time for Laes to vanish in a burst of flame. Their claws were like a storm of blades and the creatures were terribly strong. She met the oncoming blows with a swing of her flaming blade, claws tearing rents in her breastplate. But the flames were anathema to creatures such as these, and the one she had struck screeched at the burning, blistering line she'd left along its chest, golden flames lapping from the open wound. The other one would have been far more problematic had Laes not chosen at that moment to burst into being behind it, his blade embedded to the hilt in its spine. That blade was more than its money's worth, for even one burning with her god's light would have trouble inflicting such a blow.

With a roar, the half-devil ripped his blade free and tore it across the back of the other demon's knee as it turned to face him. Amberly took that as her chance. As the creature squealed and fell, she sliced deep into its neck, viscera spewing forth. But the blade did not strike deeply enough, and the demon still had the strength to swing out with both claws, catching both devil and paladin across their thighs. Its claws only scraped off her armour, but they cut deep into Laes' leg as he finished it with a downward slash to its skull. That was three of the four. The last stood upon the crypt of broken, skinned children, hissing black words in its abyssal tongue, words that tainted the air and hurt Amberly's ears. It raised its hand and a line of pale yellow streaked from its finger towards Amberly's breast.

Laes shouted two words and a shield of red light spawned over Amberly. It absorbed the brunt of the spell, but still, she was left with a searing wound on her shoulder; the flesh blackened from contact alone. That arm wasn't having a good day, but at least it wasn't her sword arm. Laes incanted another spell of his own, forming a ball of ash and fire in his palm and hurling it for the beast, right as Amberly flipped her sword and flung it like a javelin for the creature in turn. The demon leapt to the side to evade the fireball, but only succeeded in throwing itself into the path of the sword, which skewered it through its gullet and sent it sprawling, its spine cut.

Laes hobbled over to it hurriedly, cursing with every step, his free hand clutched to his wounded thigh. With one strike, he finished the beast.

"Laes!"

Just in time for one of the cultists to leap at his back with a dagger. The blade cut into the devil's flesh but, without magical properties, didn't seem to press in far enough to cause more than a flesh wound.

"Oh." Laes turned to face the man, the movement twisting the dagger out his grasp. Hell and Heaven alike had come for the cultists, and many of them were already running, but the ones that stayed had fear and madness in their eyes. They knew their only way out was to kill the two here or die and descend for the reward from their demon lords.

"You should not have done that," Laes told the fool with the dagger, yanking it from his back and sending it skittering across the floor.

The man turned to run, but Laes was quicker, catching him on the small of his back with his blade. Spine cut, the man's legs went out from under him. The half-devil made a point to stand on his neck and make sure he felt every last moment before he rammed his blade into his heart.

What followed after was more akin to a slaughter than a battle. Laes used his magic to mop up any on the run, whilst Amberly cut a path through those who were foolish enough to stand and fight. Only one of the cultists was smart enough to attempt to surrender. All that got him was the pommel of Amberly's blade to his temple. She left his unconscious form on the floor to focus on finishing the rest. She had almost forgotten about the figure in the shadows until one of the cultists called out to them.

"You said you would help! You said the mothers would protect their children! Why have you abandoned us?!"

But the figure was already gone. Mention of "mothers" inspired a thrill of worry in Amberly, however. The Mother's Hand were an infamous cabal of vampires spread across dozens of nations. When one of their members entered into a region, there was no telling what damage they could inflict, controlling men and beasts alike from behind the scenes to match their unknowable agendas. The most infuriating thing about them was how difficult they were to nail down. By the time their presence was discovered, they had usually already disappeared. Such as was the case with the mystery woman in the shadows, but with her already gone, Amberly decided to put her out of mind for the time being. She'd tell her superiors and see what they made of it. For now, she focused on a far more enjoyable task, mopping up the remaining cultists.

When they were finally done, Laes and Amberly walked back towards the room with the children. Even the half-devil was thoroughly winded.

"Okay, Laes…"

Laes looked at the paladin beside him curiously, wondering what she wanted. She was about to reply when the smell of this place finally caught up to her. Adrenaline had kept it at bay until now, but all at once, her stomach started doing flips as her gorge rose. She collapsed to the ground, vomiting violently across the floor. The half devil took a step to the side to avoid getting it on his boots.

"Take your time…"

"I was going to say… Oh, Soel…" She made the mistake of looking up, catching eye contact with one of the dead, skinned children. A fresh wave of bile coursed up through her throat.

"Let me guess. You were going to say, 'You're wonderful, Laes. Please take me to dinner'," he said, offering a hand to help her up.

"I'll let you think that if it brightens your day." She groaned as he pulled her to her feet, both their eyes catching on the hall at the same time. The light of torches was growing closer. Boots on stone echoed down the hall.

"More cultists?" Amberly mouthed to Laes beside her, wiping her lips clean of vomit as the pair of them turned to face the growing light. A few of the children behind them were crying, but Amberly had to suppress a snicker when one reached out to touch Laes' leg and the half devil practically leapt out of his skin.

"Thank you, Mr Redman…" the little boy said. Amberly managed a little smirk.

"Yeah, yeah, sure, whatever kid. Just keep quiet for now, okay? You'll all go home soon," Laes said, taking a step away from the door to put him out of reach of the children.

"Not a kid person?" Amberly teased him as the pair readied their swords.

Whoever was coming down the hall was about to come round the corner. She wasn't honestly sure she could handle more of this: what the demons here were doing, what the people here were doing. Regardless of the satisfaction she got today, this place, those poor skinned children, all would haunt her dreams for years to come.

—

THE NEXT DAY WAS IMMEDIATELY off to a better start than the one before. Syline woke up, tucked in against a tree, with her new raven friend dozing happily in her arms. Thanks to the location of her little campground, she'd been well protected from the elements over the night, and her fire had burned for a good hour or two after she dozed off. To get ready for the journey ahead of her, Syline caught two more rabbits for her breakfast with her arcane missiles. She apologised to them, but this time, she shed no tears. They suffered much less than they would have at the teeth of a more bestial predator. This island seemed rampant with rabbits; she could have easily caught five or six more, had she wished it. The place mustn't have had much of a predator population for the animals to breed so freely. She prepared them in the same way she had prepared the one the previous night, and her little raven seemed happy to chow down on the parts of the rabbit she herself wouldn't eat: the guts, gristle and the like.

As she was enjoying a rabbit kebab, a thought occurred to her.

"I suppose I need to give you a name, don't I?"

Her raven looked up at her silently, rustling its feathers.

She ran a hand down its spine as she thought to herself.

"How about..." She giggled gently to herself. "Corax. It means both raven and battering ram in the old trade tongue. What do you think?"

The raven let out a caw at her, before hopping up her chest to nestle into her scarf.

"I'll take that as an 'I love it, Syline, you're great at coming up with names'," she told the raven, snickering. It was a bit of a silly name, calling a raven "raven", but, if anyone asked, she'd tell them it meant battering ram. It'd probably just confuse them more.

After breakfast, she opened up her spell-book and studied four spells to memorise for the day's journey. Three or four was her limit for what she could generally remember off the top of her head. The arcane tongue was one that seemed naturally evasive to bring to mind, as if it didn't want to be remembered by mere mortals, and it didn't help that hers was a wand intended for beginners. Its crystals and ink could only be readied for eight spells at most. She could have relied on the book theoretically, as her focus for the day, but she always preferred casting with a wand than a tome. When casting, one always needed to have some kind of focus on them, something filled with the ink of the arcane, harvested from rare deposits in the earth. When a wizard prepared themselves for the day, they had to ready their foci to cast the spells they had in mind – a calibration of sorts that took a great deal of mental control to shape the ink within, lest the foci be destroyed, potentially catastrophically.

Syline had met a man who had lost a hand like that. Spell-books required no such thing. Once a spell was written in a spell-book, the complex enchantments hidden within the spine and covers kept the book attuned to anything within its pages.

With so many choices available to her, thanks to the archmage's tome, she took a fair while to make up her mind on what she'd choose for the day. In the end, she settled on her arcane missiles, a spell that would cause her to vanish from sight for a few moments, a spell that summoned a horse made of magic and her fire dagger. Considering her plan, she expected that the ability to summon a horse would be one she'd be very glad for by the time the day was out. At least today, she'd be setting off with a full stomach, and she wouldn't be alone.

Syline had a map of the kingdom in her room and didn't find it all too hard to recall at least the basics of it. She knew if she headed south and slightly to the east for about half a day, she should be in sight of one of the lumber islands. One named Winter's Fang after the huge, magical ice wolf the settlers had famously slain when they'd arrived on the island. She intended to head there and see if she could hire someone to act as a bodyguard. Lumber islands didn't have the larger cities' guard forces, so there were often adventurers and mercenaries hanging around them looking for work, dealing with monsters her father's forces didn't catch.

She had her coin purse in her satchel, and enough gold to surely win someone's loyalty. She just had to hope none of Lady Jane's hunters would think to look over in that area. She had to trust they'd think she was a foolish, scared girl just running down the main roads. It was a gamble, but having a swordsman to protect her would be worth the payoff even if more did come for her. A wizard's power grew exponentially with a protector to give them room to cast longer spells in combat, and having an experienced warrior would make her feel much, much safer in this journey.

With Corax riding in her scarf, Syline packed up her satchel and headed for the edge of the island. Facing out over the frozen rivers, she grasped her wand and ran through the incantation to summon forth her steed. When the last word left her lips, the horse came cantering from an illusory fog. It was beautiful, made of nothing but blue light, a huge and mighty steed indeed, already fitted with a saddle. It trotted in place before her, eager to run. Syline was glad for the riding lessons she'd taken in her younger years as she climbed atop the arcane stallion and set off at a canter. She let it go no faster than that for risk of stumbling on the ice, but at least atop the steed, she'd only be draining her magical reserves, not her stamina.

—

It was late afternoon by the time Syline reached her destination. She couldn't pretend the journey had been particularly enjoyable; her bruises still ached and each galloping step by her stallion jarred them. But eventually, that had at least settled into a dull ache. She couldn't deny the beauty of the journey either. Syline didn't leave the city all that often, and in its own way the huge open vistas only broken by islands was breathtaking. The world went on further than she could see, meeting the cloudy sky on the horizon.

During those hours, she only once saw other people. She was straying close to the borders of the kingdom and chanced upon the sight of some of the tundra elves who migrated along paths further east. There was some kind of caravan going across the waters, all riding atop huge, powerful elk or smaller does. She had waved to them, riding in opposite directions, and one or two of the elves who'd caught sight of her, returned the gesture. She had always thought the tundra elves were beautiful, though she'd never tell Alexis that, she'd never let her live it down. She would've liked to speak with them, maybe see if she could buy some food, but they clearly had their own path and no intent on stopping nor crossing the border between her kingdom and their domain.

When she did reach her destination, it was about what she expected: an island large enough to house a forest, with a number of smaller islands dotted around it, sprouting their own groves of trees. Her horse's magic finally ran out about a half hour's walk from the town, so she'd set to walking, after picking herself up out of the snow. She'd not been expecting the damned thing to disappear so suddenly. The town itself was nothing to write home about: a large lumber-mill, sheds and storehouses, a tavern, a barracks for the lumberjacks who lived here as well as a general store, and a spattering of houses for the few people lucky enough to afford one. Other than the lumber mill, they all existed on a single, long street.

It was the tavern Syline headed for. After all, it was the obvious choice. Every book she'd ever read told her that if you wanted to find an adventurer, you go to the local tavern. It was a large, two-storey building, made mostly of timber, which made sense. A pair of horses nickered to one another, tied to a post outside the tavern. Light spilled out from within, fighting against the cloudy weather. Syline removed her huge witch's hat as she stepped inside and immediately, she felt out of place. It shouldn't have come as a surprise to her that this wasn't exactly a place many women would be, but it did all the same. Looking around the room, she saw only large, powerfully built men with the weather-beaten, leathery skin of someone who spent far too much time out in the biting wind and the long beards of people with no reason to shave.

Almost all the bar turned to face her as she stepped in, and the feeling of so many eyes upon her had Syline's cheeks flushing. Right away, she wished she still wore her hat to hide from their gaze beneath it.

"Well now," the portly bartender said, "don't see many girls come this far north. Are you lost, miss?" He was a bald, older man who looked like he'd only recently retired from the lumber trade. A brutal scar, which had taken out an eye, stretched across one side of his face. He smiled, revealing he was missing several teeth.

"You gotta be real lost to end up here!" said one of the patrons, getting a laugh from the room.

"I'm…" This was harder than Syline had expected; she'd never been good with crowds, or new people, or being intimidated. She wasn't nearly as confident as she liked to think she was. "I'm looking for a bodyguard," she finally managed, looking around the bar.

To a man, they were all brutal, hardy sorts. Apart from one table. One table stood out and she found herself making her way there right away. At the comment, they had roused and the men were looking her way more intently. They looked like they'd be prime candidates as the protagonist of *The Dragonslayer's Lance*: handsome, lithe, and with rakish, charming minor scars that spoke of swashbuckling and adventure. They reminded her of her father's men, which had her feeling a little more at ease than with the huge, weathered lumberjacks.

"He-hello," she stammered out as she reached the table.

The one in the centre – their spokesperson – was the first to reply. He had carefully groomed, blonde hair in a ponytail and green eyes like emeralds, gleamed at her, alongside a pearly smile.

"Well hello, miss. Heard you say you're looking for a bodyguard?"

"Oy, missy," the barkeep drawled. Syline looked his way and he waved a hand as if to ward something away. "There's an adventurer upstairs, better sort than those bastards."

"Ignore the oaf. That man's hellblooded, miss. You don't want to truck with his sort."

Syline nodded. She'd seen hellblooded in the city, but never spoken to one herself. From her understanding, they came in all shapes and sizes, but most all were marked by their strange skin colour and horns. They were interesting from a scholarly standpoint – anyone with blood from outer realms was, but that didn't mean she didn't find them a bit unnerving.

"Better a hellblooded than someone bound for it. Tellin' ya, miss." There was a hostile air in the room. The lumberjacks were looking at the bounty hunters and Syline like they wanted a fight. She swore she could hear growls and suddenly realised she'd stepped into some long running feud. She saw a handsome, brunette bounty hunter with a crew cut put a hand on his blade, the other on her elbow.

"You should get out of here, miss," he said, looking at the blonde man with a little smile.

The man nodded and stood up.

"Come with me, miss, I'll take you back to our lodgings before this gets ugly; we can talk about the details there."

He offered her an arm and Syline took it wordlessly. It wasn't the first time a soldier had escorted her through a group of unruly peasants and his firm forearm made her feel much safer. She wanted out of that bar fast, it felt like it was a hair's breadth from bloodshed. He led her down the road and, once out of the tavern, she released his arm and looked behind them, watching the bar in case any of the lumberjacks followed. They went down a well-trodden path, marked by the passage of hundreds of feet and carriages. No snow lay here long for how quick it was trampled down into the dirt. An inkling of worry wormed its way into her stomach. This wasn't the way to anyone's house. No one would have so many visitors, and why would anyone live off the main street in such a small place.

"Now hold on one moment," she said, backing up from her prospective bodyguard. He stopped in his tracks and turned back to face her. The look in his eye set her quivering: it was a hungry, feral look. "What are you playing at, sir?"

"Ah, you caught me…" he said with a little chuckle. walking towards her. She backed up, hand going for her wand. The incantation for her arcane missiles was halfway out her mouth when the man broke into a sprint. The last syllable left her tongue right as his fist hit her stomach, driving the wind from her as a pair of little arcane missiles buried into his shoulder.

"Bitch!" he shouted.

Syline was doubled over from the first punch, and the second one he threw caught her on the back of the head. Everything went black as she hit the floor. The last thing she heard was Corax loudly squawking as the bird was caught by the man and thrown against a tree.

＝

THE NEXT MINUTE OR SO was a haze for Syline. He'd well and truly knocked the senses from her and her vision blacked out repeatedly. She had no strength in her limbs. All she knew was that he was dragging her somewhere by her leg, her body pulled along the cold dirt like a sack. Things went dark. She could see a ceiling above them. A door slammed shut, then the only sound was his heavy breathing and the wind whistling through a broken window. She was beginning to feel strength coming back to her limbs. He stood over her. There were tears in her eyes. She was sure he was one of Jane's hunters, that he had come for her to take her spell-book, to kill her. He had taken here to do it quietly where no one could get in his way.

He grinned lecherously at her as he pulled off his shirt and stuffed the sweaty, rank clothing in her mouth and tied it behind her head as a gag. It was only then that she had the presence of mind to begin to scream. She kicked out at him, but the man only laughed, hurling her sword belt to the side of the room. He lay atop her. Hands parting her robes to feel across her body.

This was so, so much worse than him trying to kill her.

She felt him kissing at her neck, his weight across her form, his hands grabbing her breast, going lower.

Syline had never had a lover in her life and she doubted she'd ever want one after this day. She screamed for all she was worth beneath the man, but it only seemed to amuse him. His dark gaze staring down at her, he looked at her like she was an object, something to be used and tossed away. How could she have been so stupid? Just because of a few handsome faces, she'd ignored the bartender's warning. Her hands batted against his sides, but she was too weak to do a thing to him. Her arms were still heavy from the blow he had struck her. She needed to do something, to get help, to do anything to escape this situation.

She kicked out. Her leg struck a table and she heard something clatter to the ground. She looked to the side as his pants reached his knees. An axe. His breath was hot on her neck, her robes open, his eyes wild. He was reaching to remove her robes entirely when suddenly, her saviour arrived.

Corax appeared from nowhere. Having gotten in through the broken window, the little raven leapt at his face, screeching and pecking at his eyes. As he did, Syline's fingers pressed as deep as they could into the wound her arcane missiles had left on his shoulder. The man roared, rearing back like a struck bear. With his weight off her, Syline swung to the side and grabbed the axe. Hand over his eyes he reached for her blindly. Syline sat up and swung for all she was worth.

Out of all the moments of that haunting event, the sound of the axe crunching through his finger bones to carve a crater through his face was the one that would stay with her the longest. He didn't roar this time, he screamed, falling to the ground and bucking about like a stuck pig. His face ruined, the fingers on his left hand taken off at the knuckle. Syline got to her feet, taking the axe in both hands. She could barely see him clearly for the sting of tears in her eyes but hate gave her blow strength and led it true. She screamed as she swung, screaming out all her anger and pain and fear and letting it ring in his ears for the last moments of his life. The axe cracked his skull open like a melon, going deep before sticking in place, blood splattered across Syline's hands.

Sobbing and feeling more hurt, more violated than she ever had in her life, Syline closed her robes and ripped the axe free from his skull. She swept up Corax, her hero, and grabbed her sword belt on the way as she fled the building. Legs shaking as she left the man – the nightmare – behind, trailing tears and spilt blood, Syline stumbled back to town.

Chapter 7

THREE MEN CAME INTO THE room, all dressed in similar garb and armour to Amberly, each held a torch in one hand and a longsword, blessed by the church, in the other. The one at the front was one she knew very well: Leoric, her mentor, adopted father and the one who had given her permission to investigate this place alone. All three recoiled at the scent and sight of the place, one of the men trailing Leoric turning to the side to vent his stomach. Leoric wrapped an arm over his mouth, calling to Amberly through it.

"In Soel's name! Amberly, what happened here and what is that?!"

This was something Amberly had not predicted. She'd thought her superiors would have had the trust in her to let her handle this place alone. Seeing as they had little faith in her hunch anyway. She could only imagine what it must look like to them: her, standing beside someone who was very obviously a devil, or at least aligned with the hells, amidst what might as well have been a charnel pit. The skin of children lying alongside corpses of demons and cultists alike. She had originally been thinking about how to approach mentioning the vampire, when she saw him next, but any thought of the woman completely fled her mind at his appearance here in the catacombs with her.

"Laes, get out of here," she whispered to her friend. He might have been a devil, but he was a friend and she wasn't going to abandon him.

"Now... Now, I can explain!" Amberly said, placing her sword in its sheath and walking forward. Her hopes weren't high. Leoric was very much the "fire and brimstone" sort. She supposed Laes was the fire and brimstone sort too, but in a very different manner.

Laes was quietly trying to slink into the shadows. Putting himself out of sight from the two aghast followers. They weren't so keen to just stand around. One drew out a knife from his belt. A silver blade. He tossed it straight for Laes as the half-devil began to chant a spell that would get him out of here.

"Laes!" Amberly shouted, giving him warning to duck the blade.

Leoric sighed. "Oh, so you even know the devil's name." He flashed some sort of signal to the men beside him. "Amberly, I always hoped... I knew you only followed Soel for the chance of revenge, but I hoped we had managed to keep your heart pure, your thoughts just. To think you would consort with Hell just to further hunt the Abyss. I shouldn't have let you off the leash so soon... I blame myself for this."

As he spoke, his men pulled goggles over their eyes and he pulled a scroll from his belt. Before Amberly could ask what it was for, Leoric spoke the trigger phrase and the scroll turned to ash as the spell within it was released into the world. With a cataclysmic bang, a huge flash of white light filled the air and all Amberly could hear was a high-pitched whining noise so loud it left her clutching her ears. The flash of white left her blinded and utterly defenceless as her arms were grabbed and tied together. She heard another spell chanted and, upon its completion, her head felt heavy, her eyelids drooped, she felt her limbs going weak, and in seconds she sagged in a powerful grip of someone behind her.

As the ringing in her ears faded, just before she blacked out, she heard a short exchange.

"What will we do with them, sir?"

"Check the children for the demon's taint, we'll do whatever we can to save them, I'll see to Amberly. She's my responsibility... My sin. It's okay my children, the dawn is here... You're safe now."

⸺

A BODY HAD BEEN FOUND on the outskirts of the city. A watchman. To be specific, one of the watchmen under Jane's control. While she had been at a dinner with her husband, the body had been hidden away in the secret chambers under her manor for her inspection. When she returned, with the just now returned Lauralee at her side, her fears were confirmed.

"That's a sabre wound," Lauralee commented idly, inspecting the corpse, "and those burns look like they're from a blade made of fire. That was the spell Syline was practising when she was in the library."

"So, she slipped the net." Jane let out a slow breath through her teeth. A girl getting lucky and managing a spell far beyond her means, that was a curiosity. This was starting to become a problem. "They said the prints led out onto the frozen lakes, correct?"

"Yes, my lady."

"Then she's smart enough to avoid the roads, but at least she's not managed her way deeper into the city, she's making her way away from us. That gives us plenty of time. There's no one out there but lumberjacks and monsters. No one she can report me to."

"Should I set out after her?"

Jane considered it, but eventually shook her head.

"No, no. There are too many open stretches of land, too far for you to travel without places to rest during the day. No." She paused, biting her lip. "I'll use my husband's connections. If the guard cannot manage it, we'll use freelancers. Adventurers, they have more experience fighting rogue mages. Money can bend them as well as I can, and their senses won't be dulled by my control. We'll organise a fallback with some mercenaries as well, just in case."

She nodded, largely to herself. Even the words that followed were more for her benefit than Lauralee's.

"Yes, don't worry, dear, this one's still under control, making her way out of the city has been her mistake. Now, what about you? How did it go with the cult?"

Lauralee paused, fidgeting.

"It–" she started. She feared Jane's mood, especially just after talking about how the guard had failed to deal with the runaway mage.

"Well, out with it."

"A paladin arrived, with a devil in tow, shortly after the summoning was completed. I had time to speak to the demons and they gave me the scroll. Then the pair wiped out the entire cult."

"Shitting hells!" Jane cursed. "We poured time and resources into that cult. They should have been better prepared, better hidden." She paused. "A paladin and a devil you said?"

"Yes, my lady, they seemed to be working together. I fled when it was clear they were going to win."

Jane looked as if she might make to lash out at her, but after a few moments, let out a ragged breath, calming herself.

"You made the right choice. If you'd defended the cult and lost, they'd have known of our hand in the activities. Still. A devil and a paladin, that's a mystery we'll need to unravel."

"I still got the scroll," Lauralee offered, trying to make the situation a little bit lighter.

"You did, you did, good girl." She paused. "Keep, keep that scroll in mind. We may be able to use it if these adventurers fail. It's another summoning, one for a hunting hound from the nethers. I had other uses for it, but if Syline remains a thorn in our side..." She nodded and began to walk away. Lauralee called after her.

"How did the experiments with the demigod go, my lady?"

Jane turned, and a broad smile spread across her lips.

"Well, darling, at least something is going well. You have no idea. Her blood. Her body. Her power. It's like nothing I've ever felt before. It was almost too much at first but" – she let out a soft, almost moan-like noise – "I don't know if any other blood will suffice again. If I keep her alive long enough, if all goes to plan, well. Soon that power will all be mine."

Lauralee smiled, but inwardly, she worried what someone with Jane's temper would be like with the power of a demigod. She hoped to be home with her own mother before she found out.

"YOU KNOW." THE FIRST THING Amberly heard when she awoke was Laes' voice. It sounded strained. In pain. "I really should have seen this coming. Nothing good comes from working with 'good people'."

She lifted her head. Pain wracked her temples like a demon's claws. Her vision was foggy but gradually starting to clear.

"I could have just stolen the one child away and disappeared into the night. But, no, whatever human part of me there is demanded I play the hero. I get the girl and save the day. Stupid! The moment I met you, I knew this would end poorly. I should have just left it at that but, no, I took a fancy to the pretty paladin. Stupid, Laes, stupid."

Laes didn't realise she was awake; it seemed like he was just thinking out loud.

"I've always been like this, you know? I always stick my head in where it doesn't belong and it's always me who gets burned. I should have just renounced the contract then and there, but the fellow was a valuable one."

Her vision cleared. They were in the cells beneath the Morning's Fury's church, where they would attempt to rescue the souls of sinners or interrogate prisoners so they could further hunt down their fellows. She was chained up to a wall. Laes was in the cell with her, on the wall perpendicular to the one she was chained to. She could see silver nails, rammed through his hands to hold him to the wall and a thick collar, embellished with symbols of Soel around his neck: ones that suppressed magic and stopped outsiders returning to their world. Sat in the cell's only window, to the right of Laes was a little, red songbird, letting out a beautiful song, but it was practically drowned out when Laes continued to rant. Any other time, Amberly would have been smiling just from that little tune, but right now, it fell on deaf ears.

"I'm a nobody in Hell; all I've got going for me is whatever authority I can bluff, and my warlocks. I've got a good collection too. Too bad none of them can hear me. With this damned collar on I can't even escape–"

"Laes…"

"Oh, good, you're awake! Now, I can really start complaining."

"Please don't. My head's pounding enough as it is… Soel help me…" She shuddered and whispered a prayer. She was afraid, petrified even. She wanted the solace of her lord, the feeling of warmth that filled her when her god granted her his favour.

It didn't come.

Her heart sank. There was no panic, only despair. Not only did her people, her church name her a traitor, but her god had also abandoned her. Maybe they were right. Maybe she was a heretic, just using them to get her revenge. She'd never exactly been the perfect zealot. She'd never make it as a nun. She only made it in the Morning's Fury because they were a bit more lax about one's devotions.

"We're going to die, aren't we, Laes?" It wasn't so much a question as a realisation – an admittance that this would be how she goes out.

"Oh, most certainly."

Despair was slowly replaced with anger. No. She'd been doing what was right. She'd been protecting people and killing demons. That's all she was ever supposed to do. If they were going to kill her for letting a devil help her save people's lives, then they could all go straight to hell with her.

"I'm just glad I'm not a true devil," Laes added.

"Why does that matter?"

"Well, because it means I at least have something of a soul, which means I'll end up back in Hell when I die. I'll likely come back as an imp... I always hated imps. But, oh well, my contracts will still stand; they'll give me a leg up on starting over."

"You seem very relaxed about this," she said, doing her best to keep up a brave face even as she fought back tears.

"... I admit, darling, it's partly an act. I'm terrified, but, well, I at least know where I'm going. Plus, growing up in Hell gives you alarming pain tolerance. No clue what'll happen to you. A zealot abandoned by her god for going too far in her pursuit of slaying demons. Sounds like something straight out of a storybook. If you're lucky, the Wanderer might take pity on you and give you entrance to his afterlife. I hear it's not so bad. It's no eternal rest, but you're basically just born again."

"And if I'm not lucky...?"

"Want to consider selling me your soul? Better to have a devil that likes you on your side than being a soul up for grabs in Hell, and it'll save you from somewhere like the Pit or the Abyss."

"I wouldn't, Amberly." Leoric was coming down the stairs. The click of his heels on the stone silenced the songbird and Amberly looked to see it flying away. "The grandmaster has decreed that you will be executed, but if you confess and repent, I might be able to make that an exile. Please, don't push your luck any further than you already have."

"Think on it, Amberly," Laes said. "We could still get that dinner together sometime. Though, I don't know how much you'd like the restaurant."

"Quiet, Hellspawn. Each word from your mouth is razors to my ears," said Leoric before cursing the devil in Soel's name, the holy words causing Laes to hiss and groan in agony.

"Leoric," Amberly said, crying, "I just... I just wanted to save the children. I don't see how what I did was wrong! Laes was doing the same thing! We both just wanted to kill the demons and save the children! What does it matter who I work with as long as good is done? I did nothing wrong!"

She raved, all the fear and outrage finally breaking free. All she'd wanted to do was good. Even if it was in pursuit of revenge, she was still doing what she was supposed to. She wouldn't have been able to save those children alone! Why couldn't they see that? Why couldn't they see that Laes had been the best option she had? That Laes had helped her save people. That neither of them had done anything evil. It was stupid, in her eyes, to turn down an ally and hate them to the core just for what they were, even if their goals were just and aligned with hers. Stupid that her god would abandon her for so little. For trying to do what was right.

Leoric did not reply. As stern as he seemed, she could see a struggle going on in him as he entered her cell.

"Please repent, Amberly. It hurts my soul enough to know you'll be executed. I don't wish you damned as well. I'm doing all I can, but you need to give me something."

"Soel has already abandoned me. I'll not repent for a sin I didn't commit. Trying to save those children was the right thing to do and I used everything I had to do it. If saving people and killing demons is a sin, then this church is the one full of sinners!" Leoric slapped her hard enough to split her lip. A sob wracked her as he grabbed her about the shoulders.

"Do you know how many times I've had to pray for Soel to forgive you? How many times I've had to beg him and the grandmaster to give you another try. How much I've sacrificed to give you one more chance!" he hissed. Amberly was stunned into silence as he continued, the dam holding back years of frustration, breaking.

"I've... I've worked so hard to try and make something of you, Amberly, but you just... you don't care! You're just guided by revenge. You've never cared about Soel, or the church, or me. You just want to use us as a path to your petty revenge for parents you barely remember. *I* raised you! *I* took you in like you were my own! *I* pulled you from their arms! *I* saved you from those demons! Is that really worth so little to you? Am I? I'm... I'm done, Amberly. I'm done. You've used up your last chance."

By the time he was finished, he was shaking, tears welled in his eyes. He let out a final sigh, and as he started to walk away from Amberley, she looked back towards Laes. He gave her a softer, friendlier smile, perhaps trying to console her or show some empathy, but it was something the devil was not used to doing.

"You want so badly to be with the devil, Amberly?" Leoric said, his voice heavy with emotion as he padded away. "You'll burn together."

—

SYLINE RETURNED TO THE BAR. As she approached, she could hear raised voices: lumberjacks and bounty hunters hurling insults at one another. Bursting inside, the door slamming wide on its hinges as the wind tore it from her hands, Syline could immediately feel all eyes upon her again. How long had it been since she'd left with the awful man? Ten minutes? Fifteen? In her mind, it felt like an eternity. She could only imagine the state she must appear in: she was crying, her clothes were dishevelled, and sitting heavy in her hands, was a bloody axe ill-fitted to her hands.

The bar was silent. There were no jokes. No seedy comments or playful jibes. Everyone wanted to know what had happened. Except for the table that already knew. The table of bounty hunters who he'd been sitting with. Who he'd been joking with. Who probably all knew his intentions when he left the tavern with the girl in tow.

The bartender was making his way over to her, but the bounty hunters got there first. They came around her like hunting hounds. As one, they demanded to know what she had done. Who she thought she was. If that was really his blood. So many questions, some of the men appalled at what their friend had done, others furious as they connected the dots, realising their friend was now dead.

Syline slowly crumpled to the floor. After all the terror she'd gone through only moments ago, this was too much for her. She felt short of breath. She felt guilty. Weak. Angry. Scared. She felt so much but didn't have the strength to do anything. She could hear Corax cawing at her from within the folds of her scarf, butting his head against her to try and give her comfort. At that moment, she felt like Corax was the only thing in the world on her side. They crowded around her, and when the bartender tried to push between them, one shoved him back.

"Leave the girl alone," the bartender snarled at them.

The one who shoved him turned to glare at the bartender.

"Not 'til we know what she's bloody well done with our mate. If 'e's dead…" He didn't expand, but with Syline weeping, and the increasing panic between the bounty hunters, it was obvious to the bar as a whole, what had been done now. Other patrons began to rise from their seats as the bounty hunters began to close ranks, beginning to panic. One man called out, saying that was his axe she held. Another began to try and defuse the situation, walking forwards with his hands splayed out, calling for the bounty hunters to calm down and step away from Syline. He was the first to get hit, a bounty hunter yelling for him to back off as he threw a haymaker for the man's jaw. He crumpled; the sense knocked out of him.

The bartender threw the second punch, catching the man holding him back in the jaw. The man went sprawling, scattering broken glass and ale as he landed on a nearby table.

"You bastards came into our town!" he roared, leaping for the man before his friends threw the bartender back. "You act like the bandits you're supposed to keep back!"

That was like the spark that ignited an inferno. Suddenly, the whole place was up in arms and everyone was fired up. Accusations were thrown at the bounty hunters. The bounty hunters accused Syline of being a murderer. The lumberjacks leapt for them, fists first. Syline screamed. The place was total chaos and Syline found herself getting trampled on as the circle of bounty hunters was broken. Some stepped over her to aid their friends, others jostled around her as lumberjacks tried to shove through them to her rescue. She should have just run. She should have just gotten out of this damned town. It was all she could do to keep Corax from getting stomped on, cradling her raven to her to keep him safe.

She was halfway through crawling beneath a table and getting out the incantation to make her disappear when one of the bounty hunters grabbed her by the collar and hefted her up out from under it.

"He was like a brother to me, and you just went and killed him, you stupid cu–" A fist came flying in from down by her side, slamming heavily into his stomach. The man's breath went out of him in a whoosh of alcohol-tainted wind over Syline's face as he dropped her. Someone else caught her, pulling her out of the way of a beer glass flying past her head. She turned to face a man unlike any other in the bar. Deep red skin with eyes of a brighter hue of the same. Huge ram horns curling down from his temples, nearly touching the gorget of his breastplate, and jutting forwards like tusks either side of his cheekbones. He was a hellblooded; the hellblooded she'd been warned away from.

"I hear that you're looking for a bodyguard?" he asked slowly, enunciating every word clearly with a deep, soft voice. As he spoke, he pulled her close and stepped them both out of the way of a charging bounty hunter.

"Yes! Yes, I am!" Syline managed, panic going through her at him wrapping his arm around her.

She wriggled away but did her best to control herself. In that same instant, he let go of her to catch one man by his extended wrist before he could catch either of them with a dagger, getting nicked on his forearm for his trouble. The man threw a punch for his head, which the hellborn narrowly dodged, getting caught on one of his horns and twisted around. He shook his head to clear the stars before slamming his forehead into the man's nose. The hunter hit the floor like a falling tree, and the hellblooded, rubbing his forehead, looked back at Syline.

"Well then, let's get you out of here. Can you stand?"

"Y-yes, yes, I can. Please, don't touch... I'll-I'll walk myself out."

The hellblooded gave her a sad frown but nodded and turned just in time to catch a bottle against his shoulder, stumbling a step back.

"Just stay behind me," he called over his shoulder.

With that said, he immediately set to putting his promise to get her out of there into action. Wading through the brawl and taking blows along the way, he proved himself solid, if not exactly quick, always putting himself between any blow that would've hit Syline. His armour protected him from much of the chaos, even if none of it looked to have come from the same source. Syline stuck close by him, using the adventurer as mobile cover from the brawl around them. He was making for a fine battering ram, forcing their way through towards the door as she moved with him, the bloody axe still clutched to her chest. The only times he threw his own punches was when he came to bounty hunters. Those, he had no compunctions of playing nice with. The hellblooded grabbed one by the scruff of the collar and threw him through a table, but as he did, another came for Syline. The hellblooded was strong, but his armour weighed him down. He cursed aloud as he spun to try and stop them.

The man had that same rakish look to him as the monster who'd taken her to the lumber mill, but their air of civility was long gone. He looked wild and furious. He rushed at Syline, trying to grab at her. Syline felt the indignant anger, fury and fear welling up inside her once more. He wouldn't touch her; he wouldn't touch her. Her protector spun, his arm raised to meet the man but instead found Syline screaming as she swung the flat of her axe for his legs, sweeping them out from beneath him, the man let out a squawk of shock, a moment before the back of his head collided with the edge of a table and he went limp on the floor.

Syline breathed a sigh of relief. She looked over her shoulder to see her bodyguard give her a smile and once more forge on, forcing their way around an upturned table and the brawl going on around it. That was when one fool was stupid enough to try and grab at Syline. She screamed as she felt the hands yanking at her hair, feeling strands ripped from her scalp as she was pulled away from the man's side. Her scream was shrill enough to get a pause from some of the people around the pair, long enough for the lumberjacks to note what was happening. The old barkeeper appeared from the melee beside the hellblooded, and together they fell on the man, a truncheon in the barkeeper's hand making quick work of the bounty hunter, alongside the hellblooded's armoured fists. Her new bodyguard helped Syline to her feet as the barkeep nodded to him, giving her an apologetic smile before he turned to try and quell the brawl. Finally, a path was open for the pair of them to reach the door. As they stepped out, Syline spied a glass flying over the crowd for her face. She let out a squeal as she tried to block with her forearms.

The man spun and slammed the door shut. Syline could just manage to hear the sound of glass shattering against it. She let out a slow sigh of relief, finally free of the bar, even if she was being shepherded by a strange, hellblooded man. Corax seemed just as relieved, poking his head out from her scarf to let out a little victorious caw at their escape before affectionately rubbing his head into the side of her neck. Her saviour trudged on. He walked from the entrance of the tavern to where the two horses were tied up. She followed.

"So."

"So?" Syline replied, looking back at him.

"Did I get the job?"

Syline stared at him incredulously for a few long moments before a limp, tiny laugh escaped her, quickly falling along with the smile that came with it.

"Yes…. yeah, yeah, just… please get me out of here. I don't want to be here; I want to leave. We can talk about payment later."

"Alright then. Can I get your name?"

She looked at the horse, running a hand down its mane, it whinnied at her. Only after a moment did she realise he had asked a question.

"Hmm? Oh… Syline… S-Syline Petranski."

"Thelonious Pugil. Do you need a hand up, Miss Petranski?"

He offered his cupped hands for her to step up into. She climbed onto his horse, moving off the saddle between its shoulders so he could sit behind her. She could have summoned a magical steed to ride but, at that moment, she didn't feel she had the requisite focus, nor energy; she just wanted to rest. She just wanted this horrible day to end.

Corax stared at Thelonious as the hellblooded mounted the horse behind Syline and set the horse on its way out of town.

"Say, ma'am, you sure you should be hanging onto that axe? S'a bit big for you."

It was only then that Syline realised she still had the axe, gripped tightly in one hand, the other holding the horse's mane for balance. She'd had it this whole time.

"Yes… I think I will, Thelonious. It… it's a good axe. Can you hold it for now though?"

He gently took the axe from her, sliding it into a loop in his saddle bags. They hit the end of the street, and he pushed the horse into a light canter.

"Where're we headed?"

"South and stay off the roads please; I'm… on the run."

Thelonious simply made a little nod. She thought she heard him quietly mutter, "Yessum", but his voice was soft enough it could've been a sigh. As the road went by around them, Syline found herself laying down against the horse's neck, too tired to keep herself upright. Soon enough, Syline had nodded off, lulled into a doze by exhaustion and the gentle rocking of the horse beneath them. She had never been so glad to have a dreamless sleep.

Chapter 8

SYLINE SLEPT HEAVILY. NEITHER THE fall of snow, nor the jostling of the horse beneath them, could do a thing to wake her. She only woke up when the ride had come to an end, and when it did, the day before felt like a terrible nightmare, surreal and unimaginable, one she'd be glad to forget. She opened her eyes to find herself being shaken gently by Thelonious. Her arms were wrapped around the neck of his horse, and she'd been using the poor mare's head as a pillow.

"Sorry, didn't mean to wake you," he said quietly, watching her stretch her arms out over her head and let out a long yawn. Corax was still dozing fitfully, nestled in her scarf.

"I didn't even realise I dozed off, thank you for letting me sleep until now."

She looked around as she dismounted, taking note of the position of the moon overhead. It must've been near on midnight. He'd been riding for a good few hours now.

"Where are we?" she asked, watching Thelonious busy himself with unloading packs from his horse's saddle. It looked like he had a tent nestled in amongst his supplies.

"Somewhere safe. Can you start a fire?" he replied, pulling down a set of folded canvas and tent poles. Syline smiled and nodded, glad to be able to do something useful, keep her hands busy and thoughts distracted.

"Then" – he left the unmade tent on the ground and pulled a short bow and quiver of arrows off his saddle – "if you can do that, I'll go catch us some dinner."

His mind must've been made up because the hellblooded trudged off into the moonlit night with the bow in hand. He was a man of few words, but she could appreciate his decisiveness. Left alone but for the horse, who seemed content to lay down in the snow and take a rest of its own, and Corax, who had not deemed her waking worthy of him doing the same, Syline set to gathering firewood. Trying not to think about the bar, trying not to think about the fact that she was alone in the woods with an even larger, even stronger man now. He wasn't like that. He'd saved her, he seemed honest. She had to believe he was honest.

By the time she'd gathered enough and cleared the ground to set up a campfire, Thelonious was on his way back. This island was a bit more open than the last she had made camp on and she could see out over the frozen water. Thelonious was dragging what looked like a doe by one of its horns from a nearby island. She busied herself with her sparking sigil to get the fire going and settled in to watch him, warming her hands by the flames. He wasn't particularly hurried, moving with a steady pace through the night, the doe leaving a furrow in the snow behind him.

"What happened to it?" she asked as he got close, taking note of a huge bite wound on its leg. One he couldn't have inflicted unless he was a very different sort of hellblooded to what she thought.

Thelonious looked at the deer and shrugged. "Wolf, probably. Herd left it behind," he told her.

Syline felt a pang of sympathy for the deer. Had she not been found by Thelonious, there was a good chance she'd have been picked apart by a different kind of wolf. She pushed that sympathy aside; she couldn't keep sniffling for every animal in her path. It was hardly fair for all the animals she'd eaten at a dinner table, far removed from the wild and the actual impact of killing them. Thelonious pulled a knife from his belt, ready to start preparing the deer, but Syline sat up and held out an arm.

"Stop, I can do that. I, er, I found a special trick for preparing animals. I should do something useful."

Thelonious looked from her to the deer, considering it a few moments. "Are you sure? Wouldn't want you to get your hands all bloodied," he said, looking at her a little incredulously, his brow furrowing softly.

Syline winced ever so slightly, eyes darting to her duelling sword.

"It's fine, Thelonious. You've done plenty for me tonight, sit down and let your feet rest."

The hellblooded relented with a shrug and sat down on the opposite side of the flames. He pulled out a metal flask and had a draught from it as he watched her.

Before she really got started however, he paused her to ask, "So, er, about my pay?"

Syline stopped in place. Of course, they hadn't actually discussed that yet, and he was a mercenary. She turned to him with a little bashful grin.

"Ah, right, well, I have a good bit of coin on me, my mother thought it was always important to carry enough to get you into or out of trouble." She let out a tiny, limp giggle as she said that, reaching into her satchel to pull out, hidden beneath her books, a velvet coin purse, filled with gold and silver coins, a veritable fortune to many less fortunate than her.

"I can pay you as we go if you would like, but my family can offer you a lot more if we manage to sort this out and get back to them." It was only as she began to speak, she realised she might have overplayed her hand, revealing to this mercenary that she had a pouch full of gold. His for the taking, with the pair of them alone out in the wilds like this. But somehow, she didn't feel like that was something she needed to worry about with him.

Thelonious didn't reply at first, taking the time to consider what she'd said, stroking his clean-shaven chin before giving a small, brusque nod. "Right, sounds good to me, no need for tapping you for all you got when we're still on the run. Hang onto your coin, we'll worry about pay when I get you home safe."

Syline lit up with a smile at that, heartened by his apparent kindness. After all, she was sure he could be doing more profitable things if he'd stayed in that town. Instead, he was going out of his way to help save her.

"Well, we have a deal then?"

"Deal's a deal. Consider me officially your bodyguard."

He let out a small chuckle, taking her tiny hand in his powerful, gauntleted one when she offered it and giving it a demure little shake.

With that settled, and a pleasant buzz about her for how well this was going so far, Syline crawled over to the doe, bringing her satchel with her. She brought forth her spell-book and scanned through it until she found that same spell of corpse sculpting. It was a grim spell to be sure, but she felt this was a better use for it than anything a real necromancer might do with such a power. She set to it, incanting the spell and working the animal's body with the skill of a master, cleaner than any blade could manage. The skin was cleanly removed, guts and bile set in a pile out of their camp and each section of meat and muscle cleanly stripped from the bone and placed down in the snow.

Thelonious watched in silent amazement. It was only when she was finished did he speak, letting out an impressed grunt before saying, "Could make your way easy with that spell."

She felt her cheeks flush red as she finished her labours. She'd kept the spell going a lot longer and used it a lot more precisely than she had with the rabbit. She didn't feel particularly tired though and that sent a flush of pride through her breast. She was growing stronger as a mage. It was always adventurers who became famous archwizards, not archivists who spent their time organising shelves.

"I could but, to be honest, I don't think I'd really want to. It's definitely a useful trick out here – especially since I have no clue how to do that without magic – but it's not something I'd like to use every day. Like you said, it's bloody work. Do you... you probably have more experience cooking than I do Thelonious, so would you mind taking it from here?"

"Sure," he said, giving her a soft smile as he rose from where he'd been sitting, guiding her back so that he could work on the meat. Thelonious set to cooking the meal, the smell of it enough to rouse Corax and have the raven sitting excitedly on Syline's lap, watching the meat roasting over the fire.

"So," Thelonious said as the meal cooked, "who're you running from? Promise I won't turn you in or nothing; my word's good. You're a noble girl, right? Petranski's the name of the king's border guard. Are you his daughter?"

Syline was quite certain Thelonious had asked more questions in that one statement than he had since he'd met her. She took a few moments to work through what he had said, working through her response, as much of a one as she was willing to give him, at least.

She sighed.

"Yes... yes, I'm a noblewoman. This really isn't the sort of place I belong. I'd barely left the city in my life until two nights ago when everything went wrong. I found something that people didn't want me to find."

She pulled out from her satchel the great spell-book, the source of all this trouble.

"This spell-book is full of all sorts of dangerous and illegal magic, the sort the king would have someone's head for and I found it in the Petrov's section of the grand library. Lady Jane caught me and tried to attack me when I cast some kind of lightning teleportation spell. I know she's sent hunters after me. People who aren't trying to catch me but trying to kill me." She took a breath.

Thelonious was silent but moved around the fire to offer his flask to her. She held it in her hands but just kept talking. It was nice for someone other than her diary and her raven to be privy to all this stress. To share it with someone.

"That's why I want to stay off the main roads. I need to find somewhere safe and secure, a way to send a message to the king, or anyone in charge, to stop Lady Jane. I can't go to the guards because I know she has plenty of them in her pocket. I've already killed one who attacked me when I woke up outside the city…"

He let out a stunned chuckle. "I'd heard the Petranski women were tough, but…" He trailed off, seeing her downcast expression. He reached to pat her on the shoulder, paused, and pulled his hand back. "I'm sure you did what you had to. But you don't have to worry 'bout that no more. I'm here now. You can take a load off." He sighed as she stared into the fire. "Looks like you could use some of that, too." He nodded for her to drink from the flask.

"What is it? It's not alcohol, is it? My mother only lets me drink wine," Syline said, leaning down to sniff at the flask curiously.

The hellblooded chuckled. "Mother ain't here, is she?"

"But…" Syline trailed off. She had no real excuse.

She gave the hellblooded a grin and undid the top of the flask. It smelled acrid and very strongly of apples. She had an experimental sip and very nearly coughed her lungs out. Thelonious slapped his knee with a hearty chortle.

"What is that?!" Syline squealed, thrusting the flask away as if it had attacked her.

"Applejack, pour a little on the meat. A bit hard to drink if you ain't used to it, but it tastes great used right."

Syline did as he suggested. She'd no intent on drinking anymore of that stuff. It smelled like apples, but she swore it tasted like nothing but death. Still, she'd had plenty of meals that were cooked in wine, so she knew at least that it might well improve the meal. She drizzled the applejack over the meat, about a quarter of the flask, before handing it back to her new friend.

"What about you?" she asked him, settling in and running her hand down Corax's spine. The raven, however, only had time for staring at the meat, expectantly.

"Mmm?" Thelonious looked over.

"Well, tell me about yourself. All I know is you're a kind, strong hellblooded who decided to save me when I needed someone most."

That put a grin on his dopey features and he scratched the back of his head.

"Well, er, ain't much to say. Grew up on a farm, good at what I do" – he took a slug from the applejack – "wasn't good at farming, not like my brothers. My thumbs are red, not green."

He frowned a bit and looked down at his hands, then looked up to see Syline staring expectantly. As if just realising then he was meant to keep talking, he straightened and cleared his throat.

"I'm good at hurting people. But I don't like people bein' hurt." He chuckled lightly and rubbed one of his horns. "I fight, so good people don't have to. I feel like…" He had a sip from his applejack. "Things ain't confusing when I'm fightin'. Sorry, I'm rambling."

Syline nodded softly, his talk of making it so others didn't have to fight, even if he didn't think he said it well, had really resonated with her.

"I think that's really admirable, Thelonious. That's a very heroic way to take things. I think a lot of people, put in your lot in life, would have gone a far darker route."

As she spoke, somewhere on the island, a bird took flight, as a branch loudly snapped deeper inland. Thelonious looked up. He gave her a smile, but seemed very distracted, eyes darting to the side. He shuffled her way, pulling out his knife to cut off a piece of meat, chewing it open mouthed, or at least pretending to.

"We're being watched," he whispered. "Get ready for a fight."

A thrill of fear ran through Syline. She did her very best to stay calm, or at least act it. Beside her, Thelonious let out a yawn, removing the harness that held his bastard sword and making a show of placing it on the ground next to him.

"Get ready," Thelonious hissed to her. She heard footfalls behind them, and suddenly Thelonious reached out and pushed her over just in time for an arrow to hit the still roasting deer, whistling right through where she'd been sitting.

A roar of a battle cry came from the woods as a man sprinted from the dark, a two-handed axe held down by his side as he rushed Thelonious. He wore the half-plate armour of a mercenary knight but didn't look as if he cared for it well. Rust and filth clogged its recesses and his stench reached them before the man did. Thelonious met the man's charge, bringing up his sheathed bastard sword in a two-handed swing, holding it by the blade. The charging warrior had no time to dodge the blow and only managed to get his arm in the way. He let out an agonised cry as the pointed guard slammed into his wrist. Behind him came three more: a man putting a bow over his shoulder to draw forth two serrated daggers, a woman dressed in thick, traveller's leathers and wielding a ruby-tipped staff, and lastly, a man in plate armour defending her, an arming sword held in his right hand and a shield in the other.

Thelonious flipped his grip on the sword and drew it, facing his opponent along with the man with the daggers who ran to support him. The charging warrior winced as he took his axe in both hands. Thelonious could already tell he'd succeeded in breaking the man's arm, but it wasn't enough to put him out of the fight just yet. He put his back to the flames to stop himself getting flanked. It was do or die. Looking around, he couldn't catch sight of her. He could only hope Syline could handle herself.

⸺

As THELONIOUS HAD RISEN TO face the two warriors, Syline scrambled out of the way of a blast of lightning launched by the staff-wielding woman. Syline brought her wand up as she turned to face them.

The woman had a cocky grin on her face.

"Oh, you think you can face a court mage, little girl?" the mage cooed to her.

Syline felt fury brim up in her breast. It hurt her to know even court mages were in the pocket of the Petrovs. The very organisation she'd dreamed of joining, now turned against her.

"So, what if I do?" she said, stalling. She didn't have time to read through a proper combative spell from the book. She had to rely on what she had memorised. Think. Think.

"Well, come on then, little witch, I'll counter any spell you throw at me," the woman said, holding an arm out.

The mage had much more experience than her; just a lightning bolt, like the one she'd just avoided, was a spell well out of her limits. At least, what she could cast without leaving herself severely drained. It hadn't even seemed to faze the mage though. Meaning she likely had more dangerous spells in her repertoire. Treat this like any other duel. Watch her. Read her. She's cocky. Overconfident. She's giving you a free shot, go for the one she won't expect.

Syline grinned back, putting on her best impression of Kat when she went to a duel: confident and strong-willed. Nothing could get in her way. Syline had to put on that air, to not let this woman know how terrified she was. She raised her wand up to her breast in a swordsman's salute, as if it were the blade sheathed at her hip. The woman didn't understand the gesture, but Syline heard a little chuckle from her guardian. He knew its meaning.

"I don't have all day, dear. Hurry–"

Syline had already started her incantation as the woman taunted her. She shut up immediately and seemed focused on working out what kind of offensive spell Syline was casting. But, Syline wasn't casting offensive magic. She couldn't play into what the woman expected. Syline cast the spell of vanishing she'd prepared that morning. It would only give her around twenty seconds. She needed to make them count.

The woman cursed the moment Syline disappeared.

"She's going to run! Catch her!" she told her guardian.

Perfect, Syline thought. She needed him away.

THE AXE WIELDER WAS AN idiot, and one easily dealt with. Thelonious had been able to disarm him after his first swing, catching his axe beneath the head and twisting it in the direction of the man's ruined arm, grinding broken bone on bone, making the man scream. It was easy after that, to yank the axe from his grasp and hurl it one way, as the man staggered the other way past him. But now, the knife-wielder was on him. Thelonious leapt back to avoid him as he came in swinging. He focused still on the axe-wielder, turning to deliver a slash across his gut that doubled him over. The lethality was lessened greatly by his armour, but not the force. Thelonious saw a flicker of movement out of the corner of his eye and stepped to the side. A throwing dagger whizzed by his head. He needed to finish this. He punched the knife-wielder to stagger him, then whirled on his still-reeling comrade and brought his blade down on the man's neck. Body and head hit the ground separately.

He turned just in time to receive the counterattack, daggers coming in from high and low. He couldn't block both on his sword, but, if he failed to block either he'd be done for. He parried the one going low out to the side. He tried to parry the blow on high with his vambrace, but misjudged, the blade cutting a red welt on the back of his hand. Panicking, Thelonious leaned into it, grabbing the blade by the crossguard and yanking at it. His opponent, desperate to not lose his weapon, slashed at Thelonious' open wrist. He tried to turn with it and was left with a thin line, just piercing the flesh beneath his leathers. He grunted in pain, but he didn't let go. This fellow was smaller and quicker than him, but in this instant, he had him trapped. Thelonious held onto the knife as the man scowled at him. He dropped his bastard sword to punch the man in the gut, forcing him to let go of the knife. Thelonious took it in his unwounded hand and skipped back a step. Now, they were even in their arms.

"You're tough, mate," the man said, giving him a wicked grin as Thelonious shook free flowing blood off his hand. "But you ain't pulling that trick twice."

He was faster than Thelonious and much more adept with the knife. When he stepped in, it was all Thelonious could do to parry his quick coming strikes. Knocking them away one after the other with his own short blade. He never got a chance to make a counterattack and had taken a few cuts on his knuckles and wrist already. This was going to be difficult.

—

Syline used precious moments to summon forth a spectral hand in the woods a few feet away; it was weak, only able to lift a few pounds of weight. It'd be enough. She only had about ten seconds left. She used the force to crack a twig. The guardian's head jerked that way and he sprinted off, trying to trample over the spot he thought she had run for. It was a good bluff, but one that would only last a few moments, just those few seconds of invisibility she had left. Those would have to be enough.

The spell ran out as she sprinted for the woman. Corax emerged from her scarf to fly for the woman's face, distracting her a moment. The woman cursed and batted at Corax as the raven pecked and flapped about her head. Syline rushed in behind her raven and dropped her wand into her pocket so that she could take her axe in both hands.

As prepared as the mage might have been to take on an apprentice wizard, she'd never expected that. She screamed. Syline did too. But Syline had already killed twice in as many days; she didn't feel ready to do so again just yet. So, with all the viciousness she could muster, she swung the flat of the axe from her shoulder in a long arc into the woman's jaw. The haft shuddered in Syline's hands with the impact of metal on skull, and her awkward swing left the edges of the blade cutting into the woman's cheek, splitting it as Syline struggled to keep her grip on the handle. The mage hit the ground in a heap.

Behind her, from the edge of the treeline, Syline heard the mage's guardian roar in fury, his footfalls rapidly approaching.

—

GODS DAMMIT, THELONIOUS THOUGHT. HE couldn't lose. Syline was holding her own, right now. But for how long? It was his job to protect her; he had to do something. He had to find an opening. Do what he wouldn't expect. *Think,* Thelonious thought. *Use your head!*

Use your head.

Thelonious leapt back a step and lowered his head, rushing as if to charge the man. He replied exactly how Thelonious expected: by leaping to the side and bringing the knife down. Thelonious turned his head very carefully and felt the knife cut deep into his horn. Cut into it and stick. The impact jarred his head terribly and hurt like hell, but it caused no real damage. He yanked back and ripped the knife from the man's grip. It stayed quivering in his horn; he could feel every slight tremor in the base of the horn, right where it grew from his skull. Gods, it hurt. But, that stupid little quickfoot was disarmed now. Thelonious shoved his own knife through his belt and took a step forward. The man was scrambling back for his bow. Thelonious grabbed his sword from the dirt.

⸗

SYLINE COULD BARELY KEEP AHEAD of the enraged guardian. It was only his armour weighing him down that saved her. She was only just staying out the reach of his sword. Wand in hand, she threw little arcane darts back at him, voicing a constant stream of incantations. Though they struck true, they barely seemed to bother him. He only roared in fury and charged through them. She could wear him down, but she wasn't much of a runner herself. She was quickly losing her breath. Getting unsteady. Slowing. She'd thrown a few volleys already and Syline wasn't used to combat magic. She felt her reserves draining rapidly.

The man with the knives, now disarmed, sprinted past her, roughly shouldering her as he passed. She lost her footing, stumbled to the ground. The guardian was over her in a second, his arming sword raised.

⸗

SYLINE WAS IN DANGER. THAT damned quickfoot knocked her over. He could wait a moment, because if he didn't step in, Syline was done for.

The man swung his blade down at her. Thelonious caught it on his own and slammed his forehead into the man's face. He stumbled back a step, giving Syline the moment she needed to crawl out from between them. Thelonious had only a split second to see her stand up before his focus was wholly consumed by the warrior before him. The two traded blows in rapid succession, both of nearly equal skill. Their blades connected and were thrown away again and again. He'd step in and the man's shield would receive him. The man would go for a blow and Thelonious would parry it on his longer blade. He'd have to abuse his reach if he wanted to end this fight.

The man was good, Thelonious had to give him that. This was more the kind of fight he was used to. It was almost fun. Almost.

⸗

THELONIOUS SAVED HER. SHE HAD a little room, now. Syline opened the grand archmage's spell-book. She'd been biting into her reserves already but was certain she could manage this. She searched further, deep within its higher destructive incantations and closer to the devastating teleportation spell than she ever had before. It wouldn't matter what state she was in afterwards, she needed to end this.

That'll do nicely, Syline thought, finding just the spell. She read the incantation as fast she dared. She saw the archer drawing his bow. She'd have to deal with him first, but this spell should take out both of them. She chanted every syllable as best she could and hoped it would be enough. The last word left her lips and she felt the magic take form. She held out her hand and blue and white searing flames burst forth, surging through the air in a crackling line. The archer had a moment to look surprised before the spear of flame scorched his bow and licked at his features. He let out a frightened squeal as he stepped back out of its path only for the flames to sputter out completely.

Syline didn't understand; her incantation had been perfect! She'd completed the spell! She'd never had one fail like this. She'd never felt a single spell make her legs so weak, make her chest hurt so bad. It was like she'd been practising for hours in just that moment. Now, at this moment, when it mattered most, Syline could barely even mourn her failure, as the ground came to meet her. Her body gave out under the stresses of the spell and darkness overcame her.

———

THE ARCHER'S SCREAMS DREW THE guardian's attention away and saved Thelonious. The guardian's blade was high in the air, while Thelonious' laid on the ground, knocked away from his bloody grip. The archer was holding his cheek, blistered red raw. Syline had collapsed, quivering on the ground. Thelonious didn't know what had happened, but he had to finish this immediately. He couldn't keep her safe from both.

The swordsman looked back at Thelonious; the momentary distraction ended. However, the swordsman found Thelonious bringing his head in viciously. It wasn't their foreheads that connected, though, but Thelonious' horn with his eye. The guardian roared and kicked the hellblooded back, but the roar turned to a scream as he did. His eye was ruined. Thelonious' horn had pierced deep and come out messily. Anger overcame the man's previous discipline, and he hacked madly at Thelonious, arm swinging high and wide each time. Thelonious was almost disappointed; he had been such a good foe until now, such a capable warrior. On one wide swing, Thelonious slapped his arm aside.

With his arm out wide, Thelonious followed through with a brutal uppercut to the man's jaw that had him staggering back and his grip going slack on his sword. A last punch to his temple and the man went limp, falling like a puppet with its strings cut to the floor.

In his time dealing with the man, the quickfoot archer regained his bearings and had closed the distance with Syline, now only a few paces away with an arrow in his hand. Thelonious locked eyes with him and hefted his sword.

"We aren't worth dying for. Just leave," he said, his voice soft, but insistent. For a few moments, the archer stared, eyes darting to Syline as if trying to work out if he could reach her before Thelonious reached him. Thelonious didn't hesitate. In that moment of judgement, he rushed the man and shouldered him back, sending him stumbling. Thelonious grabbed his arrow as he went and snapped it in his hand.

He glared at the man. "Just. Leave."

Wiping blood and dirt from his cheek, the man nodded softly and rose before slowly walking backwards, in time fading into the dark of the woods. Once he was out of sight, Thelonious listened a few moments longer, until he heard the man's feet pounding away in the dark, taking flight. Thelonious felt no need to finish them; they wouldn't be chasing them anytime soon. He sighed and wiped his blade clean before putting it back in its sheath. He used one of the quickfoot's knives to shred the court mage's robes to make himself a bandage for his hand. He tore off a few more strips and, out of respect for the man's honour and skill in battle, bandaged up the warrior's head, staunching the bleeding as best he could. He wouldn't be pretty when he woke up, but with that, his odds were improved. He did the same for the mage's face; she'd be fine apart from an ugly scar, thanks to Syline's kind heart.

After that, he made Syline comfortable on his horse and let Corax roost on his shoulder. They'd have to keep riding. Gods, he needed sleep. He grabbed the mage's pack. Wizards always had nice stuff, often potions. With them, the precious vials weren't going to get smashed like they might on a warrior's belt. He was disappointed when all he found was a wooden box with some kind of herbs in the pack, but he could at least use it to store some meat he sliced off the deer. It was good meat; it'd be enough for both of them to eat well on the road. He picked up the court mage's staff as he walked and retrieved Syline's axe. It was a nice staff, and hopefully, Syline could use it. He didn't really know how magic worked.

Finally, he sighed and yanked the damned knife from his horn and threw it into the woods. Syline stirred a moment as he roared from the pain. With the constant throbbing turned to a dull ache, he mounted the horse behind Syline and set the poor, tired mare off again. They'd just go to another island. Somewhere closer to the border. They'll get some sleep there and figure this all out in the morning.

"Thelonious," Syline mumbled. She seemed to barely be holding onto consciousness. He kept her tight against his chest to stop her tumbling off the horse. "We need to go somewhere safe. Someplace where she can't pay people off."

"I know, Syline, I'll figure something out."

Chapter 9

WHEN SYLINE WOKE THE FOLLOWING morning, she found herself lying against the side of Thelonious' horse. Thelonious was fast asleep on the opposite side of the horse, half upright against its back. The horse still dozed as well, soft whinnies leaving it on occasion in its slumber. The animal made for a surprisingly comfortable pillow. Considering the still falling snow, Syline was also rather warm, all things considered, though she quickly realised that was because Thelonious had put his coat over her before he had fallen asleep.

She sat up, stretching with a little yawn. She had probably slept nearly twelve hours over the course of last night, almost all of it spent on horseback. She wasn't sure what that said about her abilities as an adventurer, but likely nothing good. At least it was better than not being able to sleep anywhere but a plush, feather-filled bed. She had no real desire to wake Thelonious up. The hellblooded had been working very hard for her, as had his horse. So, while Corax flew off from within her scarf, likely to find himself something to drink, Syline moved away from the man and his steed so as not to disturb them and got out her journal. She hadn't thought to write in it these last few days. Maybe writing it all down would help.

WHEN THELONIOUS WOKE UP, IT was to the sound of Syline crying softly. He opened one eye and saw the young wizard's shoulders shuddering as she wrote into some little book, her raven crooning sadly as he butted his head to her cheek. He pretended to be asleep for a little while longer. Let her sort through that on her own. He didn't know what to say, never really knew how to comfort people. He only rose when his horse decided it was about time she got up as well and, with no care for the man using her as a pillow, got to her hooves. Thelonious' head slumped to the dirt and he finally conceded and sat up with a soft laugh, rubbing his sore horn. Syline shut her journal immediately. He didn't inquire. Instead, he got up and stretched himself out.

"You were real good last night, Syline."

"You think?"

Thelonious nodded. "You didn't panic, you didn't try to run. Hell, you even knocked that lady out instead of killing her. The only mistake was going for that big, flashy spell."

She couldn't help but blush at him complimenting and at the same time berating her so. Thelonious' horse butted him from the back, and the hellblooded chuckled, hugging the horse's head.

"Here, I figure staffs are more powerful than wands, right?" He pulled the beautiful white wood staff, tipped with a ruby held in a lattice of worked silver, off the horse's saddle. It was the first time Syline had gotten a real proper look at it.

"Is it really okay to have it?" she asked, her voice quiet. "Isn't that stealing?"

"Well… yeah. They attack us. We win. We get their stuff. Fair's fair. Hell, 'cept for that one nutter, we left them all alive too, so they should count themselves grateful. That's what this life is like. They knew."

Syline nodded softly, trying to process his words as she took the staff and looked it over. It was inscribed with runes she recognised as ones that would empower any elemental spell cast through it, increasing their potency. A true battlemage's staff. It must've been worth a fortune. She was terribly lucky she'd dodged that opening lightning bolt.

"That is how it goes in all the books. It's definitely more powerful than my apprentice wand. Probably a bit harder to handle, though."

"Aaah, I'm sure you can manage it," Thelonious said, clapping her on the shoulder. He turned, tightening the straps of the saddle, missing the way Syline flinched at his touch, but she managed a little smile a few moments later.

"You know," he mused, "why the axe? Aren't your family all known for bein' beautiful duellists?"

"I don't fit that role very well. I trained with the sword, but I was never very good with it and, I don't know, the one time I had to defend myself with the sword was the first time I killed someone. I know it's hypocritical, but... he looked so scared as he died. Holding the sword just makes me think of those eyes."

"Well, I don't know." Thelonious mounted the horse, turning to grin at her as he offered a hand to pull her up. "You fit the beautiful part," he teased, giving her a grin.

Despite herself, Syline blushed bright red, even her ears turned crimson as a giggle escaped her. She stepped back from his hand. She was growing fond of Thelonious, but there was still some part of her that did not want to be touched, not yet.

"I can actually conjure a magical horse. I've just been... a bit too tired to the other times. No reason to overburden your poor mare. We've been working her hard. What's her name anyway?"

"Alma. It means 'soul' in Elvish, I think."

"Alma." Syline rubbed the horse's muzzle. It butted its head affectionately into her chest and let her scratch at her ears. "It's a pretty name."

She stepped back, conjuring up her own arcane mare. Alma nickered at it; the horse unsure about this new arrival. She hopped onto its back, picking up the illusory reins.

"So, where are we going anyway? You seem to have somewhere in mind," she asked as Thelonious set off at a gentle trot. Corax came flapping back to them and sat down on the illusory mare's head. The magical horse didn't seem to mind.

"Guess I can't blame you for not remembering. I thought we'd head to Dawnsteel. See, it basically belongs to the church. If we can get to the church and tell them what's going on, we should be in good hands. At least you should be."

"Thelonious, that's a great idea!" Syline had barely any memories from what went on after she'd cast the spell last night. Even when she had flickered into consciousness it had been only momentary, hazy.

"Why didn't I think of that?" she cursed herself, chuckling softly. She had to admit, she was so glad to have him along, and not just because he was a comfort to have around and a damn good sword hand. Thelonious definitely seemed a bit more worldly than her.

"Aw, thanks. You good to get started?"

"I could use a bath, but that won't be happening out here."

Thelonious chuckled and, as they hit the edge of the island, set Alma off at a slightly quicker pace. One she'd easily maintain for the whole journey.

"I think you can wait 'til we hit town, Syline. Oh, here." He pulled out the box of deer meat and tossed it over to her. She scrambled to catch it, practically falling out of her saddle as she did. That got more of a laugh out of Thelonious.

"What's this?"

"Breakfast."

―

PERHAPS IT WAS LUCK, PERHAPS there were no other hunters after them for the moment. Either way, the journey proved uneventful. The two didn't actually speak much, both largely lost in their own thoughts. When they got to town, she wanted to do a bit of shopping, get the chance to clean herself up before she went to meet with the clergy. She'd have to be presentable as a noble heir of the Petranski family. She had to be convincing. They had to believe she was truly working for the cause of good here.

Coming into sight of Dawnsteel's rooftops was exciting. It wasn't the same kind of walled fortress the capital was. The city had once been nothing but a single cathedral and had grown larger from there, spawning and spilling out from around it. Whereas Russenholde was cramped with tight streets hidden behind high walls, Dawnsteel was all open terraces, wide lanes and beautiful parks. Whereas Russenholde did their best to warm their homes and guard from the night, Dawnsteel embraced the sun with countless windows, many of them beautifully stained frescos and tableaus. It filled Syline with a sense of hope, but so too did it bring dread. She couldn't help but think of all the ways this could go wrong. She just had to pray for the best. She wondered if the Wanderer could hear her this deep in the Glorious Dawn's domain.

They hit the edge of town and found a stable to leave Alma. Syline's arcane horse disappeared with a word of dismissal, but the same could not be done for the life and blood mare, so she was set up with a trough of water and a bale of hay. She seemed happy to be left with that. Corax stayed with his animal companion, taking roost in the hay even as she ate it. That left Thelonious and Syline free to wander up the main street of town. It was bustling, the sun shining down on its city as its people went about their business. The place was famous for its stained glass, and it seemed like anyone who was anyone had at least one beautiful window, displaying the sun or some other such religious symbology at the front of their shop. Russenholde people were welcome to worship whatever they wanted, but the Wanderer was always the focus of the cathedrals. Here, the town felt like one giant church to Soel, his icons on every corner and his words spoken on every street.

Syline felt terribly nervous walking through the street, hanging off Thelonious' arm and making a point to keep her wide brimmed hat affixed low on her head. Hopefully, it would hide her face from anyone who might be looking.

"Relax, Syline. The hunters wouldn't look for us here. Not yet. You're safe, today." Damn Thelonious for being so straightforward. She couldn't help but stress about every little thing that could possibly go wrong today.

"Come on." Thelonious pulled her along as he caught eye of a side street.

"What, what is it?" Syline asked as she was dragged along.

"Bathhouse called the Morning Dew. I think we could both use it," Thelonious said as Syline adjusted herself beside him, still holding onto her escort's elbow with both hands.

The pair made their way down the road towards it with ease. The religious people of the town parted before Thelonious, though they didn't give him trouble. They didn't seem all too happy that he was here either, many glaring, or muttering curses, when Syline was not looking; she did her best to glare back at those she heard.

The Morning Dew was a large stone building with gleaming stained glass windows of beer steins being raised in a toast to the setting sun, or maybe it was supposed to be rising, considering the name. It seemed to be both a spa and a tavern. Syline was eager to head inside, leaving Thelonious trailing after her like a good guard dog. The place was warm, humidity wafting in with the steam from the bath house attached. The bartender was a handsome young man with pale-brown hair and a happy smile on his face. He wore a pale, bone-colored doublet.

"How can I help you today, miss? I mean in all good faith that you don't look like someone here for an early afternoon beer." The man was soft spoken and smiled incessantly as he spoke. He was the kind of boy Magdova would fawn over. Syline thought it seemed a little fake, like he was hiding something under that smile. Maybe it was just her.

"I was hoping to take a bath. My bodyguard as well. S-separately, of course," Syline added hastily.

The young man let out a soft chuckle before he replied, "Of course. We separate the men and women's baths, except for a few special holidays. We aren't *that* sort of bathhouse. The men's bath is empty except for some out of town mercenaries right now, so it should be fine for your bodyguard to use it, if he's quick." He caught a barmaid's attention, and the woman led Syline through a side door.

Thelonious was directed in the opposite direction for the men's baths. Before they parted ways though, he called to her, "If I'm out first, I'll go get us some clothes and other supplies: rations, potions, the like."

Syline nodded, giving him a smile and a thumbs up. She trusted him to make good choices. As she walked to the bath, she wondered why Thelonious would not normally have been able to use the bath. She did not like the conclusions she came to.

Inside, she found a large rock pool, heated by permanent magical runes of flame beneath the water, tucked away behind bright-red, glass screens. A few women were bathing in the pool as it was, conversing happily with each other, concerning themselves with washing their body, or in one case, having a servant do it for them.

"The glass patches are very hot. They're marked red, so they should be easy to see, but please still be careful to avoid them." The barmaid bid her goodbye before departing back to the main room.

Left to her own devices, Syline was giddy to get in the bath. She stepped over to a bench and line of hooks where people left their possessions and disrobed. Public bathhouses like this were popular in Russenholde as well, and she'd been to a few with her sisters in the past, so at least she didn't feel all too awkward disrobing in front of others who weren't her personal servants like Alexis. Still, a thrill of excitement and nervousness went through her as she did. It was different when you didn't have your sisters with you. Skipping over the tiles to the bath, Syline sank in with a pleased groan. She thought of the bath she'd taken right before heading for the grand library. How she'd felt that was relieving so much stress. Gods, the thought of how little stress she'd really been dealing with then. How trivial a nightmare felt before everything she had to worry about now.

That said, this bath had similar effects for Syline. She paid no heed to the women around her, simply shutting her eyes as she reclined against the walls. The bath water softly steamed over her form and worked away the dirt, grime and stress. In no time, she slipped into a gentle doze. It was only a barmaid gently tapping her shoulder that roused her from her nap. She looked up to see the woman averting her gaze politely from Syline's form.

"Excuse me, miss, but your bodyguard is wondering when you'll be out. He says you've been here an hour already. He also brought you this." She was holding a paper parcel. Syline practically leapt from her skin at that realisation. How had she let so much time pass so quickly?

"Tell him I'll be right out, alright? Where are the…?" She trailed off, spotting the stack of fresh towels on the bench.

The barmaid nodded and departed after handing the parcel to Syline. Standing up, Syline noticed many of the women who'd been in the pool when she'd arrived were long gone, and since replaced by new bathers. She really had been in there a while. This truth was only reinforced when she took note of how pruny and wrinkled the tips of her fingers had become. She hated when that happened; it wasn't often, usually since her sisters were eager to rush her out of the bathroom to get their turn. At least it had been nice to take as long a bath as she pleased for once.

She dried herself quickly, more to give herself time to focus upon her hair than to hurry out. With so much of it, she knew she'd be unable to get it *completely* dry before she had to meet the clergy. But perhaps, with the aid of a few sigils in the spell-book, she might be able to manage something. She dried her hair off the best she could, enough so it wasn't dripping anymore, and moved to her possessions, draping her towel across her lap to open the spell-book. A few of the bathers watched her idly as she skipped through page after page of sigils, many she'd never heard of, before finally settling on just the one: a minor spell of fluid control. Murmuring the incantation, she let the magic pass through the spell-book and back into her hands, giving them a strange, oily sheen that shone with every colour of the rainbow as it caught the light. She ran her hands slowly through her hair and felt the water bubble out of it and drip cleanly onto the floor as her hands passed through. By the end, her hair was perfectly dry and silky as if she'd let it dry for hours like she normally would.

A few of the women in the pool cheered and begged to know the spell, getting a giddy grin and a wave from Syline. She could imagine other women would want to know a spell like that, in fact.

"This is the best spell ever," Syline, a girl who had suffered for her love of overtly long hair, muttered to herself.

It removed most of the inconvenience of her long hair. She had to make a few idle promises and comments to women around her about meeting sometime to teach them. Promises she had no intention to keep, but she doubted they expected her to. In truth, she barely heard them as she began to get dressed. A woman with auburn hair complimented her on her looks as she picked up her satchel. She'd be giddy from this bath for a week. Syline rarely liked being the centre of attention, but all the positive reinforcement she'd gotten from the women there, all complimenting her hair, magic or looks, left Syline feeling all fuzzy and warm. Opening the parcel, she found inside a white dress with long sleeves and ruffled hems. At the skirts it faded from white to yellow, then to orange and finally to pink. It was really quite beautiful and Syline had to admit, she was quite impressed with Thelonious' taste.

She met Thelonious in the bar. His hair was freshly styled back and much, if not all of the grime and dirt caked into his hands, had been cleaned off. He had bought a white dress shirt and red waistcoat matching his ruddy-red skin. With his frame, they made him look all the more masculine, especially with the sleeves rolled to his biceps.

"My, my, don't you look handsome," Syline said to him with a smile. He bashfully grinned and rubbed the back of his head. His dopey, farm boy looks made him seem a mite out of place in the outfit.

"I think I cleaned up alright. You're not bad, yourself," he said, giving her a grin. "That dress really suits you, Syline."

"Thank you! Gods, that bath was just what I needed. Are you ready to head for the clergy?"

He stood up, putting on his sword harness over his outfit. He wasn't about to go out without it. "That I am. Little nervous. Me and knee scuffers never really got along."

"Oh, it'll be fine. Once I tell them who I am and what's going on, we can get all of this sorted and you'll get a hefty bonus for escorting me back to Russenholde."

He grinned, following her out the door.

Chapter 10

JANE WAS SAT DOWN FOR dinner with her husband, listening to talk of the day-to-day minutiae of running his merchant empire. Their dining hall was magnificent, far bigger than was needed for only the pair of them, but she had declined guests. The tedium of the conversation was truly beginning to grate on her. Who cared about grain shipments, or the coming winter, or which transport group was running behind. Gods, she had chosen this man specifically for his mercantile holdings. She remembered a time when controlling a man like that, a business empire like that, were as far as her ambitions went. It still was for so many of her sisters.

They still didn't see the value in what she was doing, the power she was claiming. Not that they knew the whole of it. Only Lauralee did and she wouldn't be going anywhere until it was too late for any of them to stop her. Gods, the steak tasted like ash in her mouth. Her craving for a taste of the goddess was getting worse, but how could anything compare to something that glorious? She had to get back to the laboratory. She'd nearly mastered control of the creatures the scholar had gifted her as well. With just a few more tastes, she'd have the power for it to become second nature. Gods, she wanted another taste.

What was he talking about now? Oh.

"Have you heard, dear? Apparently, some kind of illness is going through the maids. Many of them are so pale and weak they barely have the strength to get out of bed."

That was her fault. She couldn't risk overfeeding on the goddess, lest her prize pass away, but she'd been hungrier than ever lately. Having another mouth to feed in Lauralee certainly didn't help. Her nails scraped along the grooves of the wood, a soft grinding noise.

"Well, I for one think it's this weather. It's no good for young girls. They need sunshine," he continued.

She almost laughed. Sunshine. Her fingers continued working into the rut of the wood. That was one good thing about this fool of a husband; he could have the discourse of an entire debate hall with himself.

She wondered how the adventurers were getting on. With an exiled court mage among them, surely they'd have no trouble dealing with a child, even if she had some promise as a mage herself. Perhaps she should fast-track the mercenaries. They were a vicious bunch, to be sure, and in numbers there was no chance of her escaping. Finding them somewhere to lodge with the border guard in town had been a trial in itself. The hunting hound would make sure they had no trouble finding her, at least. Gods, but the thing was vicious.

"Dear, you're going to go through the lacquer like that. You've barely touched your steak either."

She felt a slip of wood splinter beneath her fingers; she toyed with it, turning it this way and that.

"Dear."

"What?"

"I said you're going to… Oh, it seems you did. Are you feeling well, my love? You seem–"

The door opened. Lauralee stood waiting. Her husband understood the girl to be a distant niece who had come to study under them both in the ways of magic and business. Not too far from the truth, and with him so deep in her sway, it really didn't matter what he believed. She was glad to see her. She needed an excuse to leave this feast of ashes.

"My lord, my lady," Lauralee said, giving a slight bow. She was a good girl. Obedient. As boring as her mother, though.

"There's…" – Lauralee trailed off – "a matter you need to attend to, my lady."

A wordsmith, she was not, though. It was amazing her mother gave her to her, and not Mary. She was the one to train a daughter into someone who could command a room. Right now, Lauralee stopped being commanding the moment she started talking. At least she was rather striking to look at. White hair with those young features was certainly a look. Jane stood, placing her napkin over her uneaten meal.

"I'm sorry, dear, but duty calls," Jane bemoaned musically, pausing in her wake to plant a kiss on his cheek as she went, using the proximity to twist his strings and ensure he asked no further questions.

"Of" – he hesitated, confused – "of course, dear. See you tonight."

She left him there in the dining hall, and stepped out after Lauralee, the girl leading her unsurprisingly, to the cellars.

"So, what was so important?" Jane demanded as they walked. Not that she particularly begrudged the girl for interrupting, but it didn't pay to let them know that.

"The, ah, adventurers have returned, some of them at least."

Lauralee's shoulders were hunched, as if she anticipated being struck. That did not bode well. Jane's pace increased and she hurried on past the girl down the steps, through to the servants' entrance she had commanded the adventurers to take upon their return, which led into a rarely trod part of her wine cellar. Even if she had control of everyone in this manor, she knew well that an experienced mage could still coax answers from them, so it was prudent to ensure they knew nothing in the first place.

The adventurers were a ruined pair. Only two of them had returned. The exiled mage, the lower half of her face swaddled in bandages, covering everything below the nose. She was missing that fine staff she'd had when Jane met her. Her companion looked little better, his face livid with bruises and one eye covered by more bandages still. She could tell by the depression beneath the bandages, there was no eye beneath it. He held one arm close to his body, like one would when someone was broken, but she couldn't be sure. They stared at her for long moments as she flounced into the room, coming to rest to stare from one to the other.

"Well? Is she dead? Where's my book?" she demanded, sick of the silence.

"She," the mage began. Her voice was muffled; it sounded like it hurt to speak. "Had help, a giant of a hellblooded, true monster of a warrior. Killed one of us before the battle even began."

"And she was smarter than you let on. Used her magic well. If we'd caught her by surprise, we'd have had her, but that hellblooded heard us coming."

Excuses. Syline was still alive. She still had her book. She'd dealt with an entire adventuring party. She'd gathered the aid of some freak warrior from the hells. This was well beyond a nuisance. The adventurers took a step back.

"My lady, you're…" Lauralee began. Jane held up a hand, and only then did she notice the way embers flit about it. Motes of power trailing off her form as her choler rose.

"So," she said in a low voice, "why are you still alive? Why are you here?"

"What?"

"I told you to kill her. You gave up after one attempt? You should be hunting her now. Get fresh companions. Gather more power. Whatever. Instead, you come mewling back to me, cradling your wounds like insipid children."

She saw the woman flush. The man let out a low growl, stepping in front of her.

"The deal's off. We don't want your money. This isn't worth it. One dead, one missing, and wounds we'll never reco–"

He never finished his sentence. Jane's hand retracted from his chest as he collapsed. She'd gone right through his breastplate. How exhilarating! She'd never have managed that before.

"Here," she cooed, her tone sickly sweet, "for your efforts."

She placed the man's heart into the mage's palm, forcibly closing her fingers around it. She screamed and made to run, stumbling over her robes as she made for the door.

Lauralee was beside her as her hand closed on the handle. She tried to turn it; confusion wracked the poor woman. Why wasn't the handle turning? She looked down.

It was because her hand wasn't attached to her arm anymore. It hung from the handle, oddly despondent, right before it flopped to the floor. Her trembling gaze turned to Lauralee.

"For what little it's worth," Lauralee murmured to her, "I am sorry. You shouldn't have come back." Before her blade sliced the woman's throat, deep enough to scrape against her spine.

"Well done, dear," Jane remarked coolly, licking the man's blood from her fingers as Lauralee walked back to her side. "Though you should have made it slower, I'm famished."

Lauralee didn't respond to that. This had unsettled her. They were not monsters, they killed when necessary for their goals. This had been wasteful. Jane was known to have a temper, but not this. Any other mother would have just addled the adventurer's minds with magic, alchemy, or a bite, if they lacked her mother's bloodline talent for domination. Make them forget the whole affair or find some new use for them. Lauralee would not go against orders, she could not. But her mother would know of Jane's growing impulsiveness. This was how you were discovered. It was the blood; she was sure, the god's blood, it was changing her.

"What will we do about Syline?"

Jane took long moments to consider that, standing there in the dusty cellar full of unopened wines worth more than most would make in a month, licking blood from her fingers.

"We'll stick with the mercenaries. But I think a more subtle approach is called for. This girl has proven herself capable. Dangerous. I don't want her slipping the net again, so we'll offer her an ultimatum. Hand over the tome and leave the nation forever, or her mother dies."

Syline's family were no minor nobles, and her mother was one of the most renowned duellists in the region. Again, this was showy.

"And how will we manage that?" Lauralee offered. "Poison? Something slow acting perhaps, to make it look like an illness."

"Oh, a good idea, darling! I knew I kept you around for something." Jane patted her on the head, as one would with a pet, staining Lauralee's white hair crimson.

"Organise it, will you? Administer the poison yourself. Your mother tells me going unseen is a speciality of yours. Make sure we have an antidote ready. I'll see to having the mercenaries sent out."

Lauralee nodded and made to leave. She'd managed to salvage this hasty plan from disaster, at least, she hoped.

"Oh, but Lauralee?"

She paused halfway up the stairs.

"Her mentor, what was his name?"

"The archivist, Anatoly, I think?"

"That was it! Poison him as well, something a little more vicious. Doesn't matter if he cannot be saved, no one here will miss him."

Lauralee nodded and departed. She had a lot to do if this was going to be manageable. She wondered just how saveable she could leave the mentor without Jane noticing.

"If only I'd known all the trouble you'd cause, Syline," she mumbled to herself. "If only I'd warned you away then, you could be home safe with your mother now, without a worry in the world."

Gods, she missed her mother so. She hated it here. She longed for the comfort and quiet of Nachthelm. The routine. The logic of her mother's requests, unruffled by emotion or temper. The only things she was learning from Jane was what not to do. She daren't even speak it aloud. No daughter was ever meant to have ill-feelings to any mother that took her in but...

She was starting to hope something stopped Jane. Before she endangered all of them. Or became a danger to herself.

"I'll give you a chance, Syline... I only hope your foolish streak hasn't run its course yet."

—

THE CATHEDRAL WAS AS IMPRESSIVE as Syline had imagined. Stone blocks forming great towers, huge great doors and amazing frescoes came together to make an impressive exterior. Stained glass windows projected imagery of their god onto the grounds below as the sun caught them, glass turned into art. Braziers burned endlessly by the doors. Those doors were open and, on their approach, they could see the interior was magically lit to be as bright as day.

Just the sight of it had Syline feeling more at ease. It felt like something from one of her adventure novels, the sacred cathedral that offered the heroes protection and sanctuary from the goodness of their hearts.

Thelonious, meanwhile, noticed the whispers and looks he drew far more. This was not a place he belonged. These were not people who wanted him. The closer they got to the church, the more obvious that became. He saw the guards adjust their grip on their polearms, not exactly readying them, but making ready to do so. Just in case.

"Syline."

"Hmm?" Syline turned to look at him, her eyes bright, full of hope.

"I'm going to take a walk around town. See about my own lodgings for tonight."

Syline frowned at that, confused. Her lips pursed and her nose wrinkled as frustration blossomed in its place. She was a sweet girl, he thought, quick, too. Quick enough to realise why he didn't want to go inside.

"Thelonious, you're not a devil. You've been nothing but kind since we met. It's not like you're going to catch on fire for setting foot in a church."

"No." He caught one of the guards glaring at him and ran a hand along one of his horns. He was rarely self-conscious of his appearance, his red skin, his devilish horns. But these people made him all too aware of how he didn't fit in. "I might be set on fire, though."

Syline bit her lip, looking greatly annoyed on his behalf. "Well, alright," she huffed out. "But I'm going to talk to them. Tell them how good a person you are. It's not fair you get treated like this." Syline said that, but guilt prickled in her breast. She'd done just the same thing, judged him by the rumours of his race without ever meeting him. It was what wound her up in that woodshed. Never again.

A smile spread across Thelonious' features, and he wrapped an arm around Syline's shoulders to give her a grateful squeeze. She stiffened, her breath catching. His arm bounced back.

"Sorry, sorry, should'na." Thelonious sighed. "You're a sweet girl, Syline, thanks. Find me here later."

Syline watched him go, wanting to say sorry in return, but finding her throat tight, the words strangled mute. The man in the lumbermill's face filled her mind, grinning. She hurried into the church, suddenly cold.

The interior was truly something wondrous, as brilliant as the glimpse, she'd received from the outside, had seemed. That glimpse did no justice to standing within. The ground beneath her feet was marble. Different colours of the stone all fitted together to show the sun and dozens of star constellations spilling out from it. The pews were carved from this same stone. From stained glass windows showing the saints and angels of Soel, sunlight spilled into the church, enhanced tenfold by the enchantments laid upon the place, so that she felt as if it were the middle of summer, rather than on the cusp of deep winter. Suddenly she was glad to be a bit more lightly dressed than she would usually be. At the head of the church the altar rose, lit from behind by a titanic disc of gold, onto which sunlight was reflected from above so that it dazzled with all the radiance of the sun, casting the preacher in brilliant hues.

"May I help you, my child?" asked a priest at her back, making Syline jump.

He was dressed in white robes, a stole of brilliant orange and red hung around his shoulders. A symbol of the sun, carved from pure white marble hung at his neck. He made the symbol of Soel at his breast, hands forming a circle, before spreading his fingers down to show the rays. Syline returned it with the symbol of the Wanderer, a statement in itself, her linked fingers forming a curving bridge. He nodded his understanding.

"Ah, you are not one of our flock. What brings a daughter of our brother church to the cathedral then, miss?" he said with a genial smile.

"I'm." She cleared her throat. She'd practised this in her head but was already forgetting the "script" she'd made up.

"My name is Syline Petranski, daughter of the king's foremost and general and close friend, Peter Petranski, and–" She stumbled. She'd had a whole line of formally requesting the aid of their sister city, but all that made it out, as her voice broke, was, "I need your help. I'm in danger."

The man had been mid-way through bowing in respect to her family name, but paused as she made that admission.

"What, what kind of danger, my dear?"

"Someone." She hesitated. "A powerful mage, with evil magic, is hunting me." Gods it sounded like she was living out a chapbook, there was no way they'd believe her.

The priest's lips stiffened.

"I believe this is a matter for the Dawnguard, if it was anyone else, I may have difficulty believing it, but with your family's history and so far from home. Please, this way."

He indicated a side door, tucked in a small alcove of the cathedral's main hall, and led her through. Even in this more secluded hall, the architecture remained beautiful, glorious even. Walls were carved with frescoes that were married by stained glass windows opposite them, so when the sun was in the right position, the frescoes would be lit up in full colour. Despite the urgency of the situation, Syline found her steps stumbling, as she tried to resist pausing to admire them. The priest saw her doing so and slowed his step to let her enjoy the artistry.

"Wonderful, are they not? Do you not have something similar in the Wanderer's cathedral in Russenholde?"

The Wanderers' worship was not as active as Soel was here in Dawnsteel. Syline only went once every three months, and on special days.

"Mostly statues, I think we only have one stained glass window. A big one overlooking the altar." If she remembered correctly, it was made by Dawnsteel artisans. Maybe he was just showing off.

They passed several doors and, along the way, a number of armed men in a mix of shining armour and white robes moved by them, but near the end of the hall, he stopped at a fairly nondescript wooden door, but for a symbol of a sun and sword emblazoned upon it. He indicated a stone bench across from it.

"Wait there for the moment, please. I'll find a paladin with time to speak with you."

He disappeared inside and, folding her dress, Syline got comfortable on the bench, hoping against hope this would work, and once more rehearsing lines in her head.

—

THELONIOUS HAD DONE A LITTLE shopping. It was hard to find shadier areas in a place where the light touched all things, but no one on the up and up in this place was going to give him a fair price without Syline at his side. Those mercenaries in the baths had been able to point him in the right direction for a few things on his list at least. Nice bunch as far as sell-swords went, respected a fellow professional, and that's all you can really ask for.

That was why he was enjoying a fine imported cigar as he walked through the streets. Lodgings were next on his list, but he figured he'd check in and make sure Syline wasn't waiting for him outside the cathedral. Nice girl, but he figured if this was a sure thing with the Dawnguard, this might be where their contract ends. If that was the case, he wasn't lodging here for all the money in the world. He'd camp in the woods or try and join up with those mercs before they left town.

Thelonious' head whipped to the side as something exploded on his temple, he couldn't see, nothing but red. He was bleeding. He dragged a hand across his eyes as he moved back, blade half drawn from its holster on his back.

It wasn't blood. The remnants of a tomato came away in his hand, juices splattered his new clothes.

A child across the street, standing at the edge of a courtyard, pulled back their hand with another before their mother caught them, and dragged them away. She didn't apologise, but she at least had the decency to give him an apologetic look. He heard her hiss.

"That's a hellblooded, dear, not a devil. And he hasn't done anything, yet."

Yet. Always yet.

The child blew a raspberry at him as they went. Thelonious blew one back.

The crowd was dispersing from the courtyard now, only remnants like the child and their mother had been there by the time he arrived. That let him see to the centre, where another hellblooded, stripped to a loincloth, was bound in stocks. He was covered in the remains of tomatoes. A few rocks lay around the stocks as well. He noticed the sign: "A real devil, bound for the pyre".

Well. Surely even these people wouldn't mistake a hellblooded for a devil. Russenholde was a lot more liberal with his kind than most and they wouldn't put up with their allies burning them at the stake.

As the crowd dispersed, Thelonious approached. Gods blood! The knee scuffers had done a number on him, livid burn and whip wounds showed across his flesh and his eyes were practically stuck closed from bruising. How did you even burn a devil. He didn't seem to notice Thelonious as he approached, too absorbed in cursing out this city, the Dawnguard, some woman named Amberly, the gods, and the hells alike.

Thelonious rested an elbow on the stocks, and leaned down, offering the man a cigar.

"Oh, yes please," Laes said, pinching it between his teeth. Thelonious went for a match, before noticing the cigar was lit already.

"So, you the real deal then?" Thelonious asked, looking out at the dispersing crowd, many of whom were whispering and pointing as they noticed the hellblooded coming to talk to the devil.

"Half." Laes blew out smoke from the corner of his mouth. "You're a brave or stupid man yourself for coming up here. You know, I know they say there's a difference between us, but I wonder how much these people really care."

"Ah, they're more scared than anything, their preachers always telling them anything not in their 'all so holy light' is out to get them from the moment they're born. No wonder they're full o' hate," Thelonious mused. "Are they really going to burn you?" he asked, as he locked eyes with an old woman glaring at the pair of them. She ran when he brought up his hand in a fist, pointer and pinkie raised to make horns, a common sign for hellblooded that many of his kind took as their own.

"Oh, most definitely. Thankfully, that's not the end for me, but it's certainly going to be a lot of steps back. The real shame's Amberly, she doesn't deserve this. Doesn't deserve these people." He sighed, blowing out another stream of smoke. "You're very insightful for a…" The devil craned his neck to look at Thelonious. "Well, no offence friend, you sound like a true hayseed. A farm boy."

Thelonious laughed. "That I am, that I am. Never meant for the big city. Who's this Amberly?"

"A better person than I deserved either. Well, farm boy, thank you kindly for the smoke, but I think you should best get moving," Laes mused, nodding his head to a trio of guards, their glares a tad more serious than that of the crowd.

Thelonious nodded and clapped the devil on the shoulder, but paused as he went.

"Want me to kill you now?"

Laes nearly dropped the cigar as he laughed. "No, no, thank you, I appreciate the mercy, but if she's going to burn, she at least shouldn't burn alone."

Thelonious frowned. Giving Laes' shoulder one more pat, he walked away, musing, "You're alright, devil."

—

THE PRIEST RETURNED, LEADING HER through what looked rather like her father's barracks, but with a lot more stone and religious iconography. Warriors, calling them soldiers seemed inappropriate somehow, stepped aside to let her pass, giving curious glances as she went.

She was led into a small office, the priest bidding her farewell and closing the door behind her. Like everywhere in this place, the room was lit by sunlight pouring in from a stained-glass window. It was set behind the desk where the room's occupant sat. He was a tall man, her father's age, perhaps a bit older, with long, greying brown hair and a thick beard of the same. He looked exhausted; run down in a way she had not seen in anyone else in this place. They'd all seemed like they were invigorated somehow, call it religious fervour, but it was like the fire was out in this man.

"Lady Petranski? It's my pleasure. My name is Leoric." He stood up, giving her a bow and the symbol of Soel. She returned it with a curtsy. "Please, sit. Adrian told me a little, but I fear you have quite the story to tell."

Syline nodded, taking her seat and thanking him. It took her a few moments to collect her thoughts and figure out how to begin.

"I suppose I should start at the beginning?" Her eyes sank down to the table, fingers toying with the grain of the wood. She told him her story, starting from her decision to stay the night in the library, and hearing the glass break. She only left out two singular details, firstly, that she still had the book. In this place, she feared they may mark her as "tainted" for carrying it, or take it from her, especially with the looks Leoric gave her as she told her story about Jane. Secondly, what happened in the lumber mill. She only told him that she was attacked by the man and fought him off, then Thelonious rescued her from the ensuing bar fight.

When she was done, she realised there were tears in her eyes, she couldn't even exactly explain why. Relief, maybe? Or perhaps, perhaps she just needed to tell someone all this. Gods, so much had happened in only these last few days. She'd experienced more pain, more stress, more fear than she ever had in her life in less than a week. She suddenly felt so very tired.

Leoric nodded solemnly to himself.

"Alright, we have a matter to tend to internally, but tomorrow afternoon an escort will be organised to take you home. We'll ensure you see the king, Lady Syline. No corruption, monetary or magical, will sway my men."

"So, so you believe me then?"

He smiled softly, there was so much sadness in his eyes.

"I do. For tonight, you can stay here in the cathedral. I'll have quarters organised for you. Someone will collect you if you wait here." He made to stand, but Syline stopped him by asking, "Are you alright? You seem" – she hesitated – "sad."

The paladin let out a melancholic chuckle, knuckling his eye.

"Is it that obvious, is it? You are a kind girl, to worry about me with so much on your own plate. Yes, I am." His voice cracked. "I am well." It came out strangled. "An internal matter, one of our own was found consorting with devils and refuses to repent. She'll" – his breath came out slow, shuddering – "be executed tomorrow. She was close to me, before her fall. She was my daughter, adopted, but still. Her turn from the light of Soel weighs heavily. As does what we must do."

Syline felt all the blood drain from her. She didn't know how to take that; she didn't know how to respond. What could you say to that?

"I'm sorry," she managed, in a small voice. "Do you, do you have to kill her? Couldn't you exile her?"

"If I, if we make an exception for our own, it sets a bad example. That was the church's decision, she is to be made an example of."

Syline felt like she was stepping into another world. She suddenly realised the cultural gulf between Russenholde and its ally. They might say they are one and the same nation, but these were different people. At home, the church would never wield such power. A thought occurred to her.

"My, my bodyguard, Thelonious? The one who saved me from the tavern? He's hellblooded. That's not consorting with devils, is it? He's a kind man. He hasn't done anything wrong, but people have been glaring at him all day."

Leoric paused to look at her, she saw it there again, that judgement. But she saw pain in those eyes as well, regret. The words he spoke next came hollow, as if he spoke the beliefs of someone else.

"Kind he may be, but unless he repents the sin of his birth, the corruption of his origin will always sit upon his soul. No, speaking with him is no crime, it was not his choice to be born so, but it was his choice to not turn himself to a church for a higher purpose. It does not sound like he is a templar bound to any god, so the taint will remain. The people of Dawnsteel are not barbarians, no harm will come to him unless he harms another, but I would advise he doesn't remain in the city any longer than necessary. If he is coming with you to Russenholde, perhaps it's best if he rides separately to my men, for his sake."

Suddenly, Syline had little wish to stay in this city any longer than necessary either. As Leoric made to leave, she said again, "I'm sorry about your daughter."

She heard him clear his throat, like he was pushing something down.

"So am I," he said, almost whispering, and left.

⸺

SOME TIME PASSED BEFORE SYLINE and Thelonious were able to reconvene. She was shown where she would be staying for the night, a small, but well-appointed guest chamber hidden away in the many winding corridors of the shockingly large cathedral. She left what she had been carrying with her before stepping out to wait for Thelonious, dawdling in the open mouth of the cathedral. She found herself waiting for about ten minutes before her bodyguard came into view from a side-street. He ignored the looks the guards at the threshold gave him, but Syline did not, turning their way to glower back. It wasn't right. Perhaps it was just her guilt at her own presumptions about him, but the open hostility some of these people showed him was really rubbing her the wrong way.

"It's fine, Syline," Thelonious murmured, noticing the look.

"No, it's not, it's not right." When she looked at Thelonious, she saw he was smiling, eyes full of gratitude, but that was not what drew her interest. "Oh no!" She leant in to inspect his shirt, where splotches of tomato juice had left red stains in the fabric. "What happened to your lovely shirt?"

Thelonious let out a small chuckle, wiping at an errant tomato seed. "Don't worry about it, though, you can't clean it, can you? You know, with magic?"

Syline bit her lip, considering, cleaning magic was easy, but it was not as good for stains. Once something set in, basic sigils had a harder time dealing with it.

"I might – emphasis on might – be able to? Maybe give it to me when we have a moment, and I'll see what I can do tonight."

"Right, will do," he said with a brusque nod. "So, how did it go? Are you sorted?"

Syline beamed. "Looks like it! They said in the next few days, they'll be organising a group of the Dawnguard to take me directly to the king, not stopping for anyone."

"That's great, Syline, that's great." Thelonious let out a small sigh, glad to hear the sweet girl would finally be able to go back to her own normal life. "Not much of a need for me to look after you then?"

Syline blinked, pulled up short. "What?"

"Well, you've got the church of Soel backing you now. Ain't no need for one mercenary when you got paladins guarding you. I just figured you wouldn't want me sticking around with their kind guarding you. I know you said you'd pay me proper when we got to your family, but you really don't hafta, a few coins will see me good and there's some fellas in town I can sign–"

"No." Syline's heel clacked against the cobblestones. "No, Thelonious,

I'm not just throwing you away, just because they've said they'll protect me. I promised you, you'd receive full payment when you got me home, and I intend to see it through. Unless" – her moment of stroppy bravado faltered, as a different thought occurred to her – "unless you want to go?" she asked, nerves creeping into her tone.

Thelonious faltered in turn, why'd he expected any different? She was a sweet girl and, he liked to fancy, he probably made her feel safe after the brawls they'd been through so far.

"You sure?"

Syline nodded and surprised him by stepping in to give him a hug around the barrel of his chest. Her head didn't even reach his shoulders. "You're my bodyguard, Thelonious, and you're my friend."

Awkwardly, not wanting to spook her, knowing she could be skittish with touch, Thelonious returned the hug with one arm around her shoulders.

"That means a lot, Syl. Alright, I'll be seeing you through all the way home, knee scuffers be damned."

She looked up beaming, pulling away slightly from the hug as she did, and he immediately released her.

"Good. Now why don't we go find somewhere to eat? I don't know about you but I'm starving. Did you find somewhere to spend the night?"

"I did, but not sure it's somewhere you want to be getting dinner," he said, rubbing the back of his head.

"Well, then let's do something fancy. I don't feel like I've had a real meal since this all started, come on my treat, I've got enough to spare." She grinned, a little twinkle of cheekiness entering her eye. "Besides, I bet those 'knee scuffers' will hate having to serve you their best wine."

Thelonious laughed heartily; the word sounded so unnatural coming from her lips.

"Ah." He sighed, grinning down at her as they began to walk. "You're the best."

Chapter 11

Syline rose early that day, brought from her bed by the clamour of the church bells, which rang the moment the sun crested the horizon. She watched, bemused, as many of the congregation took up morning stretches in the courtyard, a practice that supposedly helped with flexibility and staved off the effects of ageing. To her, it looked like a lot of people dancing very slowly. After that, still yawning, whilst everyone else seemed wide awake, she hobbled her way to the refectory of the cathedral. She was treated to a breakfast of fresh fruit, squeezed juice and honey drizzled porridge. Some of the priests threw amused glances in her direction, seeing how drowsy the Russen girl still seemed. Most did not however as they seemed consumed by a solemnity that her antics could not abate.

The morning meal did help, but as she got her things together, she still couldn't fight a lingering fatigue. She'd slept the best she had since departing; it was the first time she'd been in a real bed since her runaway. Maybe that was it. She knew she was finally safe, and so the frantic, nervous energy that had kept her going was finally starting to fade away, leaving her exhausted in its passing. She wondered if she might even fall asleep on the ride home when they did leave. For now, she was safe, so she was curious to explore this city some more. Gathering her things, her spell-book included which she had no intent on leaving where the priests could find it, she made for the entrance of the cathedral. She found Thelonious waiting for her by it, inclining his head, his expression grim.

Behind him, the way was blocked by a crowd of priests and worshippers. All were here to spectate on what was taking place in front of the church. Two great bonfires had been built, huge piles of kindling and logs, above which two bodies were strung up. One of them was little more than a burned-out husk, the kindling crackling and the flames still roaring. The flames were oddly yellow and white, powered by the holy oils thrown into the flames to burn even a devil's skin. The second person still lived though and, as Thelonious and Syline pushed their way through the crowd to get a better idea of what was happening, they could hear her charges being read. In relief at her own feeling of safety, Syline had almost forgotten all about this terrible act the paladin Leoric had told her was coming.

"Amberly Penzare," began a large man, dressed in breastplate over a priest's robes, "you are hereby charged with heresy against our Lord Soel, the Glorious Dawn, the corruption of children to the ways of Hell, and consorting with devils. You were given the chance to repent. The chance to save your soul in the eyes of our lord. To redeem yourself. Yet, you refused. As is tradition, you will be given the chance to have your last words before your execution. Do you have anything to say?"

All eyes turned to the woman on the pyre. She was a beauty: half-elven with white hair and bluish skin. She wore white robes for the execution, glowing like a ghost in the bright light of the sun. Syline felt a pang of sympathy for the girl, moving with Thelonious towards the front of the crowd. Thelonious got jostled a lot along the way. The burned corpse had horns and wings. It'd been the devil she was consorting with and the people around them probably thought Thelonious was here to mourn its passing. He grimaced at the sight of the fellow, devil or no. Forcing their way forward, they found themselves standing beside a priest Syline recognised. Leoric. He was watching the proceedings with a stiff lip, his hands white knuckled at his side. He did not look at Syline as she arrived beside him.

"I was only doing what I had to do to save those children! I did nothing wrong. Even if he was a half devil, saving those children was the only reason Laes was there as well! You all care more about preserving your perfect image than actually doing good! If that's what Soel is for, then he's not any god I wish to worship. I killed demons and saved lives.

How is that evil? If you and Soel want to betray me for saving lives, then you can all go to hell with me!"

Now that pang of sympathy in Syline's heart turned into full blown anger. She sympathised all too much with the woman. She too was being hunted, having her life threatened just for trying to do what she thought was the right thing at the time. This girl was suffering it even more so. As far as Syline could gather, she'd worked with a half-devil to save some children from demons and the church had condemned them both. It seemed all too ridiculous to her. All too cruel. She made a snap decision. It was what an adventurer would do, what a hero should do. Everything she knew of what was right was telling her that she shouldn't let this girl die. Even if what the girl had done was wrong in the eyes of the church, Syline's gut told her she was good. Worthy of saving.

All at once, the fatigue and exhaustion that had gripped her since waking, was gone. It was time to act again. Her body and mind aligned in purpose and new strength flooded her limbs.

"You have to help her!" she said, turning to grip Leoric's wrist. The man reacted as if stung, ripping his arm away. He glanced in her direction, as if only then recognising her. His eyes were puffy, bloodshot.

"What?" he demanded. "Are you mad? You've heard her crimes; you've heard her refuse to repent. She wrote her own death warrant; I can't save her. Not from this. I can't betray the church."

"You're her father," Syline replied, her voice low, horrified. "You're meant to protect her."

His hand slid to the sword at his side unconsciously. He turned his gaze to her in a ferocious glare, but tears slid freely down the crags of his aged features.

"Not from this! I can't save her, I'd be betraying everything, everyone. Not from this." His voice was strangled, forcing each word.

Syline's mind was made up in that instant. Already the wheels were turning in her head, plotting how she'd pull this off. The thought that she was giving up her own safety, her own trip home was only a distant scream from the rational part of her mind which was forced down into the depths by the mad focus that had come with her renewed energy. She pulled the spell-book from her satchel, flicking rapidly to one of the pages she had marked as an interesting spell.

"Thelonious, go get her off that pyre. We're saving her."

"We're what?!" Thelonious exclaimed.

"You're what?!" Leoric echoed in a low hiss, his hand snatching her wrist. "Don't be stupid, girl! There's no coming back from this and this isn't your fight."

Syline glared back at him, fighting down the burst of fear that welled up in her breast as he grabbed her.

"No," she hissed, "it's yours. But you're running from it, so I'm fighting it for you."

Pain and hope warred in the man's eyes as he stared down at her and whispered, "If you do this, I'll have to stop you."

His hand was on his sword. Syline saw it trembling, but he made no move to draw the weapon. He was gripping it like it was the only sure port in a storm, the only thing keeping him steady.

Syline blinked up at him slowly, some part of her mind clicked into place.

"Not if you're unconscious. Thelonious, hit him."

She saw realisation, and with it, gratitude, flare in the man's eyes a second before Thelonious' fist rocketed over her shoulder. She thought she heard Leoric begin to say something as his legs turned to jelly beneath him and he hit the floor in a daze. He hadn't even tried to dodge.

People in the crowd screamed as they saw the hellblooded attack the priest, but the pair truly had their attention when Syline stepped out of the crowd, casting the spell she had picked. It was only after the last word had left her lips that she realised what a terrible idea this was, but now it was already too late to turn back. Two guards went to step in her way, she finished the spell that wracked them with a nauseating sickness, pulling on their sense of balance. One stumbled two steps forward, then violently brought up his lunch. As the second attempted to charge at Syline, he felt the spell overtaking him. Drunkenly, his body leaned to the right as he ran, and he only came halfway to reaching her before he had toppled over onto his side, clutching his gut and trying not to copy his comrade's vomiting.

"The heathen's allies have come to save her! The hells and their cults are coming for us!" someone in the crowd, likely a priest, cried.

Syline thought that was a fantastic idea and turned to another page she'd bookmarked earlier. The next spell conjured up illusions. This one was a little easier, but still draining. Cries turned to screams as, what Syline envisaged, terrifying devils clawed their way out of the ground around her. Baying at the priests who rushed to intercept. The pyre was momentarily forgotten.

"Go!" she screamed, hoping Thelonious could hear her over the crowd as she had the devils dance around the priests. She was already beginning to feel shaky on her feet.

"See!" cried a priest, but not the one who'd been reading the woman on the pyre's crimes. "See! Her devilish consorts and their warlocks step to defend her! The dark flames of hell rise against the Dawn's Light!"

Syline wondered if she'd only made things worse, but really, how could things get worse from you being burned to death after watching someone else receive the same? Clerics and guards were sprinting past the devils now with blades in hand, avoiding their reaching hands to come for their "summoner". Now was the time for her staff to prove its worth. Fires of hell were a great idea and Syline conjured up a flame dagger from her staff. Thanks to its evocation-enhancing enchantments, it was better described as a flame lance. It was as long as her arm and burned bright from the tip of the staff. She swung it back and forth wildly, moving to get closer to the pyre as the flames forced the priests to back off a step. She willed the devils to surround her. She'd figured out the rest of her plan by now. Admittedly, she was a fool for rushing in without even fully thinking it out, driven on by her horror at Leoric's choice of faith over family. Really, she was a fool all over, this was a terrible decision, but she couldn't stop now. She was certain she could manage this; she'd just need two more spells. Syline could see Thelonious on the pyre now, untying the woman from her bindings. For her part, Amberly looked very confused.

"Laes? H-How?" Syline heard her say to Thelonious.

Second last spell. The devils formed a cordon around her and, though more guards were appearing, the priests weren't yet brave enough to try their luck. She ran through the incantation directly from the book, and with each word, she felt her limbs grow weaker. This spell would be something she'd be hesitant to try and cast normally, let alone rapid fire right after two other powerful spells. After a final word, the spell ran through her staff, the ruby glowed bright-red and she swept it forward on a shaking arm. The staff felt impossibly heavy. In a circle around the pyre, flames surged two metres high, forming a wall all around it. The devils fell back into the flame so she could dismiss the illusion without the priests seeing it. One less thing taxing on her reserves. Syline fell to one knee. The magic was taking its toll now. Spots filled her vision. This was stupid, this was idiotic. Her brain felt like it was on fire.

Thelonious had the woman now. He hadn't had time to untie her legs, so he'd just slung her over one shoulder as he climbed down from the pyre. One more spell. Just one more spell and she'd be able to rest. This one was at least a simpler spell than the others. The arcane mount was one even most beginners could manage because it was a very efficient spell in terms of how much magic it consumed. As long as they didn't get too fancy with its appearance. More than that, she could cast it so it consumed it all at once, rather than relying on a constant connection; she could give it all she had left.

She could do this.

She didn't bother to rise to her feet as she ran through the incantation. Holding onto her staff for dear life, really it was all that kept her from collapsing completely. If all went well, she wouldn't need to stand. The horse was drawn from the last vestiges of her power and Syline let go of her staff, struggling to remain conscious. She really needed to practice casting one spell after another like that if she was going to call herself a real mage. The strength of her legs left her. She began to slump to the ground, just in time to feel Thelonious' strong arm wrap around her stomach and throw her up onto the horse. She landed across its shoulders, but barely felt the impact, at this point just wholly focused on keeping her breathing steady and getting feeling back in her limbs. The rest would be up to Thelonious.

—

IN THE LAST TWO DAYS, Thelonious had carried Syline while the girl was barely or not at all conscious far more than he would have liked. People might spread rumours about him if that kept happening. It didn't help that across the horse was a girl still tied around her ankles, holding on for dear life. At least that position left her keeping Syline in place as well. Now, came the exciting part. He'd always prided himself on being a pretty good rider, and this horse wasn't afraid of anything. He could push it in ways he couldn't push a flesh and blood horse, such as leaping straight through the quickly dwindling wall of flames Syline had conjured. Going high enough that all the girls got was a bit of a hot flush across their cheeks as they soared.

The priests scattered from the horse's landing. It looked like they'd been preparing some spell to clear the flames but when a huge horse of blue light leapt over the wall of fire, those thoughts were right out of their head. The crowd scattered in the path of them; they'd be stupid not to. Thelonious loved this spell already, for the horse it conjured was a huge and powerful beast worthy of some great hero. Not even the guards and priests were fool enough to try and stop them. Not since Thelonious drew his bastard sword and waved it with great bravado in his charge. A hellblooded warrior, with two women indisposed across his arcane mount, waving a sword about to scare off sun worshipping priests. Gods, what would his mother think?

Now that they were on the open road, things were easier going. The woman they'd rescued looked up at Thelonious as he rode on. "Who are you?" she blearily asked.

"Thelonious, nice to meet you, ma'am."

"Amberly. Why, though? Are you friends of Laes? I'm sorry, but you were too late…" She sighed.

"Nope, sorry, ma'am. I did meet him at the stocks though, seemed a good fella for a devil."

"Then why?"

"Syline there thought it was the right thing to do."

"And you?"

Thelonious chuckled softly, resisting the urge to say he just hadn't been quick enough to stop Syline. They could hear the guards in the distance, horses were called for. Priests yelled after them, calling them heretics, devil fondlers, children of the hells. It reminded him of the other times he'd tried to get along with sun-loving knee scuffers.

"Ma'am, I'm just the bodyguard. Though, I'm happy to thumb my nose at the church or the hells. Consider it a last kindness to a fella brave enough to go to the pyre for someone else." He pulled a knife from his belt and handed it to her. "There's a stable just at the edge of town. I'll be getting off there. You can ride a horse, right?" She took it, sawing at the ties on her legs while holding tight to his arm with the other. She cursed furiously as he had to swerve to avoid an oncoming carriage and nearly sent her flying, the arcane horse whinnying at the true flesh and blood animals as they went by. He was pushing it for all it was worth. If the guards caught up to them or reached the edge of town before they did, they were surely done for.

"Of course I can ride a horse. Where do I go?"

"Go due east. Towards the border. There's an island s'posed to be filled with nasty stuff. Knee scuffers would take their time working up the balls to follow us."

She let out a little laugh, sounding half like a sob. "Gods. You sound like him too. Not as sarcastic, but it's in there."

"Ma'am?"

"Don't worry about it." She had her legs free now and swung up to put them to either side of the horse, sitting up properly now. Just in time too. Thelonious pulled up towards the tavern where they'd left Alma and Corax and leapt off the horse before it truly had time to stop.

"Get moving! I'll be right after you!"

"Stay alive, okay!" Amberly called back, pushing herself into the saddle and spurring the horse off once again. "I don't want to have to save my saviour!"

Thelonious chuckled and drew his sword as he went for his horse. He'd be cutting this damned close. Alma greeted him with a pleased snort as he ran into the stable, trotting his way. Corax fluttered up onto his shoulder. He wasted no time, grabbing Alma's reins and hurrying both animals from the stable just in time for a pair of guards to come tearing towards him on horseback. More of the guards would be coming; he couldn't waste a single moment, or they'd never get out of here. He slapped Alma's haunch to get her trotting out of town and crouched in a ready posture, blade held low to the side. The guards had their swords drawn and were coming at him fast, just a small space between them. He felt the world slow down, it was only this moment that mattered. If he made a mistake, he died. If he didn't, he'd win. That's how every fight was. Every fight closed the entire world down to nothing but the moments between heartbeats, the tiny spaces of time between each breath.

The horses were right before him. He dived forward beneath the rider's swings, holding his blade out to the side in both hands. He felt it almost torn from his grip as it scored along a horse's leg. He hit the ground hard as he heard the horse scream. There was a tremendous clatter of armoured men hitting the ground fast and the meaty sound of horses slamming into one another. Just as he hoped, the horse he hit had tripped straight into the path of the other. Both had gone down in a tangle of limbs. One of the guards was trapped under them, and the other was struggling to his feet, nursing a broken arm.

Thelonious jumped to his feet and charged him. The soldier desperately tried to muster a defence, but he had dropped his sword in the fall and only had his buckler. He expected the swing from the bastard sword and got his shield in position to parry as best he may. Thelonious' hand wrapped around the man's throat picked him up using his momentum to drive them both onwards and slammed the man to the ground. His breath went out of the guard in a great bellow. Nothing permanent, but Thelonious doubted he'd be following after him. He ran on, leaving his fallen foes in his wake. He didn't kill either of them, but he doubted the injured horse would be any good to the watch after that. Hopefully the other would be alright. He liked horses.

Speaking of, Alma whinnied at him as she saw him approach. Corax had flown back to her at some point. He'd barely noticed the bird even when it was on his shoulder, let alone when it had left. He got a foot in the stirrup without even slowing and nearly went right over Alma's head as he pushed himself up into the saddle. Readjusting, he got himself properly seated before spurring the horse on. Soon enough, he'd disappeared into the woods. The sky overhead had clouded over and, as the trees surrounded him, it started to snow.

—

AMBERLY RODE ON ATOP THE magical steed, worried by how transparent it seemed. Syline, the one who'd rescued her, now dozed against the horse's neck, leaving her largely alone for the moment. Thoughts were going through her mind at a mile a minute. Did these people have some kind of link to Laes? Did she deserve to be dead? Had she been right in her choice? Had luck and fate seen her right, sending new allies to lead her to safety?

She could hope.

She was off the island that Dawnsteel lay upon now, pushing the horse east. The snow-covered waters fell away behind her as it galloped tirelessly onwards. The only thing out here with them was a little red songbird flying overhead, as if it were following them. She hoped that strange hellblooded fellow, Thelonious, had gotten away alright. Going off the few landmarks that the tundra had – or more accurately, the few uninhabited islands she could recognise – she was about half an hour from the border now. She'd been riding flat out for almost two hours, and her body ached to high heaven. She had never given them the confession and they had made her suffer for it. Hot irons, blades, beatings, whatever they could do to force the confession, she had no faith left to spare once Leoric had stepped back and the real confessors had stepped in. Soel would get nothing from her if he was so willing to abandon his followers for trying to do what was right. The girl in front of her stirred as they hit the border. Amberly was glad for it; being alone with her own thoughts was starting to get to her.

"Hey, are you alright?" she asked the girl, taking one arm off the reins to help her in sitting up properly.

"My head's pounding, I'll tell you that Thel…" The girl trailed off, her voice husky, but soft. She looked behind her. "Where's Thelonious?" she asked.

"He stayed behind to get something from a stable. I'm going to guess your horse."

"Oh, I do hope he's alright."

"Me too… Hey, we've not introduced ourselves yet," Amberly said, trying to draw the topic away from that. She should be happy right now, she knew. After all, she was still alive when she fully expected to have burned to death by now.

"I'm Amberly Penzare," she said. "I'm told I have you to thank for my rescue. So, er… thanks… I can't say I saw it coming."

Syline turned her head back to look at Amberly. Amberly had to admire her hair; she'd never seen someone with hair so long that didn't look like a wild bird's nest.

"You're most welcome. I'm Syline Petranski, second eldest daughter of the Petranski. I don't suppose Thelonious explained much; he's not a talker."

"He said something about you being hunted. Why did you pass out like that? Those were some amazing magics, but you just collapsed right after."

Now, Syline seemed bashful. Her cheeks were bright red, though much of that was probably from the cold wind blasting into their face.

"I have a spell-book with a lot of very powerful spells in it, but I'm actually only a novice. I had to push myself way past what I usually would to cast spells of that power. I admit I've been doing that a bit more than I'd like, of late. Three times in the past four days, I've collapsed from exhaustion. I doubt I've even given myself the time to truly recover, I've been doing it so often. Maybe don't push the horse too fast, a sudden impact might be enough to dispel it."

"Well, to cast spells like that at all is pretty amazing. I don't know how you managed it so quickly if you're a novice, so I'd say you're a little bit past that."

"Thanks." The girl seemed a bit shy, and it surprised Amberly. She'd have expected someone who'd willingly go up against the church like that to be all guts and pride, but this girl seemed exactly what she expected of a shut-in, scholarly wizard, not the sort that went on adventures. She also seemed tired, dreadfully tired. The girl said it and Amberly could see it: pushing herself so hard again and again like this was taking its toll. She looked drained, sweaty, her eyes sunk in their sockets. Most people of this region were pale, but her skin was starting to have a distinctly unhealthy pallor.

"Why don't you catch a bit more sleep? You look like you need it. We're about two hours from where we're headed anyway and then, when we get there, we need to wait for the big guy."

"Are you sure? I mean–" Syline probably had things she wanted to say. Things she decided would be a bit tactless.

"I'm sure. Carrying you away is the least I can do after you saved me from my own execution. I'll wake you up when Thelonious shows up, alright?"

Syline let out a yawn and nodded, that confirmation having broken the last of her resistance. She lay back against Amberly and was pretty quickly fast asleep. The ex-paladin smiled softly, wrapping an arm around Syline's stomach as she focused on the path ahead.

—

THELONIOUS CAUGHT UP TO THEM about half an hour after the pair had arrived at the designated island. The fact that Syline's magic steed had disappeared some fifteen minutes away and sent both girls sailing into a snow drift gave him plenty of time to catch up. For all its reputation as a warren for beasts and monsters, the place seemed deserted. Though, a few broken arrows, an abandoned sword and a makeshift grave told Amberly the king's monster hunters had probably been here recently, enough that while something likely had lived here, it was now long dead or gone.

She left Syline by a fire she built in a little nook of trees to do some exploring and quickly confirmed her thoughts: she found a pile of burned corpses. Dead. Definitely dead. They were what looked to have been a pack of kobolds and goblins. Judging by the other, larger corpses, they must've been led by a pair of orcs. Once Thelonious arrived, the pair quickly decided it wasn't worth waking Syline. Thelonious set up his tent and gently got Syline settled inside beneath a blanket. Hopefully, their rest tonight wouldn't be interrupted and she could finally recover.

The pair of them talked for a while. Syline taking the time to tell her a bit of her and Thelonious' story: why they were on the run and who was hunting them, but it quickly derailed into inconsequential small talk. Neither were in the headspace for difficult conversations.

The sun had set by now and both felt utterly exhausted. Thelonious had spent the majority of the day on horseback and his legs were paying for it. The pair decided quickly enough that they, too, should get some sleep.

Before they dozed off, Thelonious retrieved magical potions of healings from Alma's saddlebags, passed one to Amberly and woke Syline to feed her another. The vials were filled with a slightly luminescent amber liquid that moved thickly, like honey; tasted like it too. A unique export of Dawnsteel, few islands could create healing poultices of this power, this purity, this efficacy. As they swallowed them down, a faint warmth rolled over them, like stepping outside on a sunny day. As it passed through, it healed them in its wake, with an almost tickling tingle around each wound, itching ever so slightly as their flesh reknit itself, healing naturally, just at a pace accelerated a thousand times over. Sadly, only the most expensive ones hid the scars. He only had been able to afford three – he would've had more had Syline given him her purse, but she hadn't thought to. Amberly's bruises and cuts, Thelonious' aches and the gashes and lacerations to his arms, and Syline's exhaustion were healed. In the morning, the three would be ready to face the world once more.

On Thelonious' insistence, Amberly took her rest in the tent, facing away from Syline but sharing the sleeping mages blanket. The gentlemanly hellblooded insisted he would be fine with the cold. It was the two girls who had been through so much who deserved the rest. Once the flaps of the tent closed, the three finally got their much needed slumber. Far away from even the kingdom's borders, alone in untamed lands but for each other.

Chapter 12

TEAGAN RUBBED HER EYES WITH finger and thumb. This was a strange job and it was already becoming more annoying than it was worth.

The mercenary captain sat on a box of supplies in the midst of her camp, just far enough from Dawnsteel to go unnoticed. Piecemeal, her men had come and gone from the city to gather supplies and information and get some well-earned rest and relaxation after the hard ride to get here on schedule. She couldn't, she'd stayed out here. Yaldabaoth, the demonic hound their employer had loaned them, only listened to her, and she couldn't exactly bring that monster into the region's religious hotspot.

"And you're certain it was her?" she asked again.

"Sure as the moon rises," her man, Lukas, replied, a flabbergasted smile not leaving his face since he'd arrived. Gods, he was a snide little idiot. If he wasn't so quick with his knives, she'd have cut him loose long ago. "We went to the bathhouse to clean off the road, and some of the boys struck up a chat with a hellblooded in there."

"Seemed an alright fella," put in Ewan, her best archer and Lukas's partner in shenanigans. "Our type, I told him where he could get some supplies without the prices being hiked up too much for him having horns and all."

"Right, so there we was, thinking he was just some sellsword on the end of a contract," continued Lukas. "Was thinking of offering him riding out with us, since he said his job was just about done. Then we hear that some devil's going to be burned at the stake, with his paladin croney to boot."

"And we're like, 'Surely not! That won't be the fella we just washed up with, will it?'" Ewan took up the story once more, the pair might've been brothers. "He wasn't no devil–"

"Sure as the moon rises," cut in Lukas.

"But we still have to go and look, after all you can't trust knee scuffers to know the difference, and how many hellblooded could be running around Dawnsteel? Besides, not every day you see someone being burned at the stake, especially not a paladin. So, we rolled up to the back of the crowd. The devil wasn't him, coulda fooled me though, the fella on the pyre looked just like him."

"Don't be racist, Ewan," put in Martha, their camp mother, from where she stirred the stew pot. He put up his hands defensively.

"What? I'm not! They really did look alike and not just the horns and redskin. Coulda been brothers."

"Sure as the moon rises."

"Anyway, we watch the devil fella burn. Awful sight it was, all this black stuff leaking out into the golden fires, him screaming and cursing. Sad thing was, we heard him telling the paladin girl it'd be okay and not to be scared, before he burned. Never thought I'd see a devil with a heart."

Ewan accepted a bowl of stew from Martha. By now, most of the band had gathered around to listen, even those who had been there for it. Lukas took a bowl but focused on finishing the cigar he'd purchased in town first.

"Guess the devil knew what he was talking about, and hell, guess they *were* brothers," he said, turning to glare reproachfully at Martha, "because right when the paladin girl's about to go up in flames, our pal Thelonious punches one of the Dawnguard big wigs and runs in to rip her off the pyre. Suddenly everyone's screaming, guards are collapsing left and right, walls of fire are springing up around the pyre, and this crazy little wizard girl's swinging a spear with a blade of fire around like she's a kid playing soldier. Devils are bursting out of the flames and the whole place is losing its head."

"Then, our friend the hellblooded, bursts through the flames on a horse made of stars, his little wizard passed out on the front, and the paladin's holding on for dear life. They go streaking out of the town, and the Dawnguard make a show of following, but it seemed like they were holding back a bit. Didn't follow them far before someone called 'em back. Meanwhile, off they go streaking out across the tundra 'til they're nothing but dots on the horizon."

Silence reigned for a few good moments as they all ingested the story. Callum, one of the strongest in the crew put in, "Are we sure about this job, Teagan? If they're mad enough to fight the Dawnguard–"

"And win, sure as the moon rises," put in Lukas.

"Then are we sure we want to be fighting them?"

Yaldabaoth lifted its head from where it lay on the ground by Teagan's feet, baring teeth as long as daggers, all the flesh of its muzzle rolling back until it was nothing but bone and muscle as a growl shook the trees around them. Callum held up his hands, as Teagan hissed a command to the creature in its hideous tongue. After a moment of glaring, the creature settled and all there suppressed a shudder. Teagan looked at Callum, her eyes imploring him not to argue.

"This is a job we can't back out of, Callum. If we were going to, we'd have had to when we were still in Russenholde."

The two mercenaries shared a long look, before finally, the strong man placed his head down in one hand, raising the other in a supplicating shrug.

"What do we do then? How do we handle this one?"

Teagan sat back, looking up. The stars were clear tonight. Idly, she began marking the constellations, like her father had taught her. It let her mind drift over the problem, circle it like the hunters and animals on show up there.

"We scare them. Best case scenario, we never have to fight them at all. You know the deal the boss lady gave us. She does as we say, we play nice. We just have to come in with enough shock and awe that she doesn't even consider there's another option. Make ourselves as big and scary as possible, you know, like we're scaring off a bear..." She trailed off, thoughts running rampant, and as they did, a small chuckle bubbled up to her lips.

"Does that mean we're getting 'scary Teagan' again?" Lukas asked with a melodramatic sigh, after the silence had hung for several moments.

Teagan chuckled again. "Sure as the moon rises, Lukas. Sure as the moon rises."

THEIR REST DID NOT LAST as long as they would have liked. If any of the three had had their way, the trio likely would have slept all through to the next afternoon. Sadly, all three were awoken just after the sun had begun its ascent, not that they could see it. The sky – no, the world – was grey. Fog and snow blocked the view of what lay just beyond their camp.

Thelonious was the first to be awakened, the cold picking at his bones until it roused him from his slumber. He awoke to find himself half buried in snow already, more falling with a ferocity that could mean only one thing.

Thelonious pulled himself free from the snow and shook the girl's tent frantically.

"Blizzard!" he yelled over the roaring wind. "We need to find shelter!"

If the blizzard continued, that tent would be no protection for the girls, to say nothing for him and Alma. The horse was already panicking, pulling at her reins where they were tied to a nearby tree. While the girls extracted themselves from the tent one after the other, Thelonious got the horse free, holding tight to her reins so she wouldn't run off.

"Head inland!" Amberly shouted, holding her cloak tightly around herself as Syline slipped out of the tent behind her, wrapping Corax in her scarf so the little raven wouldn't freeze. Syline was still barely awake, stumbling to Thelonious' side. With that, the trio set off with Amberly leading the way, a destination seemingly in mind. Thelonious followed after her, dragging his fearful horse, and Syline stayed right behind him, clutching his back to have him act as a windbreak for her. They struggled on; the wind was too great for them to exchange any words. Syline conjured forth a pair of magical lights, one for her and Thelonious, one for Amberly, so the trio wouldn't lose each other in the grey, endless fog.

The journey only lasted ten minutes or so, but to the trio, it felt like an eternity. Each step was difficult and each breath froze their lungs more than the one before and made the one to follow even more of a trial. Amberly slowly led the others around a great hill that took up the centre of the island. On the other side of it, only found by Amberly guiding herself with a hand along the rocks, was an opening, just large enough for two people to move abreast. In the fog, she could have easily walked by it ten times over, and for all they knew, she had.

"Come on!" she yelled to them, disappearing into the dark of the cave as it turned away, deep enough for her to escape the wind and chill for whatever lay inside. Thelonious sent Syline running after their newfound friend before he set to guiding the fearful horse in through the thin opening. It took a lot of assurances and less than gentle encouragement, but he managed to get himself and his beloved steed out of the cold to stand with the girls in this hidden sanctum.

Past the small entrance way, they now stood in a fairly large, oval-shaped cave. It dipped off towards the end, going down in a wider opening leading deeper beneath the dirt. The magical light provided by Syline didn't go far enough to show what lay beyond, but it lit the cave in warm, orange hues, making it seem positively cosy in comparison to what they had just escaped.

As the trio dusted the snow off themselves, Corax squawked and flapped his way free from Syline's scarf to roost on her shoulder. Alma decided this was all too much stress for this early and lay down, the horse's breath coming in great shuddering billows through its nostrils.

"How did you know about this place?" Syline asked Amberly, looking back and forth.

She stretched herself out with a little yawn – she had to admit, she felt better than she had in days, despite their rude awakening. She'd woken briefly, and considered striking up a conversation, but both girls mostly just wanted to sleep and had woken up tucked in against each other for warmth when Thelonious had come shaking the tent. She hadn't felt that jolt of fear from Amberly being close, that she did even with Thelonious.

"When we first arrived on this island, I did a little bit of exploring while Thelonious set up camp. I get cold feet sitting around in a new place. I spotted the entrance, thought a bear might be better than a blizzard. At least we can stab a bear." Amberly sighed and looked outside. The blizzard raged on, snow building up before the cave's entrance. If it kept going like that, they'd be snowed in, in no time.

"Good thing you did," Thelonious put in, brushing snow off Alma's coat. "We're going to be stuck here until the blizzard clears up. We should probably explore deeper in, make sure there aren't bears or anything worse."

"What could be worse than bears on an island like this? Surely, all the monsters were already killed by Syline's father," Amberly said, getting a grin from Syline.

Syline snickered. "Hornbears?"

"Icebears?" Amberly added, grinning.

"Dire bears?" Syline continued.

Thelonious chuckled gently as he drew his sword out of its harness on Alma's saddle. "Or any other kind of 'something'-bear."

Amberly looked down at herself. All she had were the white robes. No belongings had been on the pyre with her, of course.

"I'll need a weapon unless you two want me to stay back here with the horse and – no offence to Alma here – but I think you two are probably better at conversation."

Syline knew that Amberly was – well, had been – a member of the Morning's Fury. Chances were, out of the three of them, she might be the best swordsman. It would probably be a pretty close contest, though. Thelonious was pretty damn impressive.

"Syline, do you want to give her something? You've got an axe and that sword on your belt."

Syline perked up a bit. She hadn't drawn her sword since she'd killed that man just outside of Russenholde and she didn't really want to, either. Whilst the axe had saved her from a man who she felt was more evil than anything she had faced thus far, the sword. She could only think of that man's eyes. But it was her family sword, and yet. She silenced her endless internal back and forth with herself by removing her sword belt and offering it to Amberly.

"I'll want it back eventually, alright, Miss Penzare?"

"I'll take good care of it, Syline. I'll take it as an honour that a Petranski is giving me her sword," Amberly said with a little smile, buckling the belt around her waist.

"Amberly, I don't suppose you still have any of that knee scuffer magic?" Thelonious asked, standing up from his horse and starting to walk down towards the slope. The magical light followed him, just above his left shoulder. He already liked it. He could see better in the dark than most, but not perfectly; having a little floating ball of light freeing up his hands from a torch was a valuable thing.

"No, no, I don't." An agonised sigh left her, her words coming choked. "Soel has left me, just like the church."

"What did you really *do*, anyway? We've caught the basics, but what's the full story?" Syline asked, curious.

Thelonious quickly glanced her way but shrugged and kept walking, leaving something unsaid. They descended into the depths once Syline fetched her staff from Alma's saddlebags. Alma was content to stay behind and the horse merely watched them as they left. Syline had tried to get Corax to stay with the mare, but each time she put him down, she would find the raven hopping after her again only a few moments later. Eventually, she relented and the raven was once more happily roosting in her robes, which she'd wrapped around her new dress rather than take the time to get changed. Through their mental connection, she received feelings of love and affection from her familiar, warming her heart, even if the blizzard still left the rest of her frozen.

"I'm an orphan," Amberly began. "My family were travelling here from the east. Past Dawnsteel. My mother was a tundra elf, my father human. I can't" – she shrugged – "I was very young, I can't really remember our home. I do remember a woodfire, a bearskin rug, my mother's smile watching some kind of festival, that's it really. I can't even remember their names, but I was a child, I knew them as my mam and dad." She let out a hollow chuckle. "I wonder what they'd think of the turns my life has taken."

"My ma never wanted me to become a sellsword. Even though, even though I was a 'cost', the price to pay, she loved me like any of my brothers," Thelonious said with a gentle chuckle, rubbing the bridge of one horn. "I think Pa always knew I wasn't made for the farm though."

Syline let out a small chuckle.

"I don't know, I can easily see you bailing hay and tending cattle." Thelonious shot her a smile, but didn't respond, letting Amberly continue.

"Well, when we were crossing the border into Dawnsteel's domain, our caravan was ambushed by demons, awful stilt-legged things, claws the length of swords." A shuddering sigh left her, as the memories returned back to her in a swell, her pace was slowing, and the other two slowed to match her. "The guard did what they could to defend everyone, but I saw demons shred them like they were nothing but wet paper. Then my mother hid us under a blanket, hoping the demons would pass us by. Gods, I barely remember my father, but my mother. I'll never forget that moment, it haunts my dreams even today. Her holding me to the bed of the cart, the smell of brimstone and blood hot in the air, as my mother told me again and again to just keep looking at her, and that it would be okay." She stopped walking, wiping an eye with the base of her thumb.

Syline spoke up. "We don't need to talk about this if it's bringing back bad memories, Amberly."

"No, no, it's fine, I'm fine, it's just been a lot these last few days. I only really talked about this with Laes." She sighed. "It wasn't okay though, one of the demons must have heard her, smelled her, I don't know, but a claw went right through her back to stab into my breast. Still have the scar. It, she didn't die right away, she hugged me close, told me to stay quiet, told me to wait. Gods, she was so brave, so strong, she knew she was dying, but told me to stay right where I was, she wanted to protect me even as she breathed her last. I did as she said, I stayed right where I was for hours, in the arms of her corpse. She was smiling, I remember that, she died hoping I'd be okay, died knowing they'd passed us by for now. Once they stabbed her, they moved on to eat other prey."

"She sounds like a wonderful woman, Amberly," Thelonious offered.

"She was, I wish I'd gotten to know her better." She sighed gently. Her arms slid around herself. "In the end, they arrived just in time, the Dawnguard. I could hear the demons snuffling around the cart, looking for more meat. I heard one growl. I knew it had heard me crying and I saw its claws easing under the blanket. Then I heard them, their battle cry and the creature's attention was elsewhere."

She smiled sadly, almost wistfully, as a memory surged up.

"When Leoric pulled the blanket off my mother and me, I nearly gutted him with her paring knife. He took me up in his arms then, told me it would all be okay, told me I was safe, that the dawn had come, and the night had fled in its path. I just cried. I'd kept myself quiet for so long, it was all I could do. I cried until I had no tears left. After that, the Dawnguard took me in. I could have been a simple priestess but well, I wanted revenge, I knew what was out there now, waiting for us in the dark, and once I had no tears left to shed, I wanted to make sure no other kid would wind up like me. Leoric was like a father to me and wanted me to follow in his footsteps, become one of the leaders of the Dawnguard but I never really fit in." She sighed. "All of them were so concerned with rules and what Soel wanted. Worship came before any real practical concern. They didn't." She let out a growl. "To me, it always seemed like they wasted so much damn time. So many more lives could have been saved if they didn't spend all this time with procedure and ceremony. If they did whatever had to be done to stop the demons, instead of all this posturing about purity and 'ensuring we remain uncorrupted', maybe if they wasted less time, my family would still be alive."

Syline's breath halted in her throat. She wanted to speak, but couldn't bring herself to, she simply placed a hand on Amberly's wrist. Amberly gave her a little smile, brushing her white locks behind her ear.

"Then I met Laes, the half-devil. You saw him" – she sighed – "being burned. He was everything they weren't: witty, practical, willing to get the job done. But he was a devil, we were meant to hate each other, but I always found it easier to talk to him than any of them, even Leoric. Maybe it was always going to work out like this. But Laes." She bit her lip. "Laes cared. He saw me as a person. He knew I struggled sometimes, he knew I had nightmares, and he wouldn't tell me to just 'pray to Soel and he may shed light on the taint of your soul'. Laes would sit with me, he'd tell me, 'No, it isn't alright, but it's not happening now, and now you can do something about it'. He was good to me, in a way priests just didn't know how to be. Never thought you'd get that from a devil, huh? We'd work together when we encountered each other, everything went wrong when he and I were taking down skin-stealers who'd kidnapped a bunch of children. Apparently, one of the kids was the child of one of his warlocks. That was when Leoric and the other paladins found us together."

"I met him at the stocks," Thelonious put in. "Seemed like a good fellow, as far as devils go. I offered him a quicker way out, but he said he didn't want you to burn alone."

Amberly laughed, but it was a choked, painful thing.

"Did he really? Gods, maybe all that flirting really had something behind it." She trailed off, her smile turning from sad, to an angered grimace. "I just wish Leoric understood. I didn't want it to turn out like this but he's just so damned blinded by his stupid faith, his stupid rules. I did love him, you know? He is my father, really but… he let this happen." She gestured vaguely. "Obviously the church is more important to him."

The silence hung for several moments, Thelonious didn't know what he could say to that, but Syline eventually cut in, breaking the uncomfortable air.

"I'm not so sure," Syline offered. "I met him, he was organising my trip home, but at your execution, well, he was so close to acting, it looked like it was killing him to stand by. I tried to get him to act, but something in him couldn't cross that line."

The anger in Amberly's eyes didn't fade. "Sounds like he made up his–"

"But he knew Thelonious and I were going to stop it, he said he'd have to stop us or he'd be betraying the church. Then did nothing to stop Thelonious knocking him out, so he couldn't. He looked" – Syline shrugged, the moment playing back in her mind – "grateful."

Amberly looked up, confusion warring in his eyes with pain and hope. Slowly, they all turned to a grateful sorrow.

"Idiot," she murmured. "He always was an idiot. Never could act when it really mattered."

She wiped at her eyes, something halfway between a laugh and a sob left her.

"Always had to have someone else take the first step. Maybe he does believe I was doing the right thing after all?"

Syline stepped close to her, holding her hand to give her comfort.

"I would have done exactly the same thing. I don't think you did a single thing wrong, and if Soel and the Morning's Fury think you did, more fool them. Though" – Syline chuckled, giving her a weak little grin – "maybe we're both in this mess because the two of us think like that," she said with a little sigh.

"What, like heroes?" Amberly offered with a grin, forcing herself to perk up from the melancholy she'd fallen into.

"Aye," said Thelonious as his eyes roved ahead of them. "I've never had time for knee scuffers. The church is far too up themselves. Don't like devil lovers either, but this Laes fellow seemed more reasonable. Even if it was for his own reasons, he was still helping you save those kids."

"Exactly." Amberly sighed. She felt lost. She knew in her heart she was the one in the right and it was comforting knowing her newfound friends agreed with her on that point, but still, the church had been the basis of her life for so long. She didn't know what she would do now that she was gone from it. She was glad for the pair of them, because it seemed like Syline had a mission all her own, finding her way home and free of those hunting her. Until it was done, it could be Amberly's mission too. At least until then, she had a focus for her life. Something to guide her.

"You look a lot like him, you know. Laes, I mean. You've got a bit of a longer face but there's a resemblance past the red skin and horns."

"Is that so? Know how old he was?"

"No, though I know hellblooded like you live a very long time, so who knows how long a true half-devil could live. Maybe he doesn't even know. Why do you ask?"

Thelonious shrugged as he suddenly stopped walking, the two women pulling up behind him. Syline nearly walked into his back.

"Never knew my father, my real father. Only knew my pa. If he looks like me – and you said he talks like me too, for all I know – he might be my father after all. Shame." He shrugged again as if reinforcing that thought didn't overtly bother him. "Hey, is it just me, or have we been going down a really long time?" He had suddenly shifted topic before Amberly could reply. The thought clicked with them as soon as he said it. Syline looked around with a newfound curiosity, having been lost in Amberly's tale up 'til now.

"Well, we probably don't have to worry about any bears at this point. We'd have found them by now. I know there are a few passages to the deep elves' subterranean home scattered around the kingdom. Maybe this is one of them?" Syline offered.

"Into the Sea Without Sky? I don't think so…" Amberly replied, looking further ahead. The tunnel seemed to suddenly drop not all too far from them, only darkness past that. It looked like that drop connected it to some other tunnels beneath, but she couldn't see properly from this far off.

"Think we should turn around now?" Syline asked, looking to Thelonious, the experienced adventurer among them, for guidance.

He gave a little smile. "Have to admit, I'm kind of curious."

Syline grinned a little, herself; she'd always wanted to be an adventurer. She'd grown up reading the stories of them and was the daughter of two herself, even if both of them now moved onto more "proper" professions. Out of everything they'd done so far – aside from rescuing Amberly – this felt the most… adventurous.

"Then I'm all for it!" she declared. "Maybe we'll find a deep elf outpost, or treasure, or some kind of terrible monster. Oh, or a beautiful princess in need of saving."

"That last one doesn't happen as much as it does in the books, Syline. Besides, the king doesn't have any daughters and I think the Prince of Russenholde can probably handle himself," Amberly said with a little chuckle.

Syline sniggered back, thinking about the prince briefly. Her family was close to the king's, in fact King Drahzan was her god-father and she'd spent the day with him a few times when she was younger, and listened to him and her parents relive old stories whenever he came to their home. The prince had always had a thing for Kat; he'd even had Syline give her an anonymous letter once. She wondered how he was getting on, how everyone was getting on, if she'd ever see them again… She forced herself to stop thinking about it, before she spiralled into despair.

With none of the three against the idea, Thelonious started leading the way off towards the hole, Amberly in quick pursuit, sword drawn already. Syline refreshed their lights before chasing to catch up. Coming closer to the hole, Syline sent one of the lights down into it so they could get a proper look. Now that they stood around the rim, they could see the hole looked as if it had been broken into the rock, likely by something humanoid considering the debris lying on the floor below and jagged pick marks on their level. It was very definitely a floor as well, for down below was worked stone, floors, and walls that looked fit for any castle. Syline exchanged a look with Amberly as Thelonious dropped to his knees, grabbed the lip and began to lower himself.

"Are you… I know I was all for it a moment ago, but it looks like this place belongs to someone," Syline said.

"As far as I know, there are no deep races living here," Amberly said. "If they did, chances are the island would have more signs of it, and the border guard would have no need to clear it. This place has probably been abandoned for a long, long time."

Syline nodded, but she couldn't deny her unease. Perhaps it was just the way the air coming from below felt warmer, or the worked stone, or whatever else preyed upon her nervous mind, but something just felt off, here. "You're right–"

"Syline!" Thelonious interrupted from down below. He held his arms out. "Jump down and I'll catch you, then you, Amberly."

"Er, just a moment!" Syline threw her axe and the staff down, Thelonious jumped a bit to the side to avoid them catching his foot. He only had a moment or so to look grumpy before Syline followed them, landing in his arms with a little squeak. Thelonious gave her a little grin before depositing her on her feet and catching Amberly next. The trio took a moment to look around the long hallway they were now in. There was a doorway to their left nearby, but what lay beyond was still too dark to see. In the other direction, the hallway slowly curved away, making it impossible to know how far it went just yet.

"Which way do you think?" asked Syline, summoning the globes of light back to her shoulders.

"Let's follow the hall, see how far it goes, first. We can check that room on our way back. I'll take the lead. Amberly, watch our backs. Syline, keep the globes between us."

With that, Thelonious set off. Syline thought he seemed quite confident down here in the unknown. She knew he had much more of a history of adventuring than her. She wondered how many tombs and catacombs like this he'd explored in the past. Walking through the hallway was quite a different experience from the caves above. They were deep enough now that they could hear and feel nothing of the storm anymore.

It was actually quite warm down here, if not a bit musty, like burnt dust. It reminded Syline of a library, in its own way. That made her feel a little bit better. The hallway went on for another two minutes or so of walking without a word. The place had a certain solemnity to it that seemed to kill any urge the three had to speak to one another. Thankfully, they did eventually escape the hallway, stepping out into a much larger room. The fact that this was under an island was astonishing, though the leaks in the ceiling and pools of water on the floor hinted how far from the island they had actually wandered.

The room seemed as large as the grand library's grand foyer, but with no bookshelves, it seemed to stretch on and on, with four great pillars holding up the ceiling. The centre of the floor of the room dipped down into a bowl shape, full of water, though none leaked from above. Each of the pillars gave off a soft, blue light from runes inscribed into them, easily lost in the beautiful artwork scribed into each one were it not for that glow. The edges of the room had stone desks, ones that came up to around Thelonious' chest, meaning they were around head level for Syline. Behind them, in alcoves worked into the walls, were old books.

Whilst Thelonious and Amberly's interest went to the pillars, Syline practically sprinted for the alcoves. The idea of ancient, lost tomes sent a thrill through her. She had to work hard to hide her disappointment when, upon opening the first, the second and the third book, most all of them had been ruined by water damage. She hadn't noticed until now, but the stains along the walls hinted that this place had been flooded more than a few times in the past. She could barely make out anything in these books, and no mending spell she knew could fix damage like that. Not with so much time having passed.

"Syline!" Amberly called, waving her to come see one of the pillars that she had wandered over to. "I don't suppose you recognise this language?

The runes definitely look elven but I'm having a hard time reading it. It reads like gibberish when I read it as elven, and I doubt whoever built this place was illiterate."

Syline bounced over and looked the text up and down before shaking her head.

"No, no, I can't read it, either. I mean, I almost surely speak less elven than you. But, I might be able to figure it out. I did a little study on cryptology. There's something familiar about this handwriting."

Amberly nodded as Syline mused upon it and stepped back to let her get closer. Syline beamed at her, before stepping in, pausing to think. Syline felt a fair bit of pride. She was doing proper exploring and, for all her fears of what they might encounter down here, right now, it just felt like they were discovering something. Perhaps someday, she could come down here with proper linguists or a spell of...

She opened the archmage's spell-book and began flipping through the pages. Surely, there would be something for this in here; what kind of archmage wouldn't have a utility spell like that? He'd never taught her, but she knew for a fact that Anatoly had one like it. A spell of language! She settled down to work through the book, enjoying this little mystery.

"This one isn't elven," Thelonious called, waving Amberly over. As she passed through the small zone of darkness between Syline's light and the one at Thelonious' shoulder, a chill went down Amberly's neck, even though this place was almost uncomfortably warm. She really wished Syline had given her one of those as well, but considering she'd seen the girl collapse, she wasn't sure how far they should try and push her.

"It's Teuflisch. I can read it," Thelonious said as she reached his side, leaving Amberly feeling a little out of place, seeing as both her newfound friends were able to translate – or at least try and translate – these pillars, but she pushed that down for a more pertinent question.

"Why can you read Teuflisch? I thought you said you never knew your father and didn't truck with devils."

Thelonious gave a light shrug, rubbing along one of his horns.

"Just... always been able to. Met a warlock once who wanted to hire me as a bodyguard. Probably for the image of it. Didn't take the job, the man didn't wash, but while I was there, he had me look at some scrolls. I could just... It's not even like I look at the words and read them, I see them and I just sort of understand."

"Hmm... well, I have heard that almost every hellblooded gets some curious natural talent. I've met ones who can turn invisible or talk to insects. With that in mind, I guess reading Teuflisch is probably about as mundane as they could come."

"And I don't have any want to know what a fly's last words are before I swat it," he said, giving her a little grin that she returned. "So, do you want to know what it says?" he asked, getting back to the point.

"Well, go on then."

Lo, gift bringer. Icaria, Scholar of Ascension, holds dominion below these frozen lands. If it is knowledge thoust seek, a parley mayhaps, but woe, if thine tribute is unworthy, foul attentions thy shall call. Warned thus, leave now if thine gift is wanting. If thine heart fills still, call I, thine steward, thusly, call me with my name, Daidallos.

Thelonious paused. "I – er… I think I should probably stop reading," he said. He looked up and over to Syline, who gave him a vaguely concerned look.

"This one says the same thing. I think we should leave these things alone. This is court mage business," Syline said, a little unsettled; she swore she could see a silhouette inside the pillar when the light caught it right.

"A parley," Amberly mused. Syline stood up and padded back to the pair of them. Corax was quivering in her scarf. Something about this place was making the bird very uncomfortable, and he was letting Syline know as much through the impulses he sent her way.

"Shhh, it's okay, Corax," Syline cooed to her familiar, petting him as she rejoined them.

"This place seems… a bit beyond us; let's leave before someone touches something they shouldn't," Thelonious said to Syline's nodded agreement.

The pair of them had a bit less experience in sunken ruins and old catacombs than Amberly. There was a shift in the air, like a door opening far away and a fresh breeze rolled in. Syline wasn't sure why, but that terrified her, sending hairs raising all across her arms as she retreated to stand beside Thelonious. She didn't seem to be the only one who noticed it either, as both her companions instinctively drew their weapons, looking around with a new wariness.

"We should get going back the way we came," Syline said just a bit too loudly, as if she were addressing someone unseen in the room, or whatever lurked in these tunnels, letting them know they wouldn't hassle them anymore. "The… the blizzard will surely have passed by now."

The other two were all too happy to go along with that plan, and all three began moving with a bit more haste down the hall the way they'd come. Their fear was proven all too warranted when, about halfway back, an unearthly roar shook the hall. It sounded like a man's scream, echoed and distorted a thousand times down a tin pipe. It shook their very bones.

"Run!" Thelonious roared loud enough to compete with the sound, shoving at both girls backs to hurry them forward with more haste.

The trio reached the hole with the sounds following close at their backs. Whatever the source of the sound was, it was definitely getting closer and it wasn't their only problem. When they reached the hole, they found that eerie, pale green lights had lit in the room they had meant to check on their way back. Inside, they could see silhouettes. Dark, humanoid figures, their bodies far too thin and heads far too large to be human. Some seemed to have horns curling up from their heads, others had tendrils rising from their backs and shoulders which shuddered in unseen winds. The lights were at their backs, and in a slow, shambling gait they were coming for the trio. As they approached, a horrible smell, which brought up Syline's gorge, grew with them, the stench of rotten eggs and infected flesh.

"How are we getting back up?" Amberly demanded, facing the oncoming beasts as Thelonious faced the hall they'd come from.

"Syline!" he said. "Find us some kind of spell that'll get us up there! Flight, levitation, a ladder, whatever! We don't have time for me to push you two up. We'll hold them!"

Just as he finished his command, the source of the roars rounded the corner. It was just as hideous as they'd imagined – no, far, far more so than that. It had the silhouette of a dragon, but in place of legs, it had long tentacles, with the texture and colour of a rat's tail. Its wings were tattered, each hole in them weeping pus. Its face was the worst of all: terribly human, still possessing a mop of brown hair, stretched down its neck like a mane. It looked as if someone had taken a human face and stretched out their jaw, like so much putty, until they looked more akin to a horse than the dragon or whatever mad god had made this beast, must have tried to emulate.

It let out another sound, but without the halls to echo it into a roar, it sounded more pitiful, more pained. The creature stopped just before them, gazing down as the silhouettes stood waiting in the hall behind.

They were waiting for something. Syline looked to her allies, trying to get some sense of what was happening. Thelonious looked tense, his hand on his blade, his breath held. Amberly though was somewhere else, her eyes gazing at nothing. Syline heard her mutter, "Mother," under her breath, as Syline tapped her. Suddenly, she brushed Syline's hand away, her eyes centring on the silhouettes in the dark as she drew out her borrowed blade.

"Can't you smell it? They're demons! Kill them all!" she roared, and at the yell, the dragon-like monstrosity screamed as well. Rushing forward with sudden anger, Thelonious added his own roar to the chorus and rushed to meet it as the silhouettes began to shamble forwards into the light.

Syline did not roar, it was all she could do not to scream.

Chapter 13

NOTHING. THE MINE IN THE foothills, west of Russenholde, had been their last lead, a known den of smugglers that the watch had left alone until now. Kassandra had come down on it with the full force of the border guard, the watch and a dozen footmen loaned by the Petrov family. The smugglers had been run from their den like rabbits before a hunting hound and not a single one of them knew anything about the missing Petranski daughter. The border guard's sorcerer, Ioann, had torn through them like a wildfire but had been left just as disappointed as her; the young man had been her pillar through all this. He and Kat, each of them a whirlwind of energy in their own way, never faltering in their hunt for Syline, never losing hope, unlike her.

Despair gripped Kassandra's heart as she rode back with her men, her heart pounding anxiously in her ears like a war drum. They'd turned the city upside down, ripped apart a half dozen criminal organisations in their hunt and scoured nearby towns for any sign of her. The only possible clue they'd found was a guard, dead and frozen in the snow outside the city. His burns suggested he'd fought a mage, but Kassandra could not understand how that mage could have been Syline. Why would she have fought a guard? Why was she outside the city to begin with? The only possible conclusion was the kidnappers had a mage of their own, which lined up with them stealing the tome from Jane's vault.

It was just all so much. She wished Peter was here. She wished she had more men. She wished she wasn't so damned tired. These last few days, she'd barely had the strength to lift her blade, her hand shaking every time she drew it. She'd come on this expedition but had barely even drawn her blade before it was over, hanging to the back to avoid being in the way.

Her mind felt lost in a fog, struggling to focus, easily falling into despair and maudlin thoughts rather than focusing on the path forward, the path she'd bring Syline back home on. She'd still not found the right path, still hadn't even taken the first step. All she wanted was to hold her daughter again. She realised then that all she could hear was her heart pounding. She could not hear the men around her, the crunch of hoofs on snow, or the jangle of equipment and saddlebags. She looked up from her horse's neck; the world around her was blurry and hazy, her breath rolled under the pound of her heart, faster, panicked. It came to her in hoarse gasps. No matter how hard she tried, she couldn't fill her lungs.

She turned to Ioann, riding beside her, and tried to raise an arm to him. She couldn't; her arms were slack by her side and no matter how she struggled, she couldn't raise them. She couldn't breathe. Her heart pounded louder, louder. With each sucking gasp, phlegm and mucus rattled through her chest. Black spots danced across her vision, then white. White growing closer fast until it hit her, cold and wet. She realised belatedly she'd fallen from her horse. She could barely hear her men yelling her name and she felt arms shaking her and lifting her from the snow. It all felt so far away and only growing further as her vision faded with every pounding drumbeat of her heart.

THE NEXT THING SHE KNEW, she was waking up in her bed, the concerned eyes of the Petranski family's physician, Galen, staring down at her. He was wiry, bald, and weathered by age, like old leather. He blinked at her from behind his spectacles. He'd been her physician since she was a girl and had been one of her father's closest friends before his passing.

"I told you; didn't I tell you? I told you; you need to rest. You're going to kill yourself if you keep going on like this, then who's going to find her?"

"Galen?" Her voice was a whisper, unfamiliar. She felt a cough coming on seconds before it hit, wracking her entire body. Dark phlegm, flecked with blood, hit her palm as she held it over her mouth. Galen stroked her back until it stopped, then handed her a handkerchief.

"I need to get back out there. We'll head south, past the border; maybe we'll find sign of her in the city kingdoms."

"Go on then," Galen said, stepping back. There was an air of challenge in his words and she took the bait immediately, turning to stand off the side of the bed. Her legs trembled and she only managed half a step before she began to fall. Only then did Galen step in to catch her. Old bastard. He guided her back to bed with an air of superiority.

"I told you, what did I tell you? *Rest*, exhaustion was already taking its toll, but taking a fall from that height into the snow? You'll be lucky if flu and a fever are the worst of it. You're not the only one hunting for her, Kass. Let someone else shoulder the burden. I swear, you and Anatoly both. He collapsed just the same way last night, damned fool, pushing his magic far past its limits for 'divinations', I'd bet. If Syline comes back to find her mother and mentor have stressed themselves to death waiting for her…" He trailed off with a rueful smirk.

"She's my daughter, Galen, I need to." She tried to push his hands back as he pulled the sheets up on her. Her hands shook so badly and she could barely close her fingers over his. He sighed, watching the display.

"But a few weeks ago, you could have tossed me across this room like sackcloth; now look at you. A stiff breeze could blow you over. You can't save her if you can't look after yourself, Kass. I'll instruct your maid on how to administer your prescription and good hearty foods to help you recover quickly."

She gave in. What else could she do? She couldn't even stand. He was right; he almost always was, a fact he'd been very smug about her whole life. He made her feel young, with that smugness, an uncle in all but blood. He let her be weak. A sniffle left her as he fluffed up the pillow. Tears budded at the corner of her eyes.

"I'm so scared, Galen."

He sighed, placing a hand on her head for a moment, just as she would for her daughters. "I know. But she's a Petranski, Kass, and your family breeds them tough. She'll come back to the nest, I'm sure of it. Let's just focus on making sure you're upright to see it, hmn?" He patted her shoulder softly. She could only nod, but the tears came freely now and harder than before, permission finally given for the dam to break.

"I'd like to be alone," she managed through gulping breaths, thick with tears and mucus.

"Alright, dear. Ring the bell if you need anything. I'll be around for a while longer to talk to your maid." With that, he rose, making his way out the door. When it closed behind him, she truly gave in, wracking sobs filling the room.

⸻

IT HURT MAGDOVA IN WAYS she could barely comprehend to see her like that. Her mother, her unbreakable mother, crumbling. She and Kassandra, who was practically glued to her hip these days, had planned to go and check on her and make sure she was alright. Kassandra had been sure a hug would've helped, but as the pair looked in through the barely opened door, Magdova knew there was no making this better. Not until Syline came home safe, and if her mother was crying like this, they must still be no closer to finding her than the day she'd disappeared. Her mother had her head in her hands, her entire body rocking with the weight of her sobs of her despair. Beside her, Kassandra whimpered to see it, tears beginning to well up.

"Hey, hey, shhh," Magdova whispered, pulling her back from the door and clicking it closed before she hefted her sister up. She wanted to cry so badly herself, to give in, to scream and rave and beg the gods to bring her sister back, but right now, they both needed her to be strong. Her mother needed this space and her sister needed a shoulder, so she gave her hers, hefting Kassandra into her arms and stroking her hair as she carried her away. It was for the best that her sister buried her head into her shoulder when she began to bawl. It meant she didn't see how Magdova's lips quivered.

Please, Wanderer, guide her road home, she prayed, for it was the only thing she had left.

⸻

THELONIOUS FACED DOWN THE CREATURE before him. It looked tormented, but he knew full well that wouldn't make it any less dangerous. It was horrific, and was far, far larger than him. *You don't need to kill it,* he told himself, you just need to hold it back. *You just need to survive. You just need to keep it away from Syline. Give her time.*

The creature let out another awful undulating, distorted roar and the smell of its breath – rotten eggs, pus and acid – brought his gorge up. It reared up, fore-tentacles writhing wildly. It was hard to keep track of them, harder still to tell how to reply. So, he went on the offensive. He had no faith in his ability to defend against something this big. There was little room around the aberration, no way he could squeeze past it or get behind it. Staying afar would only have it charge in closer and pressure Syline all the more, so he'd have to get in close and keep those awful tentacles busy as best he could. Thelonious let out another battle cry, ducking the first lash of one of its tentacles. It used them as whips, lashing at the air around him rather than just swiping wildly. Maybe they weren't as strong as they looked. Still, after a glancing blow to his shoulder nearly tore it from its socket, he was certain he wouldn't be getting back up if those hit him head-on.

He ran for its front. Reared back, it was exposing its underbelly, which was formed entirely from scar tissue that showed signs that looked worryingly like suture marks, unlike the scaley, hard flesh on its back. This close, it hopefully wouldn't be able to bring its whips to bear. He swung for its chest. He didn't expect to do any real damage to a monster like this, but he had to make sure it didn't lose interest in him. It let out a shriek that shook the walls as thick, brown blood smelling of vomit and salt wept from the wound. If it bled, he could kill it.

Thelonious felt a bit more confidence brimming up in him. It was big, but it was wild. He might be able to deal with this thing, after all. He'd been right in his guess that it would have a harder time bringing its tentacles to bear right up close to it, but that didn't mean it was defenceless. By no means was it that. Thelonious found himself immediately on the back foot again as it swung its head down to bite at him with its distorted, equine-like, blocky teeth. Thelonious scrambled backwards, the creature's awful, foetid spittle showering over his face. He forced down his gorge yet again as it pushed him back far enough to have Syline at his back, a bite scraping off one of his pauldrons and denting the steel in against his flesh.

Damn his curiosity, why'd they have to come down here?

—

WHILE THELONIOUS WAS FIGHTING ONE gigantic horror, Amberly had been tasked with taking on many smaller ones. None were quite as horrifying as the beast breathing down her neck, but Syline was certain she'd be having nightmares about these things all the same. A dozen, maybe more, of the shambling, melted flesh horrors advanced towards her with the finality of a death sentence. Syline was trapped between both fights, forced to keep an eye on both as they closed in on her. The silhouettes looked as if they had once been people – deep elves to be specific, considering the nearly black, purplish flesh. It wasn't right to call it skin anymore.

Each of the creatures looked as if they'd been placed in a sculptor's kiln and left in until their flesh was runny and soft, just like so much clay. Then, whatever mad sculptor had created these monstrosities, had flicked and played with them, adding new parts: a horn here, tentacles there, a third arm there, it was hard to tell their exact numbers with their silhouettes so distorted, so wrong. These extra parts looked solid and thought over, but the rest of them were never fixed, their flesh runny and hanging in great folds from their body. To be them must be sheer, never-ending agony, but looking in their eyes, Syline could see nothing. No emotion, no flicker of sentience. They were empty shells.

While Thelonious pushed the huge, draconic monstrosity back, Amberly had been fighting hard against the creatures, striving to drive them away. She managed to dodge between them and fight unabated for the most part. Watching her left Syline jealous. She did such an astonishing job managing so many foes at once and her expertise with Syline's own sword far exceeded anything she'd ever managed. She might even be a match for Kat. Only once did they manage to land a blow on her, but that single blow floored the demon hunter, letting the horrific monsters get to Syline. She scrambled away and frantically cast a flame dagger from her staff. She swung it back and forth, screaming as she tried to drive them back. Drive them back she did. The creatures had seemed terrified of the flames, and hurriedly moved away from her, some even breaking their silence to wail as they retreated.

"Syline!" Amberly said, looking back to her with a twinkle in her eye, "find the biggest fire spell you can cast."

—

THE CREATURE LUNGED IN FOR a bite, which Thelonious met with an over-the-shoulder slice that cleft its muzzle. It reared back, squealing and very nearly took his sword with it. He yanked it back with a curse, just in time to see the bone he'd cracked beneath the flesh already knitting itself back together. The wound he'd left on its chest was doing the same. Okay, maybe he wouldn't be able to kill it after all, but he could annoy it, at least.

"Any luck, Syline?" he called. If this thing regenerated from whatever he did, then she was their only real hope.

"Nothing for flying, yet! Amberly has something in mind!" Syline squealed behind him.

She was on her knees, frantically flipping through pages as Amberly held back the oncoming horde. *Come on, come on, she had to have something!* Syline could feel the panic rising in her breast, her friends needed her magic. Here and now, she was literally their only solution and none of the spells she had bookmarked or memorised were useful at this moment. She glanced across another page in her frantic search: a great cone of flame, a simple spell, but one that only grew more powerful the more one's reserves were poured into it.

"Keep looking!" Thelonious called to her, leaping to the side to avoid a lashing tentacle. He swung down at it, lopping it off, the severed end wriggling wildly. The creature retracted the tentacle, squealing. It'd probably grow back in a few moments, but that did give him an idea. He ran towards the beast, dancing around tentacles, then he heard Syline cry out behind him.

"I've got one, Amberly!"

"Use it!" came the panicked reply.

He didn't have time to look back; he could only pray they'd manage. For now, well, he'd spent enough time at a lumber town to know how to chop something down to size. It might be able to heal from any wound, but if he cut off all its tentacles, surely even *it* would take a while to come back from that.

—

AMBERLY HAD JUST ENOUGH TIME to scramble to the side of the hall as Syline unleashed her spell. Flames washed over the hall from behind her, and immediately, the horde she'd been holding back erupted in distorted wails, the smell of burning meat overpowering even their natural acrid stench.

"Great! Do the same for Thelonious!" Amberly said, leaping back into the fray. She grabbed Syline's axe off her as she went, and Syline let out a little cry. She didn't mind lending her duelling sabre, but that axe was special. Though, as Amberly started taking heads left and right with it, she thought it best not to argue. She was putting it to good use.

Syline felt pride well up in her. She hated feeling worthless, and between the two warriors, able to do little else but scour her spell-book for a way to get them all out of this situation, for the whole of the fight, she'd felt like little but added weight, until now. Her flames had set the awful creatures Amberly was facing on the back foot, and Syline was glad to watch the woman wade into them with abandon, the wounds she inflicted no longer healing, foul brackish blood leaking from porous, burned flesh. Perhaps they could win this, after all, if the secret to these hideous creatures was that they couldn't take flames. If it worked on the small ones, it might work on the terrible beast Thelonious was holding at bay.

She found him ankle deep in torn flesh and severed tentacles, each cut off as fast as the beast could grow them. Thelonious was chopping them off again and again, but it didn't seem to be getting him anywhere. The creature was wild with fury and Thelonious had a fair few bite marks and gashes in his flesh now from where it had gotten a hold of him. One of his arms seemed slow and Syline could see him wincing with every swing. He was just barely managing to keep ahead of it. Thank heavens it wasn't smart enough to bring its rear tentacles to bare. If things kept progressing like this, it was only a matter of time until Thelonious tired so much that it truly caught him.

"Thelonious!" Syline shouted.

They couldn't flee at this point. She hadn't found anything, at least not anything that would get all three of them out. The stupid tome was hundreds of pages long and with no real organisation to it. It was like the archmage had just scribbled down the spells as he found them, and chances are, he had. That left their only methods of escaping this place victory, or death.

"Bit busy, Syline!" A tentacle burst out of a stump, growing as fast as it was moving, and it was moving right for Syline. Thelonious roared as he swung down at it. He caught it a moment too late, and not hard enough. The tentacle struck Syline in the side of her chest, and she was thrown from her feet. She barely managed to cover her head to stop herself from taking any real damage as she tumbled across the stone, standing as quick as she was able.

"Shitting hells! Sorry! What is it?" Thelonious yelled back her way, returning to the fray with new fury.

"Duck! Then aim for anywhere I hit!"

She was heartened to see that her bodyguard had faith enough in her to duck without any further questions, immediately he hit the floor, and Syline let the flames surge out of her, rolling over the creature. This time, she wasn't just going to sit here and let others fight. If they were going to have to kill this thing, then she'd be right there in the thick of it. She conjured up her flame dagger from the tip of her staff, making it as strong as she dared. She was certain she'd grown more powerful because, despite the magics she'd been putting out, she was sure she had plenty to spare yet. Blade of flame ready, she charged in after her wave of flames to join her bodyguard.

<hr />

SYLINE SAID, "DUCK," SO HE went down. When he came up, it was like he was entering a whole new fight. The creature was screaming, but now, fear had entered alongside that mad, unending pain. Now, it knew they were a real threat. The creature's flesh bubbled and blackened, blisters bursting forth and popping immediately beneath the flames, and thick, foul-smelling blood oozed from the cracks and sores left in its flesh. This thing definitely didn't like fire. Best of all, to Thelonious, Syline had caught its front tentacles in the blast, and the things wriggled and writhed like dying snakes right up until he hacked them off at the base. This time, they didn't grow back.

The creature was on the defensive now, but that didn't mean it wasn't going to fight back. Its huge maw came for Thelonious, and he knew full well he could only meet it head on with his blade. His already aching arm would give out. He'd be lucky if it didn't shatter. Hell, he'd be lucky to survive this.

But none of that ever came to pass. As it came at him, Syline, that stupid, brave little wizard came running in at his side, screaming a high-pitched battle cry full of fear and forced bravado. She jabbed at the creature's eyes with that flaming staff of hers, and suddenly the fear was back in its cries. Rearing back, it pulled away from them as Syline harried it with the flames. Thelonious allowed himself to release the breath he didn't know he'd been holding. A cold feeling of relief washing through his form like a cool breeze.

Then, reality, oh so quickly, caught up with him again. Syline was in a melee with that beast. Syline, his tiny, stupidly brave and terrifyingly frail ward. Panic rushed through him; if a glancing hit could nearly tear out his shoulder, its attacks passing *near* her might well kill Syline. He ran in after Syline and set to slashing at the beast's chest and shoulders. He aimed for its head whenever it came in reach, but it was smart enough to keep that at the top of the tunnel, away from the flames. At this point, its face was badly burned – along with much of its chest – and Syline's spear of fire was leaving deep, black wounds with every jab. She must've been eating through her magical energy damned fast to burn it that hot, but they were winning.

But when a beast like this is put in a corner, it's at its most dangerous. He knew that, still, he let bravado and cheer at seeing that they were winning, get the better of him. That's why he felt they had no one to blame but him when the creature's rear tentacle came over its shoulder, coiled around Syline's waist and lifted her screaming into the air. He should've known it would go for the source of the flames, since the cuts he inflicted only seemed to annoy it. Syline's staff clattered to the ground and Thelonious cursed as the creature began shaking her back and forth. He *had* to kill it now. There was no way they were leaving without Syline.

"Thelonious!"

He looked behind him. Amberly was sprinting his way, Syline's axe held in both hands.

"Give me a lift!"

It took a moment for it to click with him just what she meant, but when it did, he could barely keep a grin off his face. Both these girls were lunatics. At least things were definitely lively with them around. Thelonious dropped his sword and cupped his hands together, going low on his haunches to get ready. Amberly came sprinting at him and the moment her foot hit his cupped hands, he pitched her up, throwing with all his might. He roared as he felt his right shoulder give way; that one would hurt for weeks. But it did what it needed to, and Amberly went right up over his head, high enough to meet the creature eye-to-eye as she screamed her own battle cry. The creature had time enough to meet her gaze – and probably wonder just what in the hell she thought she was doing – before Amberly buried the axe in its forehead, the whole of the axe head sinking deep into the burned flesh and bone.

Just like that, it was over. The wax-work elves had already moved like puppets, but that image was impressed upon them all the more as the draconic creature collapsed to the ground as if its strings had been cut. Syline squealed as the tentacle flailing her about suddenly went slack and she landed upon another one, severed upon the ground. A better landing, at least, than if she had fallen straight onto the stone. Amberly tucked and rolled as she hit the stone, more athletic than Syline, she came up standing and clutching her side.

None of them escaped the fight without injury. Syline's sides would surely bruise, something had definitely pulled in her stomach as she was shaken, and her breathing was laboured as she struggled to catch it. Thelonious was nursing a sprained – possibly broken – elbow, and his shoulder was in no better state. Amberly had broken at least two ribs and had taken another blow to her shoulder when she'd been clearing up the burned and flailing waxy horde.

But the fact remained they had won. It took a few moments to sink in for all of them. All three just stood, looking at one another and catching their breath until, slowly, grins began to break out on all their faces. Amberly was the first to start laughing and Syline quickly followed, but it was Thelonious who laughed the loudest. He punched the air and immediately regretted it, but that didn't stop his victorious roar. They'd done it.

The two girls joined him, all three yelling until their voices echoed through the terrifying place. This time, nothing roared back at them, only the echoes of their victory. The place was dead again. Once more, it was a tomb for them to explore. The oppressive air that had hung over the place had fallen away, as if it had come with the creatures, and faded with their deaths. Still full of adrenaline, Syline looked between the pair of them.

"Should we explore a little more? I mean we know how to beat them now!"

Thelonious burst out laughing. Gods, she was so brave, so damned utterly mad. One big meaty hand came to muss with Syline's hair, provoking a pout from the girl.

"A little further then, just a few rooms, but the moment I feel like we're in danger, we run for it. Okay?" Thelonious offered as a compromise. Gods, even if they did know how to fight these things, he doubted he could take another battle. Neither could the girls, despite Syline's enthusiasm, he could see how hard a time she was having trying to catch her breath and he doubted it was just the adrenaline.

"I'm doing the best out of us, let me lead the way," Amberly offered. "Besides, if these things were demons." She let out a slow breath, the smell of them was sending the memories soaring through her mind. "If they were demons, we need to make sure this place can't summon more."

Thelonious gave a slight shrug in response. That was as good a reason as any. Though he did worry about the fervour in her tone when it came to demons, after all, those things hadn't attacked until she'd kicked things off.

Syline refreshed the lights hovering at their shoulders, and with Amberly taking the lead, they pushed through into the chamber the creatures had come from. The butt of Amberly's borrowed blade pushing aside the remnants of the door frame.

Syline gagged. Thelonious swore. Corax leapt out of Syline's scarf where he'd been cowering the whole while to flutter up to the rim of the exit. Only Amberly seemed to not be overtly affected.

The place was a charnel house. Fused flesh and melted bodies covered the walls and floor, more of those same waxwork elves, writhing, still living, but fused into a helpless mass. It was like they were dough, mashed into the corners of the room by their more whole compatriots. Who knows how long they had been here. Who knows how long it had taken for them to be reduced to this state. Questing tendrils and unformed arms reached up towards them as they entered.

Syline vomited. Bile and acid burned at her throat as the acrid stink filled her nostrils.

Thelonious looked at her; his scarf held over his mouth.

"Wait outside, Syline," he told her.

He was trying to ignore the fact that the face in the ground she had vomited on was still moving. Trembling, Syline nodded limply and retreated to wait by the door.

"We need to burn this place," Amberly said, more to the room and to herself than Thelonious.

"Not gonna argue that, but not 'til we're leaving, I don't want to suffocate," he replied, careful with his steps as he moved towards the back of the room. A glint of metal had caught his eye.

"Will there be more rooms like this? More of these... horrors?"

"I couldn't say. If there are, I'd say that's a problem for Syline's pa. It's well beyond us. Let's not die here today and just settle for the finder's fee."

"But what if these things." Amberly paused, turning to see Thelonious pushing to the back of the room, using the tip of his blade to push flesh aside. "What are you doing?"

"I saw something. I don't think we're the first ones to find this place."

Thelonious reached down, a hand reached up to him, he took it, and pulled. The sound of waxy flesh peeling from the stone would haunt him for a long time, but a great lump was dislodged, to shudder and wail quietly, as he found what he'd looked for. There was a man under there. Not a monster, not one of these waxwork horrors. A man. His body had long since rotten, but the leather and metal of his armour remained. As did his sword. That was what had caught Thelonious' eye. It was a bastard sword, like his, but of much finer make than his weathered blade. The edge was almost sky blue, fading to near black at the centre of the blade, and the crossguard was shaped into the form of two sets of antlers, rising from the centre. The hilt was two different types of wood, lovingly wound together into a single, firm grip.

Thelonious let out a whistle, prying the blade from the man's grip. He pulled out two silver coins from his purse and placed them into the man's hand in its place.

"Sorry, fella, bad way to go," he murmured, wishing him an easy journey to wherever he wound up. He looked to Amberly, lifting the sword.

"Well, would you look at that," she cooed. "Looks like tundra elf make, though bastard swords aren't usually their style, as far as I know. Maybe it was a commission."

"Either way, it's real nice. I'll get Syline to check if it's magic for me when we have the chance," Thelonious said, managing to put a bit of a brighter shine on this place, at least for himself. "Wonder how the poor bastard got down here…" He trailed off, then looked to Amberly. "Are we happy to get out of here now?"

Amberly nodded. "For now, if Syline's father doesn't come here in force, I'm finding someone who will."

They retreated from the chamber and found Syline finishing off the dregs of her waterskin, trying to clear her mouth of the taste of vomit. She jumped slightly when Thelonious said her name and turning to look at them, cheeks flushed.

"It's time we got out of here," Thelonious told her, "but not before you burn that place to the ground."

Syline gulped. Pulling her scarf up around her nose.

"Alright, but it's your fault if I throw up again."

WITH THE AWFUL STENCH OF burning flesh, and a few pitiful wails of pain following after them, Thelonious helped the two girls up through the hole, and it was with a fair bit of groans and pain that they pulled the far heavier hellblooded up with them. With that, the trio set off back to the surface.

"I swear, if the blizzard still hasn't ended," Syline joked as they walked. She was moving with the aid of her staff and was still finding it a bit hard to get her breath. Still, her good mood was having a hard time fading; she couldn't deny the rush that came with coming out victorious against such a seemingly impossible challenge.

"Well, we'll just have to find something else to kill," Amberly said, shooting her a grin. "You were the real hero of that fight, Syline. No way we would have won without those flames. Shame you couldn't find a spell to get us out, but I suppose, in the end, it didn't matter."

Syline smiled but let the conversation trail away. She was struggling to keep walking, let alone talking and the visions of that awful room kept playing through her mind. Thelonious seemed to realise this for, without asking for a word of permission, her bodyguard came up behind her and swept the little mage up into his arms in a bridal carry. She felt a rush of fear, followed by a little guilty thrill at it but didn't argue, resting into him even as Amberly gave Syline a cheeky grin. It slowly faded as she stared at Thelonious and the trio kept walking.

Finally, she asked, "So, you said Laes might be your father?"

"Could be." He paused. "I mean, Ma did say it was a proper half-devil. Don't think there's all that many of them running around the kingdom."

"Right." Amberly looked conflicted. She let out a little sigh and looked to the ground as she walked, nursing her hip.

"I don't suppose," she put in. "I don't suppose you'd know a way to summon him?"

"Sorry, Amberly. Never met him and I'm no warlock just 'cos I'm a hellblooded. From what you told me about him though, he seems a pretty good one to have as a father. Shame I never met him."

"Maybe we can." Syline coughed and wriggled out of Thelonious' grip; it was starting to feel awkward, being the only one not walking. It wasn't as bad with just her and Thelonious, but with another girl forging on, it made her feel like the odd, weak one out. "Maybe we can find a way to summon him when we have a bit more access to components. I'm sure the book has something on summonings, but from what I know, summoning an outsider involves a bit more than just the incantation and magic, so it'll probably have to wait until this is all over."

Amberly shot her a little smile, nodding her thanks. With that, the trio largely fell silent. The going was hard enough with their wounds to spend too much time speaking. It took them a fair bit longer than the walk down had, but eventually, they found their way back to the surface and the rather ecstatic Alma. Corax fluttered out from where he'd been hiding in Syline's robes during it all, to land on the horse's head as the horse butted it into Thelonious' chest. The hellblooded let out a laugh as he stroked at the horse's ears.

"It's so cute that she worries about you," Syline said, smiling at the exchange.

"Me and this horse go a long way back. People don't think horses care, but I think they're a lot like dogs, at the end of the day. You care for a horse and that horse will care for you." He patted the horse's neck before fetching off her saddle bags a bag of salted, dried meats.

He let the girls grab however much they wanted, before getting a good and proper handful himself and shoving most of it into his mouth. It only occurred to him then that he hadn't eaten yet that day.

"Wonder what time it is," Thelonious mused, heading for the cave entrance. Alma tailed him, and Syline and Amberly quickly followed, chewing on their "breakfast". He had to shovel out a fair bit of snow, cupping his hands and flinging it away to free the entrance enough for them to get out. While the blizzard had raged on, it had filled the entrance to the cave enough so they'd have a bit of a hard time getting Alma out. The storm was over, though the snow sat heavy on the ground. The sky was finally clear, bright and blue setting the snow in a sparkling array.

One by one, they eventually made their way out with a bit of pushing from the girls to get Alma to dive into the snow, the horse's legs sinking deep into it. The trio shared quiet smiles, enjoying the warmth of the sun upon them before Syline finally said, "What now? Where do we go?"

"Well," Thelonious started, "I suppose we can start by heading back north."

"You can start by dropping your weapons and getting on your knees," said a woman in dark leathers waiting at the entrance in the clearing beyond, flanked by a monstrous hound. "I've got a message from Lady Jane and there's no reason for this to get violent."

Four men stepped out from behind the trees ahead, aiming their bows at the trio.

"So, I strongly suggest all three of you play nice."

Chapter 14

THELONIOUS WAS THE FIRST ONE to drop his weapon, slipping off the harness that held his bastard sword and doing his best to make it very clear that he had no intention of drawing it. Syline followed suit, dropping her axe along with her staff.

"And the spell-books!" called the woman. "Both on the ground, and a wand if you have one."

The archers all trained their bows on Syline. They knew that, at this distance, she was the only one who could pose a threat to them. Syline sighed and lowered her satchel to the ground, then pulled her wand – which seemed insignificant beside the staff now – and placed it inside the bag. She held up her hands to show they were empty. Now, only Amberly had not given up her weapons. The leader of these hunters let out a soft chuckle.

"Keep your blade if you must, little paladin. We all know you're no threat now your god's abandoned you." Her voice was melodic, playful. Syline swore she heard Amberly growl louder than that demonic hound.

"Anyway."

The woman clapped her hands before her, seemingly a signal, because two of her men stepped in front of her, lowering their bows and drawing short swords. The rest of them seemed to relax somewhat, their bowstrings lax.

"Lady Petrov has sent me here to make you an offer, resolve this peacefully. Isn't that nice of her?" she cooed, sickly sweet. Brushing her hand through short cropped blonde hair.

In black leathers, with short hair, daggers all over her body and a scar across her lip that put her face in a permanent sneer, the woman looked like she'd put work into perfecting the image of dangerous beauty.

She stood, waiting, expectant. It took Thelonious nudging her for Syline to realise she was waiting for her to reply.

Syline did her best to seem confident and in control. In her mind, she ran through every incantation she had memorised and wondered if she'd be able to use a single one of them before the woman's men filled her with arrows. She'd need her staff to use them anyway, so really, she was helpless. Gulping down her fears, she stepped forward. Amberly began to as well, but Thelonious, the calm presence amongst them, grabbed her by the arm. At that moment, he did not trust Amberly to not go rushing at them. The fire and fury in her eyes were enough to burn a thousand sinners. Syline was left desperately trying to hide her fears behind an air of bravado as she racked her brain for what a hero from one of her books would do now.

She gulped again against the dryness in her mouth before stammering out, "It's proper to introduce yourself before speaking to a noblewoman!"

The woman laughed playfully, a grin breaking out on her features.

"Oh. Where. Are. My. Manners? Here I was, talking to you as if you were just a fellow adventurer but oh no, no, you're Syline Petranski. Mustn't forget that. My apologies, Lady Petranski." She lowered herself in a mocking bow. "I am Teagan Austere, and this is Yaldabaoth."

She patted the head of the demon before her who snarled; its lips pulling back until its muzzle was nothing but muscle and bone. It had a terrible intelligence in its eyes. It wasn't just a simple hound, and its eyes locked wholly on Amberly.

"There," she continued. "Does that settle your sensibilities, milady?"

Syline's nose wrinkled and her brow furrowed. She really didn't know what to do from here and she couldn't think of anything to say, so she simply nodded.

"Lady Petrov has, well, actually, more than a deal it's probably better to call this an ultimatum."

"Get to the point," said Thelonious.

"Thank you," said one of Teagan's henchmen in the back.

"Fine, fine." The woman grumbled something to herself before standing up straight and addressing Syline.

"Your mother and your mentor have both been poisoned. He has maybe three nights, her, a fortnight. Obviously, we couldn't target a noble-head with an *obvious* poison, but no one's going to miss an old archivist."

Her voice was sickly sweet, the grin never fading. That sent shock radiating through Syline's form. This was the worst possible outcome to her. They had gone after her family: her mother, and the man she thought of as much like a father. They couldn't reach her, so they hurt those they could. It was her fault; it was all her fault. A strangled gasp wracked her, tears coming to her eyes.

"Now, now, no need to cry, love. No need to cry," Teagan said, waving her hands to calm her. "All *you* have to do is hand over the book and disappear. Leave the kingdom with your friends here, and don't come back. Then, they'll both get cured."

As Syline reeled from the suggestion, Teagan distracted herself, looking up at the sky and tapping her chin. Whilst she did, her demonic hound pulled forwards on its chain, getting closer to Amberly and Thelonious, intent on ripping the hellblooded and the ex-paladin alike to shreds. Amberly's face was just as ferocious as the hound's, but she seemed to be forcibly holding herself back, not giving into the fury she had earlier in the place below. The beast snarled, eyes flicking between them, but when Amberly spat at her feet and let out a snarl of her own, its eyes settled fully on her.

"Tell you what, this wasn't in the deal, but I hate making a cute thing cry, so, when we escort you south, you can write a letter to your mother. Tell her you're okay, as long as you make it very clear not to raise a fuss and not to come looking for you. I'll deliver it to her myself. Unseen of course. Isn't that kind of me?"

"Syline, only you can make this choice," Thelonious said, but it was clear what he thought the correct choice was.

There was no winning this. Her family, the people she cared for, were in danger, but this would mean she'd never get to see them again. She'd never get to go home. Never get to finish this. She'd lost. She sighed, the fight going out of her as she limply picked up the satchel, making it very clear she was not trying to open it. Holding it out in front of her, she slowly approached Teagan, who moved to do the same, her swagger full of pomp and confidence.

"You're making the smart choice," Teagan assured her, placing a hand atop the satchel. Then, a roar shook the world. The demonic hound couldn't abide Amberly any longer: it tore from its chains and leapt for the paladin. Teagan cursed as she leapt back, yelling for both her archers and the hound. In the next instant, Amberly had rolled beneath the leaping hellhound and was running for Teagan and Syline, Teagan's nearest guard moved to intercept. Amberly met the guard in full charge, her blade smashing his aside before plunging deep into his heart. Ahead of her, archers readied their bows, and the paladin held on tight to the man.

Syline still stood, holding out the satchel waiting for someone to take it, tears in her eyes and mind filled with thoughts of never seeing her sisters again. She hadn't caught up with the world as it went mad around her.

With all that going on, few noticed Thelonious had pulled a hidden blade from within his armour before he grabbed Teagan by the wrist, his face contorted in anger. The hellblooded yanked her close and stabbed his blade into her side. The woman screamed but was able to kick him off and pull away, retreating behind her men with her hand at her side.

Both archers loosed arrows at Amberly, which impacted into the corpse, the dead man making for a charnel shield. Teagan was in full retreat. Thelonious threw Syline behind him as some arrows were loosed their way, blocked and deflected by the man's armour. Only a few moments had passed since Yaldabaoth had yanked free.

It'd taken Syline that long to realise what was happening. Reality snapped back to her. The choice had been taken away from her, they were fighting anyway, even though she'd tried to make the smart choice. Even though she hadn't rushed in blindly this time.

"Wait! Stop!" she cried out, from behind Thelonious. No one heard her, not even Thelonious seemed to hear her. "I agreed to your terms, we don't have to fight!" An arrow landed by her ankle and she leapt with a yelp. No one was listening. It was all falling apart and it was all because of that demon and—

And Amberly.

But it was too late to think about that now. Whose fault this was could come later, for now, she had to survive this. She threw the satchel's strap over her shoulder as she thought through what to do next. One man was dead already, a second mercenary was running after the pair of Amberly and Yaldabaoth. Teagan had produced a scroll and was speaking the trigger phase. Syline feared it was going to be a fireball until the fast bleeding on Teagan's side slowed, then stopped.

The last pair of men were drawing fresh arrows back, trained on

Thelonious. In the moment of chaos, he had dropped the dagger and grabbed the fallen mercenary's shortsword. He charged at them, drawing their focus wholly on him. One loosed their arrow before he could close the distance, and Thelonious caught it in the meat of his bicep with a growl. The other arrow went wide, and he was forced to relinquish his bow to Thelonious' off hand to avoid being yanked into the man's thrusting blade. Thelonious reflexively hurled it into the woods as he swung at the man, the blow barely parried by the first archer who had not even drawn his shortsword, simply catching the blade on the scabbard to save his comrade.

Help Amberly deal with the swordsman, Syline thought. *She knows best how to fight the demon. Then, stop the archers.* Thelonious could deal with the other three better than her, and once she eliminated this one, she could back him up. Keep an eye on Teagan in case she has more dangerous scrolls or items in her repertoire.

Syline thought it odd; she realised she wasn't all that afraid. At least, not for herself. Her main fears now were for her family. Right now, all she had was focus on getting out of this. If only that hellhound hadn't leapt, if she'd just been able to give the stupid book up. They couldn't die. Not for her curiosity. She had her spell-book. Thelonious and Amberly were both still armed. They had just bested far more terrible, if far more stupid, foes than this. They could defeat some hunters. With Thelonious keeping them busy, Syline had a few moments of respite and she used them to pull forth her beloved wand. The staff lay out of reach and she didn't dare waste any more time. What spells did she have memorised? The classic arcane missiles, a spell of vanishing, flame dagger, and the arcane mount. She hadn't bothered searching for anything new since she'd set out. The flame dagger wasn't worth much without her evocation staff, not in a full-fledged battle such as this. She'd have to make do with the arcane missiles. She hadn't the time to search the spell-book for a more powerful incantation just yet.

As she ran for the swordsman and Amberly, she spotted Thelonious' discarded dagger and grabbed it off the ground, even as she began her incantation. Syline didn't need to take aim; she simply raised her wand and from it came three arcane darts, one after the other with perfect accuracy at the ankle of the man harrying Amberly. She hadn't the strength of spell to kill him outright, but three magical darts to the ankle were enough to trip up most anyone.

The man stumbled to the ground, getting a face full of snow. Syline ran for him in that moment of weakness. She fell to one knee in her sprint and stabbed the blade into the back of his thigh. A painful wound, one that would leave him out of the fight and rolling in agony, but not a lethal one, she hoped, Thelonious or Amberly might've gone for a killing blow, but as long as he wasn't getting up, that was enough for her. The blade sank halfway to the hilt into his thigh. The man shrieked, shrill and incoherent with agony. Syline's heart fluttered with guilt before she forced it to harden.

Corax, startled, flew up and out of Syline's robes.

"Corax! Help Thelonious! Get in the archers' faces," she called to her brave little familiar, even as she prayed the bird would be alright as he flapped away.

Her eyes were on her goal ahead as she scrambled back to her feet past the man, her staff and axe left behind in the snow. She thrust her wand down her robes; if it fell out, she could retrieve it later. For now, it was fairly snug there. She went as low to the ground as she dared and didn't slow as she grabbed her staff and axe, actually skidding through the snow a bit as she turned back to the fight. She was out of breath already. That damned dragon beast had left her sides aching and she was still finding it hard to catch her breath.

Thelonious was harrying his foes, his sheer mass and rage pushing them back as they struggled to form a fighting front, but Teagan had joined the fight. Their numbers would give them an advantage if Syline didn't intercede. That came to her when one split off from the trio, his fellows redoubling their assault to stop Thelonious going after the man as he came for Syline, seeing the wizardess alone. She had her staff now and she felt a fair bit more confident with it in hand. The man was rushing for her at full pelt. He wore no true plate armour like Thelonious, just studded leathers, and carried a small buckler in one hand, a short, jagged blade in the other. He ran with it held back and the buckler forward as if expecting a blow to deflect.

Syline didn't give one to him, murmuring an incantation, she held the staff up as if to attack him with a spell and disappeared.

The man pulled up short and cursed, head turning this way and that. Syline ran to the side, but unexpectedly, the man followed. Heading straight for her. He swung wildly at the air and received a squeal as his blade opened a deep gash along Syline's bicep. She floundered, stumbling.

"I can see your feet in the snow, you daft bitch!" the man cackled.

Syline would have cursed herself a fool if she had time. Instead, she used the advantage she still had he couldn't see her movements. Nor could he see as she ducked under his next swing. Dropping her axe and grasping her staff in both hands, she stabbed it like a spear, right between the man's legs.

Her mother would curse her out for it, but in a battle where they were so massively outnumbered, Syline didn't feel all that bad for not fighting "fair". The man made a noise all too similar to a stuck pig, hands instinctively going to cover his crotch. Right as Syline's invisibility spell ended, she pulled the staff back, ready to stab the butt of it into his nose as he doubled over. That was when she felt a terrible weight slam into her back, and she found herself sent sprawling, pain blossoming all down her right side as she was thrown into the snow. Bounding past, both her and her opponent, was Yaldabaoth, Amberly on its back, barely holding on as the demonic creature bucked wildly.

Syline heard the crunch of foot on snow and turned just in time to hold her staff up, blocking the slash the man had thrown at her back. He bore over her, grabbing the staff and wrenching it down as he flipped his grip on his sword. Syline began to panic, not just at the situation but at the memories it brought out. Her heart raced. His face melded with that of the man in the woodshed. Syline kicked out, striking him in the crotch yet again. He held on, but his eyes widened. He tried to strike down, but she jerked her body to the side and the blade embedded in the snow, just beside her head. She screamed her defiance and kicked again and again, but the man's only reply was to wrap an arm around her throat and hold her in place as he slowly brought his dagger down to her. His grip was shaking, his eyes watering, but he didn't let go.

Syline had begun to cry as well, tears streaming down her face as fear really did fill her now, when the man suddenly tumbled off her in a heap with Amberly, who had leapt from Yaldabaoth's back to protect Syline as they passed. The man shoved her off and Amberly was quick to her feet. The man was a fair sight slower, his legs shaking with agony, but he still managed to deflect Amberly's opening thrusts on his buckler. That did little to help him, however, when Syline rose, trembling with terror and trauma-fuelled fury and came running in behind Amberly, swinging her staff at his knee like it was a great club. A most terrible crunch followed as the man's leg bent in entirely the wrong direction. He screamed, tumbling to the ground, holding his leg and shuddering, as he still vaguely waved his buckler above him to protect himself.

Content that he was no longer a threat, both girls left him there. Syline turned to Amberly, smiling through the pain wracking her.

"Thanks, er, thanks Amberly." She couldn't get it out of her mind that this fight only began because of Amberly and that creature.

Amberly didn't reply. Instead, she interrupted any further words by grabbing Syline and tackling her into the snow right as a rush of flame went over both their heads. Amberly's beautiful, white hair blackened and burned. Her robes smouldered and she grit her teeth against the pain. Syline screamed as Amberly fell over ribs which were most surely broken now, even if they hadn't been before. Amberly rolled up to her feet, facing Yaldabaoth once more. She offered a hand down and helped yank Syline up to her feet to face the beast with her. Flames still licked at its chops as the beast snarled at them, pawing at the snow, ready to charge.

"Syline, I've got an idea. Hold your staff out sideways."

The beast was charging. Syline didn't question it; she did as she was told, and Amberly grabbed the head of it.

"Rush it!" she yelled, and with a fair bit of wincing from Syline, both returned the hound's charge.

It seemed almost confused by this suicidal bravery, but it was too late for it to pull back from its charge; the pair met the joint of its front legs with the staff. It very nearly yanked Amberly from her feet, and indeed, Syline did go tumbling into the snow, but so did the beast. Its balance thrown off, it slipped on the snow and went end over end with a shocked yelp.

Amberly had run for Yaldabaoth before the beast had even stopped tumbling. Syline pushed herself up to her feet, holding onto her staff for support as she watched Amberly leap at the wolf. Syline's duelling sword held in both hands, she plunged it down into the demon's eye. It squealed, bucking and heaving side to side, but Amberly did not relent, pressing deeper and deeper until the beast went limp and began to burn away into nothing. Its death in this world, banishing it back to its own.

Yanking the blade from the dog's skull with a grim satisfied expression, Amberly ran right after Thelonious, and Syline was soon to follow, though she struggled to keep up with her friend. The cut on her arm and the wracking pain in her chest was practically crippling her by this point, to say nothing of how hard it made it to catch her breath, which had escaped her long ago.

The pair found the fight at something of a standstill, though the way the fight was going was all too obvious. Corax flapped about the fight madly, cawing and screeching but never getting close enough to make a difference. The warriors ignored him. Teagan and her fellow fighter raining blows down upon Thelonious with a quartet of short swords, too fast for him to truly keep up with a weapon that was not even his own. The bodyguard had his back to a tree by now, and dozens of little cuts showed across his arms and any gap in his armour. The two lighter foes had taken a few blows from him in return. Teagan favoured her left leg, and one of her eyes was sealing shut, a cut above it weeping blood. Her fellow was missing fingers on his left hand and had a bad gash on his hip. But those were all Thelonious had managed in that time and he was being worn down, his breath coming to him in wet, gasping gulps.

Just as things were beginning to look very desperate indeed for Thelonious, salvation came, with a yell from Amberly as she ran into the fray.

"Your dog's dead, Teagan! Want to join him?" For a split second, Teagan's eyes flashed away. Corax – and in turn, Thelonious – were quick to take advantage.

The little familiar flew into Teagan's face, scratching and pecking. The woman let out a scream, grabbing at the bird and hurling it away to hit a tree with a squawk, but that gave Thelonious the opening he needed. Batting aside an attack from her fellow on his bracer, Thelonious hacked down brutally at Teagan. Her life was saved by a desperate defence as she threw her arm in the way. Her hand hit the snow with a wet thump. Teagan screamed anew, stumbling back and falling off her feet as she stared, aghast at the stump turning the snow around her into a red vista. She frantically scrabbled for a bottle on her hip.

Amberly joined Thelonious against the remaining mercenary, and though he matched them in the number of blades, he could not match them in ferocity. Thelonious hammered away, shaking the man's arm with every blow as Amberly snaked in, stabbing again and again. It was all he could do to dodge the majority. But he could not dodge the arcane darts that flew unerringly through the storm of blades, impacting once, twice into his stomach. He gasped for breath, blood flecking his lips, his guard thrown off completely. Thelonious brought back his fist and sent it into the man's temple, and he joined all his fellows in the snow. Thelonious looked past the man, to see Teagan tossing an empty vial aside, her stump healed over as she stood, remaining hand drawing a shaking blade. Fear was in her eyes now.

"Put it down. The fight's over, grab your wounded and get out of my sight," he grunted angrily to her before turning to look behind him. Amberly and Syline were both in sorry states, but the mercenary had to know she was beaten. Syline's bird's wing hung at an awkward angle as he waddled pathetically to its master where she leaned, gasping against a tree and pale as a ghost.

The man Syline had stabbed in the thigh was back on his feet, but with only one ally still standing, the fight was out of him. He had no intention of getting himself killed today. He'd left his weapons behind and sat on a snowdrift, packing the snow in against his wounded thigh to slow the bleeding and numb the pain. Thelonious looked from Teagan to him and waved his hand.

"Well! Get going!" he roared.

Teagan faltered a second, looking to her horses, her supplies. Thelonious was in no mood for bargaining. It had been a damned long day facing these mercenaries right after that mess in the depths. He shook his head and waved her off.

"Thelonious," Syline said from behind him, catching on to his line of thinking.

"What? Syline?" He turned to look at her, bloodied, breathless, irritated, but when he saw her flinch away at his tone, he forced himself to calm down, running a hand down his face. "What is it?" he asked in a softer tone.

"You're not really going to send them out there with nothing, are you? It's the middle of winter."

"Why shouldn't we?" Amberly asked. "It's not like they'd do us the same kindness if our positions were flipped."

"She's right, Syline, you know damn well this woman would kill us all given the chance," he said, waving his blade pointedly at Teagan, as her man slouched towards her. Syline shook her head, looking between her two friends… comrades. She knew it had been a long day but that didn't excuse thinking like that. That wasn't how you were meant to act. You honour your opponent even in defeat. She'd learned quickly that the real world didn't always work like that, but that didn't mean she couldn't make it.

"Just because she would, doesn't mean we should. We're better than that."

"Syline that's a nice sentiment but–"

"What about a trade?" said Teagan.

Thelonious turned, rubbing his temple, looking between her and Syline, who he knew he would not win this argument with. "We're listening."

Chapter 15

HOLDING THE STUMP OF HER wrist, Teagan made her offer.

"I tell Lady Jane that all three of you are dead and I have the book. You get out of the country, so she can't catch us if she ever finds you alive," she said with a tiny smirk, looking back to her man. "She doesn't think of you as a threat, you're just some girl with her book. She won't be in that much of a hurry to check on how quick we are in getting back to her with it, so you'll probably have about, oh, maybe two weeks to disappear?"

"How're you going to do that? How can we trust you?" Thelonious crossed his arms over his chest. "We can't follow you back to Russenholde."

"If you can manage a sending, little missy. We'll do it that way, the con would fall apart right away if I showed up in Russenholde without the book or at least your head," she said, looking at Syline. "I don't know what kind of spells you've got in your book, but if you can manage one. You can all watch, listen in, make sure I don't say anything wrong. I don't know how quick you'll be able to manage it though. Sendings need special materials. That's why we had Yaldabaoth, that wild mutt could do it without them. She only taught me the command phrases to get him to send messages if I needed to."

"And what do you want in exchange?" Amberly asked.

"Just let us keep our supplies, enough to get out of this place and start over."

Thelonious shook his head. "Don't even know if we can do a sendi–"

"Deal!" Syline cut him off. Stepping forward, she offered Teagan a handshake as Thelonious blustered behind her. A moment passed, Syline offered her other hand, that time, Teagan did shake.

"Syline, we don't even know if that book has a sending! We don't have the materials for it either unless you've got them stashed in your robes somewhere," Thelonious said as she turned back to them.

Syline was already shaking her head, though much of her body was shaking as it was. "This is our only chance to save my mother, Thelonious. If we report that I'm dead, Jane will give her the antidote, and that at least gives us some breathing room on what to do next! I have to try. I'll... I'll figure something out! I've always managed to until now!"

Thelonious felt rattled. From saving Amberly from the pyre, to this, Syline was terribly impulsive. He knew, maybe sooner than later, it would be the death of them. But in this case, she was right.

"Alright, alright. Well, if they stick with us 'til we find the materials, then we'll just need to keep an eye out that Teagan doesn't try for a round two." Thelonious locked eyes with her as he said it. She held up both arms in surrender.

"Look, you lot clearly have a lot to sort out. If it's all the same to you, we'll go check who else is still breathing. Tell me when you've sorted yourselves out."

"Um, I broke one of your men's legs," Syline said, pulling Teagan up. "I think he might have passed out, but he should definitely still be alive. He's just over there."

Syline waved across to where she had fought off the man with her staff, he was slumped over on his back, practically disappearing into the snow. Teagan gave her a grateful smile, nodding as she walked off, her man's arm around her shoulder to help him walk. Syline returned the smile, then opened the archmage's book, sorting through the pages until she found a sending. Her heart dropped. There was no way they'd be able to get all the materials needed in time. Where was she going to get fresh lavender in the middle of winter?

"I can't." She looked up at Amberly and Thelonious. "I don't know if we can do it. Not unless we go into a town for materials."

"What about if we found our own outsider?" Amberly suggested suddenly, rubbing her chin in thought.

"Where are we going to find an outsider? None of us have real links to Hell," Syline said, falling to her rump in the snow. The hopelessness of it all was hitting her hard. Without Yaldabaoth, they had no way to contact Jane, which meant she would kill Syline's family and there was nothing she could do about it. Her mother and tutor would both die and it would be her fault. All because of curiosity, her curiosity. Tears began to rim in her eyes.

"We could have ended this," she whimpered, wrapping her arms around her knees. She lifted her head to stare at Amberly. "If it wasn't for you and that stupid demon, no one would've died today. My family would be okay. Now" – she sniffled, anger and fear and grief welling up in her breast – "now they're going to die, and it's your fault!"

Amberly reeled back, as if struck, her brow furrowing. "Syline that demon attacked me."

"And it wouldn't have attacked anyone if you hadn't been here!" Syline stood up now, but there was little true venom in her voice. She was scared. She was lonely and now her mother and adoptive father figure might die and it was going to be all her fault. "Just like in the depths! Those things didn't attack until you started screaming about demons!"

Syline stepped in, her blow was pathetic. A balled fist bouncing off Amberly's shoulder. It struck Amberly then how young Syline was. The girl was trembling, hurt, drenched in blood, sweat, and tears. She didn't belong out here. Amberly had been training with a sword since she could lift it and facing real battles like this not soon after. Syline was a coddled noble girl. Scared, and out of her depth. Gods, she was brave.

Amberly stepped in, throwing her arms around Syline in a hug. Almost immediately, Syline collapsed in against her, quivering and sobbing.

"Now… my… family's… going… to die," she made out, between sobs and hiccups. "I hate you." There was still no real venom in it, only despair. Amberly squeezed her.

"I'm sorry." She disagreed with Syline. Those things would have attacked regardless and Yaldabaoth broke its leash before she ever made a move. But she didn't need to say that. Not to this girl who'd thrown away everything to rescue her once and had been ready to do it again to save her family. "I'm sorry. I'll be better next time."

"There won't be a next time," Syline mumbled, the struggle had gone out of her now, arms about Amberly, she was trembling. She tucked her head into the older woman's shoulder, and Amberly gently ran her fingers through Syline's long black hair, trying her best to soothe her.

"Yes, there will, I promise. Check the book," Amberly said. "Maybe it's got something for summoning a devil. It's got rituals and illegal spells." Syline didn't reply at first, so Amberly didn't continue speaking, instead she just held her. Letting days and days of fear and stress bleed out as tears on her shoulder.

"I'm sorry," Syline mumbled eventually and Amberly laughed.

"What for?"

"I didn't mean it. I don't hate you, Amberly."

"I know." Amberly leaned in and kissed Syline on the cheek. It sent a flush up the pale girl's cheeks. "Take a few minutes, get yourself together and then go through the book. We'll figure it out Syline, even if we have to go back there and cut that bitch's head off ourselves, and I'll be right there with you."

She squeezed Syline, before letting her go. Syline smiled. Her eyes looked less clouded to Amberly now. Like a weight had fallen off them. Poor girl had a lot of worries to carry. Amberly moved off, giving Syline a little space to sit down, collect herself. It was a few minutes before she felt she had the clarity to start going through the book proper. Almost as soon as she did, a new distraction came.

"Here," Thelonious said, interrupting her chain of thought. Syline looked up. He held a murky brown and amber vial: another of the Dawnsteel potions of healing, taken from one of Teagan's men.

Syline drank it down and, along with the fading aches and pains of the battle, most of her wounds mended. She calmed a little bit, able to focus more clearly. With their conversation with Teagan done for the moment, Thelonious directed Amberly to help him pack up their spoils of war. True to their word, they only took what they needed, leaving Teagan enough to start over. Giving Syline space to focus. Syline was still torn up, unsure of what their next move would be, but at least with something to focus on, she had direction. She could put her worries away for a moment. She sat cross legged in the snow and Corax butted at her from her scarf, begging for attention with a sad little warble.

"Thelonious! Do you have another healing potion for Corax?"

"That was the last of them, sorry. What happened to the bird?" Thelonious asked over his shoulder as he roped sacks of dried meat onto Alma's saddle.

"He got thrown into a tree, and I think his wing is broken."

Thelonious paused for a moment, then sighed and walked over, shoulders slumping.

"Can't heal it, but I doubt it's too bad a break. It's probably just dislocated or sprained. Maybe a small fracture. I've looked after hunting falcons before. I know how to fix up a wing."

He kneeled down and held out an arm for Corax. Syline mentally commanded her little familiar to go with Thelonious, and after a few moments of hesitation, not wanting to be away from the safety of his roost in her scarf, her familiar hopped onto Thelonious' wrist and cawed up at him expectantly. Thelonious smiled at the bird and tickled atop his head with the tip of a finger as he wandered back to Alma and his supplies.

Now, finally, Syline could focus entirely upon her study of the archmage's spell-book. Flipping through the pages she looked up a different spell than the one they needed. Before the blood on her clothes and satchel stained, she used the spell she had found for drying her hair to drain the blood from both. After a second's thought, she poured it into the vial the healing potion had been in. Syline didn't know much about summoning devils, but it seemed like blood might be useful to have on hand for that sort of thing.

Then, she set to finding the summoning ritual. It wasn't with the other spells, because in truth, it wasn't really a spell. Rituals were of their own sort. You didn't generally need magical power or talent to perform a ritual, but they tended to be of more use to mages than anyone else, anyhow.

Unsurprisingly, the archmage had a fair few rituals in his spell-book, along with his notes on enchanting magics, which Syline would have to go and read over later. Enchanting took a lot of expensive goods, and time, neither of which they had right now so there wasn't much of a point in investigating it now. There it was: the ritual for summoning a low ranked devil. A magic circle, at least a pint of blood – she'd need more than she had in the vial to be sure – and careful rune work. Other than that, there wasn't much in the way of components required, so that was a relief at least.

After asking Thelonious to fetch the dead sellsword for the blood, which he did with his usual stoicism, ignoring any looks he received from Teagan and her men, Syline set to work on the runes, doing her best to ignore the smell and the feeling of guilt as she used a dead man as a spell component. The snow was thick, and hard packed, making it perfect for inscribing the runes into. Syline used the back of her wand as her stylus and kept the book before her, constantly referencing it to avoid making any mistakes as she went. Once that was done, she shepherded Thelonious to fill each rune with blood from the man, along with the circle. The blood spread out into the snow surrounding, bleeding from the runes and staining it red. Syline hoped that wouldn't cause any problems.

"Okay, everyone! I think it's ready."

═

TEAGAN STOOD WITH LUKAS, WHO Thelonious had punched unconscious. Although woozy, they had wandered over to watch, standing just behind Thelonious. Amberly came with them, and with that, most everyone still living on the island stood in a semicircle behind Syline, bar those mercenaries still unconscious or not up for walking, watching the circle expectantly as she began to recite. Teuflisch was a difficult language for Syline: arcane was a very flowing language, like a string tied in knots you had to work your tongue through, but Teuflisch was guttural, harsh. Each word felt commanding and powerful. The blood began to burn with black flames and everyone hushed as she continued.

Amberly felt an arm drape around her shoulder.

"You should never make a summoning circle in the snow, you know. That won't contain an imp, let alone anyone capable of what you're after."

Syline stopped and everyone turned to face the man behind them. In his stylishly-made, expensive clothing, his tattered wings hanging like a cloak, hair slicked back and perfectly styled, Laes wasn't really paying attention to any of them. His eyes were wholly on Amberly.

"I watched you die," Amberly said breathlessly, staring at him a few short moments before crushing herself to him, embracing the half devil tightly. She was practically in shock, eyes brimming with tears as Laes wrapped his arms around her. "You said you could come back as an imp, but… this definitely is not an imp, Laes. It's like you never burned at all."

"Ah yes, well, funny thing that. As it turns out, some of my warlocks were more… charitable than I would have expected and a trio of them managed to source the resources to bring me back. Guess they didn't want to be contracted to an imp, couldn't blame them. Wouldn't have thought it would have worked on me since, at the time, I was an imp being trodden underfoot but..." He spread his arms with a helpless shrug. "I suppose I do have a soul after all! Confusing how that works, but I certainly shan't complain. What of you, though? Who are these people, dear? How in the shitting hells are you still breathing? Did the priests have a sudden change of heart?"

Thelonious snorted. Laes gave him a curious glance but seemed to dismiss him for later.

Amberly stepped back, wiping her eyes.

"This is Syline Petranski and her bodyguard, Thelonious," she introduced. Not really sure of the protocol for meeting a half devil, Syline gave a curtsy all the same. Laes seemed to appreciate it at least, giving a little bow of his own in respect. "They saw me at the stake right as the priests were about to set me aflame, and Syline here decided they should stage a rescue mission."

"Is that so? Well, let me be the first to thank you, Miss Petranski; I won't pretend I'm not pleased to see Amberly still breathing. Even if I am very curious. Do the two of you know her? Why did you save her?"

"No real reason, I just felt like it was the right thing to do," Syline mumbled. Even she couldn't really explain why she had saved her, and the attention of this new man reminded her a bit much of how Ioann made her feel when he grinned at her.

"You thought it was the right thing to do to save a woman who 'conspired with devils' and 'corrupted children'?"

"Now, I know full well all of that is false!" Syline countered.

"Well, we did do a fair bit of conspiring, perhaps even fraternising. Scandalous, I know. Alright, we'll leave the topic of your interesting concepts of heroism for another time." That got a laugh out of Teagan. Laes gave a smirk her way. He turned back to Amberly, about to say something when Thelonious interrupted by loudly clearing his throat. Amberly spotted Laes' jaw tense and brow furrow a split second before he turned to Thelonious with his big, charming smile.

"Yes? Mr Bodyguard. Oh! I know you, you're the one who offered to cut my head off. I'm glad to see you made it out of that haven of hypocrites. I must say for a bodyguard you do look quite the devil. I like your horns; they look just like mi–"

"Did you lay with a farmer woman named Alyona?"

Again, the jaw tense. But now, he spread his hands wide with a dismissive shrug and a hearty chuckle. "My good man, I've lain with many women, you'll need to be a bit more specific. Names escape me sometimes."

"Around twenty-six years ago, on the eastern borders of this kingdom. She had two children and a husband. You cured her husband and oldest son of crippling illness, and in exchange…"

The light of recognition entered Laes' eyes. He leaned back for a moment, smile falling to a simple, curious look. "Well now…" he said, looking between Thelonious and Amberly for a short moment. "Not all too often I run into one of my offspring *before* their deaths. A pleasure to meet you, Thelonious. I suppose you can call me father if you'd rather. I certainly see a fair bit of myself in you. Oh, but you do have so much of that cute, bumpkin look your mother had that made me want–"

"My brother's father is the one who raised me; he'll always be my pa. But it's nice to meet you too. Father. Please don't talk 'bout Ma like that, though."

"So sensitive," Laes said with a soft chuckle. He put his hands back in his pockets and turned to face Amberly again. "So, you're bandying about with my hayseed spawn, now? Well, I suppose with me gone, you needed some kind of replacement," he teased.

Amberly felt a grin splitting her features. As much as her new companions had quickly endeared themselves to her, she was glad to see Laes again most of all. She had been suppressing her usual flirting with them. Thelonious was too no nonsense, and just the hint of flirting would probably send Syline into shock.

"Now Laes, Thelonious might be your son, but he has a very different sort of charm to you, so don't think yourself so easily replaced," she said with a grin. "In fact, I think I'm still contractually obligated to take you to dinner when I have the time." Thelonious looked at Amberly curiously at that.

"You best not forget it either. I might need to punish you if you break your contract, but…" Laes ran a hand along one of his horns, Thelonious mirroring him as he noticed his father shared that habit. "Why are you trying to summon a devil? I know you're gone from the church, but reaching out for the dark side already seems a tad hasty. I didn't think I was so charming you'd run to the arms of the nearest devil."

"Please, there are devils and there's you. Don't think I'm going to be calling on a screeching maw devil for favours anytime soon."

"Well, I'd hope not, they're not very talkative. Plus, I want to keep you for myself. Now, before Miss Petranski here makes another terrible attempt at unleashing devils on the lot of you, what were you after from one?"

"It's not me who needs you, it's Syline."

"Ooh? Well, Syline, I might cut you a discount, since you've already done me a favour in rescuing Amberly. Never say that I'm not grateful."

Syline smiled a little at that, but still felt terribly nervous beneath the devil's gaze, it seemed a bit too... focused upon her. At least she knew with Amberly there, he probably wouldn't start flirting with her anytime soon.

"Yes, well, I need a sending, a message sent for me and something to get us home quickly. With our horses, preferably. If we don't, my family is..."

"Alright, alright, I don't need the full sob story. A sending and some enchanted horseshoes. Normally, that would cost you a fair bit, but you saved Amberly. Whilst I might ask for your firstborn, I've already got a third born here amongst you, so that feels a bit redundant, and I don't... particularly want to. I have enough brats running around and have yet to really profit from any of them. Really starting to think devils do it to get their jollies, not worth the investment. So." He tapped his foot, considering. He ran a hand along one of his horns again. He looked to Amberly and smirked. "Alright, fine. From Amberly, I want that dinner. Thelonious, all I want from you is the chance to talk with you about your heritage. Syline, I merely want you to promise that you will never intentionally hurt Amberly. I see rare opportunities in the three of you and have no interest in seeing you split just yet. Now, a sending, and horse – you know, I think I have a scroll for that, actually. One moment."

He disappeared, with a burst of black and yellow flames.

"Your father's nothing like you, Thelonious," Syline said. "You're much more approachable. He's a bit intense."

"Right there with you, Syline," Thelonious replied.

"Aw, come on you two, I think he's fun," Amberly put in.

"If you like playing with fire," Thelonious countered.

"You're hellblooded, aren't you? I thought you took to flames like a fish to water."

"Flames, sure, not a crucible."

"Bah, he's your father, at least humor me, he's not all bad. After all, you got your charm from somewhere..."

"Are you... dating him?" Syline asked, blushing like a spotlight.

Amberly made a face and blushed brightly.

"I can date who I like, alright? Besides, all it is, is dinner; me and him have been friends for a long time."

Right as Thelonious began to reply, Laes reappeared with a flash of fire and the rush of his perfume refilling the area.

"So, can I assume you all agree to my terms? Frankly, I can't imagine how I could make them more reasonable than they already are."

All three exchanged a quick look.

"I agree to your terms, Mr Laes," Syline said. Laes snickered at his title.

"Fine with me," said Thelonious.

"No problems here," said Amberly with a grin.

"Then the contract is sealed." Laes held up his free hand, and a scroll burned into existence with all three of their names at its bottom. "Just for the dramatics, of course, none of you need to worry about losing your soul to me from *this* contract."

That comment left Syline feeling a bit worried. What did this half devil have in mind for them? For Thelonious, with this conversation and for Amberly, with whatever he may try to coerce her into during their dinner. Those were worries for the future though. For now, her concern had to sit squarely with her family.

"The scrolls," she said, holding out her hands for them.

Laes tutted softly as he handed them over.

"In such a rush. Those scrolls will let your horses run day and night, all out, without break, nor tiring. They'll run five times the pace of any champion stallion too. It'll be the thrill of their lives. The only ones at risk of exhaustion will be you three, so be ready when you use them."

"And the sending scroll?"

"No components required! It's an expensive version of the spell for that reason – not common in the material, this one's hell-made. Just speak the trigger phrase and imagine the person you wish to speak to while saying their name. Then, you will have thirty seconds to say whatever you wish to them before the enchantment fades."

"Okay, good, good. Thank you, Mr Laes. I'm sorry if I've been rude to you, I'm just very stressed right now," Syline said, letting out a little sigh as she looked over the scrolls.

"Oh, have no fear. Believe me, your average devil's good mood is a fair sight more sharp-tongued than your bad one. I'm not all too used to dealing with shy girls. Most who come for a devil have a bit more of Amberly's audacity, but I'm certainly not taking offence from you being nervous."

"Thank you, Laes," Amberly said, leaning in to kiss him on the cheek. Laes gained a cheek splitting grin from that.

"I look forward to our dinner, darling. You, my boy, I look forward to speaking with you properly, in a better time," he said to Thelonious, who merely nodded. "Oh," Laes said, turning back to Syline with a mischievous chuckle, "and please do a little more research on summoning before you try it again. With that ritual, you would've gotten something a bit bigger than an imp, and you wouldn't hold it in at all. You're lucky I caught the scent of it and rolled in before its completion."

Syline blanched.

Laes laughed all the more and gave a lazy, playful salute. "Toodles. I'll be in touch; I might be an outsider, but I'd rather not be a stranger."

Then, he was gone, as if he had never been. Behind him, Amberly spotted that little red songbird she'd seen flying next to them, bouncing across the snow to peck at where he'd been standing. It stared at the group for a few moments, then released a beautiful little song before disappearing into the sky. Syline let out the breath she didn't know she had been holding. He might seem nice, he might be Thelonious' father, but that was still the first outsider she had ever encountered. Not counting Yaldabaoth, who she had not exchanged words with and mostly just watched be stabbed by Amberly. It was still frightening.

"Alright… We have these scrolls now. Next." Amberly took the scroll of sending from Syline and walked over to Teagan. Teagan and her men looked up, currently sharing a flask. Teagan was wearing a glove over her stump and waved it floppily at Amberly as she approached. Amberly grimaced; Teagan laughed.

"Okay, Teagan," Amberly said, offering her the scroll. "Contact Jane Petrov. Tell her you have the spell-book, tell her… tell her we're dead." Behind Amberly, Syline nodded. That should keep them safe from further hunters on their way back, they could hope.

Teagan hopped to her feet and took the scroll. "In any particular way or is that up to my discretion?" she asked with a smirk.

Amberly chuckled softly. "As long as it doesn't involve anything too embarrassing. Don't say I was crushed by a horse sitting on me or something."

"Oh, you are just no fun," Teagan replied with a playful little pout, struggling to get the scroll open with one hand before giving up. "Can you?"

Thelonious, with a rather sympathetic look to him, took the scroll from her and held it open in front of the sellsword.

Teagan spoke the trigger phrase, followed by, "Jane Petrov." The scroll burned away as the magic within consumed it, and a faint, blue glow covered Teagan's mouth for a second before disappearing. Scrolls contained spells as well as the magic to cast them, but the release of the magic stored inside, passing through the ink was too much for it to survive, and the ink would be burned away in the process.

"This is Teagan. I have the spell-book and will be on my way back now. The girl said she'd play along, then her batshit bodyguard jumped me, cut off my shitting hand. They put up a fight, but they're all dead now. Had to strangle Syline myself." She couldn't think of much else to say, so just let the magic run its course. When the spell ended, Teagan turned to the three. "There, can we go now?"

"Yes. Safe travels, Teagan. I didn't take any of your men's gold," Thelonious said. The sellsword nodded her thanks, and she and her remaining men quickly departed after loading their unconscious fellows onto the backs of their horses.

"So, should we get going now?" Syline asked.

She felt new hope beginning to kindle in her breast. Now, they had a new goal. Now, they weren't running. Now, they were going to take the fight to Jane and end this once and for all. That evil woman was going down.

"Not yet," Thelonious said, stamping out the fires of victory that had begun to burn. "It'll be a long journey on horseback; we should get some rest for now. Let's make camp. With those scrolls, we'll make the journey in a day, so even if she doesn't use the antidote, we'll have days to spare."

Syline grumbled, but she couldn't really think of much of a counter argument. In the end, the trio made camp away from the site of the battle and all tried to get some rest. Syline though, found herself far, far too antsy to sleep peacefully. Tomorrow would be when they settled this.

Chapter 16

"Well," Lauralee said, looking up from the dazed and drained maid in her lap, wiping blood from the young woman's neck, "sounds like it's settled then." She gently helped the girl sit upright, leaving her to lean against her shoulder as she spoke to her mistress. "Would you like me to go and administer the antidotes, now that she's out of the picture?"

Jane Petrov stood, radiant. Her pale skin practically seemed to glow in the dark room, and embers seemed to dance within her amber eyes. The changes brought about by the gods' blood were becoming all the more obvious, as were the instabilities. Quite a few maids had died recently. Lauralee had reserved this one for herself partially just to protect her from Jane.

"No."

"No?"

"No. No, I don't think we will administer the antidote. This idiot girl has caused me enough problems, and I never got the chance to take any kind of" – she let out a slow, hungry breath, her tongue flicked across scarlet lips – "personal revenge."

"But Kassandra Petranski is one of the most famous noblewomen in the city. Her death's going to bring a lot of attention, going to have people looking for the source, and that was a Nachthelm poison. Eyes will come our–"

Jane had stood impassive through most of it, but suddenly her face contorted in rage, as if a switch had been flicked. A slap sent Lauralee tumbling off the bench she sat on, to crack her head against the tiles. The sound was echoed by the maid, no longer with anyone to support her, flopping down onto her side and bouncing her head off the wooden bench. Lauralee's head spun, that had been like a kick from a horse. Her eyes drifted up to Jane.

"I am in charge. Do you understand, you idiot girl? You do what I say, when I say it, then, you go back to your boring bitch mother and tell her of my wonderful work here. You do not speak, you do not give opinions, and you do not tell me what to do. They both die. I'll have it no other way."

Jane stormed from the room, as Lauralee struggled to her feet, and immediately found her balance had been thrown off, as she fell straight back over. Blood dripped through her white hair down her forehead. She had to pull herself up on the bench to sit upright as she stared off after Jane's back. This madness was going to kill them all. She had to get back to her mother and warn the hand of how irrational Jane was becoming. The old court mage only had a day or two left. Perhaps if she gave him a little of the antidote it would let him hold out long enough for her to escape the city, before questions began. Damn those mercenaries, a part of her had wanted this story to end well for Syline. Now she was on her own again, with no-one else aware of Jane's madness. It was up to her, and her alone, to figure out a solution before Jane endangered the whole organisation, or at the very least, get out of here before Jane's temper killed her.

꞊

THE PARTY TOOK THEIR REST in the early afternoon and woke well before sunrise. This suited them just fine: even with their horses magically enhanced, this would be a journey and a half. Thelonious whipped them up a porridge from their supplies as Syline worked on preparing her spells. There was no real hope of turning back from today. It would be do or die and she knew that well. So, her spells were chosen with that in mind: a spell of shielding, her now almost-signature flame dagger spell, the burning chain she had used against the court mage's guard, a spell of vanishing and a spell of arcane missiles.

She pushed herself and prepared one more, one extra that she thought may help decide the day. The lightning teleportation spell.

"So," Amberly said as Syline sat with them around their fire. Thelonious handed her a bowl of porridge, and a little pouch of sugar he'd taken from Teagan, which made it a much more appetising meal. "When we get there, what's our plan exactly?"

Syline looked down into her porridge. It was hard to say just what she was going to do. She just knew she wanted to finish this.

"We can't go to the king. At this point, we know Jane has a path to my family and to Anatoly; we need to finish this without giving her a chance to touch them. We have to hope she came through on her side of the bargain of curing them, but we'll check on that when we get there."

She bit her lip and paused her planning to shovel some porridge into her mouth. It was hot and chewy. She was used to it being mushy, but they didn't have much milk out here. It was nice, though. It reminded her of a simpler time.

"If she hasn't, our only real choice is to, is to kill Jane Petrov, and quickly too if we're going to save Anatoly. Her husband too, if we must. Chances are they're together on this. Take the antidotes, cure my family, then prove to the king just what Jane and her husband have been up to. Jane's done something to herself. Something is wrong with her."

Thelonious sat up and turned to look at Syline from the fire. "Something's wrong with her? What do you mean?"

"She's... she's too strong. She's not human."

"Syline, you're the only human here," said the half-elf Amberly, getting a little laugh from the hellblooded Thelonious.

"You know what I mean. When she confronted me in the library, her nails cut straight through me, and then she threw me into a wall like I was so much sackcloth. She's far stronger than she has any right to be. I don't know if it's just spells cast on herself or something, but she's definitely dangerous. This will be a real fight." Syline took a swig from her water flask. "If either of you." She sighed. "I won't blame either of you, if you don't want to do this, since there's not really any coming back from it if we fail, but it's my family. There's no other choice here for me. We've only got so much time before she realises Teagan played her."

There was no hesitation on Thelonious' part: he slapped his knee and gave Syline a grin as he leaned towards her. "Now, what else would I be doing with myself? Try and find some other noble girl who wouldn't be half as interesting as you to protect? Nah, nah, my place is right here, Syline."

A flush grew on Syline's cheeks right away at that, but Amberly's answer had it grow all the more.

"I owe you my life, Syline. I owe you, and I haven't really done anything to make it up to you yet. There's no way in all the hells that I'm leaving before we've seen this through to the very end."

Syline ducked her head down into her scarf now, shyness overcoming her, though her attempt at hiding was ruined as Corax squawked at her intruding on his nest and pecked lightly at her cheek to ward her off, getting a few giggles from the wizard. Her smile softened and she looked between her companions.

"Thank you. I could never have gotten here without the both of you."

With those final sentiments, the trio fell quiet, sinking into their own meals and their own thoughts. Syline, for her part, couldn't deny the excitement that came with going home. She missed her family, she missed Magdova and her mother, Kat and Kassandra Jr. She missed Alexis and Anatoly and was eager to see them all again. To save them. Fear fluttered in her breast like butterflies, but her conviction and the thought that only they could do this was enough to squash them down.

When their breakfast was finished, the three brushed down their horses. Syline and Amberly took a moment to introduce themselves to their new mounts and stroke the horses' muzzles, reassuring them that they'd be okay with these new riders. Then, Syline cast the scrolls on one horse after the next, and blue mist lapped at the muscles and hooves of each of them. The horses nickered and reared up, eager to run. As one, the trio mounted up, weapons on their hips, armour strapped – Thelonious had looted Amberly a chain shirt, plate gloves and pauldrons – and supplies secure. They exchanged one last glance and a grin. It was a long way from Russenholde yet, but there'd be no stops, no chance to talk until they arrived.

"Let's get to it," Thelonious said, giving the girls a last smile before setting off without another word. Syline and Amberly squealed as one and hurried to harry their horses after Alma's furious gallop into the dark of the pre-dawn morning. Mist curled from the hoofprints left by their mounts and as one, they left the island behind, cutting a course straight for the kingdom's capital.

—

Whatever enchantments were laid upon their horses, the journey was not an easy one for the riders. They rode as fast as the horses would carry them, but even at such speeds, it took them until just after the sun had set for them to arrive at their destination, having ridden for the whole of its journey across the sky.

Twice on the journey, they had to stop to save their muscles from the endless jostling. For Syline, however long the journey may have been, it passed like a blur. Beautiful vistas of frozen water fell away behind them as they took the monumental bridges that carved a course through the centre of the nation, linking its most grand islands. They had no time to take a less direct course now and had little fear of hunters pursuing them, especially at such speeds. With the last rays of the sun tinting the sky orange, the trio approached the walls of Russenholde. For Syline, it felt like a lifetime since she had fled this city, teary-eyed and terrified, even though in truth it had been less than a week.

"I can't let the guards see me," Syline told Thelonious as they approached, still on the thickly forested road before the open plain around the city.

"Alright, why not?"

"Well, I don't know if they work for Jane or not. The last one who approached me tried to kill me on sight and I can only imagine the stories spread about me now."

"Fair. How are we going to hide you? Not like I have a carriage for you to hide under."

"We'll tie my horse's reins to your saddle so you can lead it. I'll hide behind you as we approach, and once we're in view, I'll use a vanishing spell and keep it up as long as I can. I'll wear your spare cloak instead of my hat."

Thelonious sniffed.

"Will that be long enough?" he asked, adjusting his seating so he could pull his spare cloak from his saddlebags for her. He swore he'd be walking bow legged all night and that was not something he was happy about.

"The guards shouldn't have any reason to stop you two. So, just try and get through the gate as fast as you can. As soon as you're through, I'll dismount and run into an alley before the spell runs out, then meet you around the road's bend."

Thelonious gave a nod and Amberly grinned in assent. They quickly tied Syline's horse to Alma, and Syline huddled up behind Thelonious, shushing the groggy Corax who cawed as he awoke, having slept through most of the trip. They approached the gate from there. Powerful, imposing, and a good six metres high, the wall was the bastion that kept the city safe. A pair of guards stood high above it, cast in silhouette by the torches behind them. The snow had just begun to fall; it looked like a storm was brewing. Thelonious absently brushed his shoulders. As they came into view, Syline drew out her wand and made herself disappear, holding her breath she focused on keeping the spell steady.

"Hoy, riders! What's your business in Russenholde!" yelled the guard.

Thelonious looked to Amberly. He wasn't good at thinking on his feet. Amberly threw back her hood, revealing her long white hair and pointed ears. She gave the guards a bright and sunny grin befitting her old god.

"My business is pleasure, sir! And it's my pleasure to come to Russenholde! Travelled all the way from Dawnsteel to taste the finest foods in this kingdom!"

"Ah, a holiday is it, then? Who's the big fellow?"

"He's my guard, sir! Would you set a waifish lass such as myself out on the open road?"

"Hellblooded, is he?"

"Would you not rather the scarier monsters be on your side?"

"Aye, aye, you have a point. What's the third horse for?"

"My sister. She fell ill halfway here and had to stay behind. She had gifts for cousins here, and I had not the room upon my packs to carry them, so her horse joined us, even if she could not."

"Alright." The guard had run out of questions, and Syline had run out of breath, now doing her best to breathe shallowly and somehow willing herself to not make a move that would disturb Thelonious' cloak. "Open the gate!" the guard called, and Amberly shot him yet another smile.

"Thank you, sir! Have a fine evening, now."

"You too, ma'am." The gate opened and the horses trotted through, the guards returning to their conversations.

At the first alley they passed, Syline dismounted and ran for it. She was left panting for a few moments. Though the magic had not overtly drained her, the tension definitely had. They were at the point where she couldn't afford anything going wrong. They'd come too far to fall to a bribed guard now. She threw up her hood and kept a hand on her wand as she jogged through the alleys to the next street over. A few homeless vagrants watched her, but the sight of a wand in hand and her expression as well, warned away any ne'er-do-wells. She found none of the old fear danced in her breast now. She was too focused to worry about bullies and braggarts.

"Well, that went swell," Thelonious commented to her as she met up with them, the pair still calmly trotting along on their horses. The enchantment on the horses' hooves fading as they drew into town.

"That was some nice bluffing, Amberly," Syline told her friend with a grin as she mounted back up on the third horse.

"Oh, that was nothing! Any Morning's Fury should be able to bluff their way into a cult without batting an…" Amberly's attention was grabbed from the conversation when she saw, on the sill of a shop window, that songbird, bright scarlet red. It was staring right at her and, as she looked its way, it sang a beautiful song just for her as it took flight off into the night. It was the one from the island where they'd fought Teagan, she was sure of it; she'd never seen another bird like it. But could it have followed them all this way? Surely not.

"What is it, Amberly? See something?" Thelonious asked, looking the way she had, but not seeing anything.

"Did you not?" Amberly rubbed her head. "I must be tired. Syline, what way's your manor? Lead the way."

"Right," Syline said, giving her a concerned look. "Right this way! Come on, not far now."

EVEN THOUGH EXCITEMENT FILLED SYLINE'S heart at the thought of going to see her family again, they still made a point to take it slow, avoiding any patrols if they could and always keeping Syline swaddled with a scarf and a hood. Few questions would be asked about that, especially with the snow falling heavier with each passing moment. Corax, robbed of his usual nest, sat sulking on her shoulder as they approached the Petranski manor. Seeing the great, three-storey mansion coming into view, a tumult of emotions played in Syline's stomach: fear that her mother would still be poisoned, hope that soon she'd be able to come home, grief that all of this had happened and excitement at seeing her sisters, mother, and Alexis again. Thelonious practically had to lead her horse in, for Syline sat slack in the saddle, staring at the lit windows of the house.

"Syline, that's your house. Shut your mouth, you look like a hayseed seeing a cathedral for the first time," Amberly told her, snickering. Syline flushed and brought herself back to reality as they approached the front gate.

"Want us to stay out here?" Thelonious asked.

"No, just… let's get inside the gate first. I can get a servant to fetch you both some refreshments and stable the horses, but I-I would like a moment with my family before I introduce you both, if that's alright."

"'Course Syline," Thelonious said softly. He and Amberly had both known Syline was wealthy, a proper noble girl, but seeing the mansion she'd grown up in really pressed that home for them. Syline dismounted from her horse, stroking its neck and taking her staff from the saddle before approaching the gate. The guard must've been in the foyer staying warm, but that was exactly why they had the bell. Syline reached into an opening in the stone pillar that supported the gate and tugged twice on a rope just hidden from sight. A bell could barely be heard ringing through the great, blackwood doors of the manor.

A few moments passed, and one of the home's few guards came out of the front door – Feliks, it looked like. He was probably a decade older than Syline and none too bright, but he was very friendly, stocky and strong in a similar sort of way to Thelonious. He held his cap on as he ran through the light snow to the gate.

"Hoy! Who's calling at this hour?" he asked the cloaked figure as he approached.

Syline lowered her hood and scarf from her features, letting him get a clear look at her. The man lost what little colour he had and looked about to yell before Syline held a finger to her lips.

"Please don't yell, I don't want the guards knowing I'm here. Can you let us in, Feliks, and stable our horses for us?"

"R-right away Syline, right away. We thought you were… well… No one wanted to say it, but…" He busied himself unlocking the padlock on the gate and swung it open.

Thelonious and Amberly dismounted and offered their reins to him. Syline noticed the guard give Thelonious a suspicious once over, but he didn't seem to make eye contact with Amberly. She couldn't blame him: Amberly was very pretty and Feliks never knew how to talk to women he didn't work for. He still struggled to talk to Kat sometimes.

"Well, I'm home, now." Syline felt her chest tighten, just saying those words. She stepped in through the gate and pulled herself up from sprinting for the front door long enough to thank the guard. Then, it was all her friends could do to keep up with Syline. Corax cawed in surprise from his shoulder roost at the sudden haste. Syline's composure was broken. She didn't want another second without her family, and now that they were through the gate, she no longer feared discovery.

Syline threw the door open and stepped in, white staff tapping against the floor. She shouldered it just long enough to undo her cloak and toss it onto the rack by the door, snow flitting from the garment to lay on the tiles. She looked around; she couldn't see anyone. Her heart began to race. For a moment, Syline was alone and felt terribly so. The house was all too quiet, and memories of that terrible dream came back to her. Rationality forced its way in, though, and reminded her it was right around dinner time; it was likely all her siblings were in the dining room, several halls away from here. She set off, steady at first, but as she caught the first hints of their voices, she began to speed up.

In her fervour, she very nearly slammed into a servant girl as they rounded the corner from another hallway leading into the path to the dining room and other entertainment areas. The servant girl faced away from her, and Syline had to skid to a stop along the tiles. Still, she bumped the girl's shoulder, and the servant turned to see who was behind her. Alexis dropped the plate she was holding, and neither girl noticed as it smashed across the tiles.

"Sy-Syline?" the servant girl managed before Syline threw her arms around her friend, crushing herself to Alexis as tears came out in full force.

"Alexis!" she cried, Alexis, mirroring it with another cry of Syline's name, arms squeezing around the smaller girl as tight as they could. They stood there, quivering and crying, simply holding one another for a good few moments.

"We thought you were – Where have you been?" Alexis demanded, pulling back to look at Syline. The familiar on her shoulder let out a warble of greeting as he did his best to nestle into Syline's scarf again. "A-and what's that!"

"Th-they're both long stories. I'm okay though, and after tonight, I'm coming home."

Alexis gulped back tears and kissed Syline on the cheek before pulling her tight again. Syline returned Alexis' kiss to the cheek, but slowly pulled out of the hug. "My family's in the dining room, right, Alexis?"

"Y-yes, well, no, your sisters are. Your mother, she's… she's very ill–"

"No, she isn't," Syline interrupted. "She's been poisoned."

"What?" Alexis exclaimed, hurrying to follow as Syline set off for the dining hall.

"I'll explain everything in a moment. Don't worry, Alexis. I'm going to fix this."

Alexis fell silent, looking at Syline for a moment, seeing a new woman awakening in her friend and master. Her eyes darted to the foyer, and she was tempted to ask about the two strange people standing there, but she decided it could wait. For now, there was no stopping Syline as she opened the door to the dining room to meet with her sisters once more.

⚊

STEPPING INTO THE DINING ROOM had a fresh wave of tears breaking free. Sitting at the table were all three of her sisters: Kassandra, Kat, and Magdova. Mags was the first to see her, and she dropped her fork, throwing herself from her seat to sprint for her near-on twin. Kat watched her, confused until Mags' dash led her eyes to Syline. Just like that Kat was on her feet, rushing over as Kassandra ran behind Mags, both colliding in an embrace with Syline and wrapping themselves around her.

"Syline!" both cried in almost perfect tandem. Syline felt a sob wrack her as she wrapped her arms tight around both of them. Kat touched a hand to her shoulder as if affirming that Syline was real.

"We thought you were dead," Kat said, her voice soft.

"I-I've got quite a story to tell," Syline managed with a little, limp smile. "It's so good to see you three again." She kissed her younger sisters' foreheads. "Sit, sit. I don't have much time to hang around here."

"Shouldn't we go to see Mother? She'll want to know you're, that you're not… that you're home," Magdova said, sniffling and wiping tears from her eyes as she pulled away from Syline.

Hurt gave way to relief in her eyes as she looked up at her, and it only occurred to Syline then that this was the longest she'd ever been apart from Magdova, her near-to twin. She pulled her in again to embrace her once more as she spoke, realising then how much her heart had ached for her sisters.

"She's awake? Alexis told me she's very ill," Syline said, looking in the direction of her mother's room.

"She should be," Kat said. "A maid just brought her dinner. Come on, let's save your story for her ears."

Kat led the way back to the foyer, Alexis trailing after the group of raven-haired sisters, but they all stopped in their tracks at the sight of the hellblooded and half-elf waiting in the foyer.

"Who's this, Syline?" Kat asked as Amberly and Thelonious moved to stand with Syline. Amberly giving a bright and friendly grin whilst Thelonious tried to blend into the wall behind him. He didn't do a very good job.

Syline turned to face her sisters again, standing now at the head of her little troupe.

"This is Thelonious, my bodyguard, and Amberly, a dear friend that we saved from unlawful execution," she told her sisters. Kat cocked her head curiously, whilst a gleeful little grin lit Magdova's features. Syline could only imagine what adventures her sister was thinking she'd had.

"Well, you definitely have a story to tell," Kat said, giving Thelonious a quick once over. The ram-horned hellblooded gave her a respectful nod. "Let's not waste any more time."

"You two stay here for now, alright? Alexis, can you get someone to bring them something to eat and drink, please?" Syline said as she and her sisters began to go up the stairs. Alexis seemed a little let down that she wouldn't get to hear the story straight from Syline's lips but dashed off all the same. The quartet of sisters headed for their mother's room.

—

STEPPING INTO THE ROOM AT the head of her band of sisters, Syline felt a chill go down her spine. Her mother lay in bed, thin and gaunt, her skin greying but for around her eyes and nose, where it was puffy and red. Syline had never seen her mother looking so weak; she had always been an unstoppable bastion of strength. Her mother was taking dinner slowly, a maid sitting nearby to help her when her hands shook too greatly. When the quartet of sisters entered, Syline and Kat leading, their mother's mouth fell open, before turning into a trembling little smile, tears budding at her eyes.

She held out her arms for Syline, her voice soft, as if she were short of breath.

"My little sparrow…" It was all she could manage, but pure joy welled in her eyes, relief washing away mountains of pain.

Syline stepped forward straight into her mother's arms, clutching her tight. She forced down her tears. Anger was beginning to take the place of sorrow. That monster Jane had no intent of curing her mother or Anatoly. Even though she thought she was dead, Jane was going to let them die just as petty revenge.

"I'm here now, Mother. Everything's going to be okay. I'm going to fix this."

"What do you mean, Syline? Where have you been? Who took you? I'm fine now that you're home. I'm just sick, I'm ju–"

"No, you're not," Syline mumbled, trying to push back tears still. "You've been poisoned by Jane Petrov."

Everyone went silent. Syline ducked her head down slightly, feeling the gaze of the whole of her family upon her. She started from the beginning, that night in the library, and went from there. Corax hopped around her shoulders as she told how she met him, before hopping into Magdova's arms, immediately taking a liking to his master's lookalike. She left out only one detail: exactly what had happened in the lumber shed, only saying that the man had forced her to kill him and that she had met Thelonious soon after. She finished by telling them of their battle with Teagan and how they had found out Jane Petrov's plot. When she was finished, her mother seemed aghast, whilst Kat's knuckles were bone-white from how tightly she gripped her sword.

"Now we're back here and I'm going to face Jane Petrov and take the antidotes, even if I have to kill her."

A gasp was shared between little Kassandra and Magdova. Her mother's lips were a harsh, thin line, her eyes blazed with a fresh fury that seemed to further invigorate her. Even as the sheer rage brought tears to her eyes.

"To my damned face," she hissed through gritted teeth, "she wished you well, to my damned face. Promised she'd do everything she could to help." Syline was about to ask what she meant when Kat cut in.

"You're not going without me."

"Kat – Katarina, we're… People are probably going to die, maybe even us," Syline said, looking at her older sister.

Kat dismissed their sisters, much to Magdova's protests, along with her mother's maid, then shut the door behind them.

"Syline, you say that as if I've never killed people, before," she said in a soft tone. "Also don't call me Katarina," she added, giving a little smile to try and lighten the mood.

Their mother spoke up. "Little sparrow, you've grown so much. You seem like a different, much stronger girl, but do you not want to wait for your father? He can handle this, you don't. I don't want you going back out there. The runners will surely have found him by now, he can't be more than a week or two away.

Syline shook her head. "I'm sorry, Mother, but it's now or never. You probably have a week left without the antidote, but the poison she gave Anatoly was much faster acting. I don't think I even have time to visit him, I need to go tonight."

"Are you sure about this, Syline? You'll be risking your life… I can't lose you, not again," their mother said, wishing she didn't have to send her daughters off to fight her battle.

"We can't trust the guard. We can't trust anyone. I can't turn this into the authorities until I stop her, and whatever she is, I doubt a normal watchman could handle her, anyway. We're the only ones who can do this."

"I'm… I'm so proud of you." Her mother had begun to sob, relief pouring from her, warring with fear for what was to come. "You've suffered so much and only come out stronger. I'm so, so sorry all of this happened to you."

Syline leaned down to kiss her mother's cheek, holding her tight.

"It's okay, Mother. It'll all be okay. I'm finishing this tonight, no matter what. I love you."

"I love you too, Syline. Please come back safe, both of you. You *need* to come back safe. You're both so much more important to me than I am."

"I won't let anyone lay a finger on her, Mother," Kat promised. "I love you too."

She gave her a small embrace and a kiss on the cheek as well before leaving the room with Syline.

"What did you mean, 'as if I've never killed people before'?" Syline asked her sister as they headed for the stairs, where they could hear Amberly retelling the tale to Alexis and, chances are, both her sisters over again.

"There've been people who've wanted our family silenced in the past, after all we are practically the right hands of the king: assassins after mother, poison in our drinks. When you were a babe, too young to remember, you were kidnapped. Mother went on a rampage and no one dared anything so brazen for a long time. But as Mother's gotten older, I've taken over removing these dissidents. We thought you'd been kidnapped again. I've been stalking the streets every night looking for sign of you."

Syline looked at her sister in silent shock, mouth agape. Kat chuckled softly and patted Syline's head.

"Don't worry yourself over it, but I'm plenty ready for this. Mother's right, though; you seem much more confident now. You know, rather than go straight there, there is someone else we could get for help."

"Who?"

"Ioann Voronyakogtya, a sorcerer in Father's forces. He's been fighting as hard as we have to look for you, I swear the man never sleeps. I think he'll be over the moon to see you home." A grin was smeared across Kat's features and Syline flushed red.

"Ioann came looking for me? O-okay, le-let's get him."

"Good. He's much more handsome than that hellblooded anyway. Much better for my little—"

"Shut up, or I'll go without you!" Syline squawked. Kat laughed, giving Syline a squeeze around the shoulders as the pair descended the stairs.

"Come on, you two," Syline said to Amberly and Thelonious as they met back up. "We have one more stop to make yet. Kat's coming with us."

"Will she be okay?" Amberly asked, giving Kat an appraising look.

"She's a better swordsman than any of us," Syline said, Kat, grinning behind her at that. Syline shared one last embrace with Alexis, Kassandra and Magdova before heading out with the trio. Magdova, most of all, struggled to let her go as Kat looked Amberly over.

"I see you're carrying Syline's sword. Hopefully you swing it a bit better than her or else I'll be dragging all of you through this."

Amberly grinned. "Ooh, I like you."

Chapter 17

THEY LEFT THE MANOR, THE four of them. Corax nestled comfortably in Magdova's arms behind them, far from danger. He wouldn't be coming tonight: Syline had no wish to risk her little raven, no matter how much he protested, and she could feel his displeasure through their link even now. To fill in for him, Malir came out of the pocket of her robes and was tucked into her scarf, a reassuring pressure against her neck. Kat had given her a teasing look, but she brushed it off. With her big sister beside her now, Syline moved through the city with far more confidence. It wasn't that she didn't believe in Amberly and Thelonious' ability to protect her or her own ability to evade the watch. It was just that Kat was her big sister, her protector. The person she always knew she'd never be able to surpass.

In the past, she was afraid of many of these streets. Anything off the path she knew, anything even broaching into the winding alleys, markets, and thoroughfares, Syline would have avoided like the plague without someone with her. She feared beggars, brigands and worse. Snow fell heavily over their shoulders as they strode through the winding back routes around bonfires and between ramshackle merchant stalls. She had her sister beside her. That filled her with confidence, but even if she weren't there, Syline felt like she could have strode through the darkened, snow-filled streets without fear.

Kat led the way, heading for the barracks of their father's men here in the city. As the oldest of his children – tied only with her twin brother, Ulrik – Kat had a fair bit of presence amongst the men, especially since they knew full well, she had all her mother's fire and her father's discipline. There weren't many who'd want to risk a fight with the proud daughter. As they walked, the pair talked. Kat told Syline of what had gone on in her absence, and Syline told Kat in greater detail of moments in her travels, filling in the story as Kat asked for more.

Their talk was of no real interest to Amberly, who lagged behind even Thelonious. Her eyes and ears kept being pulled away by something else: that bird, the beautiful red, songbird. She'd seen it again, watching her through the window of the Petranski manor. Then, once more, she spotted it flying across the road as they stepped from one alley to the next. Now she could see it yet again, resting on the gutters of a tall building, singing its beautiful song, birdsong far more beautiful, far more musical, than anything a simple animal had a right to know. It was watching her. She looked up at it as they passed underneath and, on a whim, did her best to whistle the tune back to it. The bird's chest feathers puffed up, and it gleefully returned the song before disappearing over the rooftops. For a split second, Amberly swore she felt someone's eyes on the back of her neck, and a warm breath touched her cheek. She turned. No one.

"That's a nice tune, where'd you hear it?" asked Thelonious over his shoulder, feeling a bit left out with the two sisters bantering away up ahead. Now Amberly was almost certain: Thelonious hadn't seen or heard the bird. The bird that had no place being here.

Amberly hurried to get up beside him, feeling a little unnerved.

"You didn't see it?" she asked.

"See what?"

"There's a…. I keep seeing this little red songbird, it's following us. It's following me. I think it's been following me ever since Laes and I were in that cell."

Thelonious furrowed his brow. He looked at Amberly, then up to the buildings around them. "Can't say I've seen it."

Amberly looked behind them once more. A red feather sat on the snow. She tucked it into her pocket and ran after her comrades.

THELONIOUS AND AMBERLY WERE LEFT to watch outside for anyone who looked a little too intent on the barracks. It was just Kat and Syline who went inside together.

This place might've been called a barracks, but as it was purely for the elite monster hunters currently on leave, it had far more in common with a holiday lodge. A large, two-storey wooden complex, it was taken up primarily by the huge common room they entered. Here, a motley company of hunters lounged around playing pool, sharing drinks or enjoying dinner. The only break from the jovial atmosphere was a section in the corner, devoted to a map of the city, an artist's rendering of Syline pinned beside it, with areas searched crossed out. *They'd been looking for me,* Syline thought, wishing so badly that they'd found her, instead of the watchman that morning outside the walls. But that was past now and she dragged her gaze away from the map, lest she fell deeper into maudlin thought.

It looked like someone had just made a run to a food shop in one of the main streets because paper parcels and half-finished meals were scattered all around, full of butter-lathered, toasted bread piled high with cheese, roast potatoes, mince, and fish from the waters around the island. The place had a huge hearth, which made entering the room a refreshing reprieve from the cold as the two sisters stepped in.

Syline kept her scarf around her face and her hood low over her brow, disguising her identity even among men who were conceivably theirs. Thankfully, with Kat at her side, no one was about to question her presence. Kat approached the first person they found alone, a young man with huge forearms, denoting him as an archer. He wore his military coat unfastened over a simple shirt and was reclining on a sofa, half a sandwich in hand and the other half in his mouth. Upon seeing Kat, he snapped up to his feet and saluted with the hand currently holding the sandwich.

Neither sister could resist laughing at that, and Kat grinned at the man as he flushed, a stain of gravy dripping down his forehead, realising what a fool he'd made of himself.

"At ease soldier, no need to salute. Is Ioann here?" she asked, looking around.

"Up in his room, ma'am," the man replied after swallowing.

Kat tore off a piece of fish from the paper platter in his lap as she stepped away, offering half of it to Syline.

"Thank you, soldier," Kat said over her shoulder with a little grin, chewing on her stolen dinner.

The two quickly made their way through the complex, returning a few smiles, salutes or nods as they went until they reached the stairs and ascended up into the private rooms. They went along for a few moments, looking at the closed doors. Kat turned.

"Which room is Ioann's?" she yelled down the stairs.

About five different people yelled back, and the girls were back en route. On approach, the door opened itself, the sorcerer having heard the yelling. He curiously poked his head out, hair dishevelled, shirtless as usual, lacking even his coat, this time.

"Katarina? What can I do for you, ma'am? Was there...? Have you heard...?" Kat looked down at Syline, who lowered her hood and scarf. The sorcerer's mouth opened, slack a moment before it turned to a relieved – if rather bashful – grin. A little hiccup left him as he struggled to keep it in place. It was just as bright, just as awkward and just as charming as the night Syline had met him in the library, the night all this began. "Guess you heard I was looking for you?" he asked, wiping an eye.

Syline smiled back, blushing in turn. The thought that he cared enough to worry when she disappeared had Syline a bit giddy. A moment passed with both just beaming at one another before Kat sighed dramatically.

"You're both useless. Ioann. Come on. We've need of you."

"H-huh? What for? Does it have to do with why Syline went missing?"

Syline gave him an abridged rendition of what had happened, largely just telling him of Jane's involvement and their current plan. He grabbed his coat from somewhere just inside his room.

"Are you sure you shouldn't bring the whole barracks for this? There's not a man here who wouldn't fight for the pair of you."

Syline shook her head. "We need to do this quietly. We go marching in with an army, and the guard will be all over us, and worse than that, she'll see us coming. Five should be more than enough, considering who I have with me." Syline beamed at him as she said that.

Ioann scratched the back of his head, grinning. "A-alright, ma'am – er, Syline – just give me a moment, then. Just need to grab a few items." He shut the door behind him, disappearing back into his room to ready himself.

Kat snickered and elbowed her little sister.

"Look at you: middle of all of this and you've managed to get a boy smitten," she teased, reaching over to pinch her cheek. Syline flushed bright red and pulled her hood up. "And you're pretty smitten yourself. He is hot... and I don't mean his flames," Kat continued, getting a whimper from Syline. Kat laughed and hugged her sister. "With him here, I'm sure we'll have a big advantage. This'll all end well," she assured Syline, kissing her forehead.

Ioann soon emerged from his room wearing a few assorted amulets, pouches, rings and fetishes – the war gear of an experienced sorcerer. A small hatchet hung at his hip, a crossbow on his back.

"Let's be off then," he said, and Kat turned on her heel to take the lead. Syline lagged a little so that Ioann could come up alongside her.

"When this is over," he started as they descended the stairs. Syline looked up. Ioann smiled down at her. "When this is over, how about we get that coffee, and you can tell me all about what I missed?"

Syline smiled, a little blush still tickling her cheeks. She took Ioann's hand and gave it a quick squeeze.

"I'd like that." Together, they descended out into a storm, one as heavy as when they had met. Ioann blocked it all from ever touching her.

—

ARRIVING AT THE MANOR OF the Petrovs had quite a bit of the confidence, that Syline had built up, going out the window. Like her home, it was a large, two-storey estate. Most of the windows were unlit and behind its gate and walls, the manor gave off a foreboding presence. Like Jane and her husband were already watching them within. Getting in proved to be fairly easy, at least.

Thelonious and Ioann threw the girls one by one up to the lip of the wall, so they could then pull themselves over. Then Thelonious gave the sorcerer a boost so he could, in turn, drag Thelonious up it. With the snow coming down hard around them, no guards walked the grounds, most likely all huddled for warmth in the foyer or in some little hut nearby.

"I've been here before," said Kat as the group touched down. She nodded to a window on the second storey, just to the left of the main entryway. It was some four or five metres up. "That's Gehrman's study. Let's start there. We'll check for the antidote and proof of anything illegal."

"How're we all going to get up there?" asked Syline as they all moved through the snowstorm to reach the great manor itself.

Kat looked up, then at Thelonious. She sighed. "The men can throw the women up there. I'll go first and help you and Amberly through. When things go south, we yell loud enough for Thelonious and Ioann to hear, and they storm the front door. Anyone got any better suggestions?"

Ioann, who the snow never seemed to touch, and who had been shyly raising his hand in the back this whole time, spoke up. "Er, I should be able to get Thelonious and me up there. It'll just take some good reflexes on our part."

Amberly smirked, wondering just what that could mean, but Kat merely shrugged. "Alright, if you say so. Let's get a move on, I want out of this cold."

"Agreed," said Syline, quickly echoed by the rest of the group aside from Ioann who – despite being shirtless – didn't seem to mind the weather all that much.

Ioann and Thelonious positioned themselves below the window, and Kat stepped into both their hands, taking a moment to gain her balance, getting ready to use them as a springboard for her leap.

"Alright, throw me."

With that, the two powerfully muscled men hurled her up with all their might, enough to get her level with the window. Kat showed finesse and agility that would put her little sister to all kinds of shame. She grabbed hold of the windowsill in mid-flight, flipping herself up and over onto it before grabbing the window and shimmying it up out of the way so she could slide in. Kat turned and extended her arms to catch the next person through as Amberly climbed into the men's arms.

"Your big sister's pretty damn impressive, Syline," she said over her shoulder.

"Don't have to tell me," Syline grumbled as the two men threw Amberly. She didn't fly with quite as much grace as Kat, but she still managed it well, catching her feet on the wall and grabbing Kat's wrist to walk the rest of the way up.

"Alright, you next, Syline," Ioann said, giving her a smile. Syline climbed up into their hands, wobbling to and fro before managing to get her balance.

"O-okay, I'm ready."

As one, they threw her up, and as they did, it occurred to Syline that both men would be able to see straight up the skirts of her robes. That distraction was enough to have Syline lose any sense of what she should do in the air, and she found herself madly flailing as her light frame went up to the window, easily higher than Amberly went, just for how little Syline weighed. If it hadn't been for Kat grabbing onto Syline's wrists and Amberly leaning over to take her staff and drag it in ahead of her, Syline probably would have gone straight back down into the snow. She caught her sister and friend sharing a snicker as Kat helped her through the window.

"You've gotten a lot better, Syline, but you're still pretty clumsy," Kat teased.

The three had a quick glance around the office. It was dark, the door shut. Just to be sure, Syline took her staff from Amberly and wedged it diagonally into the doorframe. Kat made a little hum of approval and, as one, the trio turned to see just what Ioann had in mind to get the big men up there. A quick conversation went on between the pair below that, thanks to the harsh wind and pelting snow, none of the girls could hear.

Amberly was distracted, anyway. Something felt... off. She felt a nagging pain as if she had just lost something. It reminded her of what she'd felt when she watched Laes burn. Without thinking about it, she clutched the feather in her pocket, and the pain eased but didn't go away. It was as if something was tugging on her heartstrings, trying to get her attention.

Ioann grabbed Thelonious and the snow exploded away from the pair, green magical energy lapping like flames off Ioann's coat. Thelonious leapt and went straight over not just the window, but the house; propelled on a huge stream of half-seen wind that faded as quickly as it came. Thelonious flailed in the air for a moment, but he managed to regain his focus, grab onto the top sill of the window and change his momentum to swing straight in.

The women inside jumped aside just in time to avoid being crushed by the armoured hellblooded. Ioann followed suit but did so with a little more grace than Thelonious, who stumbled into the desk and barely managed to stop it falling over. Ioann came in through the window tucked in and rolled up to his feet after hitting the floor. He looked at Syline for approval and she had to giggle, giving him a thumbs-up.

Ioann seemed pretty pleased.

"You need to learn that trick, Syline," Thelonious said as he looked around the room. "Would've come in handy in that 'Scholar of Ascension' place."

"I'll try and teach it to her later," Ioann said, grinning. "For now, let's find those documents." As one, they spread throughout the office, searching cabinets, cupboards, the desk, and even the liquor cabinet. The only one who did not was Thelonious, who knew that too many cooks in the kitchen ruined the pot. Instead, he stood by the door, watching and waiting for anything to try and enter. For the most part, they found little of interest: trade documents, mercantile records, and similar papers, but their time didn't go completely wasted. It was Amberly who first found something of note: a letter pulled from its envelope.

"Does anyone know what the… 'Materinskaya Ruka' is?" she asked. "It sounds familiar."

"Materin–" Kat started but was cut off by Syline.

"It's Old Human. These days not many people speak it; the 'New Trade Tongue' has almost completely replaced it, but that means 'The Mother's Hand', I think."

Amberly and Ioann cursed as one. "Are you sure that's what it means, Syline?" Ioann asked.

"What does the letter say?" Syline squeaked, wondering why this was such a big deal all of a sudden.

Amberly held up the letter and read aloud: *"Dear sister. The Materinskaya Ruka appreciate your efforts, but as it stands, we've no interest in expanding our operations to the Sea Without Sky. You are diligent and ingenious, Jane, but do not push beyond your bounds, or ours."*

"That confirms it," Ioann said, the monster hunter and Morning's Fury sharing a glance.

"You both seem very clever, mysterious and, dare I say, cool," Kat said dryly. "But would you mind letting the rest of us into your little talk?"

Ioann blushed as Amberly let out a tiny, quiet chuckle.

"Sorry, sorry," he started. "The Mother's Hand are a known threat within the kingdom and many others in the region, but they're too difficult to nail down or even prove their presence. It's impossible to say anything public about them, for they'll simply disappear and come back decades later. They're a group of female vampires who infiltrate positions of power and use their abilities to control the kingdom to their goals."

"I encountered one in Dawnsteel recently," Amberly offered. "They had their fingers in the cultist pie, so to speak, I think they helped organise and fund whatever the cultists were doing with the demons, but I don't think the Mother's Hand were taking part in it themselves. Dammit! I'd completely forgotten about that until now, with all that's been happening, it slipped my mind."

"So, she's a vampire, then. I knew vampires were supposed to be strong but," Syline said.

"But not as strong as you described, Syline. There's no way she should have been able to throw you like that. There has to be something else going on," Amberly said.

"Let's keep looking, then," Syline said, and went back to doing so.

As she did, a thought occurred to her: vampires could charm people and make them do almost anything, that's what made them so dangerous. The first man she ever killed. No other had looked as confused and afraid as he had; he had looked as if he had no idea why, or even how he got there. Jane must've been controlling him – not just bribing him but forcing him to hunt Syline. Guilt surged anew in her breast, but right with it was fury. Jane had forced that man to his death. She was more at fault than Syline, even if her blade had killed him. It was a bizarre thought, but she had it all the same. She wished to avenge the man.

They slipped into silence, searching again. It was amazingly lucky that no one tried to come into the study, but so late at night, the Petrov patriarch likely had no interest in the business. It was odd his wife was storing such illicit letters here, though. They had a near miss or two, the entire group freezing as they'd heard footsteps going by the door. It was so easy to forget how deep in enemy territory they were, and more than once, they were all left holding their breath until the footsteps faded away. It was Syline who next found something of worth, pulling a letter from within the pages of a diary in a desk drawer. A chill went down Syline's spine, and a strangled gasp escaped her.

"What is it, Syl?" asked Kat, moving by her side.

Syline ignored her, looking to Amberly and Thelonious.

"I'm paraphrasing it, half the words don't make sense, but this letter is… she traded something called a 'tome of deific ascension' for the spell-book and for a caged, powerless demigod. She traded for them with the Scholar of Ascension."

"The who?" asked Kat.

Syline quickly filled her in on the story of their venture beneath the earth and their encounter with the horrific, waxy elves and that mutated, draconic beast, and the invitation they'd found on the pillars there. Amberly was more focused on another idea, though, turning the feather back and forth in her fingers. The nagging pain grew worse when Syline told her about the god.

"If a vampire drank the blood of a demigod, I can't even think of what would happen, but I'm going to say that's the source of her strength. We need to settle this, and now."

It's you, isn't it? Amberly thought. *You're calling out to me.* She stared at the feather, turning it to and fro, feeling the gentle warmth it gave off.

"We've got proof she's a vampire and that she's been dealing with terrible things," Kat said. "These letters will be enough to protect us when this is all over, but if we turn them in now, she'll just disappear. Are you all ready? There's no telling what she'll be able to do."

Kat drew her sword, a far larger sibling to Syline's own duelling sabre, heavier and weighted for a master's grace.

"For Mother and Anatoly, let's do this," Syline said, drawing her axe off the harness on her back and taking the staff from the doorframe. Thelonious pushed in front of her, drawing his bastard sword.

Amberly clutched the feather tight against her breast and drew Syline's sword. *I hear you*, she thought. *I'll save you. Please, help me do it.*

"We can't pussyfoot about here," Ioann said. "The more time we give her, the more dangerous she is. We fight like a raging bear. Trap her, give her no chance to collect herself," he added.

Thelonious nodded and opened the door. For all their drama, it was almost disappointing when they weren't immediately assailed by guards upon stepping out. The hall was empty.

Syline stepped out behind Thelonious, eyes scanning back and forth.

"Find Jane."

She pushed Thelonious towards the main foyer, guiding him to take the lead. She wasn't afraid of any guard; she, Amberly and Thelonious had managed everything Jane had thrown at them up to this point. They could handle a few charmed soldiers. They moved through the hall as a group. All the windows in the hall had their curtains pulled shut, keeping the place in a state of near total darkness likely for the vampiric Jane's benefit. They came to the main foyer lit by gas lamps and classically impressive with the same kind of architecture found in Syline's own home. Dual staircases led from the second floor, joining together to make an impressive, grand rise, flanked by statues of beautiful women in states of ecstasy.

The group was taking a short moment to consider which way to go next, looking from the first floor to further along the second, when Gehrman Petrov came wandering from out of view to the foyer below, talking with a maid and holding a mug of coffee in both hands. He was an older man, older than what Jane appeared to be by at least a decade or more. It was hardly a secret that she married him for his money. In his younger days, he'd actually been a soldier, and served as one of the founding members of Syline's father's forces. Back then he had been in fine shape. Now, though, a gut replaced once powerful abs, his hands shook when he tried to focus and his bones creaked when he tried to work out.

His eyes locked with those of Thelonious, staring at the group for a few moments as the rest of them came to the balcony. For a moment, only confusion showed in them, as if he was trying to comprehend what he was seeing. Then, all at once, the moment of serenity came to an end. His mug of coffee was dropped, and by the time it shattered on the tiles, the man had taken off running, dragging the maid behind him by the elbow.

"Guards! Guards! Jane, my love, they've come for you! Syline has come for you from the dead!"

Syline thought that might have been a little dramatic, but it was not wholly incorrect. There was no hiding their presence, now. Syline shot Thelonious a look and took off running down the stairs, holding the skirts of her robes up as she went. Thelonious and Ioann bolted straight past her on far longer, surer limbs as Amberly and Kat skipped the stairs all together, vaulting over the balcony and rolling to their feet.

Syline felt a little put out by their athleticism, making her own bravado look paltry as they all reached the ground floor before her. They all stood together on the bottom flight of the stairs as, from every direction, guards came running. These weren't the normal retired watchman and ex-adventurers most nobles hired as their protectors. They looked much more like Teagan's men: hard, vicious sellswords in a motley assortment of armour. The only unifying aspect was that each of them held an arming sword in one hand, the back side of which was brutally serrated.

Coming up behind them was Gehrman. He held a longsword in both of his shaking hands, standing protectively before the woman who came striding up behind him. Just like when Syline had last seen her, Jane Petrov was dressed in an evening gown wholly unbefitting for the weather. But now, she did nothing to hide her terrible presence. Her eyes were tinted red, skin impossibly pale and radiant. She wiped her lips clean of blood, leaving them bright red against her alabaster skin. Her lips were held in a charming grin of good humour, exposing vicious fangs, even as her eyes blazed with deathly fury. Something had changed. Before, she had radiated grace, poise, and lethal intent, it was like looking upon a snow leopard, a great hunting cat. Now, the undercurrent of madness, the quivering hands, the faint flecks of embers dancing around her, and that not quite straight smile, she looked…

Like a nightmare.

"You know, Syline, I admire you. I'd have never expected an idiot, wannabe wizard to come this far: to defeat all of my hunters, gather your own little army, and even trick me into thinking you're dead. I honestly thought this was finished, but after tonight, it will be. No one is leaving this building alive. No one. Kill them."

Chapter 18

JANE WAS CALLING HER. SHE could feel the pulse of her mind, the call that only her true mistress should be able to give, that only her mother should be able to beckon her with. She fought every step. She knew Syline was here now, she'd somehow survived and if Syline had come, so had the end. Knowledge was a virus, and if the truth of them was out, it would spread like a plague across the city. Any of Jane's sisters would have fled already, they would have cleared up the evidence of their presence in the city and disappeared into the night to return home to Nachthelm. If Syline was here, then the watch would not be far behind. However powerful Jane had become, Lauralee did not believe for a second she could take on the entire city.

And still she called for her. Her voice pounding, screaming, raving within Lauralee's mind, wrapping about her thoughts like a chain and pulling her towards the foyer.

Lauralee's possessions lay half packed around the small room allocated to her. As she took a heavy leaden step towards the door, she crushed her favourite comb, mother of pearl, beneath her foot. The sharp teeth dug into her sole, eliciting a gasp of pain from her. She focused her mind upon it, the chain pulling at her thoughts yanked her another step forward, but as she did, she ground her foot into the comb, breaking the skin of her sole. Old blood oozed from the wound as pain danced electrically up her leg. She seized hold of that lightning and guided it to the chains wrapping about her, letting it dance back across their bond to Jane's own thoughts. She felt the chain slacken.

What do you think you're doing, child? Jane's thoughts were like razors, all sharp edges, hurling into the meat of her mind. *Our home is threatened and you hide from me? You cower and quiver? Your mother said you were a warr–*

Lauralee slammed her head into the corner of the doorframe. Something cracked. She hoped it was the doorframe. She licked blood from her lips as it ran down slowly over them from her scalp. The chains shattered.

Lauralee let out a slow, quivering breath and slumped to the floor as her balance left her. The feeling of another inside her thoughts always sent waves of revulsion through her. Only loyalty suppressed those feelings when it was her mother. She felt no such kinship with the mad creature Jane had become. It would be better for all involved, this city and the Mother's Hand, if Jane died here tonight.

Lauralee looked back over her shoulder; her maid slumbered upon her bed. Together they could flee now.

After taking a few moments to select some choice items from her possessions, she shut the door behind her and made for the foyer. She had no intention of getting involved if she didn't have to. But perhaps Syline could soften her up enough for Lauralee to finish the job.

—

THE FIGHT ERUPTED. TEN HARDENED mercenaries rushing five motley adventurers. Some made for Syline, still on the stairs. She backed up, knowing her best chances here would be with spells, not her axe. Forces clashed with one another below her. Syline tried to get a look around, but before she could really judge how any of her friends were faring, a more immediate problem presented itself. Two men were climbing over the guardrail of the staircase to avoid the fight and get straight to her.

Syline moved to the other side of the stairs, readying her staff in one hand and axe in the other as the men drew their blades. Behind them, she could still see Lady Jane Petrov watching the fight impassively alongside her husband, who still held a longsword like he wasn't sure what to do with it. As she watched, Jane let out a barking yell, seemingly at nothing, turning to glare over her shoulder at the empty hall. She put them from her mind for now. If Jane was so cocky or so cowardly that she was just going to watch the fight from a distance, then she would be punished for it in time. For now, Syline had to do her own part in this fight.

Her first foe had managed to get tangled in the overly fanciful banister, but his fellow was running for her. He knew full well she was unarmed and swung with the cruel, serrated edge, hoping to inflict a wound that would end the fight before it began. She had to act fast.

She frantically retreated to avoid it and the sideswipe that followed, beginning her first incantation, one of several she'd chosen for tonight, as she moved. The man was quick to follow, but not so quick that Syline couldn't finish the spell. A crackling blue aura like lightning surrounded her, and when his next stab came for her, the aura solidified into a shield, stopping it a mere inch from her flesh. Over her foe's shoulder, she saw a man at the base of the stairs hold up a fingerless hand as Kat retracted her blade. Her sister seemed to be faring well.

Syline did her best to give the man a cocky grin and put him off his guard. In reality, she had no clue how long that shield could hold against their attacks. His fellow had disentangled himself from the banister and was climbing the steps. It looked like he'd hurt his leg in the process. She'd have to end the fight with him before he and his fellow could put up a concerted attack. The man grinned back at her, gripping his blade with both hands to force it through her shield. Syline replied by raising her staff threateningly, beginning to incant. In truth it was nonsense, but she trusted the man didn't know enough arcane to recognise that. What she needed was enough space to bring out her more offensive spells, and he gave her just the opportunity to make that space.

Thinking she was going for a spell, the man rushed up the steps at her, his fellow just a few steps behind, but as he lifted his leg to push himself up, Syline lashed out. Lowering her staff to the ground and using it to balance herself, she kicked him full in the chest, using the high ground to compensate for her inferior strength. Though she might not have been the strongest, the kick was enough to send the man reeling, and a further shove with the butt of her staff had his arms flailing as the man cursed, crashed, and tumbled his way to the foot of the stairs, landing in a heap, bloodied and bruised by his descent down the stone steps. He knocked into his fellow as he went, and the man stumbled back several steps, cursing and grabbing onto the banister to avoid going with him.

He landed by Kat, and without ever looking directly at him, Syline's older sister sliced her blade across his chest as she stepped to defend Thelonious, who was struggling against a pair of foes, his footwork awkward from the day on horseback. Both of Kat's foes were already on the ground. One bled from a puncture through his throat, and the other laid, missing a hand and holding a mutilated arm. Thelonious was struggling, even with one of his foes at his feet already. He'd fought worse in the past, but their long travels must have exhausted him. Syline had no time to help, for the once-tangled man was upon her, and even the fallen mercenary was rising again, already gone from Kat's mind as he slipped past them.

The man coming up the stairs had a scar that split his face, leaving his mouth in a constant sneer. He held his sword low, serrated edge out like his fellow, but in his off hand, he had drawn a throwing knife. It looked like he had sprained his ankle when it had gotten caught, for he seemed slightly hobbled. Syline began casting and the man hefted the knife, throwing it ahead of him as she finished her spell. The knife flew right for her head, whilst out of her staff exploded a pair of crackling, purple and blue missiles of arcane energy. Both were dead on to their mark. His dagger struck her blade-first right between her eyes, while her missiles thudded into his chest.

But Syline had a shield spell. He didn't. The knife caught in her shimmering aura and clattered to the ground as the man stumbled back a step, blood on his lips from the missiles. They didn't cut, but he was likely bleeding badly internally from the pure force of them. He wasn't finished though, and neither was her first opponent: both were making their way for her now. Another knife flew her way to cease her casting. Again, it crackled against her shield spell, but cracks formed as it solidified. It was weakening. Syline backed up a few steps further, standing on the first landing as her shield continued to crackle dangerously, on the point of breaking. Crackling. That gave Syline an idea. She'd only cast the spell once before, and when she had, she'd vented all of her magic at once to send herself as far as she could, but surely, if she limited the power of the spell down to a minimum and kept her sights within this room alone, it would be a powerful weapon. She'd readied it, thinking to use it as a last resort escape, but perhaps there were better uses.

The two men had their blades up and ready now, right within her reach as they pelted up the steps. There was no more time to think, only to react. The blade of the man on her right scored across her shield, and she swore she could hear it splintering. The other stabbed at her shoulder, her shield flexing and the force enough to stumble her, even if it didn't penetrate. Clear a little space. The incantation was short – she'd only need a few seconds. Try not to panic. Both are wounded already. Trust in the shield.

The shield, of course! Syline swung her axe up at one, forcing him to leap back. She used that opening to jump straight between them, putting them off their guard as she leaped straight down a half dozen steps, landing with a flex of her knees and grabbing at the banister to avoid falling any further. The men hurried down the steps after her. Both were hurt and took care not to take another tumble, giving her a scant second to begin an incantation and swing her axe wide towards them. The most wounded of the pair backed up a step, but the other caught it easily on his blade. It was almost a little shameful how little difficulty a real warrior had against her meagre strength.

Still, her axe was quite good in such a situation, even if her foe was the stronger. She twisted it, caught the head against his blade and yanked forwards. He hadn't expected the counter and tripped down the stairs, bashing his head against the edge of a step. But while she'd been focusing on him, his fellow moved around to her side. She turned his way as she finished the spell, his sword was coming for her chest with all his remaining strength that hadn't been stolen by his wounds.

The blade never touched her skin, for suddenly Syline was gone, and both men received a nasty shock as a burst of electricity came from where she had been. The one who had fallen, screamed. The other shuddered, a groan of agony escaping him as his muscles spasmed and teeth chattered. His eyes frantically scanned around for where their foe had disappeared to.

He didn't see Syline, because by then she was a good few metres in the air above him. She tucked her staff into her armpit and took her axe in both hands as she rapidly fell towards the man. He didn't even look up as Syline slammed into stairs behind him, the flat of her axe coming down hard on the back of his skull. Alive or dead, Syline couldn't have said, but at this moment, she didn't have the time to spare for guilt as the man collapsed, limply rolling down the stairs. Syline at least knew how to land: she'd had a passing interest in acrobatics when she was younger and Kat had taught her how to take a fall. She flexed her knees as she landed, absorbing much of the impact. She still nearly landed on her rump.

The other man looked up at her and struggled to get to his feet, blade still held in one hand. Syline stepped forward, repeating her hammer blow once more, the haft of the axe slamming into the man's jaw. The man went down like a puppet with his strings cut, body limp. Syline was starting to think she should invest in a club.

She allowed herself a momentary sigh of relief. A moment to catch her breath. They were winning. She had won this fight all on her own – okay, Kat helped her out a bit, but still – and if she could do it, surely the rest of them would be okay dealing with their own opponents.

She looked up. Thelonious and Kat were mopping up their opponents. Thelonious had taken a cut to his arm, the bracer on his left arm rent with blood weeping from the gash to the metal. Kat was unharmed. As Syline watched, Thelonious caught the serrated edge of one of their opponent's blades on his sword, and the big, hellblooded warrior let out a roar as he ripped the blade from the man's hands. It clattered across the tiles as Thelonious cut him down. His fellow leapt back as blood splattered across one of his eyes. Kat wasted no time, stepping in and spearing her blade straight through him in the moment of distraction.

Ioann and Amberly seemed to be faring just as well: Ioann's foes both lay burned and smoking upon the ground, brutally decimated by the sorcerer's burning blade. Now, he and Amberly worked in concert to finish off her foes, both backing off in tandem, but with Ioann's reach, they had no real ability to reply.

A flash of movement caught Syline's eye.

"Ioann, watch out!"

Amberly's eyes flashed up, her blade reaching to try and cut down the flash, but she misjudged. Depth perception struggled against something moving that fast. But she did stop it from hitting Ioann. Amberly screeched at the top of her lungs, staring at the arrow embedded straight through her wrist. Syline winced at the scream as she searched for the archer responsible. There he was, the eleventh mercenary right by Jane and Gehrman, drawing his next arrow.

"He's mine! Take down those last swordsmen!" Syline shouted to Ioann and raised up her staff. A word from Jane had the man's attention moving from the melee to the wizard on the staircase. He drew his arrow back, but Syline was already moving, already casting. The arrow soared past her cheek, cutting a nick on it. Syline squealed, losing concentration as her hand went to her cheek. She could see Jane grinning as the man drew another arrow. Kat and Thelonious moved to flank Ioann and Amberly's foes. Four on two. This man was the only one Syline had to worry herself with now.

He knocked another arrow, but Syline was casting far faster this time, pain lending her fresh focus and sending words flitting from her lips one after the other. The archer's eyes widened, and he let his arrow go skittering half-drawn across the tiles before turning to try to run for cover. The gemstone at the head of her staff lit up a glorious crimson, and the roar of flames filled the air. A burning arc of light flew over the battle to strike the man full in the chest. His dying screams filled the air as, with a final syllable, Syline sent the arc for Jane. She'd expected as much, but watching the vampiress easily flip over the arc, not even singed by it, still left Syline disappointed.

Jane laughed. "Not bad, Syline, not bad," she cooed, watching the last of the mercenaries die to her friend's blades.

As one, they turned on Jane, ready and eager to end this fight.

"But," Jane drawled, "did you really think I would trust my defence to simple mercenaries?"

She spoke the words of calling.

A chill of terror went down Syline's spine as she felt the staircase shift beneath her. The staircase splintered and cracked, Thelonious had time to yell for her to run, but there was no time to do it. Suddenly, Syline found herself sailing through the air as a terrible, familiar bellow filled the room. Rubble and shrapnel flew around her, and she shielded her eyes from it, covering her face with her forearms. She could only pray she'd land on something soft. Thankfully, Thelonious caught Syline out of the air, cradling her to his chest and grunting in pain as he skidded back along the tiles before putting her back on her feet.

"I suppose it's about time I step in, as well. Gehrman, dear, you can go put the kettle on, if you like. This shan't take long. Oh, and dear? Leave the sword; you're liable to hurt yourself," Syline heard Jane say to her husband, sounding for all the world like any other noble woman. Amused and gentile.

Syline lowered her arms and looked to the stairs. Extracting itself from the rubble was one of those awful, stretched, draconic beasts. Those terrible things that looked like a man, tormented and reshaped by the whims of a mad sculptor. Rather than having tentacles, however, it had huge, brutal claws: four long talons on each limb that scrambled for purchase as it brought itself over the rubble of the grand staircase. Behind it came more of the waxwork deep elves, their forms melted, contorted, and shifted, but with more purpose than the last ones they'd fought. All their arms ended in shafts of bone; the bones of their forearms twisted around one another into twin spear points. Their heads were split in absence of any real thought, nothing but mouths filled with terrible fangs and wild, flailing tongues.

"Scared, Syline? This is what it looks like to have truly powerful allies to call upon."

Syline grinned, laughed even, looking for all the world as if she was completely confident. "Scared? We've fought these before. We know how to kill them," she said, feigning as much bravado as she could.

It worked, for Jane seemed confused, disturbed even.

"What? How could you? You've been to the – you're bluffing."

"No, I'm not. Thelonious, Kat! Keep her back as best you can! Amberly, clean up after me and Ioann. Ioann! They're weak to fire! Burn them to a crisp!" Her allies jumped to their tasks with relish. Thelonious and Kat exchanged a glance and moved side by side to stand ready against Jane, who screamed in frustration and their lack of despair, composure fracturing against the party's will to go on.

Syline gave Ioann a smile and shouted over, "I've gotten better at it!"

"At what?"

"Your spell!"

Syline conjured forth her flame dagger from the tip of her staff, shaping it into a grand spear of blue fire, holding back sheer power to avoid draining herself. Even with the staff bolstering it, she couldn't afford to burn through all of her reserves. Ioann grinned and summoned his own forth with a confident roar as the wax work elves rushed ahead of the draconic beast.

"They're stronger than they look!" Amberly warned, moving in front of Syline with her off-hand limp at her side. She'd snapped off the arrow at both sides but hadn't pulled the shaft out; she couldn't risk the extra bleeding right now.

Ioann nodded.

"Fire beats brawn!" he said with a laugh, running into the fray.

Watching Ioann in action against monsters was a sight to see. These waxwork elves couldn't really hope to compare to his grace, his strength. The sorcerer was far more experienced than any of them at fighting undead and similar beasts. He weaved in between their blades and blows, his burning blade passing through their forms with enough heat to burn limbs off entirely and leave torsos black and still burning. He worked his way straight through the centre, apparently happy to kill what he could and leave the others screaming and reeling from his flames for Amberly to mop up. He took a few cuts to his arms from their bone spear arms, but his reflexes allowed him to stay ahead of taking any serious, real wounds.

For a few short moments, Syline was distracted, simply watching him until Amberly laughed. "Swoon later, Syl! Burn them up!" she called. Syline blushed.

Amberly stealing her sister's nickname for her was a cheap shot. She didn't know how long she'd be able to push her magic reserves. She'd already used spells which had left her exhausted in the past, but for now, she felt alright. She hurried on after him, spearing for creatures' heads, or whatever she found that looked like a head, in an attempt to blind them, or searing her fire blade along their blackened limbs, where the flesh turned brittle.

By now, most of the creatures were aflame. Syline shot Amberly a smile and, side by side, the two rushed forward. With them reeling, it gave her the freedom to drop her axe through any blackened wounds or still-burning limbs. The weight of the axe was enough to do most of the work for her against the brittle, charred flesh. Jane couldn't have expected the fight to go like this, but against these creatures, Ioann was a trump card with little comparison. A renowned fire sorcerer, whose speciality was beast hunting? The creatures stood no real chance. Syline's fire spear and Ioann's blade were used to great effect, their reach so superior to the creatures that it took away any chance at a response, leaving the poor, ruined wax work abominations wailing and aflame. Once aflame, the quick bladework of Amberly and Syline's heavy axe made short work of them. In under a minute, the trio had dealt with nearly twenty-five of the creatures.

This left the draconic beast before them, its hind quarters finally fully extracted from the cavity beneath the stairs. Now finally out, it roared at the trio, and Syline knew full well this fight would be very different from that against the waxwork creatures. She spared a short glance over to Kat and Thelonious and was relieved to see the pair of them holding Jane at bay. Jane had grabbed her husband's blade and wielded it with a speed and dexterity that would make Kat jealous, despite it being a blade made for a man to wield two handed. In her off-hand, she held a slim, black wand. Between parries and counter-strokes, she fired off rapid spells: arcane missiles, shunts of force, streams of acid from the tip of the wand. It was only Kat's speed and grace that kept her from being overtly wounded. Thelonious, though, had nothing to rely on but his armour and fortitude, worn down by the magic even as the pair kept her on the back foot. It would only be a matter of time. Unlike them, a vampire would not tire, and the pair had barely inflicted any damage.

That quick glance was all she had time for, as the contorted abomination went on the assault, not content to wait any longer. Its foreclaws raised up, slamming down one after the other. One came down for Ioann, the sorcerer nimbly skipping back, even as the other came for Syline. She squealed, leaping back, and found herself going a good three metres from the tiny leap. She stumbled as she touched down on the tiles, Ioann's green-tinted licks of wind fading from around her ankles.

He winked at her. "Fireworks on this one as well, right?" he asked, rushing it even as he said it.

"Same rules!" Amberly called, coming in behind him.

"Burn, then cut, so it can't grow back," Syline finished.

Ioann had given her a little space and she intended to make use of it. She quickly cast a shielding spell and reduced the power of her flame spear spell to let it last through her future castings. Then, she went right into a fiery arc to supplement Ioann's flames. Ioann was fighting at its ankles, avoiding each and every swing of its claws and keeping it busy as Amberly scored cuts across any flesh he left burning. But the creature's form was so thick and fleshy, the duelling sabre couldn't hope to inflict any dire wounds. Not with Amberly fighting with only one arm.

Syline made the strength of this arc greater than the last, but not too much so, limiting its range to only a single target. She was relying on the staff's power to boost the spells destructive potential. While usually, the spell would be wielded with grace and dexterity to take down multiple foes at once, now Syline just wished to smother its head in flame and leave it open to a finishing blow. This time, she hoped to give it to the muscular and agile Ioann, easily able to reach its skull. The arc built up within the flame spear, burning forth as a great line of orange-blue fire, hot enough to singe Syline's cheeks, even as she held the staff up. The creature's skull was wreathed wholly in the inferno, flesh not just set aflame but bubbling clean off its skull. Its arms flailed wildly, and it screamed horribly, the terrible roar reverberating well past the walls of the manor. The creature stumbled across the ground, sending Ioann sprawling as the side of its forearm caught him full in the chest. That left things up to Syline. She'd been ready to throw her axe to Ioann, but with him rolling across the floor and Amberly nursing her wounded arm, only she stood ready to make the charge.

"Ioann! I need wind!" she shouted to the sorcerer as she broke into a sprint at the creature, dropping her staff to take her axe in both hands.

She could only hope that Ioann had heard her and would get his magic ready in time. The creature was blinded, its eyes seared shut, but it heard her footsteps coming for it. Panicked like a cornered animal, it lashed its forelegs her way and Syline only just managed to drop to her knees, sliding right on under the swing. She was utterly unashamed to admit that she felt very graceful. She really felt like a sister of Kat doing that. Now was the do-or-die moment. Its head lolled; she might've been able to reach its snout at best without the magic. Her knees tensed and she leapt for all she was worth. She felt the force beneath her, felt herself sailing.

He'd heard her. Syline let out the greatest battle cry she could manage and threw all her strength into an overhead swing. The creature's skull cracked like porcelain beneath the blow, not merely cleaved in twain but shattering beneath the flesh as the axe sank into its brain. The creature collapsed, bringing Syline back down to the earth as, with a climactic crack, it hit the tiles, shattering all beneath it.

"No! Enough!" she heard Jane yell, as she yanked the axe clear. "All I've done!" The vampire screeched and Syline turned to see Jane grab Thelonious by both horns and slam him down into the floor so hard that the tiles cracked beneath his head. He didn't get up. "All these years I've worked!"

Kat tried to take advantage of her rage and reckless movements, going for a swift stab. Jane let it go straight through her abdomen, uncaring of the wound and pain as she cast. She yanked Kat closer so that when the burst of force erupted from her wand, it hit Kat full force in the chest with the strength of a dragon. Syline's untouchable older sister flew across the room like a ragdoll to slam bonelessly into the far wall.

"I'll not have all he gave me, all the power I've shed blood sweat and tears for, all my plans, all the good I could do for this city taken away and ruined by some stupid little girl! None of you understand. Not you! Not my idiot sisters, or their stupid, worthless daughters! You'll all see, when I'm done, this city, no, this nation will be *perfect*, and *mine*."

It was at that terrible moment Syline realised, until now, Jane had been playing with them. Until now, she'd not taken them seriously nor cared about what they did to her forces. It was only the death of the dragon that truly angered her and only now was the vampire showing her true strength. She realised this as Jane ran at her. She would have reached her, killed her in an instant, if it hadn't been for Ioann. It must've been so much of his magic, likely all he had left, that sent the sorcerer flying at her. He and the vampire went down in a heap and Jane's wand skittered across the floor in their wake, broken in two. For all her strength, she was light, and momentum did a lot when your foe didn't see you coming. Syline began to have hope, however slim. She retrieved her staff, ready to join the fight when Ioann screamed. It was a terrible scream of agony with no compare. Ioann went tumbling across the ground, leaving blood in his wake.

Jane stood and threw Ioann's severed arm away.

"I will not be stopped."

She charged yet again, eyes black, face contorted with veins of the same. Her dress was in flames from the last of Ioann's blade. It blazed around her, but she seemed so unbothered by it all as she charged for Syline once again. This time, Amberly stopped her, desperately stepping in her path and trying to slow her as all their efforts proved for naught.

Jane slammed her hand into Amberly's stomach nails-first. Amberly collapsed to her knees and Jane tore her hand free, fingers bloodied to the knuckle. "Not" – she licked her fingers clean – "by some stupid, meddling, idiot child."

The woman in the dress of fire had caught up to her. Syline knew then that ruin had surely come.

Chapter 19

ALL SHE COULD DO WAS run, and even that wasn't enough to keep the vampire back. Jane was too fast, too strong. Stone and tile cracked under her footfalls as she raced after Syline, cursing her out and calling her a child, a fool, a weakling, a dead girl. Syline had no hope of fighting back. Watching her throw away even Ioann and Kat like so much driftwood, left her certain of that. They'd lost. Jane was beyond anything she had ever faced in the past. Why did they even think they had any chance of defeating a vampire who feasted on the blood of gods?

The only advantages were that Ioann had broken Jane's focus and the two spells that kept her alive. Jane was the person that she'd stolen the spell-book from, and she was famous as an incredibly skilled mage. If Jane was able to bring her magical skills to bear, she'd die in an instant. Syline's own magical skills had been reduced to a pair of spells, uttered over and over and over, going into the next the moment the first ran out: the spell of vanishing and her lightning teleportation spell. The sight of the lightning seemed to enrage Jane all the more: that spell caused her pain, and the jolts and shocks she was receiving, again and again, every time she got close to the evasive Syline left the vampire screeching in frustration.

"Just die, you little worm!"

Syline wished she could just escape all this and run away forever. But she couldn't abandon her friends, even if all she could do for them was keep Jane busy. She couldn't leave them to die, and she had to believe they still lived. If they were all dead... No, she couldn't think about that. She teleported again. Each casting hurt more and made the nausea worse. She couldn't keep this up much longer. She was fairly certain she'd already run out of magic a few castings ago. Each spell made her chest ache all the more. At this point, she was sure that any other time, she would have passed out by now – she would have already given into fatigue. Now, she wasn't draining her magic. She'd pushed past that. Now, she was doing something Anatoly had warned her of, something she'd been told to never, ever do. She was pulling on her life itself, each casting putting her a little closer to death as she drained her very soul to keep fighting.

But what else she could do? All she could do was keep running, keep casting, because the moment she stopped, she died. More importantly than that, the moment she died, Jane would turn her attention on all her friends. The only way she could protect them was to keep Jane busy and pray for a miracle. Pray for something to change. Pray for something to give her some kind of hope.

—

AMBERLY OPENED HER EYES. THE world around her was grey, little but curling fog. If she focused, she could catch vague details: walls, a huge silhouette of something that looked like a dragon dead on the floor. A body at her feet. She focused on it, leaning down.

It was her own.

"I'm... dead?" she whispered, her voice catching in her throat. Was this place what awaited her for spurning both Soel and Laes?

"Near to it, but no, you aren't dead," cooed a woman's voice. Just the sound of it sent tingles down Amberly's spine. Sultry and soft, with just the slightest raspiness to it. Her eyes flicked up. The fog ahead of her was turning red, seemingly catching alight and clearing away, leaving a clear space, in which she could see her.

Naked and glorious, the woman stood before her, smiling. Her skin was a soft, copper hue, her hair and the huge, angelic wings at her back, the colour of freshly spilled blood, and her eyes, molten gold. Her hair hung long down her back and covered her breasts with a fringe parted on her brow by small horns that rose from her forehead. Her form, her figure, her face, she was the most beautiful creature Amberly had ever seen.

"Wh-who are you?" she managed, stepping into the cleared mists towards the woman.

The woman smiled and held a hand out to her.

"I'm the princess in the castle you've come to save, my beautiful knight in shining armour."

"You're my princess? I'm what? Wait." Amberly stumbled over herself, trying her best to decipher the woman's words as she stepped closer to her. The warmth of the woman alone was enough to beat back the cold. She took the bronzed woman's hand as it was offered to her and found herself pulled in close.

"You're the songbird? You're the caged goddess who kept calling to me?" she asked. It was all sinking in now; she was the only one who heard the birdsong because she was the only one this goddess wished to hear it.

"Yours was the only heart I could reach, and you were the perfect heart for me. We both long for something. I long for a worshipper to give my all to, to protect and to care for, and you long for a god to devote yourself to. Even as weak as I am, your heart drew mine to you."

"So… you want me to worship you? Why? What makes me worth it?" Amberly asked. This situation already felt so far beyond her. She was just trying to catch up and make sense of it all. For all her years praying to Soel, he'd never spoken back, and now she was in the arms of a demigod who could only be described as divine. This woman was what every painter and sculptor strived to emulate when painting images of heavenly beauty.

"You gave everything to pursue your passion for hunting demons and saving the innocent. You were willing to go against everything you knew to do what you thought was right. That is exactly what I long for in a worshipper, in a saviour, in a lover."

That last note confused Amberly. She cocked her head at the goddess' words, wondering just what she could mean by that.

"You're a goddess of demon hunting?" she asked, looking at the horns. Maybe a god of hellblooded? Then why didn't she go for Thelonious, instead? With the feathered wings and the horns, the demigod looked like something in between angel and devil.

The goddess laughed – a beautiful, melodic sound that set butterflies fluttering through Amberly's stomach – and shook her head.

"*No.*" She leaned in and kissed Amberly, holding her tight as Amberly felt life burning back into her breast and the wonderful warmth of the goddess spreading through her form. With it came knowledge. Knowledge of who she was.

"You're…" Amberly pulled back, staring into the goddess' eyes, breathless. "You're the demigod of passion."

The goddess grinned and closed her wings around them both.

"I am. I devote myself fully to whoever I care for, whatever I do. I will not care for you as my worshipper, Amberly. I will love you with all my heart, and all I ask from you is your own love and affection in return, and that you never deny yourself your passions. Now… say my name, Amberly, my knight, my love. Give yourself to me, and together, we'll save the day."

She felt the goddess softly stroking down her cheek and holding her around her waist. The goddess' eyes were hopeful, nervous: very rarely did a goddess need to ask someone to worship them, and – if the notes were true – this was a demigod, who thought far more like a normal mortal than a god's distant view.

That was the last wall of her resistance down. She wanted a goddess, wanted the light and safety of worship again, wanted to not feel so empty without a god at her back. She'd seen now that Soel did not care for the individual; he cared far more that his laws were followed, not that right was done. A more personal, a more… human goddess like this sounded perfect for her, and she had to admit, there was something exciting about the idea of being a god's only worshipper. It sounded much more like a relationship between people than that of some uncaring being and a mere mortal.

She leaned in and whispered, "I give myself to you, my goddess, my princess… Rion."

Rion leaned in and kissed her on the forehead.

"Then I will give you all that I have left, I cannot promise much, but I will give you your chance at victory." Her arms unwound from her new worshipper as she stepped back and Amberly felt herself pulled back to reality.

AMBERLY OPENED HER EYES. SHE felt strong, she felt reenergised – reborn, even. Most of all, she felt a familiar warmth: a god's touch upon her. Her powers as a paladin had returned, the golden light of Soel replaced by the vibrant flames of Rion's passion. The wound in her stomach was now just a dull ache, healed by the flames within.

She climbed to her feet just as Syline dashed past her, eyes wide and face ashen. Syline stumbled to a halt as she saw her friend.

"A-Amberly, you're okay! What's happened to you? What's the – Look out!" Syline yanked Amberly to the side right as Jane's elongated, bloody claws cut the air where she'd been standing. Amberly faced the vampire and pushed Syline behind her. Jane glared, hunched over like an animal, arms wide and fingers clenching and unclenching, cutting furrows into her own palms that healed by the time her fingers pulled away.

"So, you got yourself back to your feet. Impressive," Jane went to say, a smug arrogance smothering the bestial rage in her voice.

"It's okay, Syline." Amberly spoke over Jane as she picked up her sword. "It's all going to be okay. You did so well to keep fighting, but now…" Jane's face contorted in confusion and anger as the flames of Rion's passion spread across the blade, turning its metal a vibrant, cherry red. "We're not alone now. I'm not alone now. We have a god at our back, unlike this godless whore," she cooed playfully, taunting Jane.

The vampire screamed, stepping in and clawing at Amberly. The reborn paladin barely parried the first and caught her other arm by the wrist, sliding backwards under the force of the blow, but keeping it from her chest. She locked her arm, elbow screaming with pain in protest, but she'd stopped the blows all the same. Jane snarled and grabbed for Amberly's blade, ready to tear it from her hand. Her eyes went wide and she let out a gasp as she pulled her hand away.

Terrible burns crossed her wrist and palm, injured from grabbing the blade. They weren't healing. Amberly grinned at her and levelled her sword again.

"The light and flames of passion are with me! Fear darkness!" She slipped back into the role of the Morning's Fury, roaring her battle cry as she felt the power of her new god swell within her. "For the dawn…" Jane stumbled away as the light emitted from every inch of Amberly. "… has come!" The entire room was filled with a burst of light, blinding Jane and Syline both. The wizard stumbling back from her friend, blinking spots from her eyes. Jane shielded her own eyes to little avail, skin blistering. Amberly lowered her sword as Jane lowered her arm. The vampire seemed… lessened now: her skin was red, her arms blistered, and the wounds Amberly had inflicted weren't healing.

"That's all I have, Amberly; this'll be up to you now. I hope this has been enough, my love."

Amberly felt the words of Rion more than she heard them, settling in her mind and memories like a kiss on her neck and a warm embrace.

This will be plenty, thank you, Amberly thought, hoping Rion could hear her. She looked over to Syline. "She's weakened now, let's finish this."

Syline felt as if she would keel over then and there if she tried to cast another spell. Any more magic would likely kill her, but this is when she'd need it most. She struggled through the words to the flame dagger, body shaking as she did. Already, Amberly was running ahead of her, sword still flickering with dying flames nowhere near as vibrant as when Amberly had first woken up, the blade's edge rapidly returning to bare steel as the goddess' presence faded. With the last word, a weak, flickering flame appeared over Syline's staff: this was all she could manage, but she hoped flame would be as useful against Jane as it was against the waxworks. Other than that, all she had to rely on was Amberly and a trembling axe arm. Syline glanced down at her hands, and past them, she saw her reflection in the tiles.

She barely recognised herself: her flesh grey and pallid, veins flush against the skin, eyes sunken in their sockets with dried blood rimming around them like old tears and her hair hanging slack like some terrible hag from a horror tale told around campfires. Her magic was killing her.

She came in just behind Amberly, charging the vampire on unsteady feet as Jane still struggled to see clearly, her arms waving blindly before her. Amberly had her blade raised, already coming down for the vampire's throat. Syline was far too committed to her charge when she realised Jane's ploy. All at once, the confusion went out of Jane's movements. Amberly was caught by the wrist, and the sound of cracking bone echoed around the room right as Jane's other hand caught the staff just behind its gemstone head, and yanked Syline in close.

"You see, you two, your mistake was thinking that by stripping away a little of my power, you'd put me on your pathetic level." She grinned at Syline as she yanked Amberly by the arm and swung her like she weighed nothing. She was sent tumbling away, screaming with every bounce as she landed upon her arm, having just healed from an arrow wound, now crushed and crippled all over again. "I might not heal anymore, but I am still a vampire, Syline."

Her grip tightened and the staff cracked. Syline's grip went slack as the hope went out of her. Jane pulled the staff away and crushed its haft, the arcane ink splattering out over each of them and splattering Syline's face and arms.

"And you are still terribly, terribly human. Fear, little light, for the night has come."

She tickled Syline's chin almost tenderly as the young wizard stood before her like a deer in the hunter's eye. Not even a god's grace had saved them. She didn't even try to dodge the blow as Jane slammed her flat palm into Syline's breast, sending her flying and her ribs cracking.

Syline tumbled back across the ground, body impacting against the tiles time and again after Jane's brutal shove. When she finally rolled to a stop, body bloodied, bruised and wracked with pain, she felt a hand close on her wrist. She screamed. Jane had her. This was all over, she was going to die, they were going to die–

Ioann pulled her face-to-face with him with his remaining arm. He was pale and shivering, his tanned skin turned ashen from blood loss.

"Ioann, you–"

"Don't let go... You can still save us..." Ioann whispered, struggling to lift his head to look her in the eye. "Whatever happens... don't let go," he whispered before he began to scream. Syline held tight to him as the man convulsed and shook. Suddenly, she felt life returning to her, magic returning to her. Her reserves filled, then spilled over with a fiery power like nothing she had ever felt in the past. Flames and wind burst from Ioann, racing along his skin and sending her hair billowing behind her. Finally, he fell still, staring up at her as blood dribbled from his mouth.

"I gave you my magic... All of it... Kill... Her..." the sorcerer rasped, even as consciousness faded from him.

"I hope you realise that whatever you're doing is just prolonging the inevitable, Syline," cooed Jane, chuckling as Syline heard her coming closer, her footsteps clicking on the tiles.

Syline felt... reborn. Refreshed. Her skin had taken on a new, healthy hue, and she felt a terrible burning in her chest replacing the encroaching cold. Ioann's magic roiled through her entire being, leaving her feeling as if she were about to explode. She could barely even imagine how the sorcerer contained it. She looked at Jane as the woman came closer. Syline began casting and she saw Jane falter as if breaking from a stupor. It only lasted a moment and she began running to finish Syline. Jane's hand reached for her, coming in an arc that would tear Syline's throat out.

It stopped dead only inches from Syline.

The blue shimmer of a shield hung in the air, cracking under the pressure. Syline locked eyes with Jane for a split second, long enough to say: "I disagree."

Jane snarled and backed off, her eyes roving over Syline. They widened as she realised how she could cast at all: neither of them held a focus, but they were both showered with the ink from Syline's broken staff.

In that moment of study, both went into new incantations. Knowing that offensively, the vampire would surely have her beat, Syline teleported once again. She arrived with a corona of lightning at the foot of the stairs, a rush of wind following suit – an effect of Ioann's wild, sorcerous magic. Jane took a slow, deep breath and regained her gentile aura as she momentarily abandoned her spell.

"So, the sorcerer gave you his power?" she called after her as she strutted over the bloody tiles towards Syline. "Fantastic! All you've succeeded in doing is making this more interesting, little whelp."

Jane began casting again. Syline cut off any reply she might have made to do the same. She was too slow. She heard a sizzling, popping sound as a thick green fog settled around her, melting at the tiles and very quickly through her shield. Panicking, she looked within herself for a solution. Ioann's power gave it to her. Great winds blustered from behind her, blowing the acidic mist back towards Jane.

Syline barely had a moment to feel relief: she only just stopped the mists spreading to her friends. A sigh barely escaped her when Jane flew from the acidic fog, her skin singed and bubbling in places. Syline didn't see Jane until her burning fingers were piercing through her shield. Syline's stomach dropped as her shield crumbled and Jane snatched her wrist and arm both.

"Get back in there," the wild and manic Jane snarled at her.

Her claws cut gashes into Syline's bicep and waist. Syline found herself hefted into the air and sent flailing back towards the cloud of caustic fog as if she were nothing but a doll Jane was finished playing with. Her axe left her grip, clattering across the ground, as she flew. Syline began renewing her shield, finishing it just before slamming into the ground, but not before her exposed flesh was left blistered and red. By the time she rose, she'd tumbled almost the whole way out the other side of the fog. Her shield absorbed most of the impact, but she was still left rattled. That wasn't her greatest problem. She couldn't see Jane, that meant Syline wasn't her target anymore, she was going for one of the others.

Panic swept through Syline and that panic summoned forth further strength from Ioann's magic: a great geyser of wind to launch her skyward, like how the men had reached the window, which catapulted her back out of the mist. A spell was already on her lips but what she saw momentarily halted her tongue.

———

NEVER LET IT BE SAID that Lauralee was a coward. Cautious, careful, patient. She was all these things because her mother had trained her to be all these things, but a coward, she was not. She saw the way Syline was fighting Jane, from her hiding place by a pillar. She saw that Syline may truly have a chance. The girl was pushing Jane harder than she could have imagined, however terrifying her mad mistress had become. If she gave her an opening, Syline may be able to finish this. Syline's axe, smeared in the ink, had clattered down beside her. Syline had disappeared into the fog and Jane was going for one of her friends.

Lauralee picked up the axe, moving the scroll she'd retrieved from her belongings to her other hand, ready.

As Syline emerged from the green, acidic mists, Lauralee pulled back her arm and hurled the axe.

———

SHE FOUND JANE STANDING OVER Amberly, pressing her heel down on Amberly's broken arm as she watched the mist for Syline's return. But as Syline came into view, she suddenly stumbled forward, the young wizard's axe buried into her shoulder. Syline didn't have time to think about the source of her good fortune, her teleportation spell went off before she even hit the floor.

As she arrived, she did so with all her momentum intact. Right by Jane, barrelling into her with all the speed of her flight intact, sending both sprawling away from Amberly. For a split second, Jane was left shuddering on the floor as the lightning from the spell coursed through her and sent her into a seizure, but already she was pushing herself through those tremors and back to her feet. Syline rose out of her tumble to face her, using Jane's momentary agony to put some distance between them after yanking her axe from the vampire's shoulder. There was a terrible wound there now, their fall had pushed it deeper into her back, and now her arm hung mostly slack. Syline didn't dare take her eyes off her, but she gave a silent thanks to whoever was aiding her.

Jane didn't give her any more time than that. Giving up on physical assault, she once more began an incantation, the words of the spell spilling from her lips like a waterfall. Syline, thinking on the spot, did the same. Surely, Jane's spell would be more powerful than hers, so she needed to keep her from finishing it. Her incantation was much shorter than Jane's, sending off dozens of arcane missiles in a storm of unerring magic. Normally, this would have pushed Syline to her limits and beyond, but right now, she barely felt the drain upon her in the slightest. Disappointment welled up in her as the vampire weaved, flipped and twirled, evading almost every one of the supposedly "perfectly accurate" bolts of magic. The ones that did hit impacted hard, bringing bloody welts across her flesh, but that didn't stop her incantation. Jane's willpower was too strong to falter now and Syline ran for a pillar to take cover from whatever was coming, incanting a shield as she went.

What came for her seemed like something from a wizard of legend: answering Jane's call was a titanic, ethereal dragon, made of crackling lightning and searing blue flames. It rushed forth and tore through the pillar like paper. It was only Ioann's seemingly limitless magic that let her survive by endlessly repeating the incantation to strengthen her shield. Even as a terrible heat leaked through and burned her lungs, she forced herself to focus on nothing but her own counter-casting. When the spell finally passed, Syline shuddered and found herself taking cover against nothing but rubble. She stepped out, holding her axe in steadier hands and taking solace in its solidity. She had to keep casting. Keep fighting. Ioann had given her everything, and no matter how astonishing Jane's magic was, she wouldn't let herself give in.

Jane was panting as Syline rounded the remains of the pillar. Even the vampire looked drained by such an astonishing spell. Despite that, she flashed Syline a grin.

"See now? This is the power of a true mage. All you have going for you is stolen power, little girl. Stolen from me, stolen from him. You're nothing but a little thief."

Syline didn't reply, instead appearing by Jane's side in a flash of lightning. Electricity crackled through the vampire and she let out a scream as she pushed herself away from Syline. The little mage swung wildly at Jane, trying to take the vampire down in the moment of weakness. Jane hurried back, unsure of just how reliable her claws would be while they shook from the lightning's touch.

"Enough! We finish this now! I don't care if he granted you his power. Even that has its limits." The vampire wiped the blood from her lips. "I'll just have to push you to them and beyond."

By the time she finished speaking Syline's own follow up spell had already finished. Flames gathered at the axe's edge in a burning, terribly focused line of azure. She glanced down a moment, surprised that the flame dagger had come from there and not her hand. Then, she noticed how her axe was splattered with the ink too. She looked up with a tiny smile, the next spell on her lips even as Jane, too, was chanting. Syline brought her axe up over her head and began to rush towards the vampire hoping to put her on the back foot. She hoped false bravado would ring true at that moment.

Terrified, Syline knew she was inches from disaster, that Ioann's power would only keep her going for so long, she knew one false step would kill her. But she forced it all down beneath a shield of focus and determination. A shield of calm that would make her mother proud and most any other duellists ashamed.

She could only hope Jane would fall for her feint, for the spell on Syline's lips was not a shield.

Jane ignored the charge, finishing her chant by the time Syline was a few paces from her. She clasped her hands together and from them burst forth a bellow of flame like a dragon's roar. Black, heavy smoke poured from the flames as they washed over Syline like a ceaseless tide. The vampire held them there, the rush of flames filling her ears as she chanted and chanted, keeping the spell going past even her own limits. *Surely, Syline's shields could not hold up against all this punishment,* she thought. When they cleared, there'd be nothing but ash left of the girl.

But Syline had never been touched by the flames: the moment they obscured Jane's sight of her, she had disappeared one last time in a flash of ozone. This time, there was no lightning. Syline appeared behind

Jane, the sound of the flames hiding her footfalls, yet still, Jane heard her, spinning with preternatural awareness, her spell changed, a shield springing into life, it's half-real mass ready to intercept the blade. Jane's eyes were wide with rage and fear.

—

LAURALEE SAW THE FINAL MOMENT. The instant where her actions would matter most. She finished reading the counterspell scroll she'd brought with her. With all the hope her dead heart could muster, she prayed for Syline's aim to be true.

—

THE SHIELD FIZZLED LIKE IT had never been there, disappearing before the axe even made contact. Jane felt the terrible burn of the superheated edge pass through her neck.

Then nothing at all, ever again.

Syline lowered her axe. Jane's headless corpse toppled to the ground. Syline stood, panting for several long moments as the body rolled down the stairs. It was over.

She'd won.

—

"*Go to your friends while you have the chance,*" Amberly felt Rion tell her. "*I think I should have the strength to heal them, or at least… keep them alive, I'm sorry I'm so weak. I'm not much of a god, especially after all she took from me.*"

Staggering to her feet, Amberly could see Syline standing over the body of the vampire. They'd won. At the very least, that gave her relief, but as things stood, many of them could still die if she didn't save them. She felt a pressure on her crippled arm like someone held it tight, keeping it steady, and a soothing warmth spread through it. It wasn't good as new, but it was usable. It'd have to work. She'd pour her energy into healing everyone else first, their wounds were more vital. If she had the power left over, she'd fix her arm.

One by one she ran to her friends and deep-red embers scattered from her open palms. Kat's broken jaw was set, and the bleeding from her scalp slowed, then stopped. By the time she blinked herself back to consciousness, Amberly had moved to Ioann, healing his severed arm with scar tissue.

Rion was still so weak, and each casting drained the pair of them. By the time she healed Thelonious' broken nose and cracked skull, she was struggling to remain conscious and the feeling of Rion's presence with her was fading away.

Thelonious opened his eyes with a gasp, a hand coming to one of his horns. It had been broken clean off right where it began to curl forwards, blood dripping from the tip of it. He forced himself to ignore that terrible ache though, as Amberly collapsed over him. The hellblooded bodyguard caught her in one arm, propping himself on the other as her head fell to his shoulder. He looked up, wary of what he would find. When he saw Syline standing vacant over Jane's body, a bloody axe ablaze with a blue flame in her hand, he couldn't believe his eyes. She'd done it. That damned little bullheaded wizard had done it.

"It's okay, Amberly... It's okay, we won... Syline won. The vampire's dead." He let himself fall slack against the tiles and spent a few moments simply breathing. It came easy.

—

THE FIGHT FINISHED, SYLINE'S KNEES began to shake. Adrenaline that had kept her mind going a mile a minute, until now, ebbed away. The feeling of Ioann's power slowly began to fade from her, flames cooling in her breast as the world finally began to slow down. Her axe trailing embers, her robes ruined, and only her trusted satchel protecting the all-important spell-book, she ran to the sorcerer only to find him still on the ground. A smile was on his lips, the colour back in his cheeks. Syline allowed herself a sigh of relief as she saw his chest rise and fall. He was okay.

"I knew you could do it," she heard Thelonious say behind her.

She turned to see him and Amberly, the hellblooded struggling to push himself up onto his elbow. Both looked a few paces from death's door. She couldn't think of what to say. Really, it hadn't even sunk in that they'd won, just yet. She just gave the pair of them a dazed smile before jogging to help her sister up.

"LET'S GIVE HER A LITTLE space," Amberly said, trying to stand. "She's probably still in shock."

With a groan, Thelonious pushed himself up to his feet and brought her up with him, holding her against his side to support her. Inwardly, she was glad for it. She doubted she'd have stayed on her feet without it, at that moment.

"Soel took you back?" he asked.

Amberly laughed and shook her head.

"Soel is done with me and I want nothing to do with him. This was all thanks to the god Jane has held captive... Her name's Rion. She'd been calling to me all this time. I can... I can stand."

Thelonious let her stand on her own but kept a hand on her shoulder to steady her as she recovered herself. "Let's... Come on, let's go find her. Get her out of here and to... wherever she belongs."

"Will you two be alright?" Syline asked, having returned with Kat behind her.

The older Petranski was tired and drained, but hardly as much s Syline, who was beaten, bloodied, and with skin that looked like ash. Her wounds were not obvious, but it was astounding she stood at all. Amberly wished she had the power left to help her but knew that she likely wasn't looking that much better herself.

"We're... we're great, Syline," Amberly said with a smile. "Well done... we'll see you back at your house soon, I'm sure."

With that, Syline nodded and disappeared elsewhere in the house as her far stronger sister slung Ioann over her shoulders and struggled towards the door, grunting under her breath about sorcerers not pulling their own weight.

"Syline's going for the antidote. I'll see you two soon," Kat called before disappearing into the snow.

The pair smiled and dipped off into the hidden passage beneath the ruined stairs. Somehow, Amberly knew Rion waited for them there. Descending the steps, they entered into a vast room full of alchemical equipment, a huge brass canister, cages full of strange creatures and chests full of gold and jewels. In the centre of it all was her goddess, Rion, as beautiful as she had been in that place between life and death, radiant and magnificent, beyond any man or woman she had ever seen. She was chained down to a table, and each of the chain links blazed with glowing runes. The demigod lifted her head as they entered, and a grin split her cheeks even as Amberly heard Thelonious gasp behind her. She couldn't blame him – she couldn't hope to compete with the goddess, even in so reduced a state.

"Rion! Hold on, I'll get you unbound."

"Don't worry, Amberly… You've already freed me," her goddess cooed to her as they came in close.

"What do you mean?" Amberly asked, confused. She came to stand beside her goddess, a hand impulsively reaching out to stroke Rion's hair. The demigod leaned into it, making a sound deep in her throat not far off purring at the impulsive affection.

"Now that I have a worshipper, I can finally return to the land of gods and spirits. It was being forgotten that had me trapped on the mortal realm, more than any of these chains. I just wished to stay to meet you in person as soon as I could. I can return, but I'll be there a long while recovering before that day. Until then…" The goddess' golden eyes drew Amberly in closer until Rion leaned in and kissed her softly on the forehead. *"We'll speak again as soon as my strength allows it, I promise, my lovely Amberly, my knight in shining armour, my hero…"* the goddess cooed, her body slowly turning to embers, whisking away on the unseen wind.

The pair stood still for a few long moments of silence, before Thelonious finally said, snickering, "Well, that's the kind of god I could bend the knee for."

Amberly laughed raucously and elbowed him in the side.

"Come on. Maybe I'll convert you later, but for now, let's get the hell out of here."

━

SYLINE JOGGED DOWN THE HALL, the feelings of power fading as she ran along. The halls weren't empty, though. As she went, maids and servants poked their heads out of doorways, ducking back in when Syline drew close. They all had a dazed look about them as if they were waking from a dream and were still not totally clear on what was happening around them. She paid them no mind, not right now. Later, she may worry over providing them assistance, making sure the poor things had not lost their minds or something, but right now, she only had the wherewithal to focus upon one thing. She needed to find a lab, a storehouse, or something. Wherever Jane was keeping the antidotes. That's what this was all for, if she couldn't find them, it wouldn't matter at all in the end.

She didn't find any such room. Instead, she found two familiar faces. Gehrman Petrov, Jane's husband, owner of the house, looking dazed and unsteady, kept on his feet largely only by Lauralee, Jane's white-haired assistant, who stood at his side, holding one of his arms with both of hers, helping him stay upright. Hearing her footsteps on the tiles, they looked up. Unlike the others, they did not shy away.

"So," Gehrman said, "she's... it's over? Jane is dead?"

That was something Syline hadn't planned for: the fact that Jane, however awful she might be, might have people who cared for her. She found it a little hard to meet Gehrman's gaze as she awkwardly nodded.

"She is. Er... Sorry. No, I'm—" She was cut short before she said what, on a moment's thought, would have been pretty stupid, by Gehrman limping closer and embracing her. The old man was crying.

"Thank you. We're... I'm finally free."

Syline was unsure of how to react, so she just softly patted him on the back. She was even less prepared for gratitude, than she had been for the anger she'd been expecting.

"She came to me years ago and so much after that is a blank. Only rarely would her magic on me fail. The things she did to the servants, the things she made me do. I was myself but my strings were hers to pull, however she liked. Thank you. Don't worry, I'll make sure no one makes you the villain in this. You've saved more people than you know. Who knows how many people in this city she's been controlling?"

Pride swelled in Syline's breast; she felt like a hero from a story. Until now, this had been all so personal. Knowing she'd helped people beyond her own circle made this all the better.

"You're... uh, I guess you're welcome, Mr. Petrov, sir. But Jane poisoned my mother and mentor; do you know where the antidotes might be?"

"I do," offered Lauralee. She looked ashamed; her pale eyes didn't meet Syline's. "I'm sorry Syline, on her orders, I'm the one who poisoned your mother and mentor."

Syline stiffened slightly, a flush of rage momentarily welling up in her, but it was snuffed out before it could really take root. It was not this girl's fault, she'd been under Jane's control, just like the rest of them. Looking at her, Lauralee might have had it even worse, she was so very pale. Syline quietly assumed that must mean Jane had been drinking her blood. Was that why her hair was white as well?

"It's fine, Lauralee," Syline said gently. Placing a hand on Lauralee's own. "Like Sir Petrov said, you've not been yourself for a long time. I can't blame you for that."

Lauralee did not correct her. Syline was a kind girl. She needn't suffer any more than she had. This could be the end of all of this. They'd never see one another again and this kind, bizarrely timid and yet heroic girl, could go back to her normal life.

"Not always," Lauralee said. "Sometimes I'd realise what I was doing. I'm strong, she made me do…" She let crocodile tears well up, she was never the best at faking emotions, but a lot of stress had finally come off her shoulders, the tears weren't entirely fake. "I came to myself a little, at the end, I tried to help."

Syline blinked slowly and a smile spread across her lips.

"You were the one who threw the axe?"

Lauralee nodded and then became as stiff as a board as Syline stepped in and embraced her. Syline smelled nice. Of course she smelled nice to Lauralee, because the scent of blood and ash clung to her in bucket loads. She wasn't used to this. She quelled the urge to breathe deep, ignoring how easily she could sense Syline's heartbeat, still going a mile a minute, sending life raging through her form. Lauralee awkwardly hugged her back. Funny, all full of fear and adrenaline, it was almost the same as Syline had smelt the first time they'd met, when she was just some scared noble girl, running from a thug.

"You saved my life, thank you," Syline murmured. She was still quivering.

"Not as many lives as you saved, but I'm glad I could help," Lauralee said, unsure what to say. Gratitude was not something she was used to. "I'll," she couldn't keep this moment going, it felt so unnatural, to hold another when not feeding upon them, "I'll go fetch that antidote for you, shall I?"

Syline nodded and let her go. Gerhman gave her a last, grateful smile, before Lauralee helped him depart. Following in his wake to find the antidote. Only whilst Syline waited for them, standing alone in that dark hallway, did she realise her hat was no longer atop her head. She spared a moment of grieving for it, allowing herself a little pout and petulant scuffing of the floor. She loved that hat.

Lauralee returned to the hallway alone, without Gehrman in tow.

"I found something else that I think might be yours," she said as she approached.

Syline began to ask what she could mean, then flinched back slightly as Lauralee reached up towards her. The other girl blinked; she looked as if she might blush, but it did not quite reach her cheeks.

"Ah, I'm sorry that was a tad forward of me." She turned her hand, so Syline could see what she was holding, a slim platinum hair pin, with a beautiful blue gemstone, the one she had lost in the library. Lauralee smiled slightly as she saw delight light up Syline's features. This time, Syline did not lean away as Lauralee stepped in to pin Syline's hair back, just above her ear with the pin.

"There, back where it belongs. Now…" She held up a slim wooden box, opening it to show Syline two small vials. "Mix them with a teacup of milk. It will help them go down. They're very harsh on the stomach, but if you go now, they should be just fine."

"Even." Syline's breath choked slightly, as the thought occurred to her. "Even Anatoly? He mustn't have much time left? They said she gave him a faster acting one."

"In…" Lauralee rubbed the back of her neck, telling this was risky, but the girl deserved comfort. "In one of my moments of clarity, I reduced the poison's dosage for him, just enough to give you more time. I wanted to believe this could end well."

Syline crushed her in another embrace, the air left Lauralee.

"Thank you." Tears dropped onto Lauralee's shoulder. She felt Syline's lips press to her cheek. She didn't know what to think of that. "Thank you."

"You should get going, Syline, your family's waiting for you," Lauralee said, gently trying to ease from the hug.

"Right, right." Syline released her, rubbing her eye. "If you… If you're ever looking for work, let me know, I'd make sure my family gave you whatever role you asked for."

Lauralee smiled and waved for her to go. "I'll keep that in mind, thank you. Now go."

Syline nodded one last time and set off at a run. Stepping outside, the chill didn't touch her as much as she feared it would. In fact, the snow seemed to sizzle away right before it touched her. Perhaps some of Ioann's powers remained. The thought that he'd always be with her in a way left her grinning as she ran into the night, finally moving through her beloved home city without fear for the first time in what felt like years, despite having only fled days barely a week prior. Despite the moon being high in the sky, it felt like the dawn of a new day.

Chapter 20

LAURALEE WATCHED HER GO. SOME part of her, buried long ago, almost wished she could accept that job offer. To live a quieter life, with a mistress she had much in common with. To escape the dangers of her new existence.

But it was a small part. She knew full well how close she'd been to killing Syline, or being sent to, numerous times in Syline's adventure. She would have, as well, if it was what the Mother's Hand required. Some part of her wondered if it was Jane's instability that had saved the girl. At the very least, if not for that, Syline likely would have been in exile now.

But none of that mattered now. She could be quietly pleased for Syline within her own thoughts, but now her focus had to lie on the next task ahead.

She looked around, the hall was largely empty. So many of the maids were likely already fleeing this place. That was going to be a pain. She'd need hands to help her load the carriage. A small sigh left her as she set off at a quick walking pace to find Gerhman. He remained where she'd left him, sat by the fire in his own study. Staring into its flickering depths. The man looked hollowed out, being under domination for so long could do that to someone. He was so used to having a presence within his thoughts, now that it was gone, his mind felt as if it lacked something, some integral part of it. He didn't look up as Lauralee entered, quietly closing the door behind her, he just sat, fingers wrapped about the head of his cane.

"I'm going to be leaving tonight, before the sun rises."

"Oh? Is that right?"

He hadn't really heard her. She approached, lightly placing a hand upon his shoulder. He looked up, his eyes dancing with the firelight.

"Did you hear me, Sir Petrov?"

He seemed to blink slowly back into reality. He knew who she was, what she was.

"Oh, yes, yes, my apologies, Miss Lauralee, not quite feeling myself. Leaving, did you say? What will that–" He cleared his throat. "What will happen to the staff and I now, then?"

Lauralee looked around his study, stepping to a cabinet, she poured the man a glass from the bottle of brandy hidden at the back. She knew it to be his favourite, only pulled out for the special occasions. She placed it in his hands, before sitting down in the armchair across from him.

"Oh dear. Must be bad then," he said with a grim little chuckle to himself, taking a gentle sip of the drink, before looking back up at her.

"All of you have suffered plenty, Sir Petrov, and I have no wish to be a cruel woman. Jane was... mad, even by our standards. But knowledge of my presence cannot leave this household. If it does, it will create... problems. Problems you won't like our way of rectifying. Who knows of me as more than just her assistant?"

Gehrman turned back to the fire, taking another gentle drink of the brandy. He took a long time to respond, long enough that she almost tried to drag his attention back to her, but right before she did, he spoke.

"Not many, thankfully. Until the end, Jane was cautious about that sort of thing. Plenty of the maids may know she was a vampire, I expect all of them, depending on what they can remember from." He waved his hand vaguely. "But I believe only myself and those you fed on would know what you are. Jane didn't allow them to speak of... that sort of thing."

She let out a small sigh of relief – that made her life much easier.

"Good. Good. I'll be taking them with me, in any case. I will need attendants on my way back home. So, it's only you I have to worry about."

He looked at her in a solemn, sad sort of way.

"That's it then." He took a deeper pull of the brandy. "Do be gentle about it, if you can, dear."

Lauralee stared at him for several moments, the smallest smirk quirking her lips.

"You're a braver man than I thought, Gehrman. But no. Some others would definitely kill you, but that would be" – she paused – "unsubtle. Syline saw you before leaving. She would know something had happened to you, that you had not been killed during the battle."

"Ah." He drained the rest of the brandy. "Well, that's fortunate. What then?"

Lauralee could not use magic. She would never be Jane, nor even Syline. But her condition, her bloodline, did come with certain abilities, nonetheless. Her mother's speciality, and so also hers, was control. Lauralee found it distasteful and did not use it if she could avoid it, but it was likely that natural inclination that had allowed her to resist the pull of Jane's mind that night. She stood up, placing her hand on Gehrman's chin, and guiding him to look up into her eyes.

The man looked as if he might blush. She resisted the urge to roll her eyes, she had to maintain eye contact.

"Promise me, Gehrman. No, swear to me, on your life. Swear to me that you will forget all about me. If anyone asks, I was a simple aide, and a distant cousin of yours, nothing strange about me. Your half-sister's daughter, brought here to learn business at your side, then take under Jane's control upon my arrival. After Jane died, I returned home to my family and to my country. I hired the maids to come with me and had to leave in a rush, so they could not say goodbye to their family. Swear it."

He went to blink and found he couldn't. His voice came in a slow drawl. Terror wrapped around his heart, claws gripping tight. All he could think was, not again.

"I swear it."

She felt it take hold. The mantle of her will settling upon his own, the expression of her focus feeling like a weight pressing down upon her soul. She was inexperienced and that feeling would likely linger for some time. That clouded look that had been over Gehrman's eyes when she entered, had returned. She released his chin and his head drifted back towards the fire. She stood and watched for long moments. The clock behind her tolled loudly and his head drifted back to look at it, pausing to focus on her.

"Lauralee? I thought you'd already left."

"I just came to say goodbye, Uncle Gehrman. Take care of yourself, alright?" She smiled, leaning down to kiss him on the cheek, giving him a gentle hug. The old man returned it, patting her on the shoulder.

"I will, dear. Give your mother my best, alright? Take a book for the road, it'll be a long journey home."

"I will, Uncle." That was a good idea actually. "Your bell is on the desk. Remember to call a maid if you need anything."

He nodded softly and released her. Lauralee closed the door behind her and set off to find the maids she would be taking with her. She was hungry, come to think of it.

—

IN THE END, IT TOOK her until the sun was almost cresting the horizon to get everything together. One of her maids had already left the manor and returned home to her meagre apartment in one of the lower quarters. Stealing her away without the matron of the house noticing had been a minor diversion. Lauralee had assisted her in packing what few possessions she had, once the girl accepted, she would be coming along. It would have been a waste of time to leave her to pack everything herself, and time was the commodity Lauralee had the least of at that moment.

But she had made it, it was a close-run thing. Indeed, it was the shadows of the city's tall roofs that had protected her in the end, the sunlight splashing across open courtyards, but kept back yet from smaller avenues.

It was in one of these she had loaded up her carriage. Her own possessions, and the maids, loaded onto the back and strapped down by the driver, the same man who had brought her to Jane some months prior and knew better than to ask why they were suddenly departing. He was a man of Nachthelm, her home, and was loyal to the Mothers and Daughters without any need for magical persuasion.

Now they trundled along the thoroughfares of the city, carriage bouncing slightly as it went over the cobbles. Outside, the noises of a city just beginning to wake reached Lauralee's ears. It was an unfamiliar sound, for this was an hour she was very rarely awake, let alone outside. But the sights of the waking city did not reach her, as the carriage lacked any windows bar a slat that could be pulled closed for speaking with the driver.

Three maids sat with her, or dozed, heads lolling against one another's shoulders. The three who knew the truth of her identity and purpose here. Amber, who's tumbling red locks and "cute as a button" cheeks were something the austere Lauralee fostered a quiet envy for, and who's blood had a vibrant, almost spiced texture to it that made it hard to resist taking more than her fair share at times. Myra, a quiet thing, with her dark hair cut in a bob cut, dozed against Amber's shoulder. Lauralee had been feeding from her just the night before, and the girl still felt woozy from it. Lastly, Sasha, who's blonde hair was cut similarly to Lauralee's own, but the difference in their height and features would never cause anyone to say they carried any sort of resemblance. She looked the most nervous of the three to be leaving her home.

"Sasha?" Lauralee asked quietly, putting down the book she had just started to open.

"Yes, mistress?"

"Come here, please."

The other girl shuffled over to sit beside Lauralee, fear dancing in her eyes. The bite had many benefits, sating her hunger of course. Rejuvenating her vitality and stamina. But more than that, those who her kind fed upon regularly, found it more and more difficult to refuse them. Sasha tilted her head to the side obediently, exposing her neck, as a thrill of predatory instinct rushed through Lauralee. The want to feed and feed and not stop until she was coated in blood. It was always there, that thirst. Controlling it was what separated true vampires from mere beasts.

She lay a gentle kiss against Sasha's cheek.

"Don't be scared. It's not going to hurt, you know that."

Then her arms wrapped about the girl and she sated her thirst, for now.

***

AFTER THAT, EVEN LAURALEE DEIGNED to sleep. The warm carriage pulled her into a doze for several hours, arms still wrapped about Sasha. This was to be a journey of at least a week or two, maybe more, depending on the weather. Her driver was still mortal and could not ride at all hours. They'd be stopping at a number of waystations and taverns along the way so they could get proper rest. They'd be hitting the first of them late in the following evening, he told her through the slats of the wood. That gave her time to begin her report, now that she had fed and rested. She was feeling much more herself, more than she had in some time, perhaps since Jane's madness truly began to come clear to her. Gods, what she'd do for a bath, but that would have to wait.

She rummaged through the things she had within the carriage with her, looking for a pen and parchment to begin her report. Her hand paused against the book she had with her. *Wyvernclaw Chronicles*. She flushed, for she had fed recently enough to do so. She'd meant to return that to the library, and that nice blind dwarven librarian before she left. She'd likely never do so now. She paused at the thought, and a small chuckle left her lips. That was hardly the worst of her crimes, and was in many ways, a bizarre thing for one such as her to feel even an ounce of guilt for. Yet still she did. Curious.

There it was. Her hand found the pen case where it hid from her at the bottom of her satchel. She shuffled about in the carriage so she could pull down the board in the wall, specially designed to serve as a miniature writing table in moments like this. The maids were quietly talking amongst themselves now, but she paid them no heed. She nibbled on the back of the pen, trying to figure out how she would even begin this report.

—

Dear Mother,

I hope this missive finds you well. I am not ashamed to admit I miss you most terribly. This city and its people have ill-suited me and I pine for the comfort of the manor once more. I send this missive ahead of me as an early warning of the strange tidings I have to tell, but first I feel I should lead with the most tragic news. Mother Jane is dead. I would name her assailant, but in truth, I place the blame of her death squarely at her own feet. Whilst I have been with her, I have seen caution and propriety flee before the oncoming hordes of bluster and madness, brought about by a strange acquisition.

Mother Jane treated with a strange, terrible creature that named itself "Icaria, Scholar of Ascension". Its servants are creatures of moulded flesh and whimsical mutation, brought about by the desires of their creator. She traded this creature a mystical tome, the secrets to which I am not privy. But its value must've been great, for in exchange she received not only a spell-book curated with the most dangerous of magics, as well as a small force of the scholar's creations to serve her will. Nay, she also received a demi-god, recumbent and indisposed within a coffin. I believe this demi-god's blood was the source of her madness. For once she had acquired it, she began to feed upon it regularly, not in lieu of other sources of vitae, but in addition to. Many servants died to her hunger in the following weeks. But great power did she receive from this creature, for Jane's magic, strength and will reached levels I had thought impossible even for those of our vaunted kind. However, her confidence in these abilities would prove to be her downfall.

A noble girl stole into Jane's vault within the royal library, apparently with the intent of repairing a broken window, but chanced upon the gifted spell-book, and saw within the illegal spells that this scholar had gifted Mother Jane. Jane threatened this girl, and when she retorted with the knowledge of these spells, Jane did attack, provoking the girl into flight with the spell-book, using the magics within. After she defeated all sent against her, with the aid of sellswords she encountered on the roads of the nation, Jane did then decide to poison her parentage, to provoke her into self-exile. This appears to have been the catalyst to provoke the girl into forward action, for she did arrive at the manor with allies in tow. It was my belief that Jane did act far too publicly in these matters, as more and more known warriors died at her behest, and more and more servants disappeared from our manor. She did deal with this girl to have her parentage cured of the poisoning but was remiss in following through. In my humble opinion as your daughter, the public poisoning, with quite insidious and fast-acting poisons, unique to Nachthelm, against, not only well-known nobles, but close friends of the king, was far too public an action. It was at this time I did decide that Jane's bluster had made her a threat to the mothers and daughters as a whole. I admit, I did not aid Jane during the battle, and indeed, it was I, in disguise as a maid, who provided the girl with the antidotes to the poisons, before they could be identified by physicians who would lead her back to Nachthelm. It is my *belief that it was better that Mother Jane perish, being thought of as a solitary force, or a rogue agent, than as a member of our family, working in concert with us. I have collected or disposed of all references of her affiliations with us in the hopes to reduce the impact of her folly, but I fear that despite my efforts, the name of the Mother's Hand will be known in Russenholde for time to come. I advise great caution in how we proceed. Seeking vengeance against this girl will only draw greater attention to us. However, I believe that this "Scholar of Ascension" creature bears further investigation. It is my belief that the level of power it is able to give away so freely insinuates that it holds even greater power back for itself. This creature could prove to be a threat not only to Russenholde, but the region as a whole, Nachthelm included. This belief is only doubled with the knowledge that Mother Jane has given unto it something with value and power it believes equal to a spell-book worthy of an archmage, a force of its creations and a demigod.*

Addendum: It is worth noting the demigod appears to be active once more and has returned to the celestial realm. Mother Jane kept me at arms-length, so my knowledge of the creature is lacking, but in the final moments, the demigod appeared to aid the noble girl's companions in defeating Jane, by creating a burst of sunlight. To my surprise, this sunlight only weakened Jane momentarily, rather than destroyed her. This speaks to just how much power its blood was able to provide, but I do not believe the madness was a worthy trade. As you have taught me, what is power without wisdom?

P.S I miss you. I look forward to coming home.

Your loving daughter,
Lauralee

She folded the letter carefully, after dusting it with sand and giving it time to dry, then slid it away into an envelope. The next time they stopped, she'd find a messenger company to run ahead. With the ability to switch horses and riders, they'd get the letter to Nachthelm days, if not weeks, before she arrived. She sealed the envelope with a dollop of wax, stamped with her mother's symbol.

Then she looked up and let out a small sigh. That had killed a few minutes at most. She had weeks of travelling in what amounted to a tiny coffin to endure. Once they were properly out of Russenholde territory she was going to insist they stop so she could have a run while the moon was high.

For now, she settled into her seat. Sasha looked sidelong at her, wondering if she was going to address them. She shook her head, but reached into her satchel, retrieving a pack of cards she flicked in the maid's direction. Give them something to busy themselves with.

She picked up her book. Finding her place and trying to get comfortable.

She remembered briefly that Syline had asked they meet for coffee sometime, that they come together to discuss the series. Her lips turned to a half-smirk. What a different world that would have been. Now, she knew it would be for the best for all involved if she and Syline never saw one another. Perhaps in another life, or, well unlife, they could have been friends.

≡

ALMOST TWO WEEKS LATER, FAR south, in the city-state of Nachthelm, a letter was opened. The pearl-handled letter opener was set aside, as the reader settled into their high-backed leather chair to read. Outside, the city was empty. Those who valued their lives knew better than to be out after curfew in Nachthelm. The steady percussion of the city regimentary marching down the streets was even muffled by the gentle snowfall. Nights like this put a smile on her face. Nights like this were a vision to what she imagined other nations could become, with their guidance. Orderly, safe, prosperous.

She read the letter. A small smile found its way to her lips at the final note left by her daughter, but it fled quickly as the rest of the news resettled itself within her mind. She turned to the maid standing by the door.

"Fetch my mage, I need a message sent to all my available sisters. I need them here by the time Lauralee returns."

The maid nodded and departed. She turned in her chair to face the window once more, looking up at the moon.

"Jane's dead," she mused aloud, letting the words curdle in her mind.

An oil slick smile spread itself across her cheeks. But this "Scholar of Ascension", that was a worry. That was something she knew nothing of, and she did not like to feel in the dark about anything that went on in her domain, and whether or not it fell within the borders of Nachthelm, this entire region was her domain, as far as she was concerned.

She gently placed a hand on the letter, looking over the final words one more time.

"I am sorry, dear," she said to no one. "It looks like you won't get to stay home long after all."

Epilogue

SYLINE TURNED TO AND FRO before the mirror one last time, inspecting herself for any last flaws. Nerves plucked and played with her heart, sending it fluttering in her chest.

"Are you sure this dress is okay?" she asked Alexis beside her, looking at her maid in the mirror.

"This is the third dress, Syline. Yes, I'm certain," Alexis said with an exasperated sigh and a chuckle. "You look absolutely beautiful, trust me."

It had been two weeks since the battle in Jane's manor. An investigation had begun, but it very quickly ended when Gehrman came forward and explained who Jane had been, along with all of his wife's crimes. Others throughout the city had started funnelling to the watch to report their own entrancement by the vampire, including a fair few critical members of the city watch itself. Thelonious and Amberly were staying in the guest rooms of the Petranski manor; the party was unable to leave just yet, for the king wished to thank them formally. Thelonious had been paid far more handsomely by Syline's family for protecting her than the girl herself had ever dared to promise. Syline had come forward with the spell-book and it had been taken from her to be thoroughly studied, destroyed if need be. She'd been sour but held out some hope that she'd get it back, at least in part.

"You should trust her on that, Syline. She's right," said Magdova, sneaking in through the door of Syline's room.

Syline sighed, forcing herself to quell her worries beneath the praise. She wore a light, sky-blue dress and a matching cloak with white furs hung around her shoulders. Her waist-length, black hair was tied into a braid just like her mother's, pinned with her platinum family seal to keep her loose fringe out of her face. She stared at herself in the mirror for a few moments longer, before Magdova spoke up again.

"Syline, the carriage man is waiting. If you fret any longer, you'll be late."

Syline looked to Alexis, alarm racing through her as she ran to grab her satchel.

"You said I still had twenty minutes!" she exclaimed as she threw it over her shoulder.

"That was twenty-five minutes and three dresses ago," Alexis replied with a snicker, stepping forward to adjust the strap of the satchel before giving her a kiss on the cheek. "You look beautiful, I promise. Don't worry so much."

Syline smiled softly and gave her maid a quick hug and kiss on the cheek in return. "Thank you for putting up with me."

"Always," her dear friend cooed as Syline pulled away to give her sister a kiss and hug as well.

"Now remember, Syline, a kiss on the first date is fine, but mother will have both your hides if you wind up in his bed," Magdova said, a cheeky grin on her face as she squeezed her older double. A huge blush rose on Syline's features and she let out a grand harrumph before stomping her way out of her bedroom, followed by the cackles of her sister and servant.

At the front door, she was met by Kat and Kassandra Jr. Both sat in chairs by the window, watching their mother and father sparring in the yard.

They looked over as Syline approached.

"Excited?" Kat asked.

"Terrified, more like."

Kat laughed. "You've faced down a vampire powered by the blood of a god but going on a date terrifies you. Gods, I hope you never change, Syl. Have a good time, okay? Don't do anything I wouldn't."

"Thanks, Kat," Syline said, leaning down to kiss her sister on the cheek, giving one to Kassandra as well, who wrapped her arms tight around Syline's shoulders for a few moments. She'd been clingy to her ever since she'd come home. She hadn't even realised how attached her youngest sister was to her.

"You're not leaving again, right?" she asked quietly, pressing her cheek to Syline's.

"I'm not going to disappear again, I promise. I love you, Kass."

"I love you too, big sister."

Syline beamed at her, pulling away and walking into the yard.

Her parents were clashing blades as she stepped out. Her mother, the picture of a duellist: slim, tall, and as quick as a viper. Her father, Peter, a powerful bear of a man. He had a glorious, black beard and long hair that hung like a mane off his shoulders. He fought with a blunted longsword, struggling to land a single hit on his wife as she tapped him again and again, her darting sabre sneaking by his guard every time. Syline paused to watch the pair of them and they came to a halt seeing her standing there.

"So, you're off, little sparrow?" her mother asked, panting hard and sheathing her blade as she stepped towards her.

"Mhmn!" Syline squeaked, feeling small by her mother and father, like a child again before the gaze of the two veterans.

"Let me know if he gives you any trouble," her mother said. "I'll punish his commander for you." She grinned back at her husband as he stepped over, smiling.

"Ioann is a fine young man, Kassandra! Considering Syline's adventures, I'd say she's the one we need to worry about being trouble. She's definitely your daughter." He laughed, leaning down to kiss Syline on the forehead and pulling her in tight to his chest.

Her father had returned a few days after the battle against Jane to find his wife well on the mend. Ulrik, Kat's twin brother had come home with him, but the younger ones were still far afield with other platoons. He'd decided now was as good a time as any to take a little holiday and spend some time with his wife and daughters until Kassandra had fully recovered from the wasting the poison had brought upon her.

"That she is! I never thought it'd be you who was the adventurous one amongst your sisters, but I couldn't be prouder. But you should get going, dear, because that's the coachman's third smoke. Anymore and the ride over will ruin your perfume."

Syline had meant to just give her parents a few quick words of thanks and love before she ran to the waiting carriage, but as she went to leave, her mother caught her by the wrist. She pulled her back and gave her another swift hug.

"Before you leave." She reached into one of her pockets and pulled out a slim little black box. Syline felt her breath catch in her throat. "I think defeating Jane is a little more impressive than Magdova, however fine a duellist your sister might be." She opened the box and removed the silver hair pin, twin to the one Syline had been given before all her adventures began. She slipped it into her daughter's hair and kissed her gently on the cheek. "Go on then, before I start crying again."

Syline giggled and squeezed her mother once more before finally pulling away and climbing into the carriage, doing her best to waft away the smoke. She called to the driver that she was ready to set off and, with a crack of the reins, off they went into the city, heading for the finest cafe – in Ioann's opinion – for the pair to finally have coffee together, as they had promised before all the drama began.

—

PULLING UP AT THE FRONT of the cafe, which faced the king's palace in the large public square before it, she saw Ioann stand up from a table outside and walk over to open the door for her. Syline had always thought the gentleman and the weak lady act was very silly, but when someone was doing it for her – especially someone like Ioann – it left her a little giddy, just for the thought of him putting in that extra effort for her. She wasn't the only one who had dressed up for the occasion: Ioann wore a handsome, sleeveless red tailcoat over a white shirt with red, slitted sleeves and tight, black dress pants. It was the first time she'd seen him wearing a shirt. His severed arm had the sleeve pinned up against his shoulder.

He opened the door for Syline and offered her his remaining arm to help her down from the carriage, which Syline took, trying not to giggle if only from the butterflies fluttering about her stomach.

"You look beautiful today, Syline," Ioann told her, leaning down to kiss her on the cheek. The butterflies multiplied tenfold and a nervous giggle escaped Syline, getting a curious look from him, even as she leaned up to kiss him on the cheek in return.

"You look very handsome yourself."

"Did you have trouble getting here? I was starting to get worried," Ioann told her as he walked with her inside the warm cafe.

"No, I just, I wasn't sure what to, I couldn't decide what to wear," Syline admitted bashfully as a waitress waved the pair towards an open booth against a window.

"Well, as I said, you look beautiful: that dress really suits you," he said, this time a flirtatious tone clear in his voice.

Syline wasn't really sure how to reply to that. She blushed, she smiled. It was pretty obvious to her that he was interested, and so was she but…

"How's your arm?" she asked, switching topics as they were each handed a menu.

"Mmn?" He looked down at his good arm.

"N-no, the other arm."

"What other arm?"

Syline stared, uncomprehending for a moment before Ioann gave her a grin and shook his head.

"It's fine, Syline. I'm a soldier, I knew I could die. Losing an arm's not so bad in comparison, and your father says we may be able to find a healer among the tundra elves who could restore it."

"That's good, at least," Syline said with a little sad smile. She paused as the waitress approached. "I'll have herbal tea and some buttered toast, please? Heavy on the salt."

"Black coffee and the blueberry muffin." Ioann gave his own order to the waitress and she took both their menus before fading back into the milling public in the cafe.

"Healing your arm is the least my family could do for you after you gave up your magic. It's really all gone, isn't it?"

Ioann nodded solemnly but smiled. "My sorcerous magic, yes, you took all of that, and I don't regret it at all. If I hadn't, we'd all be dead. Has it had any lasting effects on you?" he asked hesitantly. A sorcerer passing along his power like that wasn't exactly common and the effects on the wizard were not always the same, nor the best recorded.

"Er, yes, actually. My, I mean, I'm certainly no sorcerer, but my magic seems to come back to me a lot faster than it used to: what would once take a full night's rest to recover takes me only half a day now. Though, I still don't have your reserves. But Anatoly insists I have the potential to be an archmage if I keep casting and practising."

"Great! That's great! I'm glad it's stuck around for you. Makes it feel even more worth it. I actually have some good news."

Syline perked up.

"Now that the sorcerous magic is gone, I've found out I've got some talent as a wizard! I've hardly got your talent, but Anatoly says I could become a fine wizard, with training. I thought I'd test myself with a sigil or two, and after plenty of success, I've well… Anatoly has said he'll take me on as an apprentice. It'll be months until I can rejoin your father, so I certainly have the time."

A grin spread across her lips and Syline found herself practically bouncing in her seat with glee. It felt as if a huge weight had fallen off her shoulders: the guilt of having taken such a defining aspect of his identity away from him.

"That's fantastic! Maybe you can…" She let out a little coy giggle and leaned over to place her hand on top of his. "Maybe when you've really recovered, you could leave my father's forces and come with me?"

"I'd love nothing more."

—

"LAES?" AMBERLY ASKED THE AIR, climbing the steps up into the hidden little lounge. The doorman went to halt her, but a word from one of the men inside let her through.

It was a small place, all burnished wood, red carpeting and the crackle of a hearth, and it sat on the second floor of a building which held an assortment of small shops. A large window that took up one wall overlooked the church of the Wanderer and the large public square below, filled with closed stalls, civilians and clergy preaching to the wind, inviting those without a bed for the night into the church for soup and the hardwood of a pew to sleep upon.

Amberly walked towards the man who'd told the doorman to let her in. Softly tanned skin, slicked back hair and an unfading, rakish grin that made it look like he was laughing at a joke you weren't in on. The greatest hint was his eyes: those, at least, hadn't changed at all.

"A whiskey lounge in front of a church, Laes? You definitely have… unexpected tastes," she said as she sat down in a plush, leather armchair across from him.

The man grinned and placed down his empty tumbler of whiskey. He held up two fingers to the gaze of a waiter somewhere behind her and, in no time at all, his was refilled, and a new one was placed down for her.

"I doubt this new god of yours has any qualms about drinking," he said with a little chuckle, clinking his glass to hers as they raised them in tandem. She took a small sip, and it burned on the way down, leaving a wonderful warmth through the whole of her form. It reminded her of Rion's embrace, in an odd way.

"Plus, I thought this would be a nice place to celebrate your acquittal. I heard that the king has called off the manhunt on you?" he said.

"He did! I'm... not exactly welcome back in Dawnsteel, but the king said my actions here were proof that, even if I did not conform to what the men of the Morning's Fury thought was right, I still had good in my heart. So, he's officially announced me under his protection and forced the church to repeal their death sentence upon me."

"Good to hear some kings know that down here, it is they who rule, not gods," Laes said before taking another deep draught from his drink. "I suppose you and Thelonious are sticking on this venture with Syline back beneath... The Sea Without Sky? That place you were telling me about."

Amberly nodded and Laes gave a joking, despairing chuckle.

"So much for corrupting him into a worthy heir; with a goody-two-shoes bookworm and a paladin, I might as well drum him up as a lost cause. At least this new god of yours is better than Soel. I've only heard a little of her, but what is going on right now with you and this deity anyway? Are you now her living saint?"

Amberly looked down to her drink, watching the amber liquid swirl as she twirled the glass in a claw grip. She was going to say something about what he said about Thelonious, but she got the sense it was largely a joke. Largely.

"I don't really know. I pray to her every night, and I can feel her by me when I do like I did that night in Jane's manor, but she's silent now. She's only spoken to me once or twice since she went back to wherever the gods go. She told me to be patient, that now that she was where she belonged, she needed some time to recover so she could be a god worthy of me."

She snickered and picked up a piece of ice from the tumbler, tossing it in her mouth and crunching down on it. Laes gave her an appalled look like she'd just strangled a child. She felt one or two of the other men in the room staring at her. She didn't grab another piece.

"She said we'd have to be long distance for a little while and suggested I write her a few love letters."

Laes snorted. "Hell of a god, I suppose it makes sense if you're her only worshipper. Suppose it doesn't compare, but when I got my first pact, I spent most all my time worrying about how to do it right, if I was going to scare them off to a church or another devil, and now I've got more than I can count on both hands. Hell, I struggle to remember their names, sometimes."

Amberly let out a bark of laughter. "Well, I'm certainly glad I didn't sign myself over to you; I'm no one's mistress. I find I quite like having my god all to myself and I'd want you all to myself, as well." Laes grinned at that and went to say something, but he was cut off. "I don't suppose you'd be interested in converting to the Church of Passion?" she asked.

Laes laughed. "Ah yes, a half-devil and a paladin as the whole of her congregation... Well, I suppose the pair of us would show both sides of the spectrum and I could get behind a goddess of *passion*. Besides, knowing my soul – since it turns out I have one – has a safe hideaway. I may consider it. I'll get back to you on it when she's talking to you again."

Amberly hadn't expected him to actually consider it in the slightest. For a moment, she stared at him, mouth slightly agape. Laes just grinned at her, but if he was joking, he wasn't about to admit it.

"Are you–" she began to ask.

"I might be. Being able to be resurrected from the comfort of a cushy afterlife sounds a lot better than ending up an imp over and over, and now that I've found out I *can* be revived, I can't say I've much an interest in staying dead. Let alone being a devil. I'm comfortable dipping my toe in the hierarchy, never entering it. My father would have my hide."

That left her curious. It had never occurred to her that he might have parents, but then, she supposed it made sense. Though, considering how old Laes appeared to be, she didn't believe for a moment that his mother was still alive. She thought it best not to try to pry too deep for now and simply settled back in her seat, eyes drifting towards the window beside the pair.

"That was something I was curious about: you said one of your warlocks brought you back. I was a bit wrapped up at the time, so I didn't think to ask then. How? I've never heard of resurrection magic, at least not without divine intervention from the greatest of gods."

"Ah, I suppose you wouldn't have, no. It's not the kind of magic that they'd teach to goody-two-shoes like yourself. No, the kind of magic that brought me back is a very dark sort. A soul for a soul. It's cheaper when you're aligned to the hells. The gods there are usually happy to have their subjects out causing mischief up here. But when it comes to the divine." He paused. "Well, if someone's worth resurrecting, then they're worth keeping. It's been done, though. Great heroes come back from the dead… but dozens died to do it. Me? I'm a nobody from hell; the dark lords let me go in exchange for a pair of pure soul gems my warlock had stashed away. Lucky me, no?" he said, giving her a grin over his whiskey tumbler.

"Now, I regret asking. Souls for souls? Why would the gods make it work like that?"

"Just because a god is good, my dear, does not mean they're benevolent. I was sure you'd know that by now. If their champions are down here, they risk temptation once more. The good gods are usually content keeping their shining stars up with them in the heavens once they've passed. I imagine your Rion would be quite the jealous lover, too at least, for you. Me, I'm sure she wouldn't mind giving back for a bit more power."

"Well, least I know that one's off the table. I'm not trading anyone else's soul for mine." Laes gave a playful smirk to her as she said this.

She leaned over and lightly punched him on the shoulder. "Not to you or any god. 'Sides, all you've gotten from me is a drink, Laes. I thought we were getting dinner."

He laughed and held up his hands in defeat.

"Have you had this 'talk' of yours with Thelonious yet? I'm pretty curious to hear what it is if you're so eager to speak with him that you'd make him sign a contract to ensure he showed."

Laes put his elbows on his knees, leaning forward with his eyes resting on her still, his glass twirling between his hands. "No, not yet. It's funny you should ask, though, for once our little evening here together is at an end, I'll be going to meet him elsewhere for just that."

"Are you going to tell me what it's all about?" Amberly asked.

Laes chuckled, fixing her with a devilish gaze. It was all the stranger coming from a human visage.

"You look better as your true self," she mused to herself, only realising he'd heard her when the devil quirked an eyebrow up at her.

"Didn't expect to hear that from a paladin, of all people."

Amberly shrugged and smirked. "I worship a god with horns and blood-red wings. I've left the sun for a softer light, suits my skin better. Turns out I burn easy."

His previous chuckle turned to a cackle at that, a grin splitting his features as the devil called for another two whiskeys and asked for some steaks as well. "Fine, fine, I wasn't going to, but I'll let you in on what he and I are meeting to speak about."

Snow beat against the window and the fire crackled in the hearth, drowning out their words to all others as the pair leaned in, settling in for a few more drinks to go with their coming meal. Amberly found herself very comfortable by his side and the devil seemed in no rush to leave. In fact, he walked her back to her accommodations. When they arrived, he gave her a playful grin, a certain… expectation, in his eyes.

"May I come in?" he asked, catching her by the elbow as she went towards the Petranski manor.

Amberly turned and she knew all too well that look in the devil's eyes. Despite herself, she couldn't say she was all too against the idea, but she wasn't going to rush this, especially not with someone as dangerous as Laes. She leaned in and pecked him lightly on the cheek. His skin was very warm.

"Maybe after you take me to dinner a few more times."

Laes returned the kiss to her cheek and smiled. It seemed genuine.

"I can live with that," he said, then turned and began to walk off into the snow.

Amberly watched him go.

—

"Another beer, friend," Thelonious said to the tender.

He sat in a quiet, empty pub, somewhere deep in the mercantile district of Russenholde, about as far as he could get from the noble houses without hitting the slums, he felt a lot more comfortable in a place like this. Syline's manor was nice and all, but he always felt like he stuck out like a sore thumb, to say nothing of how intimidating being in the house of the king's general was. The night was long and Thelonious was paying this man well just to keep this place open. Tomorrow, he thought he might pay a visit to the farmlands surrounding Russenholde, or the greenhouses closer to the castle. There wasn't likely much to be doing this deep in the cold season, but he liked working with his hands and had nothing but time on them for the time being.

"You sure this friend of yours is coming?" the tender said as he poured him another pint.

"I heard somewhere that devils don't break their word, 'spose this is his chance to prove it," Thelonious replied with a sigh.

His pint was placed down in front of him right as the bell rang at the door. Thelonious and the bartender alike turned to look as a handsome man with slicked back hair in a fine, pressed suit entered.

"That's your man," the bartender said, no doubt in his voice. This man had the look of a devil.

"That he is," Thelonious replied and stood up. He tossed the bartender five silver pieces, far, far more than he was due.

"I'll take the glass with me. That should cover it if I forget. If I remember, I'll leave it by the door for the morning."

"Works for me, friend," the bartender said, suppressing a yawn as he set to cleaning up.

"You're late," Thelonious said to his father as he walked towards him.

"My apologies," Laes said, turning on his heel to match step with Thelonious. "Amberly proved far too good company to leave early."

Thelonious didn't reply. They walked into the cold together. Neither particularly noticed it.

"So, what is this about?"

"I wanted to talk to you about who you are and what that means. Your mother never would have, otherwise, we'd have met sooner."

Thelonious looked at his father curiously, thrusting his hands into the pockets of his coat. He kept a hand closed tight around a pocketknife hidden away. "Continue," he said.

"I own you. That's not a threat or to scare you or anything, it's just a fact. Your mother made a deal with me and the price was you. Not just to sleep with her and have her a son for me, but for his soul. You are my property: in soul, if perhaps not in body."

"Well," Thelonious began.

"And this means," Laes interrupted, "you already have a pact with me, you've just never known how to activate it. Whatever comes when you die, it happens. Chances are, if you do reach hell, you'll just be my right-hand man, or hell, I might let you go wherever your soul would've otherwise. I'm still not sold on this 'soul of the firstborn' thing. I feel like I've been conned but I'm not sure by who. But, until then, I have an interest in seeing you and Amberly succeed."

"A pact?" he asked. "What does that mean?"

"It means that I can lend you the strength to keep up with the girls on the journey. One has a god, and the other is a talented mage. Do you think you can hope to keep up with the pair of them as they grow? With me, you can."

"Okay, how do I use this... pact?"

"I'll give you more strength as you learn to control it, but for now, I'll teach you two commands."

The pair stopped in a quiet, snow-strewn street.

Laes turned to him. "First, do you accept the pact?"

Thelonious sighed. If his soul already belonged to Laes, then there was no point hiding from this. This was the one good thing that could come out of it for him.

"I do."

A burning sensation filled his left shoulder. Letting out a pained grunt, he peeled off his jacket and looked down his shirt to see what had happened. He found the symbol of an upturned wine glass, its stem extending out into a circle that wrapped over the brim formed on his shoulder in scar tissue. The burning faded as swiftly as it had begun.

"Now, our pact is awakened. Let me give you strength," Laes said and placed his hand on Thelonious' forehead. A rush hit Thelonious like he stood in a gale that could tear homes away. Then, it was gone and knowledge was left behind.

"Go ahead," Laes said and stepped back with a grin. Thelonious raised his hand, palm out at a snowdrift.

"*Inferflamve.*" A bolt of black fire flickering with yellow exploded from his palm and seared across the air into the snowdrift, burning a hole straight through it. Thelonious smirked, he liked that.

"And the other. This, I think, you'll really enjoy. Draw your sword."

Thelonious did so and held out before him.

"*Bergenflamve,*" he hissed and black flames spread out from his biceps, licking off his arms and up the elven blade, wreathing it in the dark, ashy yellow tinted flames. Thelonious twirled the blade around him and turned to his father, grinning.

"This... this, I could get used to."